# ROBERT
## A SEQUEL TO EXILED

## MICHAEL W. ELLIOTT

**author**HOUSE®

*AuthorHouse*™
*1663 Liberty Drive*
*Bloomington, IN 47403*
*www.authorhouse.com*
*Phone: 833-262-8899*

*Published by AuthorHouse 07/22/2020*

*ISBN: 978-1-7283-6688-3 (sc)*
*ISBN: 978-1-7283-6687-6 (e)*

*Library of Congress Control Number: 2020912928*

*Print information available on the last page.*

*This book is printed on acid-free paper.*

**Other books by Michael W. Elliott**

The Spirit of Romance
Time to Kill/The Purple Ghost
Exiled

# DEDICATION

This book is dedicated to my beautiful daughter **Crystal Renee Elliott** who has been the inspiration for everything I have ever done since the day she was born.

## Special Thanks to

My beloved parents **Edwin** and **Isabel Elliott** to whom I owe everything.
**Monna Robinson May**: for her continuous support, encouragement and belief in my abilities.
**Colleen Staub**: For her enthusiasm, support, encouragement and creative input.
**Presley May**: One of my most devoted fans!
**David Binkley**: Who initially convinced me I could write.
**Lori Parsons**: For getting me to believe in myself.
To all my friends over the years, too numerous to mention but they know who they are, who never gave up on their belief in me and have been a constant source of encouragement.
I thank each and every one of you for your kindness, encouragement and support and the motivation you gave me to see this project to its end. This book would not have been possible without you.

Cover artwork by Kimberly Roby
kmroby8468@gmail.com

# 1

"Listen to me carefully; there are a few things I need to tell you about Robert."

Julie began.

Karen looked disgusted.

"Why do we have to talk about 'him' mom? He left us; he obviously didn't want to be with us..."

Julie sighed and lifted a hand to quiet her daughter.

"That's not true Karen."

Karen rolled her eyes and stood up; she took two steps then turned to face her mother. Her words were tainted with hostility. She put her hands on her hips defiantly before speaking.

"Well, he sure isn't here now, is he?"

Her words dripped with sarcasm, her tone filled with anger. She could see the anguish in her mother's eyes but was finding it difficult to empathize with her at the moment.

Julie could sense the agony her daughter was feeling and allowed her to continue. She needed to get it out of her system before she dared tell her any more.

"He left on his own; no one forced him to go. It was all on him Mom and he left you pregnant with his child! What kind of a man would do that? What more could I possibly need to know?"

Julie closed her eyes for a moment, trying to process her daughter's words and feelings. The bitterness in Karen's words hurt but she tried to ignore the harshness of her daughter's sentiments. She knew Karen wasn't aware of the whole truth.

This only motivated her to try harder to explain it in a way her daughter might be able to make sense of what she already knew was going to sound like nonsense. She sighed softly knowing how difficult it would be to accomplish that since it barely made sense to her and she knew the entire truth. She spoke hesitantly.

"That's not true either honey."

Karen shook her head.

"Oh, leaving us wasn't his idea? I suppose he claimed it was ours."

She smirked.

Her mother shook her head.

"No Karen of course he didn't."

Karen sighed.

"Well, then whose was it? Go ahead Mom, tell me what this big secret is, why did he leave us? Oh, I know...he was kidnapped right? Really mother? You're turning this into a Lifetime movie, just be straight with me."

Julie rubbed her eyes, and let her daughter continue to ramble angrily as a pounding headache rapidly developed. She was wishing she had some of Robert's miraculous headache tabs right about now.

Putting the pain aside for a moment, and snickered silently about the television reference, fearing that by the end of the conversation it would more closely resemble an episode of The Twilight Zone.

"No, he wasn't....kidnapped, he was...well, just taken."

Julie said, and even as she spoke the words, she knew how ridiculous it sounded. She paused to give Karen a moment to react... and react she did!

Julie watched her daughter's face; she could see the thoughts and questions boiling right at the surface. Her brow was creased in a mixture of confusion, disbelief and disgust.

Karen threw her arms up in the air.

"You're talking in riddles and not making any sense. He was just taken...really mom? So, are we now starring

2

in some kind of weird Sci-Fi movie? I don't understand where you are going with this."

Julie took a deep breath letting it out slowly. If only Karen had known how close to reality that analogy really was. She patted the rock next to her.

"Come over here and sit with me sweetheart. We really need to talk."

Karen thought for a moment. She could see the seriousness in her mother's face, it concerned her. She conceded to walking over and sitting on a large rock next to her mother.

"Mom, what's going on? You're not yourself, I'm worried about you. It's not healthy to dwell on Robert mom, he's gone, and it is over. We need to move on!"

Julie bit her lip desperately trying to formulate her thoughts into words Karen could make sense of. She just needed to explain all of this without sounding certifiably insane, and she knew it was going to be a challenge.

She smiled at her daughter now sitting next to her. She reached over and gently brushed the hair from her face.

"Karen, this is going to be the hardest conversation we have ever had."

Karen looked confused.

"Even harder than..."

Julie interrupted her knowing where she was taking the sentence.

"Yes Karen, even harder than that one."

Karen pondered her mothers' answer, and then she arched her brows.

"Wow. That was a tough one at the time, kind of humorous now."

Julie managed a weak giggle over her daughter's comment.

"Yes it was, one that every mother and daughter needs

and hates to have, but we managed to get through it, and we both survived. I believe we can get through this one as well if you keep an open mind."

Julie put her arm around her daughter as Karen continued.

"Mother seriously, I don't see why we have to dwell on him, he's gone, it's over and we both just have to deal with it. It's not important anymore."

Julie couldn't help feeling anger at Karen's words. The volume of her voice rose slightly.

"I'm having his baby and you're going to be a big sister! I think that is pretty damn important don't you?"

Her mother's outburst and use of a rare swear word made Karen realize the severity of her mother's intent. Her mother never used that type of language, even in her angriest moments. It also made her regret her choice of words. She really wasn't that insensitive.

"I'm sorry, I didn't mean that. Of course I do, you know that."

Julie took a deep breath smiled a little. So far so good she thought. She lowered her voice.

"Okay then, listen closely to what I'm about to tell you, and please, let me finish before you decide to put me in a nut ward."

Karen sat quietly staring down at the ground. Her concern for her mother now outweighed her anger and skepticism. Julie noticed her daughter staring defiantly at the ground. This angered her; she was going to need her daughter's full attention if this was going to go anywhere.

"Karen Renee"

Julie scolded.

"Look at me when I'm talking to you!"

Karen looked up from the ant hill she had been studying and returned her attention to her mother.

"What mom?"

Julie put both her hands on Karen's shoulders and tried to smile. She could tell Karen was getting upset, and that was the last thing she needed now. She looked directly into her daughter's eyes.

"Remember me telling you how I have never lied to you?"

Karen nodded slowly.

"Yeah, you've have mentioned that many times."

Julie closed her eyes; she took a deep breath and silently asked for divine intervention in helping her find the words she needed to help Karen understand.

"Well, sadly this is one time I must confess I did."

Karen looked puzzled.

"Really mom, you lied to me? Just what did you lie to me about?"

Julie paused for a moment knowing she wasn't going to like the answer.

"I lied to you about Robert."

Karen covered her face with her hands in frustration and shouted out in anger.

"I should have known, Robert, of course! What else could it have been? We're still talking about him!" Karen rolled her eyes."

Julie glared at her and felt her temper rising but she kept an even tone.

"Yes, and we're going to continue talking about him until I tell you what you need to know!"

Karen groaned.

"Oh that's just great, whatever mother. You're not doing either of us any good by dwelling on him and besides, I think I already know everything I want or need to know about him!"

Julie shook her head.

"Oh trust me sweetheart, you don't know the half of it."

Karen studied her mother's face. Something in her eyes told her she really needed to listen. She still resented Robert for what he had done to her Mom, and as much as she didn't want to admit it, to her as well. She could tell this was important to her mother and she could see that she was struggling to make the words come out right. She managed a weak smile.

"Okay mom, I'm sorry, I'm listening, but purely out of respect for you. What else do you want me to know about him?"

Julie rubbed her throbbing head as her heart raced a mile a minute. She has always managed to get through the difficult times with Karen, and there had been many, but just how does a mother tell her daughter her boyfriend was an alien? This one wasn't covered in the parenting manual.

She had no prepared speech, no ideas. She silently chastised herself for not having prepared a speech for this. She shrugged inwardly and decided to play it by ear. She would just have to trust her daughter to keep an open mind.

"Karen, Robert was unlike any man either of us had ever known."

Karen threw her head back in dismay. She rolled her eyes in a typical teenage girl's response to a corny love story.

"Oh mother, please don't give me that romantic crap!"

Julie squeezed her daughter's arm.

"No honey that's not what I'm talking about at all, hear me out and please, above all, keep an open mind. I guess I should start with explaining why I lied to you."

Karen agreed sarcastically

"Gee... You think that might be a good idea?"

Julie tried to ignore the outright bitterness in Karen's response.

"I lied to you because I wasn't sure if you could handle or even believe the truth."

Karen glared at her mother.

"Did you even give me that chance mother?"

Julie shook her head with remorse.

"No, I didn't then, but I am now. Hey, even parents make mistakes and looking back at it, I guess this was a big one. I'm sorry."

Karen just groaned.

"Well that's really weak Mom, but go on."

Karen listened with skepticism as her mother continued.

"There simply is no easy way of saying this, no way to sugarcoat it so I'm going to give it to you straight.

When I told you Robert was unlike any man either of us had ever met, I meant Robert wasn't a man at all, he wasn't a human. Robert was from another planet."

Karen was abhorred.

"Oh mother please!"

Undaunted, Julie continued, her voice raising an octave for emphasis.

"You wanted the truth, so let me finish!"

Karen folded her arms and looked at her mother with frustrating annoyance and extreme defiance.

Julie felt the words rushing out before she could stop and think of the best way to say them.

"Robert came here from another planet and the reason he is no longer with us is they took him back. He was a criminal on his planet and was exiled to Earth until they could complete his sentence. Karen. He is dead, they executed him."

Karen had heard enough. She was beside herself with so many feelings she didn't understand. She just rolled her eyes again in frustration. She had trouble even responding to this unbelievable story.

"They did what? Who executed him? C'mon now what are you talking about! Seriously mother, you expect me to believe this crap? You're insulting my intelligence here! Is this the best you could come up with? Would you believe it?"

Julie threw up her hands in exasperation.

"No, I couldn't blame you if you didn't, I didn't at first either."

Karen looked astonished.

"You didn't believe it first? So you're telling me you actually do believe it now? Mother I'm not stupid. What could possibly make you believe such a pile of crap?"

Julie's headache intensified as she tried to come up with the right words to convince her daughter that what she was saying was the truth.

"The facts just can't be denied Karen, as crazy as it sounds; it's true."

Karen pounded her forehead in disbelief and closed her eyes for a moment before speaking. Her frustration was beginning to overwhelm her.

"Mom, if you had told me he left because he didn't love us, or because he had found someone else, fine I can accept that but why make up this outrageous story?"

Julie pointed her finger at her daughter and spoke deliberately.

"That's exactly my point Karen! Why would I make up such a crazy thing if it weren't true?"

Karen shook her head.

"Oh I just don't have a clue, I really don't. I don't know what to say other than I'm very disappointed in you. I'm starting to really worry about you mom."

She pondered for a moment before continuing.

"You said the facts couldn't be denied, just what facts could possibly lead you to this ridiculous conclusion?"

Julie took a deep breath. She wasn't sure if they were

making progress or not. But now she was starting to get to the heart of the story. She knew she would have to use the same factors that had convinced her that the story of Robert's origin were true, and pray they had the same effect on Karen. She knew Karen was a very bright young lady, but this would push her furthest boundaries.

"Okay let's start off with your miracle cure. Can you explain that? I'm listening."

Karen's shoulders drooped; she knew she didn't have an answer for that.

"No, I don't think anyone can."

Julie smiled figuring she may have actually won that round. She nodded her head in confidence.

"You're totally wrong there sweetheart; I can, Robert could have."

She paused for a moment.

"Think about it sweetheart. All of the doctors were amazed, they said it was impossible, yet, you were healed. Your brain was completely rewired by technology that doesn't exist, at least here. How do you explain that?"

Karen was deep in thought. Her mother had a valid point. She uttered a question without really thinking about it first.

"So you're saying, that thing, that crazy device he used on me, was something that he brought from his world? You're saying it was some kind of medical tool from the future or something?"

Julie's smile broadened.

"Yes dear, that's exactly what I'm saying, he brought it with him. Not only that, you know those awful chronic headaches I had that would drive me crazy? Well, he gave me medicine that stopped them."

Karen's eyes widened.

"He cured your headaches? Mom nothing helped you

with those! You're saying he gave you something that actually did?"

Julie nodded and smiled; now she knew she had her daughter's attention. She continued.

"Yes, they were these little Band-Aid like things you placed on your temples and the pain went away within minutes! But listen, there's even more...there was the time I was making chicken for dinner, I dropped the pan on my arm and was burned pretty badly. I had a huge burn that had blistered instantly on my arm. Robert put some kind of ointment on it that not only took away the pain but removed the burn instantly, no pain not even a hint of a scar!"

She held out her arm showing Karen there were no marks or burns.

"You know there is simply no medicine on Earth like that today, nothing that could do this, it's simply impossible!"

She paused for a moment of thought.

"Did I mention 'on Earth?'" .

Karen's expression changed to one of astonishment.

"Are you serious mom? It even removed the burn spot, just like that?"

Julie slowly nodded her head again.

"Yes it did, completely, instantly. I had never seen anything like it before!"

Karen was shocked and suddenly bombarded with a melee of conflicting thoughts. A part of her still thought the story was far fetched, but now, after watching her mother's face and listening to her words, a part of her was beginning to believe her story.

"So that letter he wrote us..."

Julie interrupted her.

"He wrote that because he thought it would be easier for you to hate him than to miss him. He was just trying to make it easier on you. He was trying to protect you, Karen."

Karen pondered her mother's words. She was emotionally worn out. She was struggling to accept what her mother was telling her, it was too much to process all at once and it was making her very tired.

"Could we go home now? I'm really beat. I just need to lie down and try to sort this all out."

Julie gave her daughter a compassionate smile.

"Of course we can sweetheart, I understand. You have to have a lot on your mind, we both do. Everything is going to be alright. You'll see, and... you're going to be a big sister soon! Isn't that exciting?"

Karen smiled half-heartedly. Excitement wasn't one of emotions she was feeling at the moment. She spoke with quiet indifference.

"Yeah mom, exciting, you're telling me I'm going to be ET's big sister, yeah that's exciting right."

Julie couldn't help but laugh at the comment and gathered her things. The two of them walked slowly down the cobblestone path back to the entrance of the park.

A large flock of Canadian geese flew at treetop level in their classic V formation over their heads. The birds were honking at each other at the top of their lungs as they flew towards the pond. This aerial display would normally draw smiles and laughter but at the moment their minds were a million miles away, more accurately, twelve light years away.

Karen silently reflected on the conversation. Her thoughts concentrated on her healing. It didn't make any sense, it never did. All of her doctors had said it was impossible, they all insisted there was simply no cure, only treatments to deal with it. She thought back on how shocked they were when they reviewed her last brain scan, and how it appeared that her brain had miraculously been completely re-wired. No one could explain that. Karen then reflected on the doctor's amazement at having to admit was actually cured. It was a lot to process.

She thought back to the device Robert had used on her and how he promised it would help her. In all the doctors' visits she had endured over the years, she had never seen anything like that gadget, and the fact that it actually worked added credence to her mother's story.

Could what her mother was telling her actually be true? She desperately fought that notion, but nothing else made any sense. That would explain her cure perfectly; he used technology we couldn't even imagine.

She was astounded to hear about her mother's headaches being cured. She knew she had tried everything and nothing seemed to help. Then the story about the burn and Robert's ointment taking the scar and pain away instantly...this was sounding stranger and stranger the more she thought about it. In fact it was getting downright weird.

Then she thought about how smart Robert was, how he knew all the impossible answers to her trivia game. Maybe he really was from a place that was far more advanced, and smarter than we were.

She shook her head back to reality and turned to her mother walking beside her.

"If this is true, then, the baby will be...."

She paused, not wanting to sound odd when she asked a question she desperately needed to know the answer to.

"Kind of like Spock, half human, and half alien?"

Julie couldn't help but chuckle at Karen's question.

"Yes sweetheart, something like that."

Karen's eyes got big and her mouth dropped at the thought.

"He won't come out with green skin and pointy ears or anything, will he?"

Julie outright laughed at this remark.

"No dear he won't. Robert didn't look like that now did he?"

Karen shrugged her shoulders.

"No, I guess he didn't."

# 2

They left the park and headed back home. After a few minutes, Karen stopped and faced her mother. She spoke solemnly conceding the possibility, at least for the moment, that her mother's story might actually be true.

"Mom, were you with him when, well when it happened? I mean, when they took him?"

Julie closed her eyes for a moment of sad recollection. A tear fell from her eye.

"Yes sweetheart. We were having coffee and just talking."

Karen sighed and chose her words carefully noticing that a tear had formed in her mother's eye. She could feel the pain the memory had on her mother and at least temporally accepting her mother's outlandish story. She finally felt some empathy for her mom.

"Wow; that had to have been hard."

Karen thought for a moment before asking a difficult question.

"How did it happen?"

Julie finally acknowledged the tears which had unexpected come to her eyes and wiped them on her sleeve. She tried to regain her composure before answering.

"Well, like I said, we were talking. You know how I cry at the drop of a hat; like now...well I went into the bathroom to get a tissue, I wasn't gone for longer than twenty seconds, and when I returned...he was gone."

Karen couldn't help but shed a tear as well; she knew that had to have been very difficult for her mother. She gathered her thoughts. She was surprised to discover that in addition to her anger and hatred of the man she thought deserted them, there was also a lingering remorseful feeling of actually missing the man she had hoped would become her new father.

"Then, is it alright that, I miss him?"

Another tear crept out of Julie's eye as she hugged her daughter.

"Of course it is, sweetheart. I miss him too, I miss him very much."

Karen hugged her mother tightly and added an uncomfortable confession.

"He was the best friend I had. He was the only one who really listened to me, understood me and seemed to really care. I mean besides you mom. He was becoming the father I had always hoped for but never had."

Julie smiled.

"He cared about you very much honey."

Unashamed, Karen now wiped her tears.

"I know he did mom. I could feel it then and for some crazy reason I can feel it now."

Julie's heart silently exploded with emotion after hearing her daughter's words. She had never felt closer to Karen than she did at this moment.

"I can too Sweetheart."

They walked the last three blocks to the apartment in silence, Karen was imagining what it would be like to have a half alien sibling, wondering if he or she would be anything like her. The thought of her soon to be sibling being half alien was hard to digest. Meanwhile, Julie was painfully reliving her last moments with Robert.

Julie smiled at her daughter walking next to her. She was relieved that the conversation was over and had actually gone better than she expected. She paused for a moment and put her arm around Karen.

"You must be getting hungry sweetheart, let's order a

pizza when we get home. I really don't feel like cooking tonight."

Karen returned the smile.

"That sounds great mom."

They entered through the front door walking through the bar to the back. Then they walked up the short flight of the stairs leading to their apartment. As they were headed up Julie heard something coming from the hallway.

Someone was knocking on a door. She stopped short, a bit frightened, but curious as well. This alarmed her; knowing there were only two apartments, hers and....the one that had been Robert's. She gave Karen a questioning glance and picked up her pace as she went up the stairs.

As they reached the top of the stairs she saw a man in a red checkered flannel shirt and khaki pants. His short, neatly trimmed salt and pepper hair and beer belly gave his identity away. It was Larry Bertlson, the landlord, knocking on the door of Robert's apartment.

Julie panicked for a minute. This was a scenario she hadn't prepared herself for. She hadn't planned on running into Larry. She knew she had to tell him something about Robert's absence.

She put her hand on her heart in an attempt to first slow it down and secondly come to grips with the unexpected situation. Her first thought was to run back downstairs and avoid the conversation that would follow, at least for the moment and give her time to prepare something to tell Larry.

All thoughts of this plan were dashed when Mr. Bertlson glanced over and saw them. The encounter was now inevitable. Her mind was racing, trying to conjure up some kind of story to tell him that would explain Robert's sudden disappearance.

She quickly turned to Karen who was waiting behind her.

"Don't say a word Karen, let me do the talking."

Karen nodded.

"No problem mom, you're on your own. Good luck."

Larry walked over to them and smiled.

"Julie, I'm glad I ran into you."

Julie sighed...this can't be good but she was a bit disarmed by his smile so she smiled back as nonchalantly as she could, and asked a question she really didn't want the answer to.

"Hello Larry, what's up?"

She asked, trying to sound as if nothing was out of the ordinary.

Mr. Bertlson pointed to Robert's door.

"Well, I dropped by to collect Robert's rent but he doesn't seem to be home. He had initially paid for a full year. It's hard to believe that year is up this month."

He said with a friendly smile.

"Have you seen him today?"

The words hit Julie like a ton of bricks. She recalled Robert saying he would be here for exactly one year when she first met him and how odd she thought it was at the time. She needed no reminder that the year had indeed come to an end. She cleared her throat if for no other reason than to buy her a few more seconds to think. She had to come up with something and quickly. She had to emphasize that sadly, Robert wouldn't be coming back.

Realizing this was a situation that would have to be addressed at some time she took a deep breath and decided that now was as good of time as any, considering there was no way of getting out of it now. Again she asked for divine intervention to give her an idea.

"Larry, there is something I have to tell you."

Larry noticed the hesitation in her voice.

"Julie, you look upset, is everything alright?"

Julie lowered her head and took a deep breath.

"No Larry I'm afraid it's not."

She closed her eyes for one last moment of deep thought. She uttered the first thing that came into her mind, one that would surely confirm that Robert was not coming back.

"This is hard Larry, but, Robert passed away Tuesday."

Mr. Bertlson's eyes got as big as saucers.

"Oh my God, Julie what happened?"

Julie's satisfaction at coming up with a clever story lasted only seconds. Now she had to come up with the details. She had painted herself into a corner and now had some quick improvising to do to try and get herself out of it. She knew she had to be clever, convincing, and defiantly decisive and all while appearing to grieve. She decided the straight forward approach would be best.

"It was a heart attack Larry. We were having dinner at my apartment and all of a sudden he grabbed his chest and collapsed to the floor. I called 911 but he died on the way to the hospital. I should have called you, I'm sorry but I have just been beside myself since it happened. It was all so sudden..."

A look of shock then sadness crossed Larry's face. He interrupted her.

"Oh Julie that's horrible, I'm so sorry. I totally understand why you didn't call, don't be sorry."

Larry wiped his brow and continued.

"I just don't know what to say. This is such a shock! Did he have problems with his heart? He was so young!"

Julie shook her head.

"If he did he never mentioned it to me. Yes it was a complete shock to me as well Larry."

Mr. Bertlson could see the sadness in his tenant's eyes.

"Were you two very close?"

Julie spoke softly.

"Yes, we were Larry. We were dating actually."

Julie's voice trailed off.

"I still can't believe he is gone. It was just so …sudden."

Larry hugged his tenant.

"If there is anything I can do Julie, don't hesitate to ask. Robert seemed like a very nice man. I don't know what to say at a time like this other than I am so sorry."

Julie thanked him and she and Karen walked towards the door to their apartment.

Larry returned to Robert's door then turned and spoke softly.

"Julie, I hate to even bother you with this, I know what a difficult time this is for you but have there been any arrangements for his personal belongings? You know, I don't want to sound cold but I have to eventually get the apartment in order."

Julie simply shook her head.

"It's okay Larry, I understand. No I haven't been in his apartment since, well since that night."

Larry looked down at the floor and closed his eyes. He took a deep breath and sighed.

"Well, I want to help you in any way I can. Did he have family that you know of?"

The turmoil in Julie's head was increasing. Her stress level was bouncing off the wall as she continued to fabricate a believable story.

"Yes he did Larry; as a matter of fact we were just planning a trip for us so I could meet his parents in Ohio. They live somewhere just outside Cleveland I think he said. I have their phone number and address. I think his belongings should go to them Larry, don't you think?"

Julie was amazing herself at the ease her fabricated

words were coming to her. She took mental notes of the details in the event the subject would ever come up again.

Larry nodded his agreement and reached in his pants pocket for the keys. He unlocked Robert's door and looked solemnly at Julie.

"Yes, I think that would be very appropriate Julie. I hate to burden you with this but I don't know what else to do."

Julie managed a forced smile.

"It's okay Larry, I know. It is something that has to be taken care of. I will call them and make the arrangements. I don't even think they know yet. They would have no way of knowing. The doctors at the hospital never asked me about his family. That's going to be a difficult phone call. I should be the one to tell them."

Julie was expecting an academy award for her performance. She was actually pulling this off magnificently. She hesitated for a moment.

"Just let me add that he liked you, he spoke highly of you Larry. Thank you."

Larry nodded and unlocked the door to Robert's apartment.

"I liked him too Julie. It was a pleasure having him for a tenant. He was a very nice young man. I will miss him as I am sure you will as well. Tragic moments like this certainly make one rethink their own mortality."

Julie sighed; she had no desire to continue this conversation. She reluctantly replied.

"Yes Larry it certainly does."

They shared a grief stricken smile as Larry continued.

"Well, here I'll just leave his apartment open for you. No one will bother anything, I mean no one but you and Karen will be coming up here anyways. I will leave the rest up to you. Just lock up when you are finished please.

Again, Julie, I am so sorry to hear about this, and I'm here if there is anything I can do for you or Karen."

Mr. Bertlson gave Julie a compassionate smile and walked down to the bar. Julie stood at the open door to Robert's apartment and a tear came to her eye.

# 3

She stood frozen in the doorway, looking inside. It was coming back to her. She scanned the living room. It was obviously just as it had been during their last moments together. No one had been in the apartment to change anything since their final moments together. She tried to compose herself but tears continued to flow.

Karen, having quietly been standing two steps behind for the whole process noticed her mother's change in mood, tapped her on the shoulder from behind.

"Mom, are you okay?"

Julie, in a mesmerized state, simply nodded without turning around. Karen put her hand on her mother's shoulder.

"Can I have the key please? I need to go lay down for a while."

Without saying a word Julie reached into her purse and pulled out her ring of keys and handed them to her daughter.

Julie took a deep breath and wiped the moisture from her eyes. She reluctantly walked into the apartment. What was once a place of great joy was now nothing but a mausoleum shrouded with bittersweet memories.

Tears now flowed uncontrollably from her eyes, her heart was racing. It was too soon, too soon to be doing this. She forced her eyes closed in hopes of stopping the tears.

She glanced at the sofa, the last place she had seen him. She buried her face in her hands and sobbed as her last memories of him overwhelmed her. She could still see him sitting there as she had gone to get a tissue. She remembered exactly what he was wearing, a power blue button down short sleeve shirt and blue jeans. Seeing the couch now painfully empty, reminded her that was exactly as it had looked the last time she saw it.

The silly painting they had bought at a yard sale still hung over the sofa. He didn't want the painting; he bought it because he knew she liked it. She thought back to that Saturday afternoon and the fun they had and how she had struggled, trying to explain to him what a yard sale was.

More disturbing yet was what she noticed on the coffee table. The two cups of coffee they were enjoying during their last moments together were still sitting there undisturbed, still half full, as if nothing out of the ordinary had happened at all. She could still taste the coffee and the sweet taste of his lips against hers.

The heartbreak was ripping her apart inside. She continued to look around the room. His shoes were neatly placed by the door. His jacket draped over the chair. She stood motionless in the middle of the living room, as if in a shrine of silent reverence. The once joyful room was now nothing more than a painful reminder that he was gone.

She took a deep breath and forced herself to continue. She wanted to get this over with. She silently questioned her sanity in volunteering to take care of his things. The pain of his absence, which she had been so desperately trying to suppress, was now hitting her like a sledgehammer.

She had to get through this, it had to be done and there was simply no one else to do it.

She took one room at a time. He really didn't have that many personal belongings.

She tackled the living room first.

The shoes and jacket could either be donated to Good Will or simply thrown out. Heartbreak overcame her again when she discovered the gloves she had given him for Christmas sitting on the end table. She picked them up, clutched them to her heart and closed her eyes for a moment of deep recollection. These she would keep.

Another moment of sadness overcame her as she noticed the small television and radio in the corner.

She thought back to the hours they spent watching various television shows and the frustration she experienced trying to explain them to him. She managed a chuckle as she recalled his derogatory comments on the music they found on the radio. She decided to just leave them, letting Larry either keep them or dispose of them in the manner he chose.

There really wasn't anything else in the living room. Robert didn't have any furniture, books or miscellaneous items of his own.

She then entered the kitchen. The first thing she noticed was his coffee maker. An unexpected smile came to her face. She remembered how he loved her coffee, saying they had nothing back home like that. She recalled how excited he was to buy an inexpensive little coffee maker and how she had showed him how to use it. She recalled the irony of the moment. Here she was; a simple high school educated, single mother, teaching a brilliant alien how to use a simple coffee maker.

He was thrilled at being able to make this wonderful drink himself. She decided to just leave it for Larry to deal with.

She opened the refrigerator to find a number of Tupperware containers filled with leftovers she had made for him. He so often complimented her on her cooking, even the simplest things. A tear once again came to her eye as she thought back to how he complimented her at ever chance he got. She had never known a man so adoring and attentive to her. Her heart was literally

25

aching from missing him at the moment. It wasn't that she hadn't always missed him, but now the little things he would do were really haunting her. She slowly walked to the bathroom.

What personal items she found in the bathroom she would again let Larry deal with. She hesitated as she moved to the bedroom. This would be the hardest room for sure. The incredible memories of the intimacy they shared there still fresh in her mind.

Sitting on the bed, she felt a whirlwind of emotions. She couldn't help but think back on the years of loneliness she had endured before meeting him, and how his presence in her life had changed all that.

She thought of the many times they made love in that very bed and how he had totally rejuvenated her. She cursed herself for allowing those thoughts to creep back in. She defiantly stood up and surveyed the room. She couldn't let herself stop living, even though that exactly what she wanted to do at this moment.

She had Karen to consider, she had to be strong and continue on. She shook her head free of the clouds; she needed to think about Karen, the responsibilities she had to her had to be the driving force in her attempt to get past the personal grief that was tearing her apart. She was confident she could pull that off because being selfish was something she had never mastered.

There was a pile of dirty clothes in the corner which were of little concern to her. What bothered her was his suitcase next to them.

The gray metallic suitcase glimmered as the rays from the sun peeked between the slats of the blinds in the window. It was as if it were being spotlighted, ominously beckoning her attention in the otherwise darkened room. She noticed two small black travel bags next to the suitcase that appeared empty.

She smiled sadly as she looked at the bare window and how she had promised him she would get curtains for him but never did.

She stared with great curiosity at the suitcase wondering what may be inside.

She was emotionally exhausted. This unexpected, painful trip down memory lane was taking a toll on her.

She decided to take the suitcase back to her apartment and open it later. She just didn't have the courage or the energy to do it right now. Besides, she needed to check on Karen. She knew it had been a rough morning for her and wanted to make sure she was okay.

She could get a garbage bag or box while she was there to collect what belongings she decided to keep.

She picked up the suitcase and returned to her apartment just setting it in the living room by the door.

Looking in Karen's room she found her daughter sound asleep. She was glad Karen was resting peacefully.

She thought about their conversation and how the weight of today's news must be doing to her. She felt guilty about having to burden her daughter with such an emotional trauma. But Karen needed to know, more importantly, she had to believe and accept the truth.

She remembered when Robert had first tried to convince her of the same thing and how her initial reaction was exactly like Karen's. The poor child's mind must be overwhelmed with confusion. She slowly closed her daughter's bedroom door and went to the kitchen to get a garbage bag and a much needed cup of coffee.

She poured a cup of coffee and walked to the living room and sat down. Her time in Robert's apartment had inundated her mind with memories of their last few minutes together, memories she had been tortured with and desperately tried to overcome.

Painful recollections she had been trying to put in the

back of her mind were now attacking her with undeniable cruelty.

She closed her eyes for a moment and could vividly see him sitting on her couch. She could hear his laugh and feel his gentle touch. She took a sip of coffee and stared at the suitcase.

The fear and anticipation of whatever lay hidden within the suitcase, bringing up even more memories, was causing a painful throbbing in her head.

She took another sip of her coffee and was determined to get this agonizing ordeal over with and try to return to her life as best she could. She decided to leave the suitcase for now and get everything from the apartment in one trip. That way she wouldn't have to face the torturous memories of being there again.

She got a couple garbage bags from under the kitchen sink and set her mind to the task ahead.

She clutched the bags and entered Robert's apartment with renewed determination. She started in the living room. She picked up his shoes and jacket and placed them in the garbage bag.

Looking around she didn't notice anything else of consequence. Robert lived a very simple life with very few personal possessions. She confirmed her intention to leave the television and stereo for Larry to deal with. She had no use for them and certainly didn't want the constant reminder of him in her home.

She took the linen from the bathroom and proceeded back into the kitchen. She smiled again seeing the coffee maker sitting on the counter. She had no use for it and decided to leave it for Larry as well.

He had no other kitchen utensils or anything of value so she returned to the refrigerator to dispose of all the containers inside. She dumped them in the second garbage bag. His constant adulation over her cooking made her wonder what kind of food he had on his planet. He so loved her cooking. She couldn't help but hold back a tear at the thought of how wonderful it was to have someone other than Karen to cook for. This thought brought up other unwanted feelings. Robert had filled so many voids in her life.

The last room was the bed room. Again she eyed the pile of dirty clothes in the corner.

She gathered them up and stopped a moment...she could smell his cologne on the clothes. Her heart sunk. She had picked out that cologne for him and smelling it again was devastating. He was enamored at the scent again claiming they had nothing like that on his planet.

She hastily massed them up into a ball and threw them in the bag deciding to just trash them as well. She couldn't bear keeping them.

A tee-shirt fell to the floor as she was stuffing the bag. She picked it up and another tear slipped from her eye. It was a Beatle tee-shirt she had bought him after he heard them on the radio and confessed to actually liking them. He got the biggest kick out of it and put it on the moment she gave it to him.

These simple memories were like daggers in her heart. But, what bothered her most was, that it was the shirt he was wearing the first time they made love, she remembered slowly taking it off him. She held it to her chest; she decided to keep this one. She checked the two travel bags and confirmed they were indeed empty.

Her attention then turned somberly to the bed. He only had one set of bed sheets and seeing them again brought more heartache. She sat on the bed and closed her eyes, reliving all the intimate moments they shared on this very bed.

Her thoughts drifted to how her life had been missing any intimacy until he came and how he completed her both physically and emotionally. The emptiness in her heart was unbearable and she could feel it ripping her apart.

She fought desperately to hold back the tears as she pondered an unanswerable question. Was it was better to have never known that kind of passion or to have experienced it only to have it cruelly taken away.

Regaining control of her thoughts she ripped the sheets and blanket off the bed and threw them into the trash bag.

She grabbed both bags and walked deliberately to the bedroom door, but, something made her turn around. She stared at the pillows sitting on the now bare bed. She had to have one. She took a pillow and kissed it gently. Holding the pillow and tee-shirt and dragging the two bags behind her she returned to her apartment.

She set the bag destined to be thrown away by the door next to the suitcase and took the other one into the bedroom.

She went to Karen's bedroom to check on her daughter. She opened the bedroom door just a crack, she didn't want to disturb her if she was still sleeping. She saw Karen lying peacefully on her bed with her back to her. She had her headphones on listening to her mp3 player. She had escaped for now into a world of her own, completely unaware of her mothers' encroachment. Julie gently closed Karen's door.

Still clutching the pillow and tee-shirt she went into the bathroom. Sweet memories tugged at her heart. She felt a need to be close to him, she decided the only way for this to come even close to happening would be to change into his tee-shirt. After the day's agonizing ordeal she needed this remorseful connection and painfully put on the shirt. The cologne on the shirt filled her senses with the sweet aroma and her heart with an excruciating pain.

She was emotionally drained. She went into her bedroom and collapsed on the bed holding his pillow tightly, fantasizing about holding him instead. She silently cried. After a few minutes she mercifully fell asleep.

She was awakened about an hour later by soft tapping on her shoulder. She rolled over and saw Karen standing by the bed.

"Mom, I'm sorry for waking you. Are we still getting that pizza? I'm getting hungry."

Letting go of the pillow she slowly sat up and smiled.

"Of course we are sweetheart. I'm sorry I fell asleep."

Karen smiled brightly. She noticed her mother's shirt, and her expression changed to one of curious interest.

"Mom, wasn't that Robert's shirt?"

She had totally forgotten she was wearing it. She glanced down at the shirt then at her daughter.

"Yes sweetheart, I ran across it while going through his apartment. I don't know, I just put it on. You know, I thought it might make me feel closer to him, it was a silly notion."

Karen looked skeptical then noticed the pillow.

"That pillow was his too wasn't it?"

Julie nodded softly trying to conceal her tears. Karen had been through enough today she didn't need to see her mother struggle.

Karen sensed there was something more to the true reason behind the two items but she didn't press any further. She simply asked,

"Are you alright mom?"

Julie just nodded and smiled.

"Yes sweetheart, I'm fine."

Karen leaned over and hugged her mother instinctively

knowing she needed it and replied with wisdom and compassion far beyond her young years.

"I miss him too Mom, but that's okay. We're going to get through

This in spite of how hard it is. We have each other!"

Recognizing her daughter's maturity, Julie smiled and hugged her tightly. Karen's gesture gave her unexpected strength.

"My little girl has grown up so fast."

The difference in her this year compared to this time last year was remarkable, and she knew they both owed that to Robert. They could never have had this tender moment a year ago; they could never have had it without Robert.

"You know sweetheart, you are my rock, my beautiful rainbow thru the raging storm. Yes, we are going to be fine. Now let's get that pizza!"

Karen beamed with joy at her mother as she slowly rolled out of bed. Her daughter was showing no ill effects from their earlier conversation. She spoke with sincere empathy.

"I know you are going through a difficult time, so I just wanted to tell you I am here for you Mom, in any way you need."

Julie's heart filled with pride as she quipped.

"Just when did we switch roles young lady? Seems like you are the nurturing adult and I am now the whimpering child."

Karen chuckled at her mother's response and finally managed a smile. Julie thought to herself, how this pleasant conversation could never have taken place before Karen's miraculous cure. How her daughter has changed. She silently thanked Robert again for what he had done for her, for both of them.

She finds this thought comforting; she knows his

spirit remains in her heart. She smiles knowing that he will be with her through Karen's new life not to mention the pending arrival of their baby.

Julie wiped the sleep, and tears from her eyes and reached into her pocket for her cell phone. She called the pizza delivery place and ordered a large pepperoni, mushroom and extra cheese pizza, Karen's favorite.

They went to the kitchen. Julie got two glasses and filled them with iced tea while Karen collected two plates and napkins.

"I'll take these into the living room mom. Maybe we can find something good on television to watch while we eat."

Julie smiled as she followed her daughter.

"Sounds like a great plan to me! The pizza should be here any minute; you know it never takes them long."

Karen placed the plates on the coffee table and noticed the suitcase by the door.

She walked over to it and examined it.

Julie entered the living room with their drinks and noticed her daughter scrutinizing the suitcase.

Karen looked inquisitively at her mother.

"This was Robert's too wasn't it?"

Julie nodded.

"Yeah I knew it was. It sure is a weird looking suitcase. He didn't get this any where near here that's for sure."

Julie snickered at her daughter's incredible sense of humor.

"No he didn't, that much I am sure of."

Karen scrutinized every inch of the usual suitcase for the next twenty minutes then the pizza delivery man knocked on the door.

Julie greeted the man, paid for the pizza and placed it on the coffee table. She turned her attention back to Karen.

"Come on sweetheart, let's eat!"

Karen took a piece of pizza then looked back to the suitcase.

"What do you think is in it?" she asked.

Julie just shrugged her shoulders trying, at least on the surface, to appear uninterested and took a piece of pizza from the box. Karen immediately saw through her mother's guise.

"Well, are we going to open it? I mean, aren't you curious about what's inside?"

Julie sighed, mildly annoyed by her daughter's persistence and still trying to ignore her question.

"Sweetheart, let's just have some pizza and..."

Karen interrupted her

"You're afraid to see what's inside aren't you."

Julie groaned.

"I wouldn't put it quite that way Karen."

Karen could tell her mother was apprehensive about opening the suitcase. She tried to console her.

"Mom, you have to open it at some point. I just thought it would be easier if we did it together. We're a team, we can do this! I'm here for you."

Karen's new found maturity continued to amaze Julie. She thought back to the quiet, withdrawn, angry daughter she used to have and how her personality had totally changed. Again she silently thanked Robert for helping them both.

"You are really something honey. I'm just so proud of you!"

Karen smiled jubilantly and replied in jest.

"So you like the new me?"

Julie just shook her head and smiled.

"Sweetheart I've always loved you and always will. Let's just say it's an improvement over last year's model."

They shared a few moments of laughter, then bit into the pizza.

Karen put her pizza back on her plate, and set it aside. She took her mother's hand and held it tightly. Her face was now somber.

"Mom"

She spoke with a serious tone.

"I know I wasn't very easy to live with. I think about it all the time now...."

Julie stopped her.

"No honey, don't give that another thought..."

Karen continued.

"No mom, I want to say this. I've needed to tell you this since, well since I got better. I really didn't' mean to make your life so...difficult. I'm so sorry. You were so tolerant of me, you didn't deserve the way I treated you."

Julie's heart was melting in a combination of motherly pride and astonishment. She beamed with happiness. She continued daily to be amazed by Karen's transformation. It was if she had become a completely different person. Again she reminded herself it wouldn't have been possible without Robert's intervention. With this thought came a tinge of sadness, she knew she owed him a debt of gratitude she could never repay.

"Sweetheart, I have never been as proud of you as I am at this moment. If it makes you feel better your apology is accepted although it is by no means necessary. Just remember, families stick together through good and bad times."

# 4

She hugged her daughter tightly and concluded.

"Now let's see what's inside that silly suitcase before it drives us both bonkers!"

Karen giggled for a second at her mother's comment then looked at her skeptically.

"Are you sure you're up to it?"

Julie smirked. Karen's empathy had given her incredible strength and confidence. She spoke with determination. She took her daughter's hand and squeezed it tightly.

"With you next to me I'm up for anything. Let's check this out!"

Karen nodded her approval.

"You rock mom! Who knows what might be inside?"

Julie shook her head and inhaled deeply silently preparing herself for what ever lied ahead. She felt so blessed to have Karen. Her daughter was such an incredible source of strength.

"You're pretty cool too sweetheart, guess we will soon find out!"

The both stood up and walked, somewhat apprehensively, over to the suitcase. They approached it with the reverence of a Priest approaching the Holy Grail; almost as if they were afraid the suitcase might actually pounce on them or something.

As she approached the suitcase Julie felt like Patricia Neal approaching Gort in 'The Day the Earth Stood Still'. She just hoped the suitcase didn't have a laser protection device like Gort's.

Julie placed it flat on the floor and looked for a way to open it.

They both sat Indian style on the floor next to the suitcase in anticipation as Julie picked it up to study it. She lifted the suitcase carefully, looking at, and feeling along the sides and top for any way to open it.

She picked up the suitcase carefully, studying the sides and top for any hinges or clasps. She didn't see any clips or fasteners, only a smooth seam running along the top extending down both sides. There was no way of telling the top from the bottom other than one side had a recessed handle. She was assuming that would naturally be the top.

Puzzled she glanced at Karen.

"Just how do you open this crazy thing?"

Karen looked surprised and shrugged her shoulders.

"Can I take a look mom?"

Karen took the suitcase from her mother and examined it closely.

She observed the same thing; a very thin seam encircled the entire suitcase without interruption. The seam was so tight that it gave the appearance of the case being one solid piece with no discernable top or bottom. There were no signs of any fasteners or clamps. She looked for someplace to put a key or maybe a combination lock but found neither.

A look of complete puzzlement creased her brow until she noticed something her mother hadn't seen.

She had lifted up the handle, which was recessed, and noticed a small rectangular strip of flat red metal underneath.

"Hey mom, did you see this?"

Julie looked inquisitively at the new discovery.

"What in the world is that? This has to be the way to open it."

Karen studied the strip for a moment. An obscure thought suddenly came to her. She momentarily reflected on all the science fiction movies she has watched. Well, if Robert is indeed from another planet, let's think out of the box.

She placed her thumb on it and pressed down. She slowly ran her finger across the metal strip and then back again.

The black seam which had been keeping the suitcase closed now turned blue and without a sound, the top slowly elevated a fraction of an inch separating it from the bottom.

A look of astonishment crossed Julie's face.

"How did you figure it out?"

Karen smiled.

"Oh I saw something like that in a Sci-Fi movie once. It worked in the movie so I just thought I would try it. Far out huh!"

Julie laughed and shook her head.

"Well, that's appropriate."

Julie stared at the suitcase. Karen noticed her mother's hesitance and tapped her on the shoulder.

"Um... mom, it's not going to open itself."

Julie chuckled.

"I wouldn't be surprised if it did sweetheart."

Karen finally took the initiative and slowly lifted the top up. The first thing they noticed was the top half featured a pouch secured by an elastic strap, very much like the suitcases they were used to.

The pouch was stuffed with neatly folded clothes. Julie pulled them out and set them on the floor. Going through them they found a pair of blue jeans, a couple button down short sleeved shirts, a couple tee shirts and three pair of white socks and three pair of boxer shorts.

Karen looked at her mother and smiled.

"Well mom, nothing unusual so far."

Julie gave her a doubting look.

"Yeah, so far that is."

Putting the pile of clothes aside they now concentrated on the bottom of the suitcase.

The first thing Julie noticed was a rectangular brown envelope sitting on top. She picked it up and set it on the floor as she continued.

Sitting on top was a black button down shirt with matching black sweat pants. She unfolded the shirt to discover a number sewn on a white square above the left pocket. '16754'.

She closed her eyes for a moment of thought immediately knowing what the shirt must be, his prison uniform.

The thought of Robert being a prisoner appalled her. They never discussed his life before coming to Earth or what led him to becoming incarcerated. He never talked about it only admitting he had committed murder.

She couldn't imagine such a kind, compassionate man doing anything like that but never pursued the issue. She simply accepted it and tried to convince her heart that he must have had a very good reason to do such a thing. She only knew him as a loving caring man and wasn't interested in learning anything about his dark side, if indeed he had one in the past.

By that time their time together was limited and she wanted to concentrate on the present and not worry about his past. She painfully refolded the shirt and placed it and the pants on the clothes pile on the floor.

Karen watched intently as her mother continued to explore the contents of the suitcase. She looked at the black uniform with special interest.

"So mom, this was his prison uniform?"

Julie nodded sadly.

"Yes dear I'm sure it was."

This discovery only added credence to her mother's

story. Karen then recalled something her mother had said earlier. She was hesitant to inquire about it but asked anyways.

"You said they executed him?"

Julie just nodded. The pain of the thought rendered her incapable of adding words.

Karen felt deep remorse for mentioning such a dreadful thought.

"That's not right! He was a great guy. Why..."

Julie interrupted her finally getting the strength to address the issue.

"Well sweetheart, apparently there was more to him than he let us know."

She took a moment to collect her thoughts.

"Perhaps in his past he was a different person than the one we got to know. You don't know what his life may have been like. Difficult situations sometimes cause good people to do things they normally wouldn't do. He may have been forced to do the wrong thing but maybe for a good reason. We are certainly in no position to judge him for his past, only fondly remember him for the man we grew to love."

Karen sadly acknowledged her mother's sentiments. She thought for a moment then tried to insert some consolation.

"Mom, did you ever stop to think that maybe we might have helped him as much as he helped us? I mean; maybe he never had anyone to care about him or love him like we did. Maybe we brought out the good side of him for the first time in his life."

Julie stopped cold after hearing that. She had never given that possibility any thought. Self confidence was never a strong point for her and the thought of her actually helping Robert in some way was as alien as he was.

The more she thought about Karen's simple but

profound notion the more it just might make sense. Maybe back home Robert was a very distraught man. It's possible he didn't have anyone to care about him, no family, and no friends and just perhaps that was what drove him to his crime. She recalled how cold he was initially, how distant and angry he seemed at first. She remembered first meeting him sitting at the bar and how evasive and impossible he was to talk to. She knew at the time something was troubling him but couldn't get anything from him.

Then, over the next few weeks, how he had gradually changed. He softened, was more open and responsive to her. Karen just might be on to something. Maybe they had influenced him in a positive way. A spark of happiness hit her; maybe she did repay that debt of gratitude after all. She had to acknowledge her daughter's insight.

"Sweetheart; that is a beautiful thought, one that never occurred to me. I think you just might be right. Thank you for bringing that to my attention!"

Julie's face lit up with joy while Karen's burst with pride for having made her mother smile again.

Julie returned her attention to the suitcase while Karen picked up the brown envelope she had discovered sitting in the back of the suitcase. She opened it cautiously. Her eyes became as big as saucers when she discovered its contents. The envelope was crammed with money. She thumbed through the bills before alerting her mother.

"Mom, I think you had better look at this!"

Julie stopped and turned to her daughter.

"What is it dear?"

Karen sat almost paralyzed for a moment mouth gaping. She thumbed through the countless bills in the envelope before finally managing to speak.

"There...there must be a thousand dollars in here!"

Her mother looked confused. She was startled by her daughter's statement.

"What?"

Karen slowly handed the envelope to her mother. Julie was baffled by Karen's last comment. She opened the envelope with keen interest. It was now Julie's turned to be shocked by the envelope's contents.

"Oh my God!"

Julie leafed through the countless bills in the envelope, her hands trembling. There were bills of all denominations all clean and crisp as if they had just been printed.

"Honey there is a lot more than a thousand dollars here, a whole lot more!"

Karen and her mother shared a moment of complete astonishment. Julie found herself trembling as Karen spoke.

"Mom, where would he have gotten this kind of money? He didn't even have a job!"

Julie shook her head.

"I have no idea sweetheart."

Karen thought for a moment.

"Do you think he was into some kind of illegal activity like maybe counterfeiting or something? I mean, he was a criminal before right?"

Julie was still in a state of shock over the bombshell she had in her hand. She tried to collect her thoughts.

"No I'm sure he wasn't. He couldn't have been."

Karen questioned her mother's assessment.

"Well then where did he get all of this money mom?"

A memory suddenly crept into Julie's bewildered mind. She recalled how Robert had given Mr. Bertlson an entire year's rent when he showed him the apartment. That was on the first day he was here. That would have been a lot of money. He wouldn't have had time to get involved in any illegal activity even if he had the notion. This relieved Julie of a train of thought she had already talked herself out of. He would have had to have brought it with him....but where would he have gotten it, and how? The fact that all the currency was crisp and clean, brand new bills only added to her confusion.

Karen anxiously asked the inevitable question.

"Well, what are you going to do with it? You can't give it back to him!"

Julie threw her hands up puzzlement. She looked through the envelope again looking for a note...a receipt... anything that might indicate where all of this came from. Finding nothing she was doubt at a loss.

"No, we can't give it back to him. I...I don't know what to do with it."

Karen badgered her mother with typical teenager exuberance over the possibility of inheriting such a windfall.

"Well then are we going to keep it mom?" Julie was a bit annoyed by her daughter's persistence.

"Karen I just don't know what we are going to do with it right now! Let's just put it aside until I have a chance to think about this. I can't be distracted right now; we still need to go through the rest of this stuff. I can't think about any money right now. This is really hard on me; I want to get it over with."

Karen, respecting her mother's request, reluctantly let the subject drop as she watched her return to the contents of the suitcase. Just then, Julie noticed a small black leather bag, like a travel bag nestled at the bottom of the suitcase. She lifted it up gently and placed it on the floor. Karen studied it with inquisitive eyes.

"Cool, I wonder what's inside!"

Julie gave her a look of bewilderment.

"Lord only knows!"

Karen smiled in anticipation.

"Well open it up mom let's see!"

Julie gestured for her daughter to slow down for a minute. She took a deep breath. Studying the bag she discovered a seal running around the entire bag, much like a zip lock seal. The seal had no interruptions or connections running from one end of the handle around to the other. She then noticed a familiar flat red metal strip on the top, again under the handle. This time she tackled the task of placing her own thumb on it and was ecstatic that the results were the same, the seal on the box changed color from white to blue and the top and bottom were separated.

Karen's eyes grew big in anticipation. Julie took another deep breath mustering up extra courage, gave her daughter an apprehensive glance and slowly opened the bag.

A glimmering gold instrument sat on top of what appeared to be first aid supplies. This was obviously a medical bag. The instrument commanded her attention for she knew instantly what it was. This was the device Robert had used on Karen. A chill came over her. She recalled how horrified she was when she first heard of what he had done to her daughter. She stared at the instrument almost afraid to touch it.

Karen leaned over and noticed the object, identifying it immediately. She too felt a chill recalling her first exposure to it.

"Mom, that...that's the..."

Julie solemnly nodded stopping her in mid sentence.

"I know; I know what it is."

They looked at each other with an uneasy feeling. While she and Karen have both been reveling in the results of its use this was the first time she had actually seen the instrument herself. For some reason the device frightened Julie.

She once again returned to her initial abominable reaction to hearing about the use of this thing on her daughter. In retrospect she almost felt guilty for doubting him but justified her feelings if for no other reason than to give her peace of mind. How else would a mother feel when she discovered a strange man had preformed bazaar medical treatments on her daughter!

How her opinion changed after she saw the results. She then looked at the object in a different light. She glanced at Karen for reassurance. Karen could see her mother's hesitance.

"Its okay mom, pick it up. Let's check it out! But don't push any buttons or anything! We don't know what all this thing can do."

Julie smiled at the strength Karen gave her but had to laugh at her last comment.

"Oh that's reassuring."

Karen smiled as her mother slowly picked up the instrument and studied it carefully. She was very deliberate in her handling of it, almost afraid she might set something off that might have global consequences. After all, she didn't know just how powerful this thing might be or what other uses it may have been designed to have!

It was cylindrical, about six inches long and made of shimmering gold, highly polished metal. It was unlike anything she had ever seen. The one end was squared off while the other end came to somewhat of a point. There were tiny slots for attaching something she assumed. It had a small panel on the side with what looked like slide adjustments and tiny dials with lights. There were four very small buttons on the panel. The blunt end had a smooth section that would have to be some kind of handle to hold it while using.

Julie looked at her daughter in astonishment.

"This is the strangest thing I have ever seen! I wonder if he left the instructions."

Karen just shook her head.

"Well if he didn't I wouldn't waste my time looking for them online."

Julie was oblivious to Karen's last remark as her attention now focused on a collection of small gold gadgets wrapped tightly in black cloth. She opened it and noticed five small attachments obviously designed to be used with the device. She glanced over them quickly and simply wrapped them back in the cloth. She had enough of this thing for now. She needed to distance herself from it for now. She still didn't feel comfortable with it.

Julie took a moment to catch her breath and collect her thoughts. She set the device and its attachments gingerly on the floor next to the pile of clothes and continued her search through the contents of the bag.

"Let's just leave that thing alone for now and see what else is in here."

Karen nodded her agreement.

The next item Julie discovered was a white tube with a cap on it. It looked like a tube of tooth paste. She picked it up and examined it. There was a label on it but the writing looked like hieroglyphics. In spite of her inability to actually read the label she knew exactly what it was. She had seen the tube before. This was the ointment Robert had placed on her burn.

"Honey, this is the salve Robert put on my burn. This is incredible stuff!"

Karen studied the tube with great interest. She noticed the label and strange printing on it.

"Wow, this must be their language!"

All of a sudden her mother's wild story was beginning to become more believable.

The next discovery was a small box with similar writing on it. Julie opened the box and saw that it was filled with the Band-Aid like patches Robert had used to cure her headache.

"Sweetheart, these are the patches he put on my temple to remove my headache. They are incredible as well!"

Karen took the box and just gaped at it.

"This is amazing mom! I'm sorry I doubted you at first. This more than proves he was, well, an alien I guess. This stuff is wild!"

Julie smiled and hugged her daughter.

"Don't apologize Karen, I didn't believe it at first either."

She returned to going through the medical bag. She found nothing further unusual. There were bandages, medical tape, a pair of scissors, gauze pads, and a package of what appeared to be some kind of antiseptic wipes. She also noticed a contraption very similar to a Swiss Army knife. This thing had a couple small blades, a nail clipper, a metal file and a few things she couldn't even identify.

She returned everything to the bag and set it aside. Her legs were cramping from sitting so long so she got up.

"I have to take a break for a minute; I'll get us some more iced tea."

She headed towards the kitchen as Karen took over her spot on the floor in front of the suitcase.

"Thanks mom, I'll take over."

# 5

Julie refilled their glasses as Karen studied the remaining contents of the suitcase.

As she was walking back into the living room Julie heard her daughter shout out in excitement.

"Mom, check this out! There is a book of some kind in here."

Julie set the glasses on the coffee table and rejoined Karen who was paging through a small book.

"Look at this writing mom it's really freaky! Their alphabet is really weird."

Julie chuckled.

"Oh I don't know. It's really not any stranger than our Chinese or Japanese writing, and I'm sure he felt the same way about ours."

"Karen nodded.

"Yeah, that's true. I wonder what kind of a book this is!"

Julie sat down next to Karen and took the book. She knew exactly what kind of book it was. She leafed through it and smiled. A tear came to her eye. Composing herself she explained.

"It's a poetry book sweetheart."

Karen gave her mother a puzzled look.

"How do you know that? You certainly can't read it."

Julie placed her hand softly on her daughter's shoulder and smiled.

"No honey, I can't read it but Robert could and he did. He would read me poetry from it. He said it relaxed him."

Karen looked amazed.

"He had a poetry book?"

Julie nodded.

"He would read you poems, really...from this book?"

Julie nodded.

"Yes, many times. He said poetry relaxed him. They were really beautiful poems too, mostly romantic and dreamy stuff. I so enjoyed the times we would quietly sit together and he would read from that very book."

The recollection caused Julie both happiness and grief. She had never had anyone read poetry to her before Robert. She thought that made him so romantic. It exposed a softer, tender side of him that she adored. Romance she was sorely missing now.

Her thoughts then drifted to what a tragedy it was for such a beautiful, caring man to meet such a horrific fate. She was consoled only by Karen's notion of how they may have given him a brief time of happiness. While the actual relief that thought gave her was miniscule it was all she had to cling on.

Her reflections were interrupted by a question from Karen.

"Mom, do you think they spoke English on his planet?"

Julie shook her head.

"I would think that would be highly unlikely."

Karen replied with a puzzled look.

"Well then how did he speak it so well here?"

Julie's face turned somber. All this dwelling on Robert was taking an emotional toll on her. She thought back to Karen's words at the park about how it was unhealthy to linger on him. She was beginning to see the wisdom in her words. She then addressed her daughter's question.

"He told me they had surgically implanted a device on his vocal chords that would translate his language into ours and ours to his."

Karen's eyes grew big.

"Wow, they really are advanced. Think about it mom, how would they even know our language to do that?"

Julie just shook her head.

"I don't know Karen, that's really not important now. Let's get this job over with."

She returned her attention to the suitcase. She noticed the only items left were two pair of sunglasses and a large manila envelope. She picked up the envelope and lifted up the top. She discovered it was filled with a number of papers, all in the same hieroglyphic writing, folded inside. She opened one up and was intrigued by not only the characters and typeface but the layout. The page had an official looking seal imprinted at the top and a number of signatures, if you could call them that, at the bottom. The signatures were small and mere scribbles making it impossible to actually decipher any names. She immediately noticed the same number 16754 that was sewn on his prison uniform in the upper left hand corner of the top document. This led her to the assumption that these must be his court papers.

The signatures intrigued her. She ran to the bedroom and returned with a magnifying glass. She studied the autographs hoping to decipher Robert's actual signature. Then an interesting thought struck her, one that she hadn't given any thought to before now. She thought about Robert the name. It was highly doubtful that was his real name. It would only make sense, if their language was different so would be their names. After all, you won't find many men in Thailand named Robert.

She dropped the issue accepting the fact that it really wasn't important and she would never have any way of knowing. Besides, it was a little late to worry about something as trivial as to what his actual name was. Yet she couldn't help but wonder how strange and exotic it might be.

She was glad this difficult task was finally over. She began the task of returning everything to the suitcase.

Satisfied she had gotten all the information from the documents she could for the moment she set the envelope back in the suitcase. She then placed the sunglasses, the medical bag and the clothes back.

Her thoughts remained on what she believed to be his court papers. She wondered if she took them to the University if there might be a professor of languages there who might be able to decipher them. If she knew what the papers said it would tell her a lot about his past. She quickly discarded the notion knowing that it would open such a huge can of worms for both her and Karen that it would be impossible to explain or to live with. Neither she nor Karen needed that type of attention at the moment. No, she wasn't ready for that at least just yet.

She glanced around and noticed the envelope of money still sitting ominously on the floor. She let out a nervous sigh. She would leave that out and put it someplace safe until she decided just what to do with the money.

She closed the top of the suitcase. Much to her surprise once the top met the bottom the case automatically closed itself with the seal conjoining the upper and lower halves and reverting back to its original black coloring. It was now sealed as tightly as it was when they first tried to open it. What amazing technology she thought!

Karen had been sitting quietly during the entire process. She had taken the poetry book and was studying it with great interest even though she couldn't read a word of it.

"Mom this is so cool. Can I take this in and show my English teacher? He would get a kick out of seeing this!"

Her mother's heart skipped a beat. She had to put a stop to this notion immediately! She spoke sternly. Karen had to know she couldn't do that.

"Karen Renee Wells think about it! Hell no you can't tell anyone about this. You can't say a word about any of this do you understand me? This, above all, is not open for discussion! That would not be a good idea at all!"

Karen frowned, showing her disappointment.

"But he might be able to translate it! He's really smart about language and..."

Julie raised her voice and stopped her daughter before she could say another word.

"I said no and that is final! I don't want to hear another word about it! Just how were you planning on explaining where you got it from? Were you going to say something like 'my mom's friend was an alien and he left this' do you have any idea how crazy that would sound! They would have us both committed to the nut ward! That book is not to leave this house do you understand?"

Karen reluctantly nodded. She couldn't really argue with that. She placed the idea at the back of her mind, not removing it completely. She couldn't help but ponder what her English teacher Mr. Norcutt would think of it.

Julie was struggling with the envelope of money. Her morals, her ethics were telling her she couldn't keep it but her logical mind was fighting back with the knowledge that there was no way she could give it back to its rightful owner. Half of her wanted to at least know what sum they were dealing with while the other half just wanted it put safely out of sight and out of mind. In this instance, logic would win the battle. She put the envelope in her bedroom dresser drawer without even counting how much was there.

Julie returned to the living room and sat down on the couch. She was feeling nauseous. Her stomach was queasy and she felt the need to sit down and relax for a minute. Karen noticed the unusual expression on her mother's face.

"Are you okay mom? You don't look so good."

Julie managed a smile.

"Yes sweetheart, I'm fine, just feeling a little weird at the moment. I just got really nauseous for a moment."

Karen sat down next to her mother.

"Maybe it's that morning sickness thing you're supposed to get when you're pregnant, you know?"

Julie raised her eyebrows surprising herself with what she was about to say.

"I have been so stressed about going through all of his things and the memories they bring back I had almost forgotten I was even pregnant."

Julie thought about what she had just said and spoke remorsefully.

"That's a terrible thing for a mother to be to say. I didn't mean..."

Karen stopped her.

"You don't need to explain, I understand mom."

Julie lowered her head and put her hands on her temples.

"This is really strange, I feel so...weak, so tired, like something has drained all the energy out of me."

Karen was now concerned.

"Is that normal mom?"

Julie lifted her head.

"Well, I sure didn't feel like this with you. I've got a doctor's appointment scheduled in a couple weeks, I think I will call and have that pushed up if I can. I can't go on like this, I just feel spent!"

Julie slowly stood up. She took a deep breath. She tried to gather her wits.

"It just hit me all of a sudden. No, I didn't feel like this at all when I was pregnant with you. Your father practically had to tie me down to stop me from cleaning and doing all the every day things I normally did. I had tons of energy but I sure don't now."

Karen tried to rationalize her mother's ailing.

"Well mom it's understandable really, you've been under a lot of stress with all of this and..."

Julie interrupted her.

"No, it's not an emotional weariness, its physical; I feel like I just ran ten miles."

Karen continued her concern over her mother.

"Do you think it's because of the baby?"

Julie just nodded.

"I'm sure it has to be. Pregnancy does weird things to a woman. Every one is different. There's nothing to worry about honey. I'll have the doctor check everything out. I'm sure everything is fine."

Karen offered a weak smile.

"Just how far along are you mom?"

Julie thought for a moment.

"Well this morning the doctor said about four, maybe five weeks."

They were both tired. The day's events had worn them both out physically and mentally. In unison they decided it might be a good idea to go to bed early tonight.

# 6

Julie placed the suitcase in the bedroom closet and decided to make an early dinner.

Karen knew how tired her mother was and happily assisted in the preparation of dinner. The conversation at the dinner table was jubilant. They bantered about how excited they both were over the coming baby. Karen again urged her mother to see the doctor and Julie promised she would try and reschedule her pending appointment in the morning. Julie told her daughter she would have to share a room with the baby since space in their small apartment was limited. Karen initially grumbled over the thought but finally consented.

They were enjoying their cheeseburgers and French fries when Karen looked up and asked a question that had been on her mind since first discovering she was going to be a big sister.

"Mom, have you given any thoughts to a name?"

Julie smiled.

"As a matter of fact I have given it a lot of thought. If the baby is a boy I want to name him Robert."

Karen thought for a moment.

"Do you think that was his real name?"

Julie sighed.

"No sweetheart, in all honesty I don't thing it was his real name but that was the one he chose and that is the one we knew him by so I want to honor his memory by naming his son after him."

Karen nodded her agreement.

"I think that would be nice mom."

Julie beamed.

"I think he would like that."

Karen nodded.

"Oh I'm sure he would! That's really cool. What if the baby is a girl?"

Julie thought for a minute.

"I don't know. I'll have to work on that one."

They finished their dinner and the two of them did up the dishes and cleaned up a bit.

Julie gave her daughter a hug and kissed her goodnight. Karen went into her bedroom and Julie retired to hers.

Julie changed into her night clothes and sat on the bed. She discovered she was exhausted but not actually sleepy. She was still feeling nauseous and weary. She was discomforted by this because she reflected on how she never felt the weariness while carrying Karen. How unusual she thought. Her first fear was there might be something wrong with the baby. She promised herself to get the earliest appointment available when she called in the morning. This was beginning to worry her. The baby's health was her utmost priority. This was Robert's baby she had to take care of it! Not only was this a natural priority to her and the baby but she owed that to him as well. This would be her eternal connection with Robert she couldn't bear the thought of anything happening to it. She had lost him but she would not lose his baby!

She was tired but restless. Her mind and body were sending her strange signals, signals she didn't understand. She knew that in her current frame of mind sleep would be impossible. She needed to relax, to take her mind off all that was burdening her at the moment.

She thought back to when she was younger she would read and escape into a book when life was troubling her. Reading would relax her which is exactly what she needed now. That was something she hadn't done in years; maybe it was time to get back to that.

She liked the idea; it was if something within her was

driving her to return to reading. She chuckled to herself thinking maybe God was telling her to slow down and relax. She wasn't completely convinced on that being the origin of the motivation though.

She walked over to her bookcase and perused her limited library. She had lost the majority of her book collection due to her many moves over the years. She had managed to maintain a current library of about twenty books. This didn't trouble her because she had really lost her passion for reading. In recent years she has rarely read anything but recipes and Karen's school textbooks while helping her with homework.

She studied her collection. There was Vonnegut, Hemmingway, Koontz, and her old favorite Danielle Steel. She remembered loving her as a young girl. Her books took her to a fantasy world of incredible romance, a romance she had been hoping to find all her life. She closed her eyes and shed a single tear realizing she had finally found that romance and how it was brutally taken from her in a single moment. No, she couldn't read her now. She glanced at Koontz, no; his science fiction stuff too closely resembled the very life she was now trying to escape from. Hemmingway...no, she just wasn't in the mood for him, too deep for her now. She decided on "Breakfast of Champions" by Vonnegut. He had always managed to make her laugh. Laughter was sorely missing from her life at the moment.

She took her book and nestled under the blankets. Looking to her left she saw Robert's pillow. She kissed it softly and placed it by her side as she opened the book and started reading.

An hour of blissful reading passed when she heard a light tapping on her door.

"Come in sweetheart."

It was Karen.

"I noticed your light was still on, I'm sorry for bothering you mom but do we have anything for an upset stomach? Mine is really bothering me and I can't sleep."

Julie got up and gave her daughter a light hug.

"I think I can find something. I'm sorry you're not feeling good. Let's see what we have."

They went to the bathroom and Julie gave Karen something for her stomach.

Karen took the medicine and smiled.

"I noticed you were reading mom. I haven't seen you read in ages."

Julie nodded.

"Well, actually I haven't. I just had this strange urge, almost a calling to get back to reading this evening for some silly reason."

Completely unbeknownst to her, Robert, even in his embryonic stage, was beginning to crave knowledge. He was also in need of strength which he began drawing from the only source available, his mother.

"Now you get back to bed and try and get some sleep. I hope you feel better in the morning."

Karen gave her mother a hug and returned to bed. Julie decided she was finally getting sleepy and put the book on the nightstand and went to sleep.

She woke up from a good night's sleep. She sat on the edge of the bed and was surprised she still felt exhausted. She couldn't shake the weariness and it angered her. She tried to convince herself she just needed a couple strong cups of coffee to return to normal. She went in the kitchen and noticed the coffee already brewing. Karen, who was sitting at the kitchen table eating a bowl of cereal, must have started it.

"Good morning and thank you for starting the coffee. You know your mom pretty well. Are you feeling any better this morning?"

They shared a hearty laugh.

"Yeah mom, I feel a lot better thanks. How are you feeling this morning? I was worried about you yesterday you didn't look too good."

Julie poured a cup of coffee and joined her daughter at the table.

"I'm fine sweetheart, just a little tired."

Karen looked worried.

"Mom, you're still feeling tired? That's not like you at all. Don't forget to call your doctor and reschedule your appointment. You need to be checked out."

Julie was touched by her daughter's concern.

"I promise you I will but for now you have to get ready for school. I will call before I go into work."

Satisfied with her mother's response Karen finished her cereal and went to her room to get dressed for school.

Julie finished her coffee and decided Karen had good advice. She got her cell phone and called her doctor before she forgot.

She was greeted by an over joyous receptionist.

"Good morning, Doctor Hart's office."

She hated to go to the doctors but reluctantly proceeded.

"Good morning. I'm Julie Wells, a patient of Doctor Hart's. I just saw him yesterday. I discovered I am pregnant and I have a prenatal appointment in a couple weeks but I was wondering if I could push that up, I have been feeling kind of strange and wanted to just check to make sure everything is alright?"

There was a moment of silence before the receptionist continued.

"How far along are you and just how have you been feeling Miss Wells?"

Julie sighed and poured another cup of coffee.

"Doctor Hart told me four or five weeks. I just feel

totally exhausted, always weary and that's not like me at all. I have a daughter and I didn't feel anything like this while I was carrying her. I'm just a bit worried and was hoping the doctor could put a rest to my concern, you know better safe than sorry."

The receptionist replied maintaining her cheery disposition.

"Oh I totally understand. You are doing the right thing. You can't be too careful when an unborn baby is involved. Let me check the doctor's schedule here and I will see what we have available. I'm sure he will want to see you. Let me put you on hold for a minute."

After a two or three minute wait the woman returned.

"Miss Wells your luck is amazing. The doctor's three o' clock appointment for today canceled, can you make it in?"

Julie had to laugh. She would hardly call her luck amazing. She was glad there was an opening and jumped at it without thinking.

"Yes that will be fine thank you."

They made the appointment and Julie hung up the phone. One more cup of coffee she thought and she might be able to fully function.

She poured her third cup of coffee and a disturbing thought came to her mind. She would have to call off work. That in itself wouldn't be a problem but her reason for it might be. She then realized she hadn't told Larry she was pregnant. How would he react? Would he still rent to her if he knew she had two children? She had a small apartment and Larry might be concerned about the amount of space they had. If he were to rent the second apartment he might also be worried about the noise level of an infant. Larry was a wonderful landlord but she didn't want to push him to the limit.

She put her hand to her forehead and closed her eyes,

a headache was rapidly developing. She really didn't need additional worries. Well she conceded to the fact it had to be done and would have to deal with the consequences what ever they may be.

She finished her coffee and checked on Karen's progress. She knew her daughter would be pleased that she was seeing the doctor this afternoon.

"How we doing, you ready for school?"

Karen was dressed and had her book bag draped over her shoulder.

"Yes I'm off. Now you take care of yourself okay?"

Julie smiled and shared the news before her daughter left.

"I want you to know I called Doctor Hart and I'm seeing him this afternoon."

Karen gleamed.

"Oh that's great mom. Tell me what he said when I get home. I love you!"

They shared a hug and Karen left for school. Now Julie had to prepare what she was going to say to Larry. Her headache was building and she remembered Robert's headache tabs were in his medical bag. She really needed one now. She resolved herself to giving one a try.

She went into the bedroom and dragged the suitcase out of the closet. Placing it on the floor she remembered the secret to opening it. She pressed her thumb against the flat red strip and again the suitcase magically opened.

She pulled out the black medical bag and again used the same trick to open it. The box of headache tabs was right on top. She peeled the protective covering off the small bandage and placed it on her temple. She examined the label on the box. The heliographic lettering so intrigued her, she so wished she could read it. She again tossed around the idea of taking a sample to the University and how Karen even offered to take it to her

English teacher to possibly decipher it. As much as she would love to be able to understand it she immediately vetoed that idea knowing it really wouldn't be a wise decision. Exposing that to anyone else would do nothing but open questions she wasn't prepared to tackle and demand explanations she simply wouldn't be able to offer without being committed to an insane asylum.

She had to laugh as she recalled something her father would tell her when ever she complained about something. He would always say 'No matter how bad things may seem they could always be worse'. That thought didn't comfort her as she prepared to call Larry. What if he asked her to leave? She was confident no local homeless shelter would accept alien children.

She resolved herself to simply telling Larry the truth upfront and letting the chips fall where they may. She had to, he would find out soon enough anyways. Pregnancy wasn't exactly something you could hide forever. She would rather he found out by her telling him than for him to notice and ask her about it.

He was a fair man, a good landlord. She would trust him to understand. Besides, she had already told him too many lies. She was somewhat reassured remembering how he would help her in any way he could. She was about to test that offer.

# 7

She dialed his number. It rang for what seemed like forever before he answered. His caller ID immediately gave him the origin of the call. He answered with his usual enthusiasm.

"Good morning Julie. How are you this morning?"

She tried to answer in a positive voice.

"Good morning Larry. I'm fine thank you. First of all I want to tell you I collected all of Robert's belongings, well the ones I wanted to keep, and got them out of the apartment. I gathered up all the trash and removed it. Now what is left you can either keep or just get rid of. Are you alright with that?"

Larry cleared his throat.

"That's fine Julie, thank you. I'll take care of what ever is left."

Now for the hard part she thought to herself.

"Hey Larry, I'm afraid I won't be able to come into work this afternoon."

Larry was taken back a bit by her words. Julie never called off.

"Oh? What's going on? You never call off."

Julie swallowed buying a few seconds to get the courage to continue the conversation.

"Well, this is kind of a special situation. I have a doctor's appointment I really need to go to and the only time they had available was this afternoon. I'm so sorry Larry."

Larry's tone turned to one of sincere concern.

"You have a doctor's appointment? Are you alright Julie?"

Julie realized the difficult part of the conversation

was now upon her. She didn't want to mince words so she got straight to the point.

"Yes thanks I'm fine, in fact I'm more than fine. But there is something I have to tell you..."

She paused a moment, nervous about what she was about to admit.

"I'm pregnant Larry. I've been feeling rather strange lately and wanted to be checked out."

She held her breath waiting for Larry's response. There was a pause before he replied.

"You're pregnant? My goodness I didn't know. Well I guess congratulations are in order."

She let out a sigh of relief that he didn't initially fly off the handle. She hardly expected him to be so receptive to the news much less offer congratulations. She realized the conversation wasn't over just yet. She felt obligated to at least thank him for his sentiment.

"Thank you Larry. I have to admit it was quite a surprise."

She knew Larry would have more to say and she wasn't disappointed. The only thing about Larry that has bugged her over the three years she had been his tenant is he is rather inquisitive, not so much nosey but he tends to pry at times.

"I see. So I assume this wasn't planned? Is everything alright with the baby? You say you're not feeling well. How far along are you?"

Julie saw no reason in pursuing this line of conversation. She had told him everything he needed to know, she was calling off work and she was pregnant. She reluctantly continued.

"No Larry, it wasn't planned but it happened and I am thrilled about it. I'm sure the baby is fine. I have just been feeling very weary and wanted the doctor to assure me everything is normal. I'm fine, I really am. The doctor told me yesterday I was about five weeks along. Being honest with you Larry I wasn't sure how you would react to this. I guess I was fearful you might throw us out."

She could hear Larry chuckle. This initially concerned her as to what might follow. She knew she wasn't out of the woods just yet. Larry had always had a curious nature about him and she was sure this would initiate it.

"Oh don't even think of such a thing Julie! You and Karen have been like family to me. I would never throw you out on the streets, especially at a time like this. You have been an ideal tenant. It has been a pleasure having you both here and this doesn't change a thing."

Julie took a deep sigh of relief as Larry continued.

"Well I do have a concern is space though. I know your apartment is small, do you think you will have room for a new born?"

She panicked. Here it comes. She hoped he liked her reply.

"Karen has agreed to share her room. Just need to make a few alterations. I'm sure we can make room for both of them. They will make do just fine. Karen is so excited about it."

Larry accepted the answer with a touch of skepticism and another soft chuckle. Hearing this gave her a huge boost of confidence that maybe this will work out after all.

"I might be able to help you with some baby items. My wife knows of a couple with a young child, I think she's about five now, who might have a crib and some other items tucked away. I'll ask her for you."

That certainly was unexpected. She smiled.

"Oh Larry that would be so kind of you. I imagine things are going to be a little tight and any help will be greatly appreciated thank you!"

She hoped the conversation would end there...it didn't. Her admittance to needing help brought up a subject she had hoped to avoid. Larry cleared his throat and asked a disturbing question.

"I have to ask one thing Julie. Will the father be involved? Julie I can't have any more in your apartment. I mean you, Karen and the baby are fine but if the father...."

She let out a very obvious sigh. Here was the prying she was so dreading and hoping to avoid. She hadn't prepared for this to be brought up. She saw no other way other than simply telling him the truth, or at least most of it.

Her face turned somber and her voice softened. Her headache, which had been terminated by the pad now returned. She interrupted him.

"No I'm afraid not Larry, Robert was the father."

Larry softly closed his eyes in a moment of grief.

"Oh honey I'm so sorry, I didn't know. Stupid me I should have picked up on that after you had told me you two were close. Please forgive me. Oh that certainly makes things difficult for you."

Julie was so relieved he was accepting this so well.

"That's alright Larry; you had no way of knowing. I so appreciate your understanding and willingness to allow us to stay. I promise you this won't be a problem at all."

Larry concluded the conversation.

"Well I'm very happy for you and I promise you can stay here as long as you like. If there is anything I can do to help you let me know. I will check into those baby things for you and get back to you.

Don't worry about work today I have the evening free I can cover for you. Now you get to that doctor appointment and make sure everything is alright. Besides, I couldn't afford to lose you as a bartender; you're more popular with the patrons than even I am. This place would go under without you."

She loved the way he ended the conversation. Her heart was finally slowing back to its normal pace. That went a whole lot better than she had even hoped. She thanked him again and hung up the phone relieved that that was one less thing she needed to worry about.

Her headache was still bothering her terribly. She wanted to get rid of it before she went to the doctor. She returned to the bedroom and opened the box of headache tabs again. She wished she could read the instructions. She wasn't sure if there was a maximum dosage she should be concerned with because that would make for a rather compromising trip to the emergency room. Placing caution to the wind she placed another bandage on her temple. Within minutes her headache vanished. She once again shook her head in disbelief...incredible she thought!

She heated up her coffee and thought about her day ahead. She had her appointment at three o' clock. That was her priority.

The morning hours flew by. She found herself tired but restless, a very uncooperative and frustrating pair of feelings. She was nervous about her pending doctor's appointment so she straightened up the apartment a bit if for no other reason than to kill a couple hours and take her mind off of things.

She fixed Karen a sandwich and placed the covered plate in the refrigerator so her daughter would have a snack when she got home from school. She thought about how empathizing Karen had been and how much support and encouragement she provides her with.

She then used what little energy she had to take a long warm shower and get dressed. She did her makeup sparingly; she was going to the doctor to see why she was so tired not to get a date.

Before she knew it she discovered it was now two

o' clock. Satisfied that she looked as good as she was going to she grabbed her purse and keys and headed for her car.

The forty minute drive to the medical building gave her time to sort out her thoughts. She wanted to have her mind clear when she talked to him. Just what was she going to tell him? She would explain she was very tired physically and honestly worried there might be something wrong. She would explain how she hadn't experienced this sensation while carrying Karen. Satisfied that about summed everything up she decided some music would calm her nerves.

While stopped at a light she sorted through her CDs trying to decide what she was in the mood for. Leafing through her book of CDs; she paused at each page. Tom Petty...ahh no, Journey...nah, Fleetwood Mac...not today. She surprised herself when she stopped at one titled 'Beethoven Piano Sonatas'. She had never been a huge fan of classical music but had gotten a couple CDs incase the mood ever struck her. For some reason this one was calling to her today. She knew it would relax her, what she didn't know was that Robert was yearning for culture. He was determined to acquire this through any means possible which, for now, were again limited to his mother. Even in its infant stages his mind was hard at work.

She arrived at the medical center and was pleasantly surprised to find a parking space right in front of the entrance. She checked her hair in the mirror and was satisfied it was presentable. She entered Dr. Hart's office; incredibly there were no other patients in the waiting room. Maybe the receptionist was correct after all; maybe her luck was getting amazing. She hoped the trend would continue. She approached the receptionist and announced herself.

"Hi, I am Julie Wells. I have a three o'clock appointment with Doctor Hart."

The woman at the desk smiled.

"Well hello Miss Wells. I spoke with you on the phone. I'm glad you could make it. Dr. Hart was called into emergency surgery at the hospital but Dr. Barnett is here to see all his patients today. You'll like him he's a great guy. I'll let him know you are here."

Before the woman had a chance to pick up the phone a young doctor entered the waiting room. He was tall, well over six feet tall, he had brown eyes and dark brown hair and mustache which was a compliment to his muscular build. He appeared to be no older than thirty. He noticed them at the desk and smiled. He spoke to the receptionist.

"I just spoke with John; he's going to be out for the rest of the day. There apparently were some complications with the surgery so he's going to stay there. Looks like you're stuck with me all day."

He turned his attention to Julie and again flashed an infectious smile.

"Good afternoon, I am Doctor Barnett, you must be Miss Wells."

Julie was caught up in his smile and charming demeanor. She also had to embarrassingly admit he was quite handsome and so young looking. She thought to herself he looked more like the star college quarterback than a doctor. She returned his smile and shook his hand.

"Yes I am. I have a three o'clock appointment."

The Doctor glanced at the receptionist who silently confirmed the information.

"It's a pleasure to meet you Miss Wells. I'm sure Carol explained I will be taking Dr. Hart's patients today. I hope that isn't a problem for you."

Julie couldn't help but smile as she replied.

"No, that's not a problem at all Doctor."

Dr. Barnett nodded.

"Great! Please come with me and we will get started."

They walked into the examination room and he closed the door behind them.

The doctor opened a folder the receptionist had given him and paged through the papers within it. He asked Julie to sit on the examining table.

"Have a seat Miss Wells while I get familiar with your history."

She smiled and sat down on the gurney while the doctor continued to read. After a few minutes the doctor looked up and smiled enthusiastically.

"I see we're going to have a baby."

Julie nodded.

"Well congratulations. Now I also see you were just in yesterday, what brings you back today?"

Julie thought about how to reply.

"Well, I've been so tired lately, really drained. I have also been feeling so nauseous but I just attributed that to morning sickness."

The doctor nodded and glanced over her chart.

"Is this your first child?"

Julie shook her head.

"No, it's my second; I have a fifteen year old daughter. This is why I was so concerned. I didn't feel the weariness with her."

Dr. Barnett acknowledged her and continued reading through her charts.

"Well all pregnancies are different. The body reacts differently as it gets older. There has been a long gap between children here; that could also play a factor. A woman's body changes a lot in fifteen years. I see Dr. Hart has you at about five weeks along."

Julie affirmed this information.

The doctor set the folder on the counter and took Julie's pulse. He then placed the stethoscope on her chest and checked her breathing and heart.

"We're looking good so far. Mom seems to be pretty healthy. So it's mostly the weariness that brought you in today?"

Julie nodded.

After checking her eyes he rubbed her stomach.

"On the surface I'm not concerned about the tiredness. Like I said, as you get older the body naturally changes, so it would be normal for it to react differently than with your first child.

Keep in mind you're fifteen years older than you were with your first child. Like I said, your body changes a lot in that time period. It should be no surprise that it would react differently then when you carried your first child.

The tiredness just might be taken care of with some supplements or vitamins. We'll run some tests to be on the safe side. I'm sure everything is alright."

Julie smiled. She liked him already. The doctor opened a cabinet and handed Julie a green gown.

"If you would change into this Julie we will get you all checked out."

Julie smiled, took the gown into the bathroom and changed. She returned to the examination room placing her clothes on the metal chair next to the examining table.

The doctor pointed to the gurney.

"Just relax Miss Wells and let's see what's going on here."

He took her blood pressure and jotted some notes in the folder.

"You check out pretty good so far. Your heart rate is good, your breathing normal and blood pressure is perfect. Now let's check out the little one. Excuse me for a minute I want to get something that will help us do just that."

He left the room and returned in a matter of minutes with a small hand held device. It had a small base with a digital readout and a chord leading to another small apparatus.

"Miss Wells, this is a Doppler fetal monitor, it is designed to allow me to check on the baby's heart beat. Now normally we don't notice any significant heart beat until around eight weeks but I want to check just to be on the safe side. I'm telling you this so you won't be alarmed if we don't pick up anything."

Julie appreciated his attention and efforts. He asked Julie to lie down on the examining table. He lifted her gown then ran the device across her stomach. He made a couple passes across her stomach then held it steady. He glanced at the readout. As much as he tried to conceal it a look of confusion crossed his face. Julie couldn't help but notice.

"Doctor, is everything alright? Do I have a reason to worry?"

Dr. Barnett withdrew the monitor and paused for a moment of thought before addressing her concern.

"No reason to be concerned, not at all Miss Wells."

He checked the device again and noted something on a page in the folder.

"This is nothing to worry about but I am noticing a strong heart beat. This is rather unusual for this early in a pregnancy. If anything this is a good sign. You appear to have a very healthy baby here."

This only makes me want to question Dr. Hart's speculation as to how far along you are. I don't normally question a colleague's opinion but I think in this case I have to. Based on what I'm seeing here I would have to say you are at least nine weeks along. I want to do an ultrasound and take a look at him or her. Trust me you have no reason to be concerned."

For some reason Julie wasn't totally relieved at this evaluation. She had to question his words.

"So you're telling me you think Dr. Hart's evaluation was off?"

Dr. Barnett could see the worry in his patient's eyes. He wanted to address her concern with caution. He didn't want to say anything negative about his colleague but placed her rights to know what he thought might be the truth above anything else.

"Well Miss Wells, don't get me wrong, I am not questioning Dr. Hart's findings, tell me did he run any tests while you were here?"

She shook her head.

"Okay, that just tells me he was working with limited information. I want to emphasize we are doing this ultrasound not out of concern for the baby's health, he certainly appears strong and healthy, but only to get a more accurate assessment on how far along you are."

Julie managed a weak smile. She really appreciated his efforts not only to ensure the baby's health but to put her fears aside. She agreed to the ultrasound.

Dr. Barnett arranged for a nurse to set up the ultrasound while he talked to Julie.

"It's perfectly normal to feel fatigued during pregnancy. The body is going through quite a change and that often results in the woman being tired, especially as we get older. So I'm not really concerned. We will see what the little guy is up to in the ultrasound."

Minutes later a nurse entered the room and told the doctor the ultrasound was all set.

Dr. Barnett led Julie to a room down the hall where the ultrasound machine was. He asked Julie to lie down on the table next to the machine which she did. Dr, Barnett activated the machine and took the scanner in his hand. He lifted up Julie's gown and ran the device across her stomach slowly a number of times pausing it occasionally.

His attention then turned to the screen. He studied the image meticulously for a couple moments then continued to move the scanner across Julie's stomach. Again he studied the screen as Julie studied his face. He made a couple adjustments on the machine and again scanned her stomach keeping a keen eye on the screen. He stopped and rubbed his chin in thought. Julie noticed his actions. She couldn't help but notice the puzzled expression the doctor was trying to hide.

"Well doctor, just what are we seeing here? You look a little perplexed should I be worried?"

Dr. Barnett gave his patient a reassuring smile. He thought for a moment on how he wanted to word his thoughts without alarming the patient.

"Oh you shouldn't be concerned at all Miss Wells. It looks like we have a very healthy baby here. In all honestly what perplexes me is his development. He appears developed beyond even my estimation of nine weeks."

That comment did nothing to ease her unrest.

"Just what am I supposed to make of that doctor?"

The doctor approached his reply cautiously.

"Well, if indeed you are only nine weeks along the baby is, how can I say this, physically developed beyond what I would normally expect at this point. I assure you it is not a bad thing he is just maturing at a very rapid pace. Everything gives the impression of a very strong and healthy baby I assure you."

The doctor wrote a series of notes in her folder and studied them.

"Miss Wells, have you been taking any vitamins or supplements?"

Julie shook her head no.

"Have you taken any steroids or testosterones?"

Julie again shook her head no.

The doctor had just one more question he hesitated to ask.

"Miss Wells, do you take any illegal drugs? Now I ask that without judgment I just need to know what we are dealing with here."

Julie sighed and answered with contempt.

"No doctor I do not! In fact I never had."

She was now beside herself in confusion. She was never given this line of questioning when she was pregnant with Karen.

She was of course relieved that the baby appeared healthy but confused about his rapid development. She didn't know whether to be overjoyed or worried. Her thoughts were interrupted as the doctor spoke.

"I would like to see you again in two weeks. What we can observe now is that the baby is healthy, appears very strong and is physically very well developed. What I would like to do is to run an MRI in a couple weeks. This will allow us to get an idea of the brain activity. I assure you Miss Wells you have nothing to worry about, your baby is doing just fine."

She was leery of that plan of action, it hinted at something wasn't right.

"Is that a normal procedure? I didn't have anything like that with Karen."

The doctor rubbed his mustache thinking the best way to respond.

"I wouldn't say it was standard no, but with your baby's rate of physical growth I think it would be a good idea to monitor the brain activity to insure it is corresponding accordingly."

Julie conceded that he knew what he was doing and agreed with his plan.

"Well I have to admit I am not comfortable with this but I just want what is best for the baby. If you say this MRI will help in accessing his well being then I guess I will go along with it. You're the doctor."

Julie shook his hand and got dressed. After getting dressed she was greeted at the door by the doctor who handed her a slip of paper.

"I'm going to write you a prescription for some vitamin supplements. They are very mild but should give you some energy back. Talk to Carol and schedule a return for a couple weeks but for now just go home with the knowledge that you have a very healthy baby!"

She thanked him and went to the receptionist to get her prescription and schedule her next appointment. Dr, Barnett remained behind continuing to study the unusual images from the ultrasound. He was more intrigued than he had let on.

# 8

He had printed out a series of pictures from the session and was studying them with great interest. His concentration was broken by his cell phone ringing. He noticed it was Dr. Hart calling from the hospital.

"Good afternoon John, how are you holding up down there?"

An obviously tired doctor replied.

"We had a Hell of a time in surgery. I just got out of there after over four hours. We almost lost a triple by pass; he started fibrillating then went into cardiac arrest just as we were closing. We had to open him up again but I think we got him out of the woods, he's hanging on. There were some complications so I wanted to stick around. How are things on the home front?"

Dr. Barnett put down the photographs he had been scrutinizing and answered.

"We're fine here John but now that I have you on the phone there is something I would like to go over with you if you have a minute."

Dr. Hart could sense concern in his colleague's voice.

"Sure Gary, just having a cup of coffee what's going on?"

Dr. Barnett picked up the pictures and glanced at them again as he replied.

"I just saw a lady, Julie Wells; she's a patient of yours."

Dr. Hart mulled the name over.

"Oh yeah, she was just in yesterday. She just found out she was pregnant. You say she was in again today? She didn't have an appointment, what brought her back so quickly?"

Dr. Barnett cleared his throat.

"No, she took a cancellation. She said she was feeling tired and weary and was concerned. I checked her out, you know, heart, blood pressure, she's fine. I just gave her a script for some vitamin supplements and told her it was normal but that's not why I mentioned it. When she was in yesterday what tests did you run on her?"

The doctor thought back for a moment.

"Well, she came in because she was feeling nauseous so I just ran a simple blood and urine test. That's when we discovered she was pregnant."

Dr. Barnett processed the information.

"You say on her file you figured her to be about five weeks along?"

Dr. Hart thought back to what he had written on her file.

"I guessed at that yeah. While checking her heart rate I ran the scope across her abdomen and didn't pick up a significant heart beat for the baby so I estimated she was only about five weeks along."

Dr. Barnett shook his head after hearing that.

"Well the kid sure has a strong one today!"

Dr. Hart was surprised at the news.

"Are you serious? That couldn't be."

Dr. Barnett continued.

"Yes, I ran a Doppler on him and he had a very strong heartbeat. John it read about 180 bpm. I think she is a lot further along than five weeks."

Dr. Hart was intrigued by this.

"That's crazy! I can't believe there would be such a dramatic increase in heart rate overnight. It wasn't anything near that yesterday; it was barely detectable at all. There is simply explanation for that. Maybe we should do an ultrasound and..."

Dr. Barnett interrupted him.

"I did an ultrasound today. This is where things get

really interesting. The extremities, the arms and legs are clearly present. Now we both know this is not something you see after only five weeks. After closer examination the fingers, toes and ears were actually starting to develop. The fetus was very active. I mean the little guy looked like he was trying to run the mile. I'm beginning to think she may be even further along. I've never seen such development even at nine weeks. If indeed she is only nine weeks, and what you say about yesterday is true, then this baby is growing at an alarming rate."

Dr. Hart was amazed at his colleague's observations. He was struggling with even what questions to follow up on. Dr. Barnett spared him by following up with an off the wall speculation.

"John, I hesitate to even bring this up because I obviously don't know her as well as you do but do you think this may be drug induced? I mean, do you think she might be taking something, maybe steroids, growth stimulators or even street drugs? There's a lot of crap out there. I asked her about it and she said no but I just don't see any other way of explaining this accelerated growth."

Dr. Hart responded directly.

"That would be a natural assumption Gary; it would make sense but not a chance. She isn't the type. Julie could have just stepped out of a Disney movie. I can vouch for her without question in this regard."

Dr. Barnett accepted the reply and continued.

"Well, I am going to have her come back in two weeks and do an MRI. I am curious about the brain activity. If the brain is accelerating as quickly as the body then we might really have something here."

Dr. Hart thought about the plan.

"Based on what you told me I would concur with that. Even genetics wouldn't account for something like this. I just don't even have a thought right now. An MRI is a good next step. I would be interested in the brain growth and it would also tell us if there is any problem with brain development or abnormalities. Yeah, let's give her another couple weeks then put her in the tube and see what it shows us. How was her demeanor? I don't want to alarm her about this."

Dr. Barnett eased his colleague's worry.

"I can tell you we have her attention that's for sure. She was uneasy about the MRI but I sugar coated everything pretty nicely so she was okay with it."

Dr. Hart was relieved.

"Good job partner. Well I have to get back to ICU so I will catch you later. Thanks again for sitting in for me today."

Julie sat quietly in the car for a moment before turning on the ignition. She had a lot on her mind. At the moment she was experiencing mixed emotions about her visit. On the one hand she was pleased and relieved to know the baby apparently was healthy and doing fine. On the other hand she was concerned over Dr. Barnett's obvious confusion over the ultrasound results and his insistence on her returning for an MRI. She didn't have one of those with Karen and his suggestion clearly meant he wasn't happy with something.

She wasn't familiar with just what an MRI was for but remembered him mentioning something about brain activity. This concerned her. She tired to put her worries aside. She wanted to get home. She had had enough excitement for one day and she knew Karen would be home and anxious to hear what the doctor had told her.

Then a thought struck her. Something she had put at the back of her mind up to now. Something she knew but had to keep to herself. She was very familiar with the gestation period for a pregnancy, a human pregnancy that is. She remembered the baby she was carrying was only half human. Could it be that where Robert came from babies had a shorter gestation period? That would certainly explain the amazing growth. As strange as the thought was she had to concede to it being a possibility. She tossed that idea around in her head. The notion brought a chill to her...what other surprises might lay ahead.

She fought her first thought, of a movie she had seen as a kid, 'Rosemary's Baby.' It was the story of a poor woman who was some how impregnated with the devil's baby. She remembered how frightened she was watching it and how the baby acted so strange in the movie. She vowed at the time to never have a baby!

She shook her head to try and rid herself of that terrifying thought. She chastised herself for even making the ridiculous connection. Okay, it might be an alien baby but it certainly wasn't the devil's baby, it was Robert's baby!

She drove home in silence. She didn't want to listen to music; she needed quiet to collect her thoughts. She fought desperately to convince herself that everything was fine and the baby was doing well.

She stopped at the drug store and filled her prescription with hopes the vitamins would restore her strength and energy. She needed all the help she could get with this tiredness; now to find a way to control her thoughts.

She arrived home and sat in the car for a moment. Her stress was mounting to an unbearable level. She had to be composed and positive when she talked to Karen. She somehow had to push her fears and anxieties to the back of her mind. She didn't want to give Karen any reason to worry and would have to conceal the uncertainties she was struggling with.

She collected her keys and purse and all the courage she could muster and walked into the apartment.

Julie opened the apartment door to find Karen sprawled out on the living room couch watching television. The empty plate on the coffee table told her Karen had enjoyed her lunch.

Upon noticing her mother's arrival Karen leaped from the couch to greet her at the door.

"Mom you're home!"

They enjoyed a quick hug and Karen started the interrogation immediately.

"Did you make it to the doctor? What did he say? Is the baby okay? Was he worried about you being tired?"

Julie laughed and tried to put at least a temporary halt to the over zealous cross examination.

"Whoa there slow down! I can only deal with ten questions at a time!"

They shared a laugh as Karen whimsically apologized. Julie continued. She was careful in her wording. She wanted to assure her daughter there was nothing to worry about while concealing her personal concern that there just might be something to worry about.

She was encouraged by Karen's exuberance over the coming baby and wanted to strengthen it not damage it.

"Okay, first of all I just got back from the doctor. Dr. Hart wasn't there so they had another doctor see me. He was very nice and quite handsome I must say!"

Karen giggled.

"Oh mom seriously come on what did he tell you?"

Julie smiled. She wanted to lighten up the mood and was satisfied she had succeeded.

"Well most importantly he assured me the baby is doing great. In fact the baby's growth had surprised him."

Karen looked puzzled.

"Mom what do you mean, surprised him?"

Julie wasn't sure how to reply to this. She regretted

mentioning it. She didn't want to raise any suspicions of anything being out of the ordinary.

"Oh it was nothing bad sweetheart. He was happy the baby is strong and healthy."

Karen nodded her head skeptically. She was a smart young lady and knew her mom well. Something in the back of her head was telling her that her mother was hiding something. She pushed her concern aside for the moment.

"What did he say about you being tired so much?"

Julie put her arm around her daughter and smiled.

"He said there was nothing to worry about. He told me every pregnancy is different and reminded me that I am fifteen years older than when I had you. The body changes over the years and it's perfectly normal for me to be tired. He gave me a prescription for some vitamin supplements which I just got filled so I'm good. I have another appointment in a couple weeks."

Karen studied her mother with concern.

"You have another appointment in a couple weeks? Isn't that a little soon? Mom, be honest with me. It sounds like they are worried about something. You admitted to lying to me once please don't do it again.

This is my little brother or sister we are talking about here. I have a right to be concerned. Level with me mom, what's going on?"

Julie looked at her daughter with a thoughtful reflection that had survived many storms. She felt such a feeling of pride looking at the incredible young lady Karen had become. She had turned out pretty good and, with the help of Robert, had become a very compassionate and intelligent woman. Julie knew she would have to tell her everything, she owed that much to her.

"My dear daughter Karen, how did you become so mature so quickly!"

Karen simply gave her mother a blank stare.

"Well think about it, I had to. Over the last six months I have been cured of an incurable brain disorder and found out my mother's boyfriend was an alien from another planet! It's been a traumatic year mom."

An overwhelming feeling of remorse came over her. Karen had indeed been through a lot over the past year. Her only consolation was the over all result was very positive, well except for the loss of Robert.

She now had to ease her daughter's troubled mind. Karen was correct, it would be her sibling and she had a legitimate right to be concerned. She had to laugh at Karen's almost psychic ability to see through her cover up.

"The doctor was just, well intrigued by the baby's rapid growth. Dr. Hart had initially said I was about five weeks along but after examining me Dr. Barnett felt I must be maybe nine or so weeks along. That's all honey I swear to you. The baby and I are both fine!"

She gave her daughter a reassuring hug.

"You're going to be a terrific big sister!"

Karen studied her mother's eyes and was now confident she was being told the truth. Julie went into the kitchen to fix a cup of coffee while Karen pondered the significance of her mother's words.

"Mom, do you think since Robert wasn't, well human, that their babies might grow differently than ours?"

Julie returned to the living room and sat down.

"I can't help but believe that might be a factor yes. My only concern is that the baby is healthy and the doctor assured me he was."

# 9

The next couple weeks flew by. Karen was struggling with math in school and Julie helped her as much as she could. She was never good at math and thought back to how Robert was such a help to Karen in that department. He would sit down with her for hours and explain things. They would laugh and make it fun. More than once she fought back tears over this.

The vitamins had been helping Julie's energy level. She wasn't feeling as tired physically as she had been but she was still struggling with stamina. She often just felt lethargic, as if something was simply draining her resilience. While she was relieved at this development she found herself worried about another.

She had been experiencing awful cramps periodically. It was if something were stretching her insides. She knew cramping was normal during pregnancy but didn't experience them to this degree with Karen. She would mention this to the doctor.

The day of her follow up appointment had arrived. Julie woke up early, got Karen off to school and took a shower. It was during the shower that she first noticed her baby bump.

She tried to remember just when she had noticed it with Karen. For some reason she didn't think it was this early.

She gently massaged her stomach feeling the bump. It was then that something happened that shocked her. As if reacting to her touch, the baby kicked! She knew this wasn't right. Startled she repeated the process with the same results. There was no doubt about it, the baby was kicking!

She remembered being anxious for this to happen while carrying Karen and her doctor told her it should start around week 16.

Now Dr. Hart had initially told her she was about five weeks along and then Dr. Barnett changed that to around nine weeks. Even at that new estimate she should be only about eleven weeks along now. There was no way an eleven week old baby should kick. She rethought her last notion. The key to that idea was normal baby. She was beginning to firmly believe Karen's suspicion of Robert's genes playing a key role in this odd development.

Julie dressed and decided to have a cup of coffee before she left for her appointment. She sat at the kitchen table deep in thought. She was trying to fight the feeling of apprehension that was currently absorbing her. She couldn't dispute the nervous feeling that was building up inside her. She knew she was going to be given an MRI examination but wasn't sure why or even what an MRI does. She knew she didn't have one with Karen and this bothered her. She also knew they don't give MRI examinations as a standard procedure for pregnancies. There had to be something they didn't like or understand. This thought did nothing to sooth her nerves.

She arrived at the doctor's office about a half an hour early and signed in at the reception desk. She was disappointed in the magazine selection. Having only Motor Trend, Popular Science, Cosmopolitan and Women's World to select from she decided to play solitaire on her cell phone. She put the phone back in her purse after trying only one game. It was evident her nerves weren't conducive to a productive game of cards.

She glanced up towards the reception desk and noticed Dr. Hart and Dr. Barnett conversing with another man. He was older than either of them and dressed in what appeared to be a very expensive Italian suit. He had a stethoscope draped around his neck so Julie assumed he was a doctor. She laughed to herself thinking he must be a very good one based on how he was dressed.

They were obviously discussing the contents of a large folder Dr. Hart was holding as he had opened it and was sharing it with the man.

Dr. Hart finally noticed her sitting at the other end of the room and motioned for her to join them. She took a deep breath and slowly walked over to where they were standing wondering silently if it was her folder they were studying.

Dr. Hart shook her hand and smiled.

"Good morning Julie, it's good to see you. I am sorry I missed your last appointment but I am confident my colleague here Dr. Barnett took good care of you."

Julie smiled and nodded as Dr. Hart continued.

"Julie, Dr. Barnett and I have been going over your charts and I wanted to bring in someone to work with us on this. He is an expert in the field of prenatal growth and development from the University Hospital. He comes with credentials as long as your arm. We are lucky he was available. Julie I would like you to meet Dr. Stepanov, he will be overseeing your MRI this morning."

The doctor smiled and shook Julie's hand and checked the folder quickly to insure he got her name correct. He spoke with a heavy Russian accent.

"Good morning Miss Wells. I am Dr. Stepanov. I was asked by Dr. Hart to assist in your MRI today. It is nice to meet you."

Julie was a bit taken back not only by his accent but strong handshake. She found it difficult to return his smile with any sincerity. The fact that the doctors felt the necessity to bring in an expert troubled her and only reassured her fear that something must be wrong. She replied as cordially as she could.

"It's nice to meet you doctor but with all due respect I have to admit to being just a bit confused here."

That was the understatement of the year. She addressed her question to Dr. Hart.

"Doctor, is there something specific that is bothering you about this? May I ask why you felt the need to consult with an expert in the field? Isn't that a bit out of the ordinary? I mean first the need for an MRI and now this? From my point of view this is all very unnerving. Now this is my baby we are talking about so don't bullshit me!"

Dr. Hart thought for a moment and replied.

"Julie, let me assure you there is nothing wrong with your baby. Based on what I have seen directly and through Dr. Barnett's tests he is very healthy..."

Dr. Stepanov interrupted.

"Doctor, allow me if you will to address Miss Well's concerns. Miss Wells, I was contacted by Dr. Hart after he studied the results of your tests. From what I have seen so far he is totally correct in saying you have a very healthy baby. It is not the health of the fetus we are looking at, it is the extraordinary growth that intrigues us."

Julie wasn't sure what to make of that comment.

"Are you saying the baby is growing too fast?"

Dr. Barnett now added his thoughts.

"Miss Wells, there is nothing to be alarmed about. We are simply questioning how far along you really are. Initially Dr. Hart had you at five weeks when he first saw you. After I ran those tests the next day it was my conclusion that you were closer to nine or even ten weeks along. My estimate was based on what the ultra sound showed."

Julie had to respond.

"Just what did the ultra sound show doctor?"

Dr. Hart now took the reigns.

"Well, we saw a fully developed embryo when we

were expecting to see a developing fetus. The baby has developed beyond what you would normally expect for a five week pregnancy. We noticed amazing growth in the arms and legs and even eye lashes, eyebrows, finger nails and toe nails. This usually isn't present until around sixteen weeks. Now this could be a result of me simply misjudging the duration initially but even with Dr, Barnett's updated conclusion this was still amazing growth. You might be further along than either of us had imagined.

Now today we are going to give you an MRI to insure the baby's brain is developing at the same pace. It will show us blood flow to the brain and also the genetic development of the cells within the brain itself."

Julie wasn't sure whether to be thankful for their dedicated efforts or terrified that they felt those efforts were needed.

Dr. Stepanov spoke up.

"This is my area of specialty Miss Wells. With the MRI results I should be able to give you a very accurate assessment of just how far along you are. Now let's get this started so we can move forward. Again let me assure you the baby is very healthy, we're just not sure how old it is."

Julie was getting tired of all the rhetoric she seemed to be getting. This was her and Robert's baby they were talking about and she wanted some real answers.

"You mean to tell me you can't determine how old my baby is? That's crazy, aren't you guys trained in that sort of thing!"

Dr, Hart responded.

"Of course we are Julie but sometimes the moment of actual conception can be cloudy and..."

Julie interrupted him. She was now getting angry.

"I understand that but how can you be weeks off?"

Dr. Hart continued.

"When you first came in and I discovered you were pregnant the fetus appeared about five weeks old. Then when Dr. Barnett did the ultra sound the next day we discovered an embryo of much further development."

Julie looked puzzled.

"You mean it grew that much over night?"

Dr. Barnett replied.

"That is what was puzzling. Yes it did appear to have substantial growth which of course is unprecedented. I shared the ultra sound results with Dr. Hart and he was very surprised at the changes. He then suggested we bring in Dr. Stepanov to get an expert's opinion."

Julie was mortified.

"Well I am almost afraid to even mention what is happening now. You might think I have Rosemary's Baby."

Dr. Hart put his hand on Julie's shoulder and pointed to the examining room.

"Let's all go in the room and you tell me the latest developments."

The four of them entered the examining room and Dr. Hart closed the door behind him. He pointed to the examining table and asked Julie to sit down.

"Now tell me about these new developments Julie."

Julie sat on the table and lifted her blouse exposing her stomach and the baby bump.

"Well, this appeared out of no where. I noticed it this morning while I was in the shower."

The three doctors looked at each other. Doctor Hart approached Julie and gently touched her stomach, rubbing it slowly.

"Well now this is interesting. You say you just noticed it this morning?"

Julie nodded. Dr. Stepanov ran his hand across Julie's stomach and sighed.

"You defiantly have a baby in there Miss Wells. This gives us a better idea of how far along you actually are. The baby bump usually appears between twelve and sixteen weeks and..."

Julie spoke up.

"Oh there's more doctor. When I touched it this morning, he kicked"

Dr. Stepanov stepped back and gave a questioning glance to Dr. Hart who had to ask his patient a question.

"You're sure of this?"

Julie nodded.

"Oh definitely, this happened twice this morning. There is no doubt about it, he kicked me!"

Dr. Stepanov rubbed his chin in thought.

"This is your second child Miss Wells?"

Julie nodded.

"Well, usually we notice the first kicks between sixteen to twenty weeks but for a second child it can start as early as week thirteen. The MRI will give us a clear picture of the baby's brain activity and growth which will in turn give us a clearer picture of just how far along you really are. Are you ready?"

Julie sighed; she was still worried and confused. She had a gut feeling the doctors were more concerned than they let on. She slowly nodded her head in agreement and the four of them went to the MRI room in silence.

The test itself was difficult for her. She had forgotten how claustrophobic she was. The fear of the closed space temporarily took her mind off everything else she had been worrying about. She was so relieved to stand up after the test. She took a number of deep breaths to regain her composure. She then turned to Dr. Hart.

"Okay, now what?"

Dr. Hart managed a weak smile.

"First of all I want to do another ultrasound on you since you are here. Given the unusual circumstances I want to keep an eye on this little guy. Then we wait for the MRI results. I'll push them and make sure we get the results in the morning. The three of us will go over them and come to some conclusions. I will call you tomorrow after we have done that. I promise you Julie we will have the answers you seek and again I want to assure you that nothing is wrong, the baby is fine. Now let's get that ultra sound done so you can go home."

Reluctantly Julie had no other choice than to agree. They all went into another room and Dr. Hart called in a nurse to run an ultrasound test. All three doctors watched attentively as the nurse passed the scanner over her stomach. They scrutinized the screen in unison.

If they saw anything unusual they kept it to themselves. She noticed Dr. Hart busily jotting down notes in his folder. As curious as she was she withheld any comments or questions, she was tired and just wanted to get home. Dr. Hart walked over to her sensing her uneasiness and put his hand on her shoulder.

"Okay, we're finished for today. I want to wait to schedule your next appointment until I can review the results of the MRI. Now you go home and try and relax."

She thought to herself that would be easier said than done.

# 10

Two days passed and she had yet to hear anything from the doctor. She found it impossible to sleep. She would lie in bed tossing and turning. Her mind was racing with anxiety. She couldn't help but ponder all the things that could be wrong. She would find herself wide awake until the wee hours of the morning.

She calmed her nerves by reading. She found her taste in literature changing from Danielle Steel to Twain, Dickens and even attempted Hemmingway. It was if she were drawn to them for the first time in her life.

Her television habits had changed as well. She no longer watched her Lifetime movies; she was now enjoying the Science Channel and Discovery channel. She was actually enjoying learning about so many things she had never had an interest in before. She had this unexplainable thirst for knowledge. She had no way of knowing it wasn't her thirst that was being quenched.

Her eating habits had changed as well. She was always snacking, something she had never done before even when she was pregnant with Karen. Her taste in snacks ranged from brownies to chips, it didn't matter. She just felt a constant hunger and would frequently eat without even thinking, almost instinctively, again she had no way of knowing it wasn't her hunger that was being satisfied.

Her cramping was excruciating at times and helped only mildly by the prescription she was given. In addition to the discomfort that was providing her there was the almost annoying kicking by the baby. Karen of course had kicked her occasionally but nothing like the constant onslaught she was experiencing now. She tried to find humor in it by thinking to herself that this kid really wants out of there!

She had also noticed her baby bump was growing at an alarming rate. She had decided if she didn't hear from the doctor by the afternoon she would take the initiative to call them. She was finally conceding that something just wasn't right.

She poured a cup of coffee and used it to take her prescription. She hoped it would calm her nerves which at the moment were driving her crazy. The anticipation of not knowing exactly what was going on was all encompassing.

She was sick of the standard medical dogma the doctor's were trying to pacify her with. She needed definitive answers and she needed them now! She mustered all the inner determination and courage she could and got out her cell phone. She had to call Dr. Hart and demand some real answers!

She got her cell phone and took a deep breath. She was confident that they would have to know something after all the tests she had gone through. She took a sip of coffee while silently asking a little assistance from God. The receptionist answered on the second ring.

"Good morning, Prescott Medical center how can I direct your call?"

Without hesitation she replied.

"May I speak with Dr. Hart please?"

The receptionist placed her on hold while she connected her. After a wait that seemed eternal the doctor answered.

"This is Dr. Hart."

Butterflies were accumulating in her stomach as she thought about how to approach this.

"Dr. Hart, this is Julie Wells. I'm calling because I haven't heard anything from you and I really need some answers here!"

The doctor replied with all the professional courtesy he could.

"Good morning Julie. First of all let me apologize for not getting back to you yet."

Julie silently groaned. She thought to herself here we go with the medical text book answers again. She wasn't in the mood for lip service.

"Doctor, I don't want your apologies I want some answers. This is my baby we are dealing with and quite frankly you all have me scared.

You subject me to tests which are not commonly done for pregnancy, call in a specialist and then tell me my baby is growing beyond anyone's wildest dreams. Just what the hell does that mean! Then on top of that you tell me not to worry because everything is fine with the baby. Well excuse me but that is not the message you are giving me!"

The doctor took a minute to organize his thoughts before he answered.

"Julie I fully understand how you feel. Any expecting mother would feel the same way. We want to give you answers but we want to make sure we are giving you the correct ones.

We know this is your baby we are talking about and we certainly don't take that lightly. What we have here is a most unusual situation, an unprecedented one. Again I emphasize your baby is very healthy. What has been puzzling us is his rate of growth."

This was not what Julie wanted to hear. She looked at his words as nothing but textbook rhetoric.

"Doctor if you tell me one more time my baby is healthy I am going to scream. What I want to know is why the concern, why the confusion on your part that merits you calling for these unusual tests and the need to call in a specialist. You can't tell me this is standard procedure because I had none of it with Karen! So stop the bullshit and cut to the chase!"

Dr. Hart cleared his throat. He was faced with leveling with his patient without alarming her any more than she already was.

"Julie, in all honesty we are puzzled by the baby's accelerated growth, a very healthy one I must add, but an unusually rapid one.

Now the ultrasound shows the baby is healthy, the tests we did on you show that you are also healthy. We are simply trying to determine the reason for this rapid development.

We're looking at two possible factors that could alter development. The first is drug induced. Now I know you well enough to know you do not use illicit drugs and you have told me you have not been taking any steroids or any other growth enhancement drugs. For the moment we are forgetting about this factor at least concerning you. I'll get back to this in a moment.

Now the second factor we have been considering is genetics."

Julie digested what the doctor was saying. She felt encouraged that at least he was attempting to explain their concerns and allowed him to continue.

"Genetics or heredity could also be a cause of unusual growth. Are any members of your family large in statue?"

Julie thought that was an odd question but replied.

"No doctor, both my parents were relatively small. In fact my mother was only four foot eleven and weighed maybe one hundred and ten pounds. My dad was about six feet tall but no one in our family was overly large."

Doctor Hart was now faced with confronting what could be a touchy subject. He chose his words carefully.

"Julie, we have to consider the father in this equation

as well. His genetics, heredity and possible drug usage are as important as yours."

Julie gasped. She wasn't prepared for this line of questioning. She cursed herself for not expecting it. Her mind was racing along with her blood pressure. She had to think quickly. Her dilemma was delayed for a moment as the doctor asked a disturbing question.

"Are you with the father? Is there a possibility he could come in and we could run some tests on him?"

She closed her eyes in an effort to clear her head and sighed. Using the only insight that came to her frazzled mind she decided to use the same story she had told Larry.

"I'm afraid that would be impossible doctor. The father has passed away."

There was a long pause before the doctor replied.

"I'm sorry to hear that Julie. Well that being the case what that leaves us with is you and we can't find anything that would cause this. None of us can even speculate on what would explain this."

Julie was glad that was over with but she did have one more question.

"The MRI, did you get the results of that? Wasn't that supposed to measure the baby's brain development?"

The doctor again paused before answering.

"Yes we did Julie. Dr. Stepanov spent a great deal of time going over the results. He even solicited assistance from his colleagues at the Mayo Clinic. They were very interested once they knew the details. One even had asked if it would be possible for you to fly up there to be examined."

This comment did nothing to ease her worries. If the Mayo Clinic was so interested that they wanted her to come that couldn't be good. She was getting aggravated and impatient.

"Just give me the results Dr. Hart."

Dr, Hart replied without hesitation.

"This is where things get really interesting. Yes you are correct, the reason we ran the MRI was to determine brain development. It seems, and the test results were undeniable, that as rapidly as the body is maturing, the brain is way ahead of it. This is truly a remarkable child you are carrying Miss Wells."

Julie was totally taken back by the remark and almost to the point of being appalled by its implications. She barked a vehement response.

"Is that all you have to say....a remarkable child? Is this supposed to make me feel better, you thinking of my child as a genetic mutation? I will not have my child looked at as a science experiment!"

The doctor grunted as he replied.

"That's not what I am saying at all. I am just saying from a medical perspective this is a very unique situation. What you need to be concerned with is again, the baby appears very healthy and strong."

Julie was at wit's end.

"Doctor, have we determined just how far along we are?"

Dr. Hart wasn't sure how to answer that question.

"That is a difficult question to answer at this point given the extremely unusual circumstances of the situation. There would be two ways of approaching it, first that we may have originally misjudged the conception date or secondly that we were correct and the growth has just been unprecedented. I am a believer in the second scenario.

If we were to accept that my original estimate was correct that would place you at about thirteen weeks along now. Well what cannot be denied is that your baby's growth is well beyond that. Based solely on the baby's growth I would place you somewhere about twenty weeks. I've taken a number of considerations into this, the physical development, the incredible brain activity, the size of your baby bump and the kicking you are experiencing all lead me to this conclusion. Even that doesn't fully explain the accelerated brain activity which is beyond even that. I hope that answers your question Julie."

She was now beyond wit's end. On the one hand she was being told her baby was perfectly healthy, then on the other hand, she was told the entire medical profession was dumbfounded by the baby's accelerated growth. She had reached an undeniable conclusion, one that she couldn't share with anyone. It had to be Robert's genetic influence that was causing this perplexity.

"Okay doctor, you have convinced me my baby is healthy but what concerns me is your emphasis on the brain activity. Just what is going on with my baby's brain?"

The doctor took a deep breath and chose his words carefully.

"Well, I'm sure you noticed during the last ultra sound I was poking you as we ran the test. To my amazement the baby's response was simply startling. It was reacting to the pokes in a manner we have never seen even at five months. It was if there was a conciseness, almost a thinking process.

When told about this the doctors at the Mayo Clinic were over whelmed. The brain itself is fully developed, something we would expect to see around six months. I wish I had the answers Julie but we simply don't have an explanation for this incredible maturation.

There really isn't much more I can tell you at this time. I would like to schedule another appointment for you for one month from today. Of course if anything comes up in the mean time contact me, we can push it up."

The doctor transferred her to the receptionist who scheduled her next appointment. Julie disconnected the call and went over to the coffee maker. She poured a cup of coffee but was thinking what she needed more was a stiff drink, something to calm her nerves.

# 11

The next two months passed quickly. Larry had held up to his promise and dropped off a beautiful maple crib complete with blankets, pillows and an adorable mobile; he also brought over a changing table and a huge bag of stuffed animals. He was very supportive as he conceded to giving Julie a number of nights off to accommodate her frequent days of cramping and nausea.

Julie and Karen teamed together to remodel Karen's room. Karen fought her initial resentment for the inconvenience of having to reorganize her room remembering this was for her future little brother or sister and eventually agreed to put her bookcase and vanity dresser into storage to make room for the baby furniture.

They assembled the crib and changing table then put up the mobile over the crib. They both had to laugh after seeing the mobile featured planets and other celestial objects. She couldn't help but think God has a very unique sense of humor.

Julie went to her doctor's appointment and was again assured that her baby was healthy and strong. The doctors continued to emphasize the baby's incredible growth and she again refused any attempts of further research. She just wanted to get this ordeal over with and begin raising her child.

The doctors couldn't stop commenting on how large she had gotten in just the period of a month. The only piece of useful information they offered was after being asked if they could determine the baby's gender they replied she was having a boy. She and Karen both enthusiastically agreed the baby would officially be named Robert.

One evening Julie couldn't sleep. She couldn't get comfortable and felt sick to her stomach. She was cramping horribly and it felt as if the baby had dropped. She panicked and struggled to make it to the bathroom.

Walking was an ordeal as her back felt like someone was stabbing her. She thought to herself in disbelief, she couldn't be having the baby, it was too soon! Her thoughts turned to the only other alternative she could think of, she must be having a miscarriage! Her mind was now filled with thoughts of sheer terror!

No....no that can't be! She refused to believe that! She sat in the bathroom and was gasping for breath. She said a silent prayer. She discovered she was bleeding. She let out a scream.

Karen heard her scream from her bedroom and ran into the bathroom throwing open the door.

"Mom, what's wrong; are you alright?"

Julie couldn't speak, her water just broke. She was in excruciating pain and managed to cry out what words she could manage.

"Karen, call an ambulance, I'm having the baby! Go... hurry!"

Karen was in a state of shock seeing her mother like this.

"You're having the baby now? Mom, it hasn't been nine months..."

Julie was frantic.

"I know that Karen! Now just call the damn ambulance!"

Robert Harry Wells was born at 5:22 AM on August 12th. Julie had been pregnant for six months and eight days. The baby weighed seven pounds eight ounces and showed every sign of being as strong and healthy as an ox. Julie chose the name Harry as Robert's middle name in honor of her father, Harry.

Julie held her new son and smiled as she noticed he was already starting a full head of hair. She looked into her son's blue eyes and closed her own for a second; the resemblance to his father was already obvious.

She so wished Robert could be here to share the moment. Then again, she so wished he could be there to share every moment.

The initial crying had already stopped. Robert silently surveyed the room, his inquisitive mind already at work. Julie held him tightly as tears of joy flowed from her eyes.

Dr. Hart walked over to her and smiled.

"Congratulations Julie, you have a beautiful son. We're going to want to keep an eye on him for a couple days and run some tests just to make sure everything is where it should be."

A look of shock crossed Julie's face.

"Is that really necessary?"

The doctor shook his head.

"Julie, you were only pregnant for a little over six months; that gives a whole new meaning to the word premature! He appears fine, it's simply amazing he is so big after only six months, but we just want to check him out and put him on a series of vitamins and supplements, nutrients he would have normally gotten from you during the last few months that obviously he didn't get.

Julie you must realize is a woman carries a child for nine months for a reason. The baby needs that time to fully develop. He draws a lot of nutrients from the mother during the last few months. Your child is missing those last three months.

I assure you this is just a precautionary thing to make sure he is as healthy and strong as he should be."

She couldn't argue with his reasoning. A six month term is simply unfathomable.

She thought about the father's genetic influence, perhaps this is their normal gestation period.

Julie reluctantly agreed to the doctor's request still holding her son tightly.

# 12

**SIX MONTHS EARLIER**....on a distant planet twelve light years from Earth, in cell 5447 Block E, deep in the bowels of Teludia State Detention Center, a prisoner was lying unconscious but slowly awakening.

The prisoner slowly forced his eyes open. An excruciating pain overwhelmed him. His entire body was throbbing in pain. He attempted to sit up but the physical agony was hampering any progress. He slowly edged his way up the pillow and eventually got into a sitting position. He took a deep breath which in itself was rigorous. He wanted to survey his surroundings but found moving his head impossible at the moment.

He was delirious and disoriented. He had no idea where he was or how he got there. His mind was racing. He realized at the present moment he didn't even know who he was...that had to be a priority. Maybe that would help him with the dilemma of where he was.

He slowly opened his eyes and painfully scanned the room. His surroundings were fuzzy as he tried to force his eyes to focus and get his bearings. He meticulously moved his head from left to right taking in every detail. After blinking a number of times and trying desperately to fight the massive headache he was suffering from he finally came to a disturbing realization, he was in a prison cell, one that he immediately recognized.

He closed his eyes hoping it would help him concentrate. He took a deep prolonged breath and reopened his eyes. All of a sudden his mind was inundated with shocking and unsolicited thoughts.

It was all coming back to him out of nowhere! It was like a part of his past that had been for some reason completely erased came storming back to him in a flash. He came to the painful realization of who he was.

The first thing he had to come to grasps with was that he was in a prison cell, one that he now knew he had been in before. That realization was quickly followed by the history of events that lead him to be initially incarnated, the murder, the trial and the sentence; it was all now vivid in his mind.

The sentence....wait, he was to be executed. What came into his mind next totally over whelmed and astonished him. He fought his latest grisly thoughts with all his might trying to understand them. He remembered the execution.

He buried his head in his hands deep in thought. It was so real, the walk to the execution room, being pushed into the chamber, the sounds of the machinery, and then the ghastly neon green glow which filled the room just before he blacked out. He remembered it as distinctly as if it were yesterday. But how could this be? Why wasn't he dead? It was a dream, it had to have been, just a nightmare for he was still very much alive. Was all of it a dream? He rethought that notion. If his execution was a dream, and it must have been for he couldn't deny for he was clearly alive, part of it was real. This was a prison cell and he was currently confined in it; that sadly was no delusion.

Two guards stood outside the prisoner's cell door. The one held a tray of food, while the other slid a card through a slot opening the door. The guards entered the cell and the tray of food was thrown on the metal desk next to the cot where the prisoner sat, finally upright.

Both guards held prod sticks in the event of any trouble and seemed itching to use them as they were pounding them in their hands. The one guard spoke.

"You better eat this quickly skumbag; the warden

expects you in his office in fifteen minutes and you will be there! I hope you enjoy it because it could be your last meal! We will be back and don't try and give us any trouble!"

The loud words were deafening to him and echoed in his head like a gong being beaten. The guards left and he thought about what they said.

The warden, oh he remembered that man and not fondly. Maybe he would be able to at least tell him why he was still alive, and for how long he could hope to remain that way.

Finally gathering his thoughts he discovered he was remarkably hungry. He couldn't remember the last time he had eaten anything. He looked down at the tray of food and stopped suddenly before he had even picked up the fork. An extraordinary thought just exploded in his head. In an instant he recalled the last time he had eaten, it was at Julie's. Julie....oh my God! He suddenly remembered her!

He closed his eyes in horror as the recollection became so real. He could now see her face, her hair, and her beautiful eyes. He had no memory of her before that moment, now it was painfully evident! Julie...his beloved Julie now filled his every thought! He reached back in the corners of his mind for any memories he could conjure on their time together.

Julie...oh God how he remembered her now! It was all coming back to him in waves of agonizing recollections. Slowly the past year was creeping back vividly to him. They were in love, she had a daughter, yes, that much he was sure of.

He suddenly lost his appetite. He so longed to be in her comforting arms again; to feel her touch and taste her lips: the realization that that would never happen actually brought tears to his eyes, something that rarely happens.

He remembered the last time he cried was his last night with her, all too aware his pending fate. He cynically laughed at the tricks his mind was playing on him. That memory was probably from just the other night but in his mind it seemed a hundred years ago. Now he had to deal with not only his pending death but the memories of the only woman he had ever loved in his life.

His thoughts went back to the initial sentencing a year ago. Death didn't bother him; he actually looked at it as a relief from his worthless life. He had nothing to live for. Now things were different. Tears reluctantly and unexpectedly continued to flow from his eyes as the memories continued.

Now he had Julie, the most incredible woman he had ever met. The thing he found most amazing was that she actually loved him in return. It was all coming back to him now. He recalled their last night together before he was taken back. She kept her hopes up that something would enable them to remain together. He knew in his heart she would be waiting for him.

Then an even more horrific thought entered his consciousness; Julie now thought he was already dead! He had told her he was to be executed. He had to lie down on the cot and buried his head in his hands. He wept at the thought of the anguish she must be struggling with.

But he wasn't dead! He was very much alive! How could her tell her and relieve her of all her grief? Even if they had no chance of ever being together again he had to at least let her know he was alive. She deserved that much so she could move on.

He squeezed his forehead in his hands. His every thought was of Julie. He closed his eyes and remembered how Julie would always pray to a deity she referred to as God when things got difficult.

She would try and explain the concept of religion and God to him many times. They had no such concept here. He was totally unfamiliar with the idea of putting your problems into the hand of an icon no one could even prove ever existed.

Everything in his world was explained by science not this thing she referred to as religion. Religion didn't exist here. He was never a spiritual man and had never given any thought to this God she was so fond of, there was no reason to create such fantasy; they had science to explain everything and it did so perfectly.

His mind was looking at things differently now. Perhaps Julie was right, he couldn't prove she wasn't anymore than she could prove her God existed. He knew Julie as an intelligent rational person so if she honestly believed in this then maybe there just might be something to it. Simply because his culture hadn't adopted it didn't mean it couldn't exist.

He pondered the idea and felt he had nothing to lose at this point; now, how to word a prayer to this God. He knew he didn't have much time before the guards would return.

If this God was as omnipotent as Julie had led him to believe he was; then surely he would find a way. He put his faith in hers and asked her God to tell her he was alive and was thinking about her.

His moment of silent reverence was broken suddenly by the sounds of shouting. The guards had returned and were standing outside his cell door. One of the guards ran his prod stick across the bars and yelled.

"Get up! You're going to see the warden, now move!"

The guards opened the door and walked over to his cot.

"On your feet get moving!"

He got up slowly and was grabbed by one of the guards and pushed towards the door. The one guard clutched him by the arm while the other poked his prod stick into his back urging him to move.

"The warden has been waiting a long time for this little visit so let's move! I'm sure you two will have a lot to talk about!"

The three of them walked down the long corridor to the warden's office. He was forced to walk quickly as the guard continued to poke him from the back with his prod stick, sending a jolt of electricity with each jab.

They entered the elevator and after a short silent ride arrived at the floor where the warden's office was located. The one guard jammed his prod stick into his back pushing him out of the elevator. They walked down the hall; his arm still in the grasp of the belligerent guard. The guard clutching his arm looked at him maliciously.

"I remember you, oh yeah you piece of crap! It may have been a year but oh I remember you! Well now it's time to pay the piper. Hope you enjoyed your vacation because now you're going to pay for it!"

He ignored the remarks and continued walking. He wasn't in the mood for a confrontation; his mind was still on Julie.

They reached the warden's office and entered through the large ornate wooden doors. One guard approached the secretary's desk and handed her their paperwork while the other remained with him.

The secretary alerted the warden he was here and within a minute the warden came out of his office to greet him.

The warden spoke briefly with the two guards and told them to remain where they were. He then turned his attention to the prisoner.

He studied the prisoner from head to foot before speaking.

"We meet again prisoner 16754, come into my office we need to talk."

He followed the warden into his plush office. The warden closed the door and sat at his desk.

"Sit down please."

He was skeptical of the warden's apparent politeness. He had remembered him as being anything but cordial in their last meeting. He sat down and took a deep breath not having any idea of what was ahead. The warden lit a cigar and again studied the prisoner. His glaring stare made him even more uncomfortable than he was before. The warden spoke.

"Before we begin let me apologize for the delay in this meeting. I realize you have been here what, two days now? Well I just got back from out of town."

He nodded, continuing to wonder about the warden's demeanor.

"You look well, I take it the last year has been kind to you."

The prisoner was totally taken back by this unusual insistence on small talk. This was not the warden's style. He decided to try paying lip service to him until he found out where he was going with this. His instincts told him something wasn't right.

"It has sir."

The warden nodded in what appeared on the outside his approval. He took a long puff on his cigar and pulled out a manila folder scrutinizing each page. Glancing up from his studies he addressed the prisoner.

"Before we go on, do you have any questions?"

The prisoner was shocked that his thoughts were even being taken into consideration here. He decided to answer the question brutally honest.

"Well sir, I can't help but wonder why I am even still alive to be honest with you."

The warden let out a contemptuous laugh.

"I guess that would be a primary concern of yours, and a good question it is. Well let me prefix my answer by saying that was not my decision. You're still alive because that is what the state has deemed appropriate. The reason I was out of town was to go over your case with the Board of Corrections. It seems in your absence they have been reviewing the facts of your prosecution."

He raised his eyebrows in surprise. Now this is getting interesting. Considering when he left he was facing execution he looked at this as a good thing, after all, their new conclusions, if any, couldn't be any worse than the old one. He spoke up with renewed interest.

"May I ask what their findings were? I mean, after all I do have a vested interest in this affair."

The warden gave him a droll smile.

"Of course you do. Well the board looked at a number of aspects of the proceedings. You remember of course the charge was first degree murder, this cannot be disputed. You did indeed murder a man. I think we can both agree on that."

He nodded in silent and remorseful agreement as the warden continued.

"Now after intense research, the Board had discovered the victim was an extortionist. Seems he was involved in a number of, how can I say this, damaging activities, which if left unattended, could cause the State a great deal of....problems.

These problems would include substantial financial consequences, the possible termination of many key figures not to mention the considerable embarrassment it would create. It would result in a public relations and political nightmare.

I might add that one board member even went as far as to suggest you did the state a favor by ridding them of such trash. I personally found that comment almost comical if not insulting. After hours of intense discussion it was even suggested you be acquitted of all charges all together. It should go without saying that I personally vetoed that outrageous suggestion."

The warden now had his undivided attention. He had tried to tell that to the prosecutors at his trial but his cries fell on deaf ears. Now they might finally realize he was telling the truth! His only question was how this new information might affect the final verdict and sentence. He was about to find out.

"With this new knowledge the State has granted you leniency, a stay of execution if you will. Well, more aptly, they have decided execution is not an appropriate action to take in this case."

He threw himself back in the chair! He put his hands to his head in amazement. His eyes popped out of his head and his mouth was gaping. His heart was racing! This was more than he even dreamed of. He searched for something to say to the warden to show his appreciation.

"I…I don't know what to say sir. I…."

The warden interrupted him.

"I do not want your thanks or appreciation, this was certainly not my decision and to be honest with you I do not agree with it. You murdered a man, whether he was a good man or not you still killed him! That is against the law in my eyes and should be met with the ultimate penalty. The members of the panel disagreed. The Board has made their decision and I am forced to respect it regardless of whether or not I agree with it."

He nodded his head. There was one important question to ask.

"Well sir, then just what is my sentence to be?"

The warden clasped his hands together intertwining his fingers, moving them back and forth in thought. He took another puff of his cigar and contemplated how he wanted to answer that question.

"The Board has left that up to me. They have given me the freedom to do what ever I want with you, sadly barring execution of course."

He looked the warden straight in the eyes.

"What have you decided then sir?"

The warden let out a derisive laugh.

"Well, let's start off with what I can't do. As we have already discussed, I cannot execute you. But I also cannot release you into the general public."

The prisoner stopped him.

"But you said complete acquittal was mentioned."

The warden shook his head.

"You don't seem to understand this. You are in possession of a lot of information that could incriminate the present administration on a number of levels. This would have severe political ramifications for years to come!

If I were to allow you to circulate in the general population and any of this information were to get out, well let's just say we can't take that chance! No, releasing you unconditionally is out of the question!"

He was all of a sudden feeling a little less enthused than he was just moments ago. He tried to think of what other options the warden would have. He replied.

"I don't imagine it would mean anything to you if I promised you I wouldn't talk about it with anyone. I would have no reason to, I just want this all behind me. I swear to you."

The warden slammed his fist on his desk.

"Releasing you is not an option! I will not be responsible for any information about this leaking out during one of your drunken or drug induced stupors! We both know your history and also both know it will continue if I were to allow you to simply walk out of here."

He stood up in anger.

"I am not like that anymore, I have changed!"

The warden gave him a stern look.

"Do not interrupt me! You expect me to put any credence in the word of a convicted murderer dope addict? No, you will not be released and that is not open for negotiations, it's final! People like you don't change!"

He closed his eyes and sighed in initial disappointment. Then out of nowhere a solution occurred to him! It would be the perfect answer to both the warden's dilemma and his personal dreams! This was going to be too good to be true! He threw up his hands to get the warden's attention.

"Sir, I think I have the perfect solution to the problem if you would hear me out."

The warden lifted his eyebrows in mock anticipation of the prisoner's suggestion.

"You...you have a suggestion? Really now; and just why would I even listen to your suggestion? I am the authority and you are the criminal here remember? I can't imagine a scenario that would give you any input into this."

He nodded.

"I totally understand and respect that sir but I think I have a solution that would solve both of our problems."

The warden couldn't help but laugh.

"The only problem I have is what to do with you. Now you on the other hand might have a lot of problems depending on what my decision is, and let me add you will have no influence on it!"

He sighed. This obviously wasn't going to be easy to convince him of his idea.

"Please sir, just humor me for a moment. You don't want to release me into the population because of the information I may leak out, okay that's fine. Then how about this, send me back to where I was. That way I will be totally out of your hair and there will be no threat of me leaking any information to anyone! Not only won't I be in the population, I won't even be on the planet!"

The warden stood up and placed his hands on his desk as an act of defiance.

"You can't be serious! You've got to be kidding me!"

He ran his fingers through his hair trying to come up with a response.

"With all due respect sir I wasn't kidding. Think about it, it would solve both of our problems...."

The warden interrupted him. He spoke sarcastically.

"You must have really liked it there."

He tried to conceal a tear that was forming in his eye.

"Yes sir I did."

The warden was now toying with him.

"Just what was so special there? Tell me, this I have got to hear."

He wanted no part of the game it was obvious the warden wanted to play. His initial thought was to level with the warden, to plea for his sympathy but then he second guessed his line of thought.

He would not make Julie a pawn in this pointless chess game. He had too much love and respect for her to put her in that position.

"It's not important sir. I just wanted to try and offer a solution to..."

Again the warden interrupted him.

"I am not interested in any solution you could possible come up with! While I am not at liberty to execute you, I will not consequently reward you for your actions. You want to go back? Well you are not going back! Just what was it there that was so attractive? Was it the drugs, the booze, a cheap hooker perhaps?"

It took every ounce of restrain for him not to rise up and attack the warden. He knew that would do more harm than good. He lowered his head in deep thought. His first objective was to forget the warden's last comment and the second one was to try and figure out what he had in mind next. He took a deep breath and answered the question as respectfully as he could. Inside he was raging mad but on the outside as cool as a cucumber.

"It was none of that. Well then I have to ask, where do we go from here sir?"

The warden walked slowly around the room puffing on his cigar. He finally turned and faced the prisoner.

"Well one thing is for certain. We cannot keep you here. I will not authorize you living here at the public's expense. We simply don't have the cell space to accommodate such a luxury. Besides, I don't want to have to look at you every day. That certainly narrows my options."

The warden returned to his desk and called his secretary.

"Get a guard in here. I want this maggot removed from my office."

He laughed inwardly to himself. This was the warden he remembered. He thought to himself about what other options might be available.

"Sir, I have a right to know what you intend to do with me!"

The warden just shook his head and chuckled.

"First of all you remain a prisoner and the only rights you have are those I give you! Now to answer your question, I don't know, let me sleep on it. You're still my prisoner and will be treated as such and don't forget that. This is a correctional facility not an amusement park! Now get out of my sight!"

# 13

The prisoner struggled through a restless night of sleep. While his physical pain subsided his mental anguish increased tenfold. He couldn't get Julie out of his mind. The struggles she must be enduring simply broke his heart, a heart he didn't even have before he met her. At first he thought there would be no hope of ever seeing her again but he had sincerely thought he had come up with a plan that would allow him to do just that, only to be shot down in flames by the warden.

It was obvious the warden was more concerned with hurting him than solving his problem. That would be an obstacle that would seem to be insurmountable. He knew that would be his only hope of ever being reunited with her.

He was rudely awakened by the sounds of the same two guards at his cell door.

"Get up scumbag; we're skipping breakfast this morning. The warden wants to see you immediately now move!"

He rubbed his head in confusion. Why would the warden want to see him again so soon? He remembered the warden said he wanted to sleep on the dilemma of what to do with him...maybe he has decided. His heart was filled with uncertainty. What little relief he got came from the knowledge that they couldn't execute him. He racked his brain for what options the warden might have. He knew one thing for certain; what ever the warden had decided wouldn't be good.

He got up as the guards opened the door to his cell. Breakfast was the last thing on his mind. The guards stood by the door and motioned him over. He complied and was once again escorted to the warden's office.

There was no talking or taunting during the five minute journey to the warden's office. It was strictly business this time. The one guard held him by his arm while the other walked behind, prod stick in his hand but by his side.

He glanced at the guards who both remained silent. This was unusual behavior for them. He wondered if they knew something he didn't.

The arrived at the warden's office and opened the doors to find the man standing by his secretary's desk waiting for them. He looked inpatient. The prisoner felt in his heart his fate had been decided.

"Thank you; that will be all guards you can leave. I can handle it from here."

The guards nodded and left the room.

The warden said something softly to his secretary and then turned his attention to the prisoner.

He studied the warden's face to try and get any clues as to what may lie ahead. The warden stood like a statue, stone faced. He could gather nothing from that.

The warden opened the doors to his office and addressed the prisoner.

"Come in Kmyviks."

His heart skipped a beat. This was the first time the warden had ever called him by his name. It was the first time anyone had called him by name in such a long time. He almost didn't recognize it. Everyone here had simply referred to him by his number and Julie; well she never even knew his real name.

His mind was overwhelmed with thoughts. What would inspire him to call him by name? He couldn't help but look at that as a good sign. To personalize the relationship had to mean the warden might be showing a faint sign of compassion, of feelings. He hoped against hope that he was correct; if he could just get the warden to listen to him. The warden noticed the prisoner's expression.

"Is there anything wrong?"

The prisoner struggled for words.

"Well sir, this is the first time you have ever referred to me by name and I was just a bit taken back."

The warden chuckled.

"Well Kmyviks, this will be our last meeting so I thought we would spare the formalities. Now come in please."

He followed the warden into his office. The warden pointed to the chair by his desk in a silent request for him to be seated; he complied.

The warden lit a cigar and sat pompously behind his desk. They stared into each other's eyes for what seemed an eternity before the warden finally spoke.

"Let's keep this short and simple. I have many things to do and you, well you have places to go. Out of respect, is there anything you would like to say before I pass sentence Kmyviks?"

The stern look on the warden's face told him without doubt this would be the last chance he would get to plead his case. There was so much he wanted to say but emotions were over coming him at the moment. His heart was racing.

He closed his eyes for a brief second and saw Julie's face. He fought back a tear. The thought of never seeing her again terrified him more than any sentence the warden could give him.

Words, he needed words. He needed words he had never used before to express emotions he had never felt before. It was now, for the first time in his life, he needed Julie's God. He found himself praying he did indeed exist.

All of a sudden her religion was beginning to make sense. It was somewhat comforting to believe that when all hope is gone there was some spirit watching over you. He now silently asked this spirit for the words he needed. Science wouldn't get him out of this one.

He panicked, he wasn't sure if anything he said would make a difference. He had to try.

"Sir, with all due respect, may I have a minute. I have never pleaded for anything in my life and I have never begged for anything before, but I am now."

The warden flashed a cynical smile; H e was enjoying seeing his advisory squirm.

"Oh now this is going to be interesting; you, pleading to me for anything? Do continue, this has to be enlightening. Do speak Kmyviks; tell me your story. I will grant you that request if for no other reason than curiosity."

Again he inwardly thought this might be encouraging. The warden was at least willing to listen to him. He had this once chance to plea his case, to pour his heart out to the only man who could save him.

He thought about his life and how he had always been a strong man, a tough, hardened man who never needed anything from anyone and never asked for any kind of help. He had always been self centered, looking out only for himself.

He then thought of his heart; that had laid dormant all his life, void of emotion, void of any feelings that didn't directly involve survival. His heart had been a mere organ whose only function was to pump the blood that kept him alive.

Julie had changed all that. She had taken that cold heart and nurtured it, transformed it into a heart that could actually experience love. His heart was now not only pumping blood but also circulating the most incredible feeling of passion he had ever felt.

His primary concern was not survival but to be reunited with her. To give back the love she had shown him. He again silently prayed to Julie's God and spoke. His first sentence stuck in his throat for it was such a foreign thought.

"Sir, I beg of you, please allow me to go back. I will never again be a burden to you or society. The state's secretes and fears will go with me."

The warden rubbed his chin. The prisoner intrigued him. He had a sincere curiosity as to what was driving this man's desire to return.

"You really want to go back there don't you, and something tells me it's not simply to escape justice. Tell me Kmyviks, just what would motivate you to want to spend your life on a foreign world? This is something I can't even begin to imagine."

He felt encouraged more than ever. The warden was actually showing interest in his plight. He cleared his throat and spoke with a sincerity he had never experienced before.

"I met a woman there sir. She changed my life. She showed me love and what it means and what it can do for a person. She loved me and I loved her in return. I have never loved anyone in my life sir, not even my parents. No one has ever actually loved me before..."

The warden interrupted him.

"Well, you haven't been the easiest person to love. I think we can both agree on that. In fact I would have thought you incapable of love."

The prisoner nodded.

"But sir, she changed me. I'm not the same person I was the last time we were together. I did something good while I was there; I made a positive difference in someone's life!"

The warden scoffed at the remark and fired back.

"The only positive influence you could ever make on someone's life is by leaving it! I'm not convinced."

The prisoner folded his hands and closed his eyes as if in prayer.

"Sir, this woman taught me the meaning of love, she taught me how to place someone else's happiness over your own. I beg of you sir, please send me back."

The warden stood up and paced the room. He wasn't expecting this interaction and was certainly shocked it was coming from the man in front of him.

"You must have really loved this woman. For a man to be willing to spend the rest of his life on an alien world apart from everything he has ever known simply for the love of a woman, absurd."

The warden puffed on his cigar thinking before continuing. His curiosity was getting the best of him.

"So you claim you did something good while you were there, you say you actually made a positive difference to someone? I find that impossible to believe. Just what did you do and for whom? There has to be a fascinating if unbelievable story to go with this."

He took a deep breath taking the warden's words as encouragement. As much as he didn't want to involve either Julie or Karen into this he thought it might increase his chances of being allowed to return to them. Against his better judgment he tried to explain.

"The woman I spoke of had a young daughter. The girl was suffering from an emotional disorder that was totally disabling. Apparently mental illness is still a problem on that planet.

Well I naturally had the means available to me thanks to the medical equipment you allowed me to bring with me to correct that problem and I did. She is now a wonderful, perfectly healthy young lady. Her mind is functioning perfectly normal now thanks to my efforts."

The warden rubbed his temples deep in thought. He stared directly at the prisoner with a disturbing cold harshness.

"Forgive me but that is quite difficult to accept coming from you Kmyviks. The man I sentenced a year ago would be incapable of such actions."

Kmyviks jumped up from his chair and addressed the warden.

"That is exactly what I have been trying to tell you sir. The man I was a year ago wouldn't have done that. The woman I met was so incredible. She saw through that and changed me. I am a better man for having known and loved her. I am a changed man because of her love for me.

Please sir, they mean that much to me. I love her more than life itself sir. Please let me go back, I am of no use to you here and I could make such a difference there."

The warden took a puff from his cigar and walked over to the prisoner.

"Oh that is where you are mistaken! You could be of great use to us here!"

The prisoner looked up in confusion.

"I don't understand. How could I be of any use to you if I remained?"

The warden returned to sitting at his desk and relit his cigar.

"Your actions have really opened a can of worms for the State. You inadvertently exposed a weakness in the very workings of the Administration. This has caused a great deal of concern.

If such men, as the man you eliminated, are able to penetrate the inner circle so easily they can cause incredible problems and embarrassment. Steps must be taken to insure this never happens again."

He wasn't sure where the warden was going with this

but instinctively knew it was going to prevent him from returning.

"How do I fit in with this sir? I've already rid you of one problem..."

The warden interrupted.

"Indeed you have! I think the state is showing it's appreciation for this effort by not executing you. Now Internal Affairs has been in session to determine the best course of action to make sure such an embarrassing situation never arises again. They had decided to form a special team to monitor the situation."

A look of worry crossed the prisoner's face. He somehow felt he was expected to be a part of that team. His focus now was to talk the warden out of his cooperation.

"You're not expecting me to be a part of this team?"

The warden smiled.

"They are planning on establishing a task force to deal with and eliminate insurgents as they are discovered. This of course will be done internally, and with complete discretion and secrecy.

They needed someone to head the team. This person would have to be of low moral standards considering the work that might be involved. He would also have to be adept at, well, eliminating undesirables. I recommended you immediately.

Yes Kmyviks you will be a part of this team. As difficult as it is for the State to admit this, you have displayed, how shall I say, a very efficient talent at handling these types of things. Your talents will be most helpful."

The prisoner stood silently gapping in horror!

"You recommended me? The Department of Corrections suggested acquittal! So it is you that is preventing me from going back! How could you? I'm going to report this!"

The warden let out a boisterous laugh.

"Report this? To whom would you report this to? Do you think you have any friends here? Do you honestly think there is anyone in your corner? I own you! Now you have no choice in the matter. You will be heading this team!"

The prisoner was devastated. His hopes of returning were now vanquished. The thought of working for the State was something he just couldn't come to grips with and would ultimately refuse to cooperate with.

"What if I refused? You couldn't execute me. Just what would you do then?"

The warden tapped his fingers on his desk and took another puff on his cigar.

"No, you are correct. I couldn't legally execute you but I assure you, accidents happen and if one were to happen to you there would be no one responsible or required to be held accountable for it. There would be no inquiry and it would be forgotten the next day. Now I would think long and hard about this before you answer."

He was torn between total rage and complete depression. He knew now he would never see Julie again, that thought brought a tear to his eye. He also knew he was staring at the man responsible for it; that brought a rage he hadn't experienced in a long time.

During his time with Julie he had never felt any anger or rage of any kind. She had rid him of that. He started to fear his old persona could be returning. The though terrified him.

He was such a good man when he was with her. She brought out things in him he never knew he possessed. Now, without her influence, there would be nothing to prevent the old persona from returning.

He could already feel the hatred, the anger, the rage building up inside him. At the moment these feelings were directed solely at the warden but he had no idea how to prevent them from coming back as a way of life, like he was before he met Julie

The warden interrupted his thoughts.

"Now you don't have to make this decision today. You are going to have plenty of time to dwell on it."

The prisoner wasn't comfortable with the warden's latest thoughts.

"Just what is that suppose to mean?"

The warden smiled.

"Well, I mentioned this project was in the works, it is. The unfortunate thing is its going to be down the road a ways. There have been some budget cuts that will force the project to be put on hold, for a while."

The prisoner didn't like the sounds of this. The warden continued.

"We're looking at a year, maybe longer. So you are probably wondering what we're going to do with you in the mean time."

Kmyviks put his hands to his head to try and squeeze out the pain he was currently experiencing. He simply stared at the warden who continued.

"I put a lot of thought into that dilemma. We certainly can't keep you here. There is no cell space and I would not expect you to live in such luxury at the public's expense so I had to find an alternate solution, which I have. The answer is cryonic suspension."

Kmyviks had no idea what the warden was talking about.

"Cryonics....dare I even ask you what that is."

The warden smiled and puffed on his cigar.

"Well I know I would if I were you because you will be spending at least the next year in it."

# 14

The prisoner was beside himself in confusion. As much as he hated to admit it, fear was starting to creep into his emotions.

"Just what the hell are you planning on doing to me?"

The warden nonchalantly ran his fingers through his hair. His reply was stoic and unemotional.

"We are going to freeze you Kmyviks. You will be in a state of complete hibernation, suspended animation if you will. Oh I assure you it is perfectly safe and unfortunately painless. This will keep you alive until you are needed, at no inconvenience to the State or cost to the general public. It is the perfect solution. They tell me it's just like sleeping. You have no concept of time. You will be out of it before you know it and then we can get to work."

Kmyviks was speechless. He didn't know what to think. Shock was mixed with anger and fear.

"I have no say in this?"

The warden laughed.

"No, I'm afraid you don't. Now I have already arranged a team to prepare the process. You see this was decided long before your little emotional romantic intercession. Your fate was determined before you even walked in the door. You will now be escorted to the cryogenics ward where we will begin the procedure. The actual process is amazingly simple.

So I guess this is goodbye Kmyviks. I am retiring at the end of the year so I am afraid I will not be around when they...thaw you out. I wish you the best of luck, I am sure you will do the State proud."

The prisoner realized he had no recourse in the matter. His heart was suffocating from despair. A feeling of hopelessness over whelmed him. He had run out of options. He was facing this fate alone without any hopes of any help. He had to accept his fate. He was backed into a corner he couldn't get out of.

He thought of Julie, the ordeal she must be going through and the heartbreak of knowing he would never see her again.

He could only ask for closure, to simply get this nightmare over with. His only thought now was asking for a brief explanation on how this was done.

"Just how is this done?"

The warden lifted his eyebrows and grinned.

"It's a most amazing process actually. We've been doing it for years now in selected cases. Of course you wouldn't have known about it because it is kept highly secretive. We have never had any trouble with reviving the patient so you have nothing to worry about. The actual technique starts ironically enough with your death."

This was not what he wanted to hear.

"What are you talking about...my death?"

The warden leaned back in his chair and relit his cigar.

"Yes, we actually have to stop your heart to begin the freezing process. Once you are pronounced dead an emergency response team begins work on you immediately. Relax; we don't want you dead any more than you do.

They stabilize all your body functions by supplying your brain with enough oxygen and blood to preserve minimal function. Your body is then packed in ice and injected with an anticoagulant to prevent your blood from clotting. Once you are stabilized we begin the freezing."

The warden called his secretary on the intercom and requested the guards to return. He then spoke to Kmyviks.

"I hope you don't harbor any ill feelings towards me Kmyviks. I am simply doing my job, this is nothing personal. No, I am not especially fond of you, I never have been but none the less I must do what is best for the State. I'm sure you understand. You would do the same if you were in my position. My hands are tied and this is the only viable solution. Everyone will benefit from it, you will see in time."

Kmyviks just gaped at the warden dumbfounded.

"You mean even after hearing my story you are unmoved?"

The warden just chuckled.

"As touching as it was it had no consequence in my decision. Sadly having a heart is a detriment to this position one that I have totally taken out of the equation. Compassion is not a luxury I can afford to have.

You and your ridiculous story will be totally forgotten the moment you walk out of this office…do we understand each other?"

The prisoner glared at the warden but, for the moment, remained silent. The warden continued.

He scowled at the warden with contempt and replied.

"Perfectly"

The warden scoffed at the comment and continued undaunted.

"This could be a wonderful opportunity for you. Once you are revived you will hold a prominent position in the Administration and you will be paid handsomely for your work. Not a bad outcome for a convicted murderer if you ask me. You will head a department that will perform a valuable service to…"

He had heard enough. His inner demons were returning from his past. The anger was building up in his soul, anger he hadn't felt in over a year now over took him. Hatred now controlled him. The old Kmyviks had returned.

"If I could I would slit your throat where you stood! I will never serve this Administration; I hope you rot in hell!"

There was a knock on the door as the guards returned. The warden opened the door and addressed the one guard.

"Escort the prisoner to the cryonic ward in D block. If he gives you any trouble, well you know how to handle it."

He then turned and faced the prisoner.

"You say you have changed? Well I certainly don't see it. You are the same monster we exiled a year ago. Just so you know; if I had my way we would have commenced with the execution! Guards, get that son of a bitch out of here before I decide to execute him myself!"

The guards grabbed him and pushed him towards the door. He fought them long enough to turn around and fire one last comment to the warden in total rage.

"You're going down warden! You and the entire administration are going down and I just wish I could have a hand in it! The people will not stand for such tyrannical abuse of power! I will die before I work for you!"

The warden just grinned.

"Be careful what you say, that could easily be arranged. Remember, just one plug will be keeping you alive! It would be a shame if that somehow accidentally got unplugged now wouldn't it?"

One guard shot a jolt of electricity in the prisoner's back with his prod stick. Stunned the prisoner fell limp. The warden smiled.

"Get him out of here! If he gives you any trouble, just kill him!"

The guards pushed his limp body out of the warden's office, past the secretary's desk and into the hallway.

The guard with the prod stick jabbed him in the back to revive him. He repeated the process until the prisoner snapped out of his electricity induced daze. Enraged Kmyviks turned to face his adversary.

"Do that again and I will use it on you!"

The guard just laughed.

"I really don't think so."

The guard jabbed him again only this time adding a mild electrical jolt to emphasize it.

"You're just not making anyone happy this morning you piece of garbage. Just be thankful I didn't turn the voltage up or we wouldn't be having this conversation, now move!"

The guard with the prod stick jammed it into his back pushing him forward while the second guard tightened his grip on the prisoner's arm literally dragging him down the hallway.

The prisoner's heart was now filled with animosity, permeated with bitterness and hate. The kindness that had filled his heart for the last year was now gone. He felt nothing but anger and rage. Deep within his soul this transformation saddened him but his current state of acerbity over took any feelings of remorse.

As he was being shoved down the hallway his mind dwelled on what was happening to him, not so much physically but emotionally. He could handle the physical pain, he had done that all his life, he had built up such a high tolerance of physical pain the guards actions hardly phased him.

What was gnawing at him was the loss of his heart. He recognized what was happening to him and it was causing him incredible heartache.

He fought the physical pain and withdrew into a cerebral fantasy of the past year. It was a defense mechanism. His thoughts turned to Julie, her daughter

Karen and the love and compassion they had showed him and brought out in him.

He remembered what it felt like to love, and be loved in return. The loss of this caused him more pain than any prod stick could hope to. It was a pain he was unfamiliar with. He had never experienced love before in his life therefore he had never experienced the pain of losing it. He wasn't sure how to handle this, how to deal with it or over come it.

The anger in him continued to rise. He now accepted the fact that the kind man that Julie and Karen had created was now dead. The monster he had been all his life was now resurfacing.

The guard grasping his arm pushed him forward. He turned to the man and fought the move. The guard grabbed him.

"I've the authority to just waste you right here so don't give me a reason!"

The guard behind him laughed.

"It's a good thing we are taking this punk to cryonics; he needs to cool off a bit!"

The prisoner turned around and glared at the guard but held his cool and said nothing. He so wanted to take them both out, and probably could have if given half an effort but decided that action would prove nothing.

There would be many more where they came from, escape was not an option. That thought went against every fiber in his body but sadly it was the reality of the situation. It still took every ounce of restraint he had not to at least try.

The three men continued in silence and without any further hostilities. They walked down the hall to the elevator. He was shoved in the elevator and pushed to the back as the guard pushed the button to D ward.

The two minute ride was silent and uneventful. The

doors opened and he was again shoved out and pushed down the hall. Scowls were exchanged but not a word was spoken. His indignation remained boiling but locked in his soul and unspoken.

The three men walked deliberately down the hall and stopped at the large metallic doors labeled "Cryonic Preservation Lab"

The guard picked up a phone to the left of the doors and called in. Within minutes a woman opened the door and glanced at the paperwork the guard gave her. She nodded her approval and motioned the men to come inside.

"We've been expecting you, please wait here a moment."

The guard acknowledged her and spoke a warning.

"Be careful with this one, he's a wild one."

Undaunted the woman walked over to a desk where a man in a white suit stood waiting. After a brief conversation the two returned.

"We'll take him now thank you. You both can leave."

The guard with the prod stick added.

"I'm telling you this jerk is crazy. He..."

The man stopped him.

"I thank you for your concern but I assure you we have the situation well in hand."

The guards nodded and took one last look at their prisoner. They walked out silently.

The man glanced at the paperwork then addressed the prisoner.

"Good afternoon. Let's get one thing straight from the beginning. Your past, your background is of no interest to us here. We are a medical facility not a penal one. You treat us with respect and we will return that. While you are here you are a patient not a prisoner. I will be the doctor in charge of the operation and this will be my assistant. Is all this understood?"

The prisoner was relieved to have finally met someone with some reason and compassion. He nodded his approval. He had no intention of giving these people any trouble. They were not the people he targeted his anger at; they were simply doing their jobs.

The doctor and his assistant smiled.

"Very well then let's proceed. I realize this is not a pleasant experience for you and certainly not one of your choosing. We respect that and simply ask for your cooperation. I am sure you understand why you are here and what we are doing."

Kmyviks nodded.

"Good, let me give you a brief explanation of how this works. You will be put into what we call a state of cryonic suspension. Your body will, in all practical sense, be totally shut down.

Your bodily functions, respiratory, nervous system, and circulatory will be shut down to a minimum required to continue life. Your brain activity will remain normal but in a dormant state, just as if you were sleeping. You will have no concept of time.

When you are revived it will seem like the next day. The process is harmless, painless and totally safe. We have done this many times without incident. We are good at what we do here. Before we proceed do you have any questions?"

Kmyviks was taken back by the inquiry. Questions... he didn't know how to answer that. Concerns maybe, fears definitely but questions? Just what was he suppose to ask?

He thought any questions would be pointless and only delay the inevitable. He accepted his fate, he had lost Julie and that was all that mattered. This was his future and he just wanted to get it over with.

He remembered his past, many times over the years

he had felt hopeless, but at those times he had nothing to lose so it really didn't bother him. He had reached the point where death was actually welcome.

Now he again felt hopeless but there was a lot more at stake. He couldn't help but feel that in this case, death would be a merciful end for he couldn't imagine going on without Julie. He sadly shook his head; no he didn't have any questions.

The doctor nodded and handed the prisoner a set of clothing that could only be described as attire appropriate for an astronaut.

"This is a thermal insulation suit. It is what you will wear while you are in cryonic suspension. It protects and insulates the body, keeping in the body heat needed for survival. You can change in that room over there."

The doctor pointed to a small changing room. The prisoner hesitantly took the suit and went into the room to change.

He entered the changing room and closed the door. The room itself was small and windowless. The room had a tile floor and the only features were a small bench and dim over head light.

He examined the suit he was given. It was a one piece jumpsuit white in color. The threads were composed of a thick fabric but he couldn't recognize the material. The gloves and feet were sewn into the suit making the outfit entirely one piece.

The suit was obviously insulated and featured connections sewn into the sleeve for external tubes or other apparatus. There was a tight seem running down the front of the suit from the neck to the naval area. He assumed this was for access to the body after the suit was on.

He hesitated deep in thought. He had to sort things out before he continued.

He was experiencing a variety of emotions at the moment; reluctantly he had to admit fear topped the list. He analyzed that sensation. He wasn't afraid of dying; he had faced death many times in his life and conquered it every time.

He wished he knew more about the process he was facing. He had been assured it was perfectly safe and that it had been successfully done before.

Doubts continued to flood his mind. How long would he be under, would they remember to revive him, questions he couldn't answer. He then remembered the warden's comment about how only one plug would be keeping him alive. If the warden decided to unplug it he would never know and obviously never awaken again.

Then his thoughts again turned to Julie. He had resolved himself to the fact that he was going to be frozen, for how long he didn't know.

He then forced himself to concede he would be forced to work for the state doing who knows what. This in turn required him to accept the scoundrel he once was would return and remain the rest of his life. His future was bleak indeed.

As much as all of this saddened him he accepted it. His heart was destroyed with the loss of Julie so his personal fate was of no concern to him. He slowly took off his prison jumpsuit and folded it placing it on the bench. He then unfolded the white cryonic suit and took a deep breath. He sat on the bench and closed his eyes before continuing. He needed one last moment of peace before he put it on.

He folded his hands in prayer like he had seen Julie do many times. He said a silent prayer to a God he had just recently discovered and whom he still wasn't convinced even existed.

He simply asked for closure, not so much for himself

but for Julie. He just wanted her to know he was alive and she remained in what was left of his heart. He asked this God to somehow, someday let Julie and Karen know he was alive and his heart remained with them.

He meticulously put on the suit slowly one arm, one leg at a time. He certainly didn't want to damage it in any way since it was going to be keeping him alive. He gently closed the front seam and stretched testing the suit's comfort. The material in the suit irritated him causing an itching.

He laughed at the trivial discomfort knowing it would be temporary and that it was the least of his current problems the room.

He exited the room and was greeted by the doctor and his assistant.

"Are you ready to proceed?"

Starting down at the floor he silently nodded. He suddenly felt totally devoid of emotions. It was if none of this were actually happening, like he was in a dream, a horrible nightmare; one he inwardly knew he would never awaken from. Apathy over took him. He just didn't care about anything anymore. He thought of it as a defense mechanism. If he didn't care maybe wouldn't bother him.

The three walked deliberately towards the back of the reception area in silence. They reached a wall made of black partitions extending from the floor to the ceiling completely separating the room from the reception area. The doctor pulled them aside to create an opening. He followed the doctor and his assistant into the room.

They were obviously standing in an operating room. In the center of the room was an operating table surrounded by a myriad of medical machines each being manned by attendants in white surgical gowns.

The doctor opened a folder he had been carrying and studied it for a moment before speaking.

"Kmyviks, if I may call you that, let me explain what we will be doing. I don't want to alarm you but I feel I owe you total honesty about the procedure. Let me prefix this by assuring you this is a totally safe operation, one that we have successfully done many times before."

He listened with an overwhelming sense of uneasiness. He wasn't sure he wanted to know anything about what they had to do or how they were doing it, he just wanted the whole thing to be over. His only thoughts were of the outcome.

He would be in a complete state of suspended animation for a yet to be determined amount of time. That was all that was important to him. Oh, and with the hopes of eventually being brought out of it alive. He rethought that, he was trying to think of a future that would be worth it.

The doctor continued.

"Now I know this is going to sound a bit terrifying but it works. Initially we will place you under anesthetics and stop your heart temporarily. The response team you see here will then inject your body with a series of chemicals that will continue the blood flowing as if the heart had never been stopped.

They will also prevent blood clotting and any damage to the brain. You body will then be cooled to a temperature just above the freezing point of water and the blood will be removed.

Once this is achieved we will then inject you with a cryoprotectant to prevent ice crystals from forming in your organs and tissues and your body will be cooled to minus one hundred thirty degrees Celsius.

We will then lower your body into a tank of liquid nitrogen at a temperature of minus one hundred and ninety degrees Celsius. This is where you will remain until revived. You will be monitored hourly to insure there are no complications or problems. We have done this many times before Kmyviks I promise you it is totally proven and safe."

Chills ran up and down his spine! He really wished he hadn't heard all that.

The doctor put his hand on Kmyviks shoulder and offered a sincere expression of compassion.

"Is there anything you want to say before we put you under?"

Words escaped him. He uttered the only thought that came to his troubled mind.

"You won't forget about me will you?"

The doctor smiled.

"No, you will be monitored hourly and all your files will be safely kept on the computer which is checked daily. We won't forget about you. When the time comes I promise you, you will be revived in perfect health and no concept of time. It will be like waking up from a peaceful night's sleep."

He was instructed to lie down on the table as the procedure began. His final waking thoughts were of Julie. As he lost consciousness he softly spoke to her.

"I'm here sweetheart. I'm alive and I love you."

# 15

**PRESENT DAY.....**Tiny Robert squeezed his mother's thumb with all the might he had. His infant eyes gazed at her with an unusual intensity. Julie took notice of these acts and smiled. They were locked in the stare for a moment. It was almost a hypnotic gaze.

Then something hit her like a ton of bricks. Her heart skipped a beat. She started to tremble. She felt an intuition that defied all logic in both its meaning and its origin. Robert was trying to tell her something. Her motherly instincts told her so. Her mind tried to process the revelation it was being given. It made no sense but none the less it was loud and clear.

He was alive! She felt it! She didn't know how but she couldn't deny it. Her heart, her very soul was screaming it at her. She had never believed anything stronger in her life. She grabbed the arm of the attending nurse.

"I have to see Karen, please get her in here!"

Puzzled the nurse politely replied.

"I'm sorry Miss Wells; your daughter can't come in here at the moment. We have to..."

Julie stopped her in mid sentence.

"Get my daughter in here now!"

The nurse nodded.

"Yes Miss Wells, I'll see what I can do."

Within minutes Karen was by her mother's bedside. Her face beaming at seeing her baby brother for the first time nestled in his mother's arms.

"Oh wow mom, he's beautiful!"

Julie grabbed her daughter's arm. She spoke with an alarming tone.

"Karen, he's alive!"

Karen looked at her mother with confusion.

"Of course he is mom, he looks great!"

Julie shook her daughter's arm.

"No, Robert is alive."

Karen was dumbfounded by her mother's statement. She was taken back by the distressful expression.

"Yeah, Robert, he's in your arms mom of course he is alive."

Julie frantically shook her head.

"No, you don't understand. His father is alive!"

Karen stepped back. She was concerned about her mother's tone of voice. She appeared to be almost in a state of panic. She thought carefully before replying.

"Mom, we both know that is impossible."

Julie squeezed her daughter's hand.

"But he is; he told me!"

Puzzled beyond words Karen tried to calm her mother down.

"Mom, Robert is gone, we both know that. Look at my beautiful baby brother mom. You should be happy this is wonderful!"

Julie was trembling, her mind racing in excitement but confusion. She had to convince her daughter.

"I know he is alive, my son told me. I don't understand how but he made that quite clear."

Karen was now scared. Her mother was in a state of panic. The attending nurse had overheard the conversation. She could tell the patient was getting upset and that was the last thing she needed to do.

"Miss Wells, I'm afraid Karen is going to have to go back. We have to get the baby into the incubator and you need to get some rest. It isn't good for you to get excited like this now."

The nurse put her hand on Karen's shoulder and

walked her to the door. Julie started to cry as her daughter was escorted out of the room.

Julie shouted out to Karen just before she left the room.

"He's alive, Karen, I just know it!"

Her mind was flooded with confusing thoughts; thoughts she so wanted to believe were true.

The attending physician walked over and took her hand.

"What is it Miss Wells? What is upsetting you? You've just had a baby, you need to regroup and rest. You have a beautiful son who appears very healthy. I'm so very happy for both of you!"

Julie so wanted to share her thoughts but knew she couldn't. She knew if she did they would transfer her from the maternity ward to the psych ward. She took a deep breath, she couldn't stop shaking. She tried her best to appease the doctor.

"There's...there's nothing wrong doctor, I'm sorry, I'm fine."

The doctor patted her arm and smiled.

"Okay Miss Wells, we want to get your son into an incubator for observation. He is considered premature so we want to take any necessary precautions and monitor him just to be on the safe side. Now I'm going to give you something to help you sleep then we are going to take you up to a room where you can get some rest."

Julie slowly nodded her head in disgruntled agreement. She knew she couldn't share her secret with anyone and that there was nothing she could do, even if her cogitations were true.

She sighed and her mind drifted to her beloved Robert. A voice was suddenly echoing in her mind as clear as if it were coming from her bedside. It wasn't just any voice, it was Robert's. 'I'm here sweetheart. I'm alive and I love you.'

She could hear these exact words so vividly in her mind it was literally as if he were standing next to her saying them aloud.

She closed her eyes and whispered "I love you too". She didn't know if he would get the message but she felt better for saying it.

They gave her a shot then the nurse told her she was going to take Robert. She asked for one more moment with him. She held him tightly to her chest and again looked directly into his newborn eyes. There was a connection, one that transcended mother and child; he was telling her something she just knew it. She kissed his forehead and whispered into his tiny ear.

"Thank you, thank both of you."

She then reluctantly gave him to the nurse and they took her to her room.

The effects of the shot were almost immediate. She felt woozy and dizzy and was already drifting off to sleep as they wheeled her to her room.

Her thoughts turned to Robert. She was delirious from the effects of the shot as she tried to create a coherent thought. She fought the intoxication with all her might. She thought back to when she was holding their son and his penetrating stare. The incredible connection they had, the almost supernatural feeling she experienced gazing into his infant eyes. Did he really give her a message? Was she imaging it? Was it just wishful thinking?

They arrived at her room and the attending nurse hooked up an IV and checked the monitors. Everything was a blur; she couldn't stay awake any longer. Just before she passed out something startled her. She could hear his voice, plain as day his voice filled her head.

Rapidly losing her battle with consciousness she was

now wrestling with her sanity as well. Her rational mind told her it was impossible for Robert to be alive much less talking to her. But her heart wouldn't be denied. Something deep within her forced her to believe both.

Perhaps she was going insane, admitting the possibility of that scared her at the moment as she drifted off into a drug induced sleep.

She drifted off into a dreamless slumber for three hours. Then all of a sudden she could feel his touch, she could feel his arms around her. Along with an exhilarating joy came an overwhelming chilling sensation, she was freezing cold. It was so real! She was trembling with cold and woke up screaming.

Within seconds two nurses ran into the room. Karen, who had been sitting in a chair by the bed, frantically grabbed her mother's arm.

"Mom what's wrong?"

. Julie opened her eyes and surveyed the room. She was shivering and hysterical. She looked at her daughter but couldn't stop shaking. Her skin was actually cold to the touch.

"He was with me, Karen he was there! God I'm so cold!"

One nurse put her hands on Julie's shoulders and looked squarely into her eyes.

"Miss Wells, I'm here, it's okay, calm down."

Julie looked at the nurse wide eyed and took a series of deep breaths. She was still very cold.

The nurse took a wash cloth and wiped the sweat from Julie's brow. She continued to hold her down trying to get the patient to stop shaking.

"Miss Wells you had a bad dream, it's over now relax."

Julie frantically shook her head and spoke in frenzy.

"It was no dream damn it! It was no dream!"

Tears were racing down her face. She turned to Karen in sheer panic.

"Tell them it wasn't a dream Karen. Oh God it wasn't a dream he was there!"

Karen was beside herself. She had never seen her mother so disturbed. She was frightened

"Mom relax, I'm here. You had a bad dream that's all."

Julie continued to just shake her head. One of the nurses had left to get a doctor, they both returned. The doctor was now holding her hand trying his best to comfort her. He found it to be cold. He couldn't understand why she would be feeling so cold.

"Miss Wells, I am Doctor Scharfrath I need for you to relax. Now tell me what's going on, we're here for you."

Tears continued to flow as she tried to organize her thoughts. She couldn't stop shaking from the cold. That was her first concern.

"I need another blanket I am so cold!"

The doctor looked at the nurse in puzzlement. Actually he felt it was quite warm in the room but he ordered the nurse to get Julie another blanket.

He felt Julie's head for a temperature. He was surprised to find it as cold as her hand was. He squeezed her hand.

"Julie, you've just had a baby, your hormones and emotions are in a state of disarray at the moment, that's normal. We need for you to relax and calm down a little."

Julie buried her head in her hands extending the IV currently in her arm to the limit. She was at a crossroad. She knew she would have to explain her outburst but also knew she couldn't tell anyone the truth.

She realized she would have to fabricate a believable story that would keep her out of the nut ward. She closed her eyes for a brief moment of solemn thought. She took a deep breath praying for wisdom and proceeded.

"I'm okay doctor, I am. Thank you."

Doctor Scharfrath wasn't convinced. He looked into her eyes. He could see she was settling down but still a little rattled. He wanted to get to the cause of her alarm.

"Julie, you were saying someone was there with you; who was with you in your dream?"

Julie was infuriated at the word dream but withheld her disdain in check. She didn't want to make matters worse. It would be hard enough to explain as it was. She had to think and think fast. Her mind was racing. She thought the best lie would contain at least a little of the truth to make it believable.

"The father, he...well he is often in my dreams."

The doctor nodded his head with compassion.

"That's certainly understandable Julie. Now it's important you understand and accept that it was just a dream, a perfectly natural dream. Now are you feeling better?"

Julie glanced at Karen who continued to hold her arm tightly. She could see the concern on her face. Her first priority was to set Karen's mind at ease. She could discuss her experience in more detail with her later. She ignored the doctor for the moment.

"Everything is okay sweetheart, I'm fine. I'm sorry to upset you."

Karen finally smiled and tightened the grip on her mother's arm.

"You had me going there for a minute mom. You looked like you saw a ghost!"

Julie squeezed her daughter's hand.

"I think I have sweetheart."

Doctor Scharfrath checked over her chart. He pulled a nurse over to the corner of the room and they talked for a short time. The doctor then returned to Julie's bedside and smiled.

The doctor looked closely at his patient. He took her

pulse and was concerned that it was weak. He checked her breathing and discovered it was very shallow and labored. Then he then noticed her lips were discolored. He was also worried as to why she was shivering so much in a warm room. He had the nurse take her temperature and was surprised to find it at 96 degrees.

"Miss Wells, as strange as it sounds it appears you have signs of hypothermia. I don't understand how this could be possible."

Julie gave him a blank expressionless stare and replied in a soft monotonic voice.

"Robert...Robert is in a very cold place."

The doctor was puzzled at her response.

"If you are referring to your son I assure you he is in an incubator and is nice and warm."

Julie panicked. She realized had said too much, they would never understand much less believe her. She immediately retracted the statement. She stuttered the words.

"Oh...oh, of course he is doctor, forgive me. I don't know what I was thinking."

The doctor processed her statement. He wasn't convinced everything was as it should be with his patient.

"Julie, you were referring to your son weren't you?"

She picked up on the doctor's line of thought, it frightened her. What was he thinking? Was he going to keep her for psychological testing?

# 16

Her mind was racing with confusing thoughts. She felt trapped. She knew it wasn't just a dream but couldn't let on to anyone about it. She knew exactly why she was cold, he had touched her and he had to have been somewhere cold. He somehow conveyed his cold to her... but how?

Perhaps she was going mad, at the present moment she wasn't sure herself. The only thing in the world she was sure of was that Robert had somehow communicated with her. Robert was alive, somehow she knew that!

Gathering her wits and finally getting warmer she tried to talk rationally to the doctor, at least tell him what she knew he wanted to hear.

"I'm fine doctor. Those dreams can just seem so real I'm sorry. Thank you, I'm feeling much warmer now."

Doctor Scharfrath still wasn't convinced she was totally out of trouble. He ordered the nurse to bring her a hot cup of tea.

"I'm getting you something hot to drink. I want you to stay under the blankets until we get your temperature up again. I'm troubled about these symptoms Julie, they are classic hypothermia.

Now dreams can be strange things, they can have many effects on a person and even in some rare occasions cause physical manifestations but to have brought on actual symptoms of hypothermia to this extent is quite unusual.

Your symptoms could only have been caused by the dream, there's no other rational explanation for it. Now what concerns me is the degree of the condition. You say your husband was in this dream?"

Julie had no other option than to continue with her story.

"Well doctor, he wasn't my husband, we weren't married but yes the baby's father was in it, he has been in a number of my dreams recently."

Dr. Scharfrath nodded.

"Have you ever experienced any physical consequences from these dreams before?"

Julie shook her head. She didn't know what to say. She didn't want to go any further into this discussion but she had to tell him something.

"No, I've never experienced anything like this before."

The doctor smiled.

"Well, the brain is a complex organ Miss Wells. It is the most influential organ in the body. If the brain convinces the body it is cold, well then the body reacts accordingly. This is what we are experiencing now. I want you to rest for a little while..."

Julie had had enough of this conversation. She regretted her earlier slip of the tongue and desperately wanted to avoid any others in the future. She interrupted him.

"Doctor, I'm fine. I'm feeling much better. How long will I be here before I can go home?"

Dr. Scharfrath rubbed his chin and sighed. He wanted to make sure she was out of any danger before answering. He felt her hands which were now warm again. He noticed her lips were also back to normal and she seemed to have stopped trembling. Her breathing and pulse were also much better. After taking her temperature and being pleased that it had also risen he replied.

"Well, the birth went exceptionally well; there were no complications. Your son is doing fine and will continue to be monitored for a few days in the incubator just to be safe.

I was initially worried about your condition when you

first woke up but you seem to be stabilized and doing much better. Let's hope that was just a one time bad reaction to a bad dream.

I think the best thing for you would be to remain here overnight, get some rest and let give your body a chance to regroup.

I want to be sure those symptoms were just the result of one bad dream and nothing we need to be concerned about reoccurring. Sleep here tonight and see how you feel in the morning. Barring any further incidents or bad dreams I see no reason why we can't get you back home tomorrow.

Now your son is going to remain here for a while longer. Remember he is three months premature. We want to monitor him and make sure things continue to go smoothly. At the moment he is sleeping and appears very healthy!

We are giving him vitamins and supplemental nutrients which he normally would have gotten through you during a normal nine month pregnancy. We will monitor him closely and run tests to insure all his levels are where they should be. These tests will include keeping a close eye on his brain activity. I foresee the need for these precautions will be short term. There is nothing to be concerned about; this is standard for all premature babies.

I must say you have quite a son Miss Wells; he is the talk of the nursery. His development for having been three months premature is quite astounding, I would call it unprecedented. He shows no adverse effects for the short term pregnancy, in fact quite the contrary. This of course is highly unusual.

He is alert, physically firm and I must say equipped with a healthy set of lungs based on his crying volume."

The doctor chuckled and continued.

"Most importantly I assure you he is doing very well. I would like to continue this for, let's say three days, and see how he is then."

Julie didn't like the idea of all this scrutiny on her son. She knew the reason for his advanced physical state, a secret she couldn't share with anyone. She was apprehensive about what tests they might perform while he was there. Everyone seemed to have such a high level of interest in him she was afraid of what any tests might reveal. She kept her concerns to herself.

Doctor Scharfrath clipped her chart to the end of the bed and turned around.

"I have to make my rounds now but nurse Wentzel will be here if you need anything. You get some rest and I will check in on you in the morning."

The doctor left and Julie turned to her daughter who had remained sitting patiently by her bed.

"Well sweetheart, looks like I'm stuck here tonight. You get in my purse and get cab fare and go home."

Karen shook her head and held her mother's hand. She managed a weak smile.

"No mom, I want to stay here with you tonight."

Puzzled her mother replied.

"There's no reason for you to sit here all night, I'm fine. Now you go home and sleep in your own bed. I'll call you in the morning."

Again her daughter defiantly shook her head.

"No mom, we're family. I belong here with you. Besides, I wouldn't be able to sleep. You need me here and I'm staying!"

Julie squeezed her daughter's hand with incredible mother's pride.

"I'm so proud of you sweetheart. You are the best daughter a mother could ask for and you're going to be a great big sister! Isn't Robert beautiful? And he's doing so well. I really appreciate your offer but there's really no reason for you to stay."

Karen interrupted her mother.

"It isn't my brother I'm worried about mom, it's you."

Julie was confused.

"I'm fine, I feel great and..."

Karen again stopped her mother.

"Mom, you never have bad dreams, at least not like this one. That's not like you at all. I don't think this was a dream."

Perplexed Julie questioned her daughter.

"What are you saying Karen?"

Karen took a deep breath before trying to explain herself.

"Mom, you don't get hypothermia like you had from just a dream I don't care what the doctor said! Your symptoms were real, they weren't conjured up manifestations from a dream; I saw them!"

Julie nodded and sighed. Her daughter continued to impress her with her maturity and compassion. She tried to console Karen with tactful honesty.

"Yes they were Karen. I don't understand it. I was just so very cold."

Karen's expression changed to one of concerned reverence.

"And you think the cold came from Robert don't you."

Julie closed her eyes as a tear fell from them.

"Yes sweetheart I sincerely do. Just don't ask me to explain why or how."

Karen slowly nodded.

"If you believe it then so do I mom. We'll get through this together!"

Julie smiled and motioned for Karen to lean over and give her a hug.

"I love you so much!"

Karen held her mother tightly.

"I love you too mom."

At moments like this Julie couldn't help but think of Robert and how his intervention had made it possible. She fought back a tear and was sure she felt his presence with them, only this time it was a feeling of warmth.

Karen was inwardly and silently worried about her mother. She had never seen her act this way before. Seeing her mother wake up from the dream in such panic scared her.

Did she honestly believe her mother had actual contact with Robert...of course not, but her unrelenting resolve to support her prevented her from admitting that to her. She wanted to probe deeper into what her mother was experiencing without exposing her personal doubts.

She tried to convince herself her mother just had a bad dream but her mother's reaction upon waking was so extraordinary she was having trouble believing that, not to mention the severe physical reaction her mother suffered from.

She put her hand on her mother's shoulder and looked her square in the eyes. She privately wished she were smarter so she could come up with just the right words to say.

"Mom, in this dream, you say Robert was with you?"

Julie wiped the tears from her eyes and spoke softly.

"Yes, we were together."

Her mother sighed deeply before continuing.

"It was so real sweetheart, unlike any dream I have ever had. We held each other and it was so wonderful and oh so real. I could feel his touch Karen!"

Karen thought for a moment.

"Mom, you said he was cold. Is that why you think you got hypothermia, because he was cold in your dream? Is that even possible?"

Julie hesitated before answering. She could detect Karen's skepticism and certainly couldn't blame her for it. The story was outrageous she knew. She had always been honest with her daughter and fully intended on keeping that tradition going now.

"Sweetheart, I've asked you to believe a lot of, well strange things recently and you have accepted them like a real trooper. I know how hard this all has been on you but I am going to ask you to believe one more thing so bear with me."

Karen squeezed her mother's hand tightly and smiled.

"I'm here for you mom, just tell me."

Julie beamed with joy and pride. She spoke with all the sincerity in her heart.

"Robert Jr. told me. Somehow his father's words came through him I just know it."

Karen's eyes grew wide with wonder.

"You mean like telepathy or something?"

Julie wasn't sure how to respond.

"Yeah, I guess something like that. There's simply no other way of explaining all this."

Karen was speechless. After accepting the fact that her step father was an alien this should be easy she thought. She was struggling with a response.

"So you're telling me you think my brother might have psychic powers? Wow; that adds an interesting element to things doesn't it!"

Julie couldn't help but smile at her daughter's strength. How she could make lightly of such a startling possibility.

"Well, who's to say what powers they might have developed? Look at the medical advancements they have! I would have to say anything is possible, we're not sure what we are dealing with here."

Karen was simply flabbergasted and a bit frightened.

"Wow, and he is just a baby, imagine what he might be like when he is my age! I guess I will have to be careful what I am thinking when I'm around him."

They shared a brief laugh. Inwardly Julie took her daughter's innocent words to heart, they made her think. If this is really true, what future surprises might Robert Jr. have in store for them?

Once she had accepted Robert for what he was she never gave any thought to what differences or powers his people might actually have. She only saw him as the man she loved and not as some creature from another planet with mystical powers. Now the thought seemed a bit more relevant.

She was totally convinced Robert's words were transmitted to her through their son. She wasn't sure how to deal with that reality. Julie put the thought in the back of her mind and smiled at her daughter. She turned on the room's small television which was suspended from the ceiling in the corner. She hoped it would supply at least a temporary diversion for them.

After flipping through their limited selection of channels Julie decided to watch the news. When the program was over she turned to Karen and just shook her head.

"There sure is a lot of strange things happening in the world today aren't there?"

Karen just smiled.

"Think about what you just said mom. If they knew about us we would make lead story."

Julie chuckled.

"You make a valid sweetheart. I can't argue with that at all."

Julie thought for a moment then added.

"It sure has been a wild ride for both of us hasn't it?"

Karen gave her mother a serious look.

"Something tells me it's just beginning mom."

Julie sighed.

"Something tells me you're right. I'm getting really sleepy sweetheart, I'm going to try and get some sleep. You can keep the television on if you want.

If you want a pillow or blanket, just ask the nurse she will get them for you. Thank you again so much for wanting to stay with me. I feel bad; I know that chair can't be that comfortable to sleep in.'"

Karen smiled.

"You're welcome mom, its fine. Don't worry about me, you just get some sleep. I love you, goodnight."

Julie enjoyed a peaceful, dreamless sleep. She woke up and noticed Karen still sitting in the chair watching television wrapped up in a blanket.

"Did you get some sleep sweetheart? I know you couldn't have been very comfortable."

Karen leaned over and took her mother's hand.

"Oh I did mom, did you?"

Julie smiled and nodded.

"Yes I did I was so tired I just died. Let's see about getting some coffee and orange juice!"

Karen smiled.

"That would work!"

Julie pushed the nurse button on her remote control and sat up. Within a minute or two the nurse appeared.

"Good morning ladies, I am Nurse Powell. How are you feeling this morning Julie? Did you sleep well?"

Julie tried to return the over exuberant smile that dominated the nurse's face but fell just a bit short.

"I feel great thanks and yes I slept very well. Has the doctor told you when we can go home?"

The nurse glanced at the chart at the end of the bed. Flipping through the pages she again smiled.

"Well, I need to check your vitals real quick here and we will go from there."

Julie nodded and the nurse checked her blood pressure and took her pulse and temperature.

Julie waited for the thermometer to be taken out then asked the nurse for some coffee and orange juice. Again the nurse beamed a smile and replied.

"I don't think that will be a problem. You check out great Julie I'm sure it won't be long before you can go home.

Oh, I want to tell you your son slept straight through the night and is doing fine! He is just so adorable, we all just love him! He's so big for being so premature. We're all betting he will be a football player when he gets older. I'll be right back with your coffee and orange juice."

Julie had to disagree with their assessment of his future. She would more likely put money on him becoming a nuclear physicist.

Twenty minutes passed and still no refreshments. Julie looked at Karen with a puzzled expression.

"I don't understand what is taking so long for our drinks, what did they have to order out for them?"

Karen snickered. No sooner had Julie finished her sentence but the door opened. It was Nurse Powell with their drinks. Dr. Hart walked in right behind her with a folder in his hand. He glanced at Julie with a stoic face.

"Good morning Julie, how are you feeling this morning?"

At this point Julie just wanted to go home. She had the reassurance that Robert slept well and is doing fine and now she just wanted to leave.

"I'm fine doctor. Before you ask, I slept well and no, I didn't have any dreams. Now can we go home?"

The doctor sighed and took a deep breath.

"Well your vitals are good and I am very glad to hear

that you didn't have any bad dreams. That of course was a concern of mine.

You will be released today but I need a few moments of your time before you go. So you two enjoy your coffee and orange juice and relax. I have to make rounds now but I will be back in a bit and we can talk before you go."

The doctor walked out deliberately before Julie could digest his words. Julie took a minute of thought then looked at Karen with an even more puzzling expression. She didn't like the sounds of what the doctor had said. Talk...we need to talk? She couldn't read anything good into that.

If she had just gotten the clean bill of health the talk would have to be about Robert. This bothered her beyond words. The nurse had just told her Robert was fine. Then what could the doctor want to talk to her about?

She was experiencing a sick feeling in her stomach. Her motherly instinct was telling her something was wrong with her baby.

Karen noticed her mother's concern and squeezed her hand.

"What do you think that was all about mom?"

Julie just shook her head.

"I don't know Karen but I don't like it. I guess we will just have to wait until the Dr. Hart comes back."

Karen was now sharing her mother's worry.

"But they said Robert was fine so what do you think he wants to talk to you about?"

Julie didn't have a response. She laid back and closed her eyes. She tried taking slow long breaths to calm down. She continued to feel in her heart that something was wrong.

Julie rested for a few minutes as Karen tried to enjoy her orange juice. She was worried about her mother and now started to worry about her new born brother. There must be something wrong or the doctor wouldn't insist on talking to them before they left.

Julie's break was interrupted by the nurse returning. She walked up to Julie and smiled.

"I just spoke with Dr. Hart. He said you could get dressed and get ready to go home. He will be back as soon as he finishes his rounds. He mentioned he wanted to talk to you before you left. He should be back within the hour."

The nurse left and Julie sat up in bed. She glanced at Karen sitting in the chair next to the bed and just shrugged her shoulders.

"Well, we're going home, that's a good thing. Before we leave I want to see Robert. You know, just to assure myself that he is doing okay. I miss him already, I so wish he could come home now with us.

I have to admit the doctor's are right in this case. He was three months premature and it's a good idea to keep him here a while for observation and just make sure he is strong and healthy. Let me get dressed quick here and we will walk down and visit him!"

Karen gleamed and nodded her head.

"That would be awesome mom!"

# 17

Julie went into the small bathroom and changed. She returned to find Karen had gathered all her belongings into a bag. She grinned at her daughter's diligence.

"Great job sweetheart, thank you! Let's just leave everything here and go see Robert. Are you ready?"

Karen nodded and the two walked out of the room into the hall way. After a brief search Julie discovered a sign saying 'nursery'. It was down the hall to the left. She pointed it out to Karen.

"Looks like that is the place, let's go."

They walked down the hall and made a left turn. There before them was the nursery. Large panes of glass separated them from a room currently occupied by about ten new born babies. The children were arranged in three rows. Each child was in his or her own little bed and a white name card with black lettering hung from the front of each bed.

Karen beamed with joy and squeezed her mother's hand.

"Which one is Robert mom?"

Julie shook her head.

"I don't know; let's see if we can find a nurse I can't read the name cards from here."

A nurse just so happened to be coming out of the door and Julie walked over to her.

"Excuse me, my daughter and I just came to see my son, could you point him out to me please?"

The nurse smiled.

"Of course I can, what is your last name?"

Julie told the nurse her name and the nurse said she would go in and point him out to her. The nurse reentered the nursery and walked down each row of children. She repeated her search before coming back out.

"I'm sorry Miss Wells; he doesn't appear to be in there. Would that be the name on the card?"

A look of concern crossed Julie's face.

"Of course it would, that's my name. His name is Robert Wells. Are you sure he's not in there? He was just born yesterday he has to be in there!"

The nurse shook her head.

"No Miss Wells, I checked twice. There is no baby with that last name in the room."

Julie tried to remain calm.

"What do you mean he's not in there? He was just born yesterday he has to be in there! Could he be with the doctor maybe having tests or lab work done?"

The nurse shook her head.

"No Miss Wells, you don't understand. There simply is no bed with that name on it in there."

Julie looked at Karen dumbfounded. Karen spoke the only words that came to her.

"Do you have another nursery that he might be in?"

The nurse again shook her head.

"No, this is the only nursery in the hospital."

Julie shrugged her shoulders and addressed the nurse with that possibility. The look of concern was now replaced by a look of worry.

"Well then where the hell is my son?"

The nurse tried to ease her mind.

"Just calm down a minute Miss Wells, I'm sure there is an explanation. Okay, you say your name is Wells and your son's name is Robert and he was born yesterday?"

Flustered Julie just nodded.

"Alright, let me check the records just give me a minute we will find your son."

Julie and Karen followed the nurse to the nurse's

station and waited very impatiently as she accessed the computer.

After a few minutes of reading the screen the nurse walked over to Julie.

"Your son is fine; he has been transferred to another room."

Julie was now totally confused.

"Transferred? Why? Where is he?"

The nurse replied without hesitation.

"The doctor ordered his transfer this morning. He is in room 304 and according to the computer he is doing fine. That is all I can tell you at the moment."

Julie was losing her patience.

"Well he is my son and I want to see him before I go home. How do I get to that room?"

The nurse shook her head.

"I'm sorry Miss Wells but that is impossible at the moment."

Julie was now losing her temper.

"What the hell do you mean that's impossible! I am his mother and I demand to see my son!"

The nurse raised her hand in an attempt to calm Julie down.

"Miss Wells; that is the quarantine room, visitors are prohibited, even the family. Now that is all I can tell you for now.

You can speak to the doctor when he arrives which should be soon. He can answer all your questions. Now why don't you go back to your room and I will get you another cup of coffee until the doctor returns."

Julie was outraged and her voice rose to a fever pitch.

"I don't want a damn cup of coffee I want to see my son! Now I want some answers! Why the hell is he in quarantine?"

The nurse took a deep breath trying to calm the situation.

"Miss Wells, all I can tell you is Dr. Hart ordered your son to be transferred to quarantine this morning. Your son is fine and being well taken care of. The doctor is finishing his rounds and will be in shortly so please just go back to your room and bear with us until he arrives."

Julie tried to hold back the anger she was feeling. It took every ounce of restraint she could muster. Inside she was exploding with a combination of exasperation and fear. She knew she wouldn't get any more information from the nurse and reluctantly conceded to returning to the room.

Her head was swimming with troubling thoughts. She was well aware of the meaning of quarantine. Why would they put him there if, according to the nurse, he was fine? That just didn't make any sense! There was something they weren't telling her.

Julie and Karen returned to the room and both sat nervously on the bed. Karen rubbed her mother's arm trying to comfort her mom the best she could.

"It's going to be okay mom I just know it. I'm sure he's fine. The doctor will explain it. Maybe it is just for precaution since he was so premature; maybe they can give him undivided attention there."

Julie marveled at her daughter's wisdom and compassion. She was a true gift to her. She tried to find solace in her daughter's words. She gave Karen a hug and managed a forced smile.

"You're right sweetheart; that makes sense. Thank you for being so strong. I don't know how I could survive without you."

She wasn't convinced of the validity of the explanation but accepted it more for Karen's sake than her own.

The nurse brought her another cup of coffee and Karen another orange juice.

"Dr. Hart just returned and will be here in a few minutes."

Julie acknowledged her with a slight nod. She tried to make amends.

"I'm sorry I chewed your head off. I'm just so worried about...."

The nurse interrupted her.

"Oh don't apologize; any mother would feel the same way. I feel terrible I can't give you any more information but all we know is what the doctor tells us.

I did speak with the attending nurse and she assured me your son is doing wonderfully."

Julie and Karen shared a look of total confusion. Julie stirred her coffee more for a nervous release than with any intention of actually drinking it. Karen just stared at her orange juice. There was a strong but unspoken tension building up in both of them. They both knew the other was more worried than they let on.

Julie couldn't help but think there was something dramatically wrong with her son. She fought back thinking the worse. She had lost Robert she couldn't bear the thought of losing their son.

While she sincerely appreciated her daughter's kind efforts she just couldn't accept the explanation she gave. You don't put someone in quarantine to give them undivided attention. You put someone in quarantine because they are sick!

Julie was restless, nervous beyond words. She tried to pick up her coffee and noticed her hand was trembling. Karen observed this and felt helpless to sooth her mother, she had her own demon's to deal with at the moment... she was worried about her baby brother.

The minutes seemed like hours as they waited for Dr. Hart to return. Finally the doctor came through the door.

"Good morning Julie. I'm sorry for making you wait, my rounds took longer than I had expected."

Julie snapped at him.

"Cut the pleasantries doctor, what's going on with my son is he alright?"

Dr. Hart smiled and nodded.

"Yes Julie, your son is doing very well. Now I have arranged a conference to discuss exactly what is going on."

He turned to Karen.

"Karen, if you could just wait here..."

Julie defiantly stood up for her daughter.

"No! Anything you say to me can be said in front of her, we are in this together!"

Karen smiled and whispered to her mother.

"Thank you mom."

Julie squeezed her daughter's hand and smiled.

Dr. Hart nodded.

"Very well, if the two of you could follow me to the conference room we will discuss this."

The doctor led them down the hall and into a small conference room. The room featured a long table with six chairs arranged around it. Already seated at the table were two men in white lab coats.

The first was dark skinned with jet black hair and bushy eyebrows appearing to be in his forties, obviously of Indian persuasion.

The second man was older, perhaps in his late sixties. He had rather scraggly thinning grey hair and wore dark rimmed glasses.

Dr. Hart motioned for the two of them to take a seat which they did directly across the table from the two doctors. Dr. Hart took the chair at the end of the table and introduced the two men.

"Julie I have asked a couple of my colleagues to join us for this discussion. Their input will hopefully help you understand what we are dealing with here. First this is Dr. Patel he is a specialist in hematology."

The doctor nodded to both Julie and Karen and they respectfully returned the acknowledgment as Dr. Hart continued.

"Seated next to him is Dr. Killian, he is from pathology."

Julie's eyes grew as big as saucers.

"Hematology...pathology...now you're scaring me doctor! What the hell is wrong with my son?"

Dr. Hart cleared his throat and put up his hand.

"First of all Julie, your son is doing fine."

Julie had heard that before. She impatiently pounded her hands on the table.

"Alright then why are we here? What is going on with my baby? Why was he placed in quarantine? I know for a fact you don't put someone in quarantine without at least suspicions he is sick yet everyone keeps telling me he is fine, now give me some honest answers!"

The three doctors all looked at each other as if in a silent motion to decide who speaks first. Dr. Patel took the initiative.

"Miss Wells, allow me to begin please."

He spoke with a soft spoken Indian accent.

"Dr. Hart performed some routine lab and blood work on your son last night. After reviewing the results he sent a sample of your son's blood to my lab and called me at home and asked me to come in and look at them. He had some concerns which, after I examined them myself, I totally concurred with."

This did nothing to ease Julie's mind. Her worst nightmares were already coming true. The testing and subsequent questions had begun.

The fact that a doctor felt the need to come back in

after being home shocked her. There had to be something dramatically wrong but she allowed the doctor to continue.

"We have found a number of...abnormalities in your son's blood."

Julie's mouth dropped to the floor.

"You found abnormalities? Just what sort of abnormalities are we talking about doctor?"

Dr. Patel opened a manila folder and glanced at it before continuing.

"Well, the first thing that came to our attention immediately was his white blood cell count. It is extremely high Miss Wells; in fact I have never seen such a high level in my career and I've been doing this for over twenty years."

Julie was visibly trembling. She was scared to death. She tried to formulate intelligent questions.

"I don't understand all this jargon. Speak English to me doctor, just what is a white blood cell and what does it do? Is this life threatening? Be straight with me doctor this is my baby we are talking about!"

Dr. Hart felt the need to intervene.

"Julie please, don't jump to rash conclusions."

Julie resented his interruption.

"Rash conclusions, you're telling me something is wrong with my baby's blood and you're asking me not to jump to conclusions? Let the man continue, he is the blood expert, I want some answers and I want them now!"

Dr. Patel took a deep breath. He was trying to use all the professional diplomacy he could find. He had to explain what was wrong with her baby's blood in an honest manner without totally unnerving her.

"The white blood cell is the body's defense against illness and disease. When a disease cell appears the white blood cells attack it to prevent it from spreading. This is a very good thing."

Julie tried to digest the doctor's words. She tried to remain calm as she answered him.

"But you're telling me my son has too many? Just what does that mean?"

Dr. Patel responded.

"Well, there is a condition called leukocytosis which refers to a patient having a high white blood cell count. This is not actually a rare condition but what is of concern here is your son's count is off the charts.

Normally leukocytosis is agreed to be anything over 11,000 per microliter of blood. The sample I received from Dr. Hart contained over 20,000. As you can see this is well over the normal amount.

Now there can be a number of reasons for a high white blood cell count. In itself its not life threatening but it could have been triggered by an infection, an inflammation, a trauma or stress but what we have to be concerned with is it also could be a forewarning of another disease."

Julie put her head in her hands. She was beside herself with worry. As sugar coated as the doctors were trying to make it she couldn't help but feel her son's life was in jeopardy.

She then clasped her hands together and tried to fight back a tear as she addressed Dr. Patel.

"So this is why you have him in quarantine?"

Dr. Patel whispered something to Dr. Killian and allowed his colleague to pick it up from this point. The doctor spoke deliberately with an unwavering, almost detached tone of voice. He was stern and strictly business to the point where it was unnerving.

"Not entirely. While your son's high white blood cell

count is a factor...there are others we need to keep an eye on."

He opened his manila folder, glanced at it and continued before Julie had a chance to respond.

"There were a number of cells in your son's blood we....well quite frankly, were unable to identify. We have sent samples to the best hospitals in the country to quickly identify these anomalies."

Julie was now in a state of rage.

"What do you mean you couldn't identify them? What kind of a hospital do you run here?"

Dr, Hart again interceded.

"Julie, we found some rather strange cells in your son's blood. No one has ever seen the likes of these before. We are currently unsure of their function or origin. They don't appear to be doing your son any harm, his vitals are all very good and he is strong and appearing very healthy. What we have to focus on is to be sure these cells are not pathogenic in any way.

That means that they are not harboring infectious diseases. We have to take precautions until we totally understand what we are dealing with."

Julie was terrified.

"But you said my son was doing fine? He isn't sick is he?"

Again Dr. Hart took the question.

"No, your son is fine. We have to consider the possibility of him being a carrier. A carrier is someone who has a disease but shows no ill harm from it personally but has the capability of spreading that disease to others. This is why he was placed in isolation, quarantine if you will.

Now I'm not saying this is the case at all. Doctors have to speculate on every possible scenario. What I am saying is we can't be too careful until we identify these unusual cells. Better safe than sorry.

Your son is being monitored very closely and getting the best care available. He is in no immediate danger."

Julie was stunned. She glanced at Karen who had been sitting silently by her side. Karen held her mother's hand. Julie fought back tears as she tried to speak.

"Tell me about these cells you can't identify. Just what could they be?"

Dr. Killian rubbed his hand through his hair clearly not sure how to answer the question. He hesitated then responded.

"They are most unusual Miss Wells. I have never seen anything like them. They are neither red nor white cells. They don't appear to be any type platelet or plasma. They don't seem to be performing any function at all that we can identify.

Like Dr. Hart stated we need to be confident about their function and that they are not pathogenic before we can expose anyone else to them.

Now genetics could be involved here. I would like to get a blood sample from you to see if you might be carrying them as well. Now I see on your records that the father is deceased, is that correct?"

Julie put her hand on her forehead. All of a sudden it was becoming very clear. This had to be Robert's genetic influence. His blood must be different than ours. She should have known this could become an issue. Karen squeezed her mother's arm in an attempt to get her attention, it worked.

No words were spoken between the two but it was obvious they were both on the same wave length.

Julie knew she had to answer the question and forced the words out of her mouth.

"Yes, his father is dead. He died of a heart attack."

Dr. Killian rubbed his chin in thought.

"Miss Wells, genetic traits can be shared with family

members, mothers, fathers, even siblings. We need to establish whether or not these blood traits were inherited from the parents. Does he have any family members we could contact about getting blood samples?"

Good luck on that one she thought. What could she tell them to get them off this train of thought? She took a deep breath and closed her eyes for a second. After a prolonged sigh she finally came up with a story.

"I'm afraid not doctor. His parents were killed in a horrific car accident when he was young and he was an only child."

Right after she said that she gasped and hoped they wouldn't do any cross referencing because she just remembered she had told Mr. Bertlson his parents lived in Ohio.

Dr. Killian jotted some notes in his folder.

"That is truly unfortunate. Well I do want to see your blood just to rule out any genetic transfer from your side of the family."

Julie agreed to the blood test. She was preoccupied with thoughts of just what other influences Robert might have on their son. She should have seen this coming.

In an attempt to lighten up her emotional burden she quipped to herself, with all those white blood cells Robert Jr. may never be sick a day in his life, that would save a lot of doctor visits and expenditures on cold medicine.

There was an uncomfortable silence before Dr. Killian spoke.

"Miss Wells, I realize this might be an awkward question but please understand that the more we know the better we can diagnose what is going on with your son. You say the father passed away as a result of a heart attack?"

Julie's heart sunk at the thought of having to deal

with anything relating to Robert. She simply nodded. The doctor paused out of respect then continued.

"Did he have any health issues that could have led to that?"

Julie was taken back by the question.

"No doctor, none that I knew of."

Dr. Killian nodded.

"Did either you or the father ever have any blood transfusions?"

Julie gave the doctor a bewildered look.

"Why are you asking that?"

Dr, Killian cleared his throat.

"Well what that tells me is that any possible genetic or biological origins would have had to have come from either you or the father. This greatly helps us narrow down the sources these unusual cells might have come from."

Julie silently acknowledged his explanation.

"No, neither of us ever had a blood transfusion."

Dr. Killian jotted down notes in his folder and returned his attention to Julie.

"Very well then, that would narrow down the source to either you or the father."

The doctor thought carefully before asking the next question.

"Miss Wells, did the father enjoy general good health? Did he have any illnesses?"

Julie closed her eyes for a moment of solace thought.

"No doctor, he was a very healthy man. I can't even remember him having so much as a cold."

Dr. Killian bit his lip in deep thought.

"That's interesting. Did he have a doctor?"

The doctor was hoping he might be able to retrieve some medical history on the father that might shade some light on the enigma.

Julie shook her head.

"No, he hadn't seen a doctor the entire time I knew him."

She knew where the conversation was headed. She was getting very uncomfortable with all the emphasis now falling on Robert. She knew this train of thought had to be deterred before it really turned into a problem.

She thought about what she had just said and regretted it. She didn't want to give the doctor any more reason to continue to investigate Robert.

She can't have him keep asking questions about Robert because sooner or later he would bark up a tree she couldn't climb.

"Doctor, so you are leaning towards thinking this was caused by genetics?"

Dr. Killian nodded.

"Yes, I have to. The types of cells we have found just don't materialize out of thin air. I'm almost certain they were inherited from one of you. Now we're not going to be able to get any information or samples from the father so all I can do is to again ask for a blood sample from you and see if that tells us anything. Let's do that before you leave today.

The sooner we can get to the bottom of this the sooner your son can go home. As it is now we feel the need to keep him in isolation just to be on the safe side."

Julie took a deep breath and agreed to the blood test. She knew in advance they wouldn't find what they were looking for it her blood and thankfully they would never have access to Robert's.

Dr. Hart could tell his patient was struggling. He tried to ease her mind.

"Julie, I know how difficult all of this is for you but let me assure you we are doing everything we can to care for your son and get to the bottom of what is causing all the confusion.

We have sent a sample of his blood to John Hopkins medical center. They have one of the best hematology labs in the country. I'm sure they will be able to give us some answers.

In the mean time we are taking real good care of your baby. He is under constant monitoring and receiving the best care we can give him, he's doing just fine.

Now you get that blood test out of the way and you and Karen just go home. We are going to get your son home as soon as possible."

Julie squeezed Karen's shoulder and managed a smile.

"Let's go home sweetheart."

Karen nodded and returned the smile. She and Karen were escorted to the lab by a nurse. Julie then was given a blood test and told she was cleared to go home.

# 18

As they were leaving the lab they were met by Dr. Hart who had been waiting by the door. He smiled at both of them and spoke some unexpected words.

"Julie, I thought you might like to see your son before you leave. I realize this has been a most traumatic time for you and you certainly deserve to see your beautiful son. I know it would ease your mind seeing for yourself that he was doing wonderfully."

Julie was shocked.

"But you said he was in quarantine and wasn't allowed visitors!"

The doctor nodded.

"Well he is but I can give you special clothes to protect you if you would like to see him for a quick moment. I think it would be important for you."

Julie glanced at Karen who was beaming from ear to ear.

"Can Karen come too?"

Dr. Hart acknowledged her with another smile.

"Of course she can, we can get her an outfit as well. Now please come with me and we will get you all set."

Julie grabbed Karen's hand and followed the doctor to a small storage area not far from the lab.

She and Karen were outfitted with hospital gowns and both given surgical masks.

The three of them took an elevator to the isolation ward. They walked down a short hallway and came to a set of double doors.

Dr. Hart took out a card and swiped it in the mechanism beside the doors which immediately opened.

They walked past a number of identical rooms before

coming to room 25. Again the doctor took his card and swiped the box next to the door which unlocked.

The three donned their masks and entered the small room.

In the corner of the room was a patrician of blue cloth connected in sections to completely enclose a crib. Lying peacefully asleep in the crib was Robert.

A tear came to Julie's eyes as she gazed upon her son. She looked at Karen who was equally touched.

Robert was asleep but looking perfectly fine. She just stood and gazed at her son. He looked so peaceful. She looked at Karen then at the doctor with joy. Dr. Hart was pleased.

"As you can see Julie, your son is doing wonderfully. We continue to monitor his vitals and everything is fine. Now you two go home and relax. We will call you when we get the results of your blood test and the results from John Hopkins. I will also let you know if anything changes which I don't expect."

Julie already knew what the results of her blood test would be...perfectly normal. Her blood would show no indications of the abnormalities they found in her son's. What she didn't know would be how the doctors would interpret them and what course of action they had planned from there. She feared what John Hopkins might find.

She remembered how much emphasis Dr. Killian was placing on genetics and that once her blood test came back normally the only other source would be the father. She prayed they wouldn't take it any further for she had no answers to give them, well none that they would believe.

She and Karen returned the gowns and masks and thanked the doctor for the opportunity to see Robert.

They went to the lobby and called a cab to go home.

Her heart was back to beating normally after seeing her son. Karen was beaming.

"He looked great mom! He is so cute! See, I told you everything was alright! I can't wait to get him home!"

She had to agree with her daughter. Robert truly looked wonderful and seemed to be very healthy. She too was very anxious to get her son home.

She tried to put all her apprehensions in the back of her mind. It was out of her control and she remembered her father preaching to her about not worrying about things you can't control. Her thoughts now turned to just how long they would have to wait to bring him home.

The cab arrived and they had a joyous ride home. They continued to talk about how good Robert looked and designed plans on what still needed to be done before he came home.

They arrived home and walked up the stairs to their apartment. As she took out her keys Julie discovered a note taped to the door. It was a hand written note from their landlord saying he had stopped by to collect the rent and for her to call him when they got home.

With everything that was going on recently the days had just flown by and Julie had lost track of the date. They entered the apartment and took off their coats. Karen went into the kitchen to get iced tea for them as Julie tried to remember where she had put her checkbook; she wanted to get paying the rent out of the way while she was thinking about it.

Karen brought the drinks into the living room and Julie was relieved to have found her checkbook in the coffee table drawer. They both took a long sip from their drinks and sat down on the sofa as Julie opened her check book.

She had remembered being disappointed that her last paycheck was a fraction of what it usually was but at the time she didn't give it another thought. Now, after analyzing her bank statement it became very relevant. She was devastated to discover she didn't have enough in the bank to cover her rent!

Julie knew she had missed a number of days at work due to her pregnancy and how understanding Mr. Bertlson had been but now it was causing a real problem. She had never been short or even late paying her rent and a look of devastation crossed her face.

Karen immediately noticed the change of moods and questioned her mother.

"Mom, what is it? What is wrong?"

Snapping out of a momentary daze Julie didn't want to alarm her daughter, this was her problem not Karen's.

"Nothing dear, don't worry about it I will handle it."

Karen refused to take that for an answer.

"Mom, I know that expression, something's wrong."

Julie conceited this was one confrontation she wasn't going to win. Her daughter was too smart and too caring to simply let this slide.

"Well, it seems I am a bit short on the rent."

Karen looked concerned.

"When is it due mom?"

Julie sighed.

"It was due yesterday sweetheart."

Karen took her mother's hand trying her best to console her.

"Mom, Mr. Bertlson is a very nice man I'm sure he will understand if it's a bit late."

Julie shook her head.

"That's just it Karen, he has been so understanding about so many things lately, I don't want to push our luck any further."

Karen hated to see her mom like this. She didn't know what to say to make her feel better.

"Well, what can we do mom?"

Julie shrugged her shoulders and took a deep breath letting it out slowly.

"I'm just going to have to figure out where to get a little extra money sweetheart."

An idea suddenly came to Karen.

"Mom, remember all the money that we found in Robert's suitcase? Could we use that?"

With everything that has been going on Julie had completely forgotten about that. She remembered she wasn't comfortable with having that money at the time and she didn't feel any better about it now even though she knew she needed it.

She recalled wondering where the money had come from and if it was even real. Was it stolen...counterfeit; did it originate from some illicit activity, could it be traced? Robert never had a job where could he have gotten that money? Dare she use it? The only consolation she could find was the fact she knew she couldn't return it.

If Robert had come to it from legitimate means he would certainly want them to use it. Her head was swimming with conflicting thoughts. She had no other savings or any other means of earning any extra money. She had to think of Karen and the baby. She didn't know for sure how Larry would take the news and she couldn't take the chance of him being upset over it. Now was not the time to be homeless.

She struggled silently with the dilemma for a moment. Against her better judgment she decided she had no other recourse than to take her chances and use the money.

The deciding factor was that she knew Robert, in spite of his tainted past, was a good person and the money had to have been legitimate. He certainly couldn't use it so he would want it to help them.

Karen tried to say something that would ease her mother's troubled mind.

"Mom, I know this is bothering you. I know how you feel about that money and how neither of us is sure where it actually came from but I also know Robert loved both of us and he would want us to have it.

I really can't see anything bad about using it. Robert would never allow anything to harm us so I am sure the money is good. In your heart you know that as well."

Julie continued to be amazed at her daughter's maturity. She knew she was right. She knew she had Karen's approval and if Robert were here she knew she would have his as well. That was all she needed. She gave Karen a hug.

"Okay, we can do this, it's the right thing. Let's at least see how much there is."

Her nerves were really bothering her. She was actually trembling. She remembered a bottle of wine Robert had gotten her shortly before...before he left. They had never opened it and it had been sitting in the cupboard. She never had the heart to open it; until now. She wasn't much of a drinker but she needed something to calm down.

She went into the kitchen and opened the cupboard. Seeing the bottle sitting on the top shelf brought a tear to her eye. She closed her eyes tightly to prevent a total flood of tears. She opened the bottle and poured herself a glass.

Returning to the living room she took a large drink and a deep breath.

"Let me get the envelope sweetheart, I'll be right back."

She went into the bedroom and got the large brown envelope from her dresser drawer.

She carried it back into the living room with the care one would normally use carrying a bomb. It was heavier than she had remembered it. She knew there had to be an awful lot of money in it for it to be so heavy. Just having it in her hands made her nervous.

She sat down on the sofa and gently placed the envelope on the coffee table. They both just stared at it then at each other. Karen could feel her mother's apprehension.

"Its okay mom, we're doing the right thing. Robert would want this."

Julie nodded continuing to fight back the tears. She appreciated the vote of confidence. She took another drink, picked up the envelope and slowly opened it.

She pulled out a number of stacks all containing crisp bills. She noticed they were bound together and organized by denomination. Much to her surprise there was a stack of one hundred dollar bills, a stack of fifty dollar bills and one each for twenty, ten, five and one dollar bills.

Both of their eyes grew as big as saucers at the discovery. Karen was the only one of them able to speak.

"Oh my God mom, I've never seen so much money in my life!"

Unable to formulate words Julie just nodded. She finished her glass of wine and was finally able to utter a response, her voice notably trembling.

"Neither have I sweetheart...neither have I."

She took a deep labored breath.

"Alright, we are going to count this. Now I will give you a few stacks and I will take the rest."

Karen simply nodded as her mother handed her the stacks with the small bills in them.

Karen examined the stacks before opening them. She discovered a disturbing fact that they had forgotten about.

"Mom, these are brand new. You can tell they have never been used."

Julie had noticed the same thing. She wasn't sure how to respond.

"Just open them up and count each stack."

Julie took out a notepad and pen from the coffee table drawer. She wrote a line of numbers corresponding to the various denominations.

"When you are finished counting a stack write the total on the paper sweetheart, then we will add them all up."

Karen understood and started with the stack of ones. Her mother began with the stack of one hundred dollar bills.

After a few minutes Karen wrote her total down. There were one hundred one dollar bills. Julie continued counting her rather large stack and finally finished. She was astounded there were one hundred and fifty bills. She wrote down the total without figuring exactly how much that added up to.

They both continued counting the remaining stacks writing down the totals until all the stacks had been counted.

They both looked at the list in amazement. Julie tallied the results. The envelope contained twenty thousand dollars! Julie tried to form words.

"Oh my dear God I can't believe this! This can't be real!"

Karen's mouth was gapping.

"Mom, it's real."

Julie put her head in her hands trying to rationalize some form of logical thought. Karen put her arm around her mother.

"What are we going to do with this money mom?"

Reality returned for a brief moment.

"Well, first of all we are going to pay the rent. Now I

can't emphasize strongly enough; do not tell anyone, I mean anyone, about this alright?"

Karen shook her head in agreement.

"I won't say anything mom."

Julie contemplated getting another glass of wine. This whole situation was so unsettling for her. She decided one more glass won't kill her and went into the kitchen and poured another glass of wine.

She remembered Larry had asked her to call him in the note and decided to get that out of the way. Before reaching for her cell phone she remembered Larry wouldn't have known she had given birth. She knew that would initiate a thousand questions, none of which she was in the mood for.

She took a long sip from her glass of wine and get what she anticipated to be an unpleasant phone call out of the way.

Larry, as usual, somehow answered on the first ring.

"Larry, this is Julie. I got your note and wanted to apologize for the late rent. You know that's not like me. I had the baby yesterday and I just got home from the hospital."

Larry was quick to reply.

"Julie, you had the baby? But it hasn't been nine months has it? Is everything alright?"

She took another sip of wine and wanted to get this conversation over with as quickly as possible.

"Yes everything is fine thank you. He was premature but he's healthy, strong and doing great. Thank you for asking. I will have your rent tomorrow if you'll be here."

Larry would not go away that easily. As always he had a thousand questions for her.

"How far along were you? You say the baby is fine, well how are you? Is the baby home with you?"

Julie shook her head at his continuous inquisitions.

She knew his heart was in the right place but it just got to be annoying at times.

"He was about three months premature Larry but I'm doing just fine. No, the baby is still at the hospital. They wanted to keep him there for observation just to be safe. I'm not sure how long he will remain there. I do have the rent for you."

Larry cleared his throat.

"Well Julie the rent is the last of my concerns. He was three months early? My God that's very unusual if not unheard of!"

Julie had had enough of this.

"I know Larry but I promise you both he and I are fine."

Larry accepted her answer.

"Well, I certainly hope so...I just want to know for sure you and the baby are both alright. So you had a boy?"

Julie had to chuckle.

"Yes Larry, his name is Robert. I named him after his father."

She could hear the sigh over the phone.

"Oh that's wonderful. I can't wait to meet him. Yes I will be there tomorrow; someone has to tend the bar until you feel like rejoining your post. I will come up sometime in the afternoon. Now you just get some rest and let me know if there is anything I can do for you; oh, and a hearty and sincere congratulations!"

Julie was pleased the conversation was going so well. She then thought about how she had been away from work quite a bit and wanted to address Larry's comment.

"I'm so sorry about not being at work for a while, having a baby takes a toll on you. If you could just give me a few more days I promise..."

Larry stopped her.

"Oh don't worry about that at all Julie. I totally

understand. I've been holding down the fort but rest assured it will be great to have you back. Everyone has been asking about you. I tell you, you are more popular there than I am."

She giggled and thanked him. She then quickly hung up the phone before soliciting any further interrogation.

She returned to the living room took notice of Karen still sitting on the sofa continuing to just ogle the stacks of money sitting on the coffee table. She smiled and sat next to her.

"That sure is a lot of money sweetheart."

Karen just nodded in total awe. She was deep in thought about all the possibilities that kind of money could open up for them. A thought popped into her head and she spoke almost without thinking.

"Mom, we could get a bigger place. We could get like a house or something where Robert could have his own room!"

Julie hadn't even given such a notion a thought. Karen did have a point. Things were going to be rather cramped now with the baby.

She had always felt a tinge of guilt forcing the two of them to live in such a small modest place. She knew Karen deserved better but it was all she could afford on her meager income.

Twenty thousand dollars would certainly allow them to acquire a larger apartment. She finished her glass of wine and drifted off into thought.

All the bills are caught up and manageable. They really have everything they need. The car is only a few years old and running good. What would they use the money for? She could keep still her job. Her wages do keep the lights on and food on the table.

This windfall was for all practical purposes spending money. Perhaps this was God's way of saying they can now get a nice place for all of them to live in, to celebrate the new addition to the family, something they could never have afforded without it.

Karen noticed her mother's silence.

"You're thinking about it aren't you mom?"

Julie smiled at her daughter and raised her eyebrows.

"Yes Karen, you have me thinking about it. I have to admit, it does make sense. It just might be the best use for the money.

Did you just come up with that idea or have you been thinking about it? I mean, does sharing your room with Robert really bother you, be honest with me sweetheart. I know it would be a terrible inconvenience but..."

Karen interrupted her mother.

"No mom, it's not that at all. I would be happy to share my room with my beautiful baby brother but I was just thinking it would be better for all of us."

Julie listened attentively. She studied her daughter's eyes. She knew Karen had been forced to make many sacrifices over the years and asking a teenage girl to share her room with a newborn infant was asking perhaps too much. She thought of how she might have felt if asked to do the same thing at Karen's age.

She also knew Karen would never come out and admit her true dislike for the situation; she would never say anything she thought would hurt her mother. Julie's top priority has always been to do what was best for her daughter and the more she thought about it the more the idea of getting a bigger apartment fit right in with those priorities.

Giving the matter even more thought she conceded to the fact that she as well would love a larger apartment for a number of reasons.

She found some mitigation in realizing that while doing

what was best for Karen was her primary motivation the move would also be a great benefit to her as well.

She again marveled at her daughter's wonderful mind. Karen had came up with such an elementary idea but one that was now doable and would greatly improve the quality of life for both of them. She chastised herself for not thinking of it first.

The more she thought about it the more sense it made and how now was the perfect time. She knew if they blew this money on other things they might not get the opportunity to make the move again. This kind of money doesn't come around every day. She was now certain it was divine intervention.

Julie leaned over and gave Karen a tight hug.

"You know what sweetheart…that's exactly what we are going to do! What better way of celebrating our new addition than with a nice new apartment!

We're going to find a great place, a place where you can continue to have your own room and Robert will have a nice nursery all to his own!

It will have a nice big kitchen and a spacious living room and a shower that always has hot water, not like this old one where it is hit or miss!"

Karen threw her fists into the air in celebration.

"Oh that's awesome mom!"

They both smiled as Julie shouted out with joy.

"You know, there have been a thousand reasons why we should have moved and only one reason why we didn't. Up until now we simply couldn't afford a nicer place but that has changed. I see no other reason to stay here! Oh this is so exciting!"

The two hugged again and Karen sighed.

"Robert would be so happy for us."

A tinge of sadness overcame Julie as she thought

about what her daughter had just said. This would never be possible if it weren't for him. She spoke solemnly.

"I know he would. He would want what is best for us. I just wish..."

Karen interrupted her mother's sentence; she knew exactly where it was going.

"I do too mom."

Julie put the money back in the envelope and returned it to her bedroom dresser drawer. She would deposit it in the bank in the morning.

She returned to the living room and noticed Karen in the kitchen fixing a sandwich. The excitement of their new plan had totally made her forget about fixing dinner. She went into the kitchen and apologized.

"Oh sweetheart I am so sorry. I was so excited about this I wasn't even thinking you might be hungry. Let me fix us something."

Karen shook her head and smiled.

"No it's okay mom. I'm really not that hungry I just thought I would make a quick sandwich. Can I make one for you?"

Julie was again taken back by her daughter's kindness. She couldn't help but think about how Karen had changed since Robert's procedure. This wonderful young lady didn't exist a year ago. Pondering this along with the excitement of moving brought a tear to her eye.

She sat down at the kitchen table and put her head in her hands. Her thoughts were suddenly overcoming her. She aversely reflected on all that has happened in the past year.

She continued to be overwhelmed about Karen's transformation. The thought of finally being able to move thanks to the money Robert left and of course her new born son. None of this would have been possible without Robert.

Then she started to weep uncontrollably....she missed him so very much. Putting the material benefits of having Robert in her live aside she reflected on her heart. She thought back on how devastated she was when Karen's father left them and how she vowed to never love again.

Then, out of nowhere, came Robert. To say he totally stole her heart would be an understatement. He brought it back to life like the Phoenix bird. He took an empty shell of a heart, void of emotions and incapable of loving again and completely reformed it. He gave her such love and unconditional devotion that she was powerless not to fall completely in love with him.

Her sobbing intensified as she silently cursed God for taking him from her. Why, after all the years of being lonely and distraught couldn't he have just let her drown in her own despair? Why did he have to tease her with love and hope only to take it away!

Karen saw her mother sitting there in agony. Her heart sunk.

"Mom, I know you are thinking about him, I'm so sorry."

Now, seeing the grief she was causing Karen by wallowing in her personal Hell only added shame to her misery. She was turning her daughter into an innocent victim, a fate she didn't deserve. She had to be strong, not so much for herself but for Karen.

She wiped the tears from her eyes and stood up. She hugged Karen tightly.

"I'm so sorry sweetheart. I'm trying so hard to be strong for you but..."

Again Karen stopped her mother in mid sentence.

"Mom, stop it please. You don't owe me strength. This is a pain we both share and we will find the strength to get through it together."

Julie was proud of her daughter beyond words and

suddenly felt remorse for cursing God. She had been blessed with an incredible daughter and now a beautiful son. She had so much to be thankful for and it took Karen to make her realize that.

Karen was again totally correct in her assessment. They would survive this and move forward. She had the love for her daughter and new son; that was all the love she would need; now to just convince herself of that.

She and Karen spent the next hour playing cards to lighten up the mood. They laughed and had a great time as Karen won three straight games of rummy. After the third game they both decided to call it a night.

Karen went into her bedroom and got ready for bed and after a few minutes Julie knocked on her door.

"Come in mom I'm just getting ready for bed."

Julie entered the room and gave her daughter a tight hug.

"Sweetheart, you have no idea what a pillar of strength you are to me. I couldn't get through this without you. We are going to be okay. We're going to find a nice big place to live and enjoy having Robert in our lives. It's going to be great! Now you get some sleep and thank you again for being such an incredible daughter...I love you!"

Julie fluffed up her pillows and reclined in bed; her head was swimming with so many thoughts. She was determined to concentrate on the future and no longer dwell on the past.

The future...okay, moving was now the focus point. Just how does one find a place to live? She had lived here for...strange, she had to think and she couldn't even remember how long she and Karen had lived there. Well it had been many years she knew that for certain.

She knew her own ways. This moving project had to be done with haste or she would talk herself out of it. Strike while the iron is hot she convinced herself of.

She had to set her mind to actually doing it or the next thing she knew it would be five years down the road and their money would be gone and she would forever regret it.

Again she used Karen as her driving force. The move would be the best thing for her and she owed that to her. When ever she uses her daughter as motivation it kick starts her adrenalin; that is what she needed now.

She woke up early after actually enjoying a night of long dreamless sleep. She felt refreshed and in good spirits. She quietly opened Karen's door a crack and was pleased to see her daughter still sound asleep.

# 19

After having slept on the idea of moving it appealed to her even more today. She was completely convinced it was the best thing to do and the most logical thing to do with the money.

She went into the kitchen and put a pot of coffee on. Watching the coffee slowly drip into the pot her mind turned back to the moving project. She was determined to make this happen and she would have to start giving the details some serious thought.

Julie poured her first cup of coffee and sat on the living room sofa. She got out a notebook and pen and started jotting down notes.

They would need a three bedroom apartment. The apartment would have to be furnished because this one was and they didn't own any furniture. On site laundry facilities would be nice; as would air conditioning but neither were a necessity.

She wanted to stay in the immediate area, first of all so Karen wouldn't have to change schools and secondly to keep the commute to work as short as possible...that is if Larry would still have her after she told him they were moving.

Then her thoughts turned to her landlord and boss. How would Larry take the news of them moving? Would he still allow her to continue working for him? Maybe he would fire her.

She took a sip of coffee and immediately forced herself to stop that train of thought. She knew she would need to continue working because Robert's money would only stretch so far. It would cover the first month, the security deposit and the movers and buy what incidental items they might need.

She sincerely wanted to stay at the bar; she loved the job, the people and working for Larry. Larry had told her repeatedly how much he liked her and how much all the customers liked her. To top it off, if Larry would fire her he would have to at least initially pick up her shifts and she was sure he wouldn't be fond of that idea. That gave her some job security. She hoped this would be the deciding factor in allowing her to stay.

After finishing her coffee Julie could hear Karen in her room. She wanted to get to the bank and deposit the money so she could have the rent when she met with Larry.

Karen fixed a bowl of cereal and told her mother to go ahead to the bank she said she just wanted to relax for a while.

Julie took a shower and got dressed. She drove to the bank and back and noticed Larry behind the bar when she reentered the building.

Thinking to herself that she would at some point have to tell him about their plans she decided that a good time would be when she handed him the check. At least she knew that would put him in a good mood and maybe make the conversation a little more positive.

She sat at a table near the door and filled out the check and then met Larry at the bar.

Larry smiled as he noticed her approaching and started the questions before she even had the chance to hand him the check.

"Julie, you are looking spectacular this morning! How are you feeling?"

She returned the smile and giggled at the compliment.

"Good morning Larry. I feel just great thanks. Here is the rent. I am sorry it's late."

Larry accepted the check and returned to behind the bar. He motioned for her to sit down.

"Do you have any idea when your son will be able to come home?"

Julie sat down and shook her head.

"No I don't. They want to monitor him for a while but they weren't specific as far as how long."

She cleared her throat in an effort to gain the courage she would need to continue the conversation. She wanted to tell him now while she had the nerve.

"Larry, I'd like to talk to you if you have a couple minutes."

Larry looked confused. He poured them both a cup of coffee and studied her face.

"Julie, you look concerned about something. Is everything alright with the baby? Is there anything my wife or I could do to help?"

She wished he could just for once start a conversation with something besides a question, as empathetic as they may be.

"The baby is fine thank you. I need to talk to you about something else. This isn't easy but I have given the matter a lot of thought. With the new baby coming I've decided Karen and I are going to need a bigger place.

Initially I thought Karen and the baby could share the room but after giving it more consideration I felt that was asking an awful lot of her. As agreeable as she was I just thought that was simply not fair to her."

Larry listened without saying a word.

"So what I am saying is we will be moving as soon as we find a suitable place. My hopes are twofold. First of all I hope you understand and secondly I sincerely hope I can remain employed here. I so enjoy working here with you Larry I don't want this decision to jeopardize that."

Larry rubbed his chin in thought and took a sip of

coffee. His smile told Julie that at least the first part of her hopes look safely intact.

After a moment of silence Larry replied.

"My dear Julie, let me first say I totally understand. I want what is best for you and I can't in all honesty argue with your reasoning. I guess I have kind of been expecting that decision.

I have come to think of you and Karen as family, I mean you have been here so long. I think it would be the best thing for you and Karen and the baby to have a larger place."

Julie took a long relieved breath as Larry continued.

"Am I disappointed in losing you as a tenant; of course, am. Good tenants are hard to find and you have been one of the best I have ever had. You have never caused any trouble, never complained and always paid the rent on time."

Julie smiled and patted his hand as it sat on the counter.

"Thank you Larry that means the world to me. This was a very difficult decision to make. You have been an incredible landlord and have been so kind to both of us."

Larry smiled and took a sip of coffee. He rubbed his chin again and Julie knew he was thinking something. She never would have expected what it was.

"Now secondly, of course you can continue working here. I don't think this place could function properly without you. You have become such a favorite with all the regulars. I can't imagine running this place without you.

Now you say you haven't found a new place yet?"

Julie sadly shook her head.

"No, that is going to be the hard part."

Larry grinned.

"Well, I think I might be able to help you there."

Julie couldn't hide her look of astonishment. Not only

was Larry being so understanding about their decision to move but now he is even offering help in finding a new place? That was more than she could have even hoped for.

"What do you mean Larry? How do you think you could help us?"

Larry folded his hands together and thought for a moment.

"Well, my brother in law, Claudia's bother you know, has a property over on Briarcrest Road in the valley. It's only about...oh say fifteen or so miles from here, real close actually. He has spent all his free time over the past couple years remodeling it but never put it on the market. It's been kind of like a hobby for him. He has just been sitting on it. He's funny that way."

Julie listened with fascination.

"It's a real nice two story house. It has three bedrooms and one and a half baths. Like I said he has totally remodeled and updated all the plumbing and electrical features. It has a nice front yard and a porch. I don't know why he hasn't offered to rent it out but with my influence I bet I could talk him into it. It would be perfect for you!"

Julie was totally speechless. She just sat there with her mouth gapping at the prospect.

"Larry, I don't know what to say! That would be so wonderful and so kind of you to even suggest it!"

Larry's face got serious for a moment.

"I would have to add though; I am certain he would want more a month than I have been charging you. He has put a lot of time and money into restoring the place and I am sure it would bring a lot on the market if he ever decided to go that route.

My influence can only go so far I'm afraid. I would have no say in what he wanted a month for it.

But then again I would think he would be happy to finally be getting some payback for all his efforts. I really can't say; he might be flexible.

May I ask how much you think you could afford and I will call him and how about I do some negotiations for you?"

Julie wasn't prepared for this question. She couldn't tell him that Robert had left her twenty thousand dollars; that would illicit questions she couldn't answer. She knew Larry's tendency to question everything and he would have a field day with that one. She said to herself 'think Julie think!'

She had to be clever to come up with an explanation that wouldn't lead to a thousand questions. It had to be something simple yet believable.

"Well, my parents left me with a number of bonds which have matured. I have been sitting on them for years now just waiting for the right time to use them. I can honestly say I believe this was the right time so I cashed them in. We're not rich but I think I could handle what ever your brother in law would decide upon."

Larry smiled....he took the bait.

"That's outstanding Julie! I'm so happy for you and Karen, and the baby of course. I will call Leonard and see what we can work out.

I so hope I can talk him into renting it and you two can reach an agreement. You would love this house it is really beautiful!"

Julie thanked him repeatedly and silently thanked God for being with her during this difficult time and apologized to him for her earlier indiscretions.

She ran up the stairs to tell Karen the good news. She found her daughter munching on chips relaxing on the couch watching television.

"Hey sweetheart, guess what!"

Karen sat up and questioned her mother's new found exuberance.

"Gee mom what are you so excited about?"

Julie smiled from ear to ear.

"I just talked to Larry about us moving. Not only is he all in favor of it but he might also have found the perfect place for us to move to! Oh sweetheart if this actually works out it will be wonderful!"

Karen leaped from the couch and hugged her mom.

"What do you mean mom? Well don't just stand there, tell me about it!"

Julie collected her thoughts.

"Larry totally understands about our situation and how crowded it would be with three of us. He said his brother in law has a house just outside town he has been remodeling and might want to rent. From what Larry said it sounds perfect!"

Julie proceeded to tell Karen about the features of the house.

"And even better yet, he said I could continue working here for him after we move. Isn't that just fantastic?"

Karen beamed with joy.

"Oh that is so cool mom! We're really going to do this!"

The beautiful expression of hope on Karen's face made all the mental turmoil she has been privately dealing with worth it.

Karen thought for a moment and had a question she had to ask.

"Did he ask you about the money?"

Julie smugly chuckled.

"Oh of course he did. I just told him a little white lie and he bought it hook line and sinker."

Karen grinned.

"Oh mom you so rock! I can't wait to start packing!"

Julie put her hands up in an attempt to curb her daughter's exuberance.

"Well let's just wait until we know for sure we have this place."

Karen nodded her reluctant agreement.

"Okay mom, I'm just so excited!"

The joy of seeing Karen's excitement only confirmed she had made the right decision. This was going to be the best thing that ever happened to them. They were going to start a new life and she was determined to make it a great one.

She finally conceded to accepting the fact that Robert was gone but his love will always be with her in her heart and that his legacy will be all he continues to do for them in his absence.

Her thoughts were now focused on waiting for two very important phone calls. One coming from the hospital giving her son a clean bill of health and telling her she could bring him home.

She had called yesterday to check up on him and the nurse assured her he was doing fine but the doctors were still waiting to hear from John Hopkins.

The other call would come from Larry hopefully with promising news about the new apartment.

Two days passed and she didn't receive either call. She understood Larry has been very busy minding the bar by himself while she had been on maternity leave. Knowing the rent for this month had been taken care of she admitted there was no actual rush. She would give him more time.

What really brought her anxiety was not hearing a word from the hospital about the results from John Hopkins.

. She wasn't sure if that was a good thing or not. She knew if anything was wrong she would have heard from them so she tried her best to look at it as a positive thing. On the other hand she was worried about what those results might tell them.

She and Karen passed the time by cleaning the apartment and double checking they had everything ready for the baby's arrival.

On the morning of the third day the phone rang. Could this be the call giving her permission to bring her son home?

She took a deep breath and answered the call. It was Larry.

"Good morning Larry."

Larry replied enthusiastically.

"Good morning Julie. I hope this call finds you in good health and good spirits because I think I might have some good news for you!"

Julie raised her eyebrows in anticipation.

"I'm doing good Larry, what is the good news?"

"Claudia and I went over to see Leonard and Edi last night. After about three hours of persuasion by me, Claudia and even Edi and half a bottle of bourbon he finally agreed to allow you to see the house."

Julie's eyes lit up and she smiled from ear to ear.

"Oh Larry, that's wonderful news. Thank you so very much!"

Larry chuckled.

"Well you should really thank Edi. She was the deciding factor. Actually it is her property, she inherited it from her parents but she has let Leonard restore it.

She was excited about finally having the possibility of getting some return on all of his hard work. She was rather persuasive in her tactics last night I must say. When you meet her you will easily understand how persuasive she can be. She's a real spitfire! Poor Leonard wasn't given much of an opportunity to resist."

Julie grinned and couldn't help but get excited.

"Did he say when we can see it Larry?"

Larry replied in a lively manner.

"He was thinking about sometime next week. Let me give you his number and you can call and set something up. I sure hope this works out for you and Karen. Just sweet talk him like you did me, remember? I'm sure things will go your way."

Larry gave her the number and they hung up. Julie was encouraged, that was one less thing she had to worry about. Now all she had to do was charm this Leonard guy into letting them get the apartment! She giggled to herself...sweet talk him, yeah sure.

She thought back to her days in high school. She was a little flirt. She could charm the bark off a tree as well as any boy who innocently crossed her path.

She then remembered her hair was a lot more vibrant, her smile a lot brighter and her stomach defiantly a lot flatter. She was a bit out of practice but she hoped she could rekindle some of her old zest if there were any left in the tank. She wasn't too worried about it because from what Larry had just told her Leonard's wife did most of the work already.

With that being started, now all she had to do was to concentrate on getting Robert home. She was going to need some help with that one.

She and Karen finished cleaning the kitchen and then took a long look at Karen's room. They were pleased with the crib and changing table being all set up.

Karen had generously agreed to giving up one of her dresser drawers to baby clothes and necessities which were all in place.

They laughed again at the mobile hanging from above the crib with its stars and planets all situated perfectly overhead patiently waiting for Robert's approval. Julie still couldn't help but think it was a divine omen.

She shook in her head in disbelieve after she caught herself actually hoping it might make Robert feel more at home.

Satisfied that everything was as in order as it was going to get they both conceded to the fact that all they could do now was wait for that fateful phone call from the hospital.

# 20

The call came on the fifth day. She and Karen were having breakfast when the phone rang. They glanced at each other both empathizing with the other's anticipation. Julie answered the phone. It was Dr. Hart's secretary.

"Good morning Miss Wells. This is Diane, Dr. Hart's secretary. How are you this morning?"

Julie was not in the mood for such pleasantries.

"I'm fine thanks, what's up?"

Diane hesitated for a moment.

"I just spoke with Dr. Hart. He would like you to come in today if you can. He and Dr. Patel would like to speak with you. Could you come in at three?"

Julie let out a big sigh. It wouldn't be a matter of whether or not she could come in at three, it would be a matter of whether or not she could wait that long.

"Yes of course."

Diane again paused.

"That's perfect we will see you then. Just come to his office not the hospital. The doctors will be waiting for you."

Julie hung up and explained everything to Karen who was waiting with baited breath right next to her.

Karen squeezed her mother's arm in excitement.

"Maybe he can come home today!"

Julie shrugged her shoulders. She was puzzled as to why the doctor wanted to meet her at his office and not at the hospital. She had felt that if they were going to allow Robert to come home he would have just met her at the hospital.

"Well, they want me to go to his office and not the hospital, that's strange."

She passed the next four hours nervously straightening up the apartment just to keep busy. She smiled at the thought of hopefully their days in this crowded old apartment will be numbered. She promised herself to call Leonard when she got back and get the ball rolling on securing their new apartment.

Two thirty finally arrived and she took a shower and got dressed. She kissed Karen goodbye and drove to Dr. Hart's office.

She couldn't help but wonder about all the possible scenarios as she was driving. It was obvious they must have gotten the reports from John Hopkins. She tried to remember what Dr. Patel did. After giving it more thought she remembered he was in the hematology department. That would make sense that he would be there with Dr. Hart since all the commotion was about Robert's unusual blood.

She couldn't help but worry that John Hopkins found something wrong and would insist on keeping Robert for further studies. If this arouse she would flatly refuse. She wanted her son home!

Julie arrived at the office and checked in with the secretary who immediately recognized her.

"Good afternoon Miss Wells. I will let Dr. Hart know you are here. Please just sit down for a moment he will be right out."

Julie took a deep breath and tried to prepare herself for what was ahead. The five minute wait seemed like hours. She was nervous and her heart skipped a beat when she finally saw Dr. Hart come through the doors and walk over to her. This would be the moment of truth.

The doctor approached her and smiled.

"Julie, always good to see you; I'm glad you could make it. Please come with me. How are you feeling this afternoon?"

Julie got up and walked with the doctor.

"Dr. Hart, I just want my son to come home."

The doctor nodded.

"That's what we all want Julie and I can promise you it will be soon."

They walked through the doors into a small conference room where Dr. Patel was already seated. Dr. Hart motioned for her to sit down and he took the seat at the end of the table.

"I'm sure you remember Dr. Patel he is our hematology expert."

Julie managed a smile and acknowledged the doctor who returned her smile. Dr. Hart began the proceedings.

"Julie, I want you to know I visited your son this morning and he is doing wonderfully. He has gained a little weight, he is eating well and all his vitals are strong."

She was getting very impatient with all the protocol.

"Then why is he still at the hospital? When can I bring him home?"

The doctors exchanged a glance and Dr. Patel spoke up.

"Miss Wells, we have been studying the results of the tests John Hopkins ran on your son's blood."

Julie stopped the doctor and glared at Dr. Hart.

"When can my son come home?"

Dr. Hart could see her frustration and impatience and tried to nip it in the bud with a straight answer to her question.

"Julie, we are thinking Friday but please let Dr. Patel continue."

She tried to calm down knowing getting further upset wouldn't solve anything. Dr. Patel continued.

"Miss Wells in all honesty I am at a loss for words. I have been in the medical profession for twenty years and after studying your son's blood and reviewing the reports from John Hopkins I have to say I have never seen anything like it before nor would I dare to say any other doctor would have."

Julie wasn't sure where the doctor was going with this but allowed him to continue.

"I can go as far as saying if I were to have been given this blood blindly, and I don't want to alarm you with this, I would tend to doubt it was even human.

You already know about his high white blood cell count. This has produced an extremely high level of immunoglobins, a natural protein. Your son's immune system is simply phenomenal. He couldn't get sick if he wanted to and I emphasize this is only a slight exaggeration!"

Julie glanced at Dr. Hart and continued to listen.

"This still doesn't answer the many questions we had about the cells we couldn't identify. After thoroughly testing your son's blood sample the doctors at John Hopkins were equally amazed and quite frankly dumbfounded.

While they couldn't identify them they were about to break them down. Now I can't tell you in good faith the results made any sense but they can't be denied.

The mystery cells were found to contain a cocktail of proteins and minerals. They even discovered strains of enzymes we only know as synthetic compounds found in cancer preventing antigens.

We found this incredible interesting because the human body simply does not produce these synthetic chemicals! I don't have a clue as to how they ended up in your son's blood!"

Julie was getting more alarmed as the doctor continued.

"Now after reviewing your blood tests we can say with certainty they did not originate from you. Your blood tested totally normal."

She didn't like the direction this was taking. It was all falling back on the father which she knew it would. This was one avenue they could not pursue! Dr. Patel wasn't finished and continued undaunted.

"The most encouraging results were they found nothing pathogenic or harmful in his blood. No signs of disease or anything to cause any alarm.

In addition to the strong presence of antibodies and proteins his blood also was found to contain a very high level of amino acids, potassium and human growth hormones we refer to as HGH.

Now amino acids perform a variety of functions related to cellular metabolism, this of course includes growth.

This would explain his rapid physical development and how he could be three months premature and still be fully developed as amazing as that is. His body was literally pushed into overdrive due to the extremely high levels of amino acids it was forced to contend with.

That being said there is simply no logical explanation for those high levels. I want to stress the point that we are now confident that there is nothing harmful about them, in fact quite the contrary, they are quite a blessing.

This young child appears to be a biological superman. He is truly a medical marvel. His blood could be described as a miraculous soup of disease fighting ingredients that are unprecedented in medical history!

If we could somehow reproduce this incredible blood all doctors would be selling cars.

Dr. Hart and I examined your son this morning and he continues to be doing well. His respiratory system is functioning perfectly. In spite of the unusual blood flowing through it his circulatory system is doing its job to perfection. All of his organs are functioning normally. He is eating well and is alert and appears to be very healthy.

You have nothing to worry about; you have a very healthy baby. This is why we are all in agreement he can go home in another day or so."

While distressed about their confusions regarding the biological origins of the abnormalities Julie was so ecstatic hearing her son can come home soon. Her joy was quickly interrupted by Dr. Hart.

"Julie I know this is a tough subject and I'm sorry for even bringing it up but it might clear some things up.

We know you are not the source of these strange blood traits. Your blood test came back perfectly normal which leads us back to the father. He of course would be the only other source of these anomalies.

Now I know he passed away as a result of a heart attack and you say you don't recall him ever being sick or treated for any illness or disease in the time you knew him.

May I ask how long you knew him?"

Julie's heart started racing. She couldn't let them pursue this line of thought.

"I knew him for about a year."

Dr. Hart nodded.

"Did he have a doctor? Could there be any medical records we could review about his general health?"

Julie shook her head.

"Doctor I already told you, in the year I knew him he never so much as went to a doctor once. He would have no records that I know of."

Dr. Hart jotted some notes on his yellow folder.

"Did you know his parents or any other members of his family?"

Julie again just shook her head.

"No doctor I never met any other members of his family."

Dr. Hart gave Dr. Patel a look of discouragement then solemnly returned his glance to Julie.

"Okay Julie again I am sorry for even mentioning it. The way things look now I see no reason why your son can't go home on Friday.

We're firmly convinced he is in good health and presents no danger to anyone. We are just going to continue monitoring him and give him a few booster shots and he will be ready to go home.

So you go home and give us a call Friday morning and we will make arrangements."

As she was driving home her frustration evolved into outright anger. It seemed inhuman to separate a mother from her new born child. There should be a law against it. She couldn't help but pity poor Robert lying there in the hospital being deprived of his mother.

The calls she gave to the hospital inquiring about his welfare only brought continued frustration. They kept telling her he was fine and healthy. Then why can't he come home! She and Karen have been going crazy since they left the hospital worrying about him.

One the one hand she logically understood the doctor's position. They had quite a dilemma to cope with having to deal with Robert's most unusual blood. She understood they wanted to be safe and not expose the world to some possible unknown epidemic. But on the other hand she was his mother and felt he should be home with her!

Arriving home she conceded to finding peace in the fact that she knew her son was healthy, safe, and being well taken care of, although she would much prefer doing the job herself. The most consoling thought was in knowing he was coming home Friday.

Seconds after opening the door she was accosted by Karen who rushed up to her.

"What did they say mom? Is he coming home?"

Julie wrapped her arms around Karen and tried to calm her down.

"Dr. Hart promised me he could come home on Friday! He said Robert is very healthy, has gained some weight and everything is fine. They just want to give him some booster shots and keep an eye on him for a couple more days."

Karen couldn't hide her excitement.

"Oh that's so cool mom! I can't wait! My baby brother is finally coming home!"

Julie fixed a cup of coffee and got her cell phone out. She wanted to call Leonard about the apartment. She got his number out of her purse and made the call.

After four rings a woman answered.

"Hello."

Julie figured this had to be his wife. She wasn't disappointed because based on what Larry had told her she was the one with the influence in this project. She was the person she wanted to talk to and it would be nice not having to make use of any charm.

"Good morning. I am Julie Wells, a tenant of Larry's. I am looking for a bigger apartment and Larry had mentioned you and your husband had one."

There was laughter and the woman replied.

"We sure do honey and I am so glad you called. Larry had mentioned you the other day when he and Claudia stopped by. He spoke very highly of you.

I have been trying to get my crazy husband to rent that place out for over a year now!

All he does anymore is work on that place tinkering with one thing or another and I rarely see him. Sometimes I think he just goes over there to get away from me.

It would be so nice to finally get some rewards from all his time and efforts."

These words were music to Julie's ears. She liked this woman already.

"Well I would be very interested in seeing it."

The woman replied enthusiastically.

"That sounds like a plan to me. If he won't show it to you I will do it myself. I'll put a fire under his butt!

I have to admit he has done a lot of work over there. It's an older place but Leonard has really turned it around. He has completely replaced all the electrical fixtures and redid the plumbing. We spent weeks over there painting it and it is looking really nice if I do say so myself.

It would be real nice knowing a family is enjoying it and I can't argue with getting a little money out of the place either."

Julie couldn't help but instantly love this woman. She hoped her husband was as nice.

"When could I see it? My schedule is pretty flexible at the moment so I can work with yours."

There was a short pause as the woman thought about the question.

"I think just about any time would work for us. We are both retired and are home pretty much all the time; that is when he isn't over there working on something. How would tomorrow afternoon work for you?"

Julie clenched her fist in victory.

"Tomorrow would be fine say about one? I am so excited about seeing it and thank you for this opportunity."

The woman agreed and gave her the address.

"I will have Leonard over there. He can show you the place and boast about all the renovations he has done. Has Larry told you anything about it as far as the rooms and all?"

Julie tried to remember what Larry had told her about the apartment.

"He really didn't mention much but did say it was a lot bigger than the apartment we have here."

The woman cleared her throat.

"Well honey, it is a house not an apartment. It has two floors. On the first floor is a very spacious kitchen, a nice sized living room, a half bath and another room in the back which could be used as a bedroom or den, what ever you need.

On the second floor are two bedrooms and the bathroom. It has a nice porch which Leonard just varnished the wood floor and painted the railing.

It has a nice small front yard with two beautiful oak trees that must have been there for a hundred years, they are huge. It also has a really nice pine tree in the corner of the yard that's always filled with beautiful birds just singing away all day long!"

It sounded just perfect to Julie. She listened attentively as the woman continued.

"Now Larry mentioned it would be you and your daughter living there?"

Julie's voice couldn't disguise her excitement.

"Yes, and my newborn son, just the three of us. The place sounds so perfect for us. I can't thank you enough for showing it to us!"

The woman continued.

"You have a new born baby, how exciting! Oh honey it is my pleasure. Like I said before, I have been trying to get Leonard to do this for ages. Now do you have any pets?"

Julie continued to enjoy the woman's outgoing persona.

"No, my daughter has always wanted a cat but Larry won't allow pets in his building."

The woman laughed.

"Larry can be a real pain sometimes, that's ridiculous!

Well honey, by all means get that child a cat! Hell you can get her two cats that would be fine with me and I'm sure fine with your daughter. Every child should have a pet. Pets are fine just please clean up after them."

Oh, I haven't even introduced myself yet silly me. I am Edith, Leonard's wife but you can call me Edie, everyone else does. I am looking forward to meeting you.

Now when you first meet Leonard he might start rambling about me but don't you listen to a word of it. He can be an old fart at times.

In fact I think men in general are nothing more than a pain most times. Hell all they're good for is making babies and keeping the yard mowed. I think the world would be a better place if they just let us women run it don t you think?"

Julie laughed hysterically. This lady was a gem. She didn't know how to reply to that.

The woman continued.

"Oh I'm sorry for rambling on like that. Okay, where were we? Oh yes, while it is true he has done most all of the renovations to the place I actually own it. I inherited it from my parents when I was young so I make the calls. He hates that but deals with it. I actually let him think he has more authority than he does. It's an arrangement that works for both of us.

From what I have gathered from our brief conversation and what Larry has said about you I don't see any problems with you and your family getting the house.

Now you and Leonard can work out the financial details. I'm going to leave that up to him. Now don't let him charge you too much. We're doing fine and I don't want him taking advantage of you."

Julie was feeling very confident that this arrangement was going to work out. Larry was right, Edie was a real spitfire and she couldn't help but love her already. Edie finished the conversation.

"Well doll, it's been nice chatting with you. I look forward to you and your family moving in. I can just tell you are good people and we all become great friends. I will have Leonard over there at one tomorrow. Goodbye."

# 21

Julie clicked off the phone and walked in to the living room where Karen was sitting watching television.

"Guess what! I'm going to see the house tomorrow!"

Karen's eyes lit up with excitement.

"Oh mom can I come too?"

Julie smiled.

"Of course you are coming. You are going to be living there too, you have a say in this. We're going to decide on this as a family!"

Karen was overjoyed.

"Wow what a great week it's been. Robert is coming home Friday and we get to see our new home tomorrow. Woo Hoo!"

Julie had to share the conversation with her.

"Yes, I spoke to Edi Leonard's wife. She is really something. She told me all about the place and...she said we can have pets! How would you feel about finally getting that kitty you have been wanting for so long?"

Karen's eyes exploded with happiness.

"Oh really mom, I can get a cat?"

Julie nodded.

"I think that would be a wonderful idea!"

Karen ran up and gave her mother a huge hug as tears of joy ran down her cheeks.

"Gee...a baby brother and a kitten this is so awesome!"

Julie was overwhelmed with delight seeing her daughter so happy. She couldn't help but think back to the sad, depressed, totally out of touch young lady Karen used to be and how wonderful it was to see her daughter so enjoying life.

These thoughts, as wonderful as they were, once

again made her think of Robert and how he had made all of this possible. She fought back the sadness of how she so desperately wished he were here to share the joy with her.

After a restless night's sleep Julie managed to make it to the kitchen and put on a pot of coffee. Change always bothered her, even when it was a positive one. She would get set in her ways and get comfortable. She looked at anything that interfered with her routine as threatening.

She knew in her heart that the changes that were happening now, the new baby, the new apartment, were both very good but still she felt vulnerable for some reason.

That was one area Karen's father was very good at, sensing her uneasiness and calming her down. Perhaps it was the fact that she was now facing these new changes without such support that bothered her.

She poured a cup of coffee and sat at the kitchen table. She was thrilled with the new baby and the thought of finally being able to get a nice house for her and Karen was a dream come true.

She reached deep in her mind for the source of her unsettling thoughts and finally came to an answer and it was all about Robert.

He was responsible for making all this happen, both the baby and the new home and she was feeling guilty that he couldn't be there to share it. That was it, she was now sure of it.

Her thoughts were interrupted by arms wrapped around her from behind. It was Karen who had just entered the kitchen. Julie was so engulfed in her thoughts she hadn't even heard her enter.

"Good morning mom! When are we going to see the apartment?"

She had to laugh at her daughter's exuberance.

"We are going to meet at one o'clock, now just calm down until then."

Karen bounced across the kitchen getting a bowl of cereal and a glass of orange juice. She sat at the table with her mother.

"Oh mom how can you relax when this is so exciting!"

Julie shook her head. Julie's insecurities came out with her words.

"This will be a big change for both of us if we do get this place sweetheart."

Karen nodded and smiled.

"It will be great! Robert will have his own room, you will have more space and I get a kitten. See mom, we all make out on this deal!"

In this case fighting fare wouldn't enter into it; she wanted that house and was determined to do anything it took to get it!

She shouted out to Karen who was listening to music in her room.

"Sweetheart, get dressed it's almost time to leave. Now put on something nice remember we are trying to make a good first impression! No dirty jeans or holey sweatshirts. Dress like a lady!

Now get moving I don't want us to be late for this!"

All she heard in return was the defiance of a fifteen year old tomboy 'oh mom'.

"I mean it! Don't argue with me. We want to look nice, today could change our lives!"

She heard a reluctant 'alright mom' and was satisfied her daughter would comply knowing what is at stake. Julie was in Heaven seeing her daughter so happy. They enjoyed breakfast together and couldn't stop talking about the possibilities of their new home.

She had decided if they do get the place, Karen's bedroom would be the room on the first floor. She wanted

Robert's nursery to be close to her bedroom on the second floor.

Karen was fine with that idea and was already kicking around ideas for the name of her new kitten.

Julie kicked herself for not asking Edie if the home was furnished. Everything in their current apartment was there when they moved in. She took a deep breath and resolved that they could easily pick up some furniture if necessary. Robert's money would more than cover what they might need.

Julie's only concern was that Leonard would like her. She was confident she had won over Edie and encouraged that she pulled the strings.

She double checked her purse to ensure she had the address, on a yellow sticky note she found the words 201 Briarcrest Road. Hopefully that would be their new address.

She was pleased by the fact she knew exactly where that was. The address was only about fifteen miles away. That would enable Karen to remain at the same school and make her commute to work very manageable.

She knew the area well. It was in a small valley just outside town. The neighborhood was very nice. She had never enjoyed living directly in the city and the new home would provide a wonderful change of scenery for them.

She showered and changed into a nice lavender pant suit. She wanted to look professional and she had been told how nice that outfit looked on her.

She then tried to remember how she had been so charming in high school. She looked into the mirror and decided to unbutton the top button of her blouse. She had to use every tool at her disposal to win over Leonard.

She knew that would at least catch his attention and from there she could turn on the charm, if she remembered how.

Julie went in to the kitchen and poured a cup of motivation as Karen emerged from her room.

Karen had chosen a flowered pull over shirt and had put on a very nice pair of jeans.

"Well mom, is this presentable?"

Julie approved of her daughter's selection.

"You look very nice sweetheart; now do something with that hair."

Karen gave her mother a disgruntled expression.

"At least comb it Karen Renee!"

Julie shook her head and sighed. She thought to herself 'do I really have to be a single parent today?'

Raising a teenage daughter should at least earn the parent a medal if not a commendation by the Queen. Sometimes she wondered what planet that girl came from....then she gave that another though; probably not the same one her brother originated from.

She finished her coffee and Karen returned with neatly combed hair. Julie got her purse and the two of them headed out.

The twenty minute drive was silent other than Julie stressing to her daughter the importance of acting courteous and polite.

Karen looked at her mother with contempt. She acknowledged her mother's words and sarcastically promised to be on her best behavior but had to add a few words of her own.

"Geese mom, I'm not a baby!"

Julie thrashed back at her daughter.

"No you're not...you're a teenager and they're even worse!"

Karen scowled making her displeasure clearly apparent.

"Chill out already mom!"

Julie gave Karen a look of antipathy.

"If you want that kitten you had better listen to me!"

Karen silently relented to her mother and turned her head to look out the side window.

Julie suddenly realized she was so edgy about the coming event and she had been taking it out on her daughter. By no means was this premeditated or intentional and she realized her mistake.

"I'm sorry sweetheart. I am just really nervous about this. I so want everything to go perfectly and we get the house. I didn't mean to thrash out on you."

Karen took her mother's hand and smiled.

"I know mom. Don't worry, we've got this!"

Julie again marveled at how mature her daughter was and continued driving with renewed enthusiasm.

They pulled on to Briarcrest Road and Julie reached in her purse for the slip of paper with the number on it.

She glanced at Karen and could tell how excited she was. It was a beautiful neighborhood. The street was adorned with shade trees and all the yards were neatly manicured with neatly trimmed hedges. What a difference it was from living in the inner city. It was almost like paradise.

She smiled as she passed children playing with dogs on a front yard and visualized Karen and Robert doing the same with her future kitten.

She thought about how she hasn't had a front yard since she lived with her parents. All the following years had been spent in low rent apartments. She made a mental note to buy a lawn mower.

Karen had so wanted this but kept her dream silent. She thanked God for finally allowing her to give her daughter the live she so deserved.

This would be so refreshing for her and Karen and Robert. This was something she had wanted for so long and she still had trouble believing it might just actually be happening.

She silently thanked Robert again for his part in making this dream come true, this time successfully fighting back the tears that normally accompany any thoughts of him.

She slowed the car up when she realized they were now in front of 201.

There before their gapping eyes stood the most beautiful foursquare design house they had ever seen.

Julie wasn't sure if it was the actual appearance of the home that she thought so alluring or what it symbolized. It represented hope, a new beginning for her and her family.

It was an older two-story house rejuvenated by an obviously fresh coat of beige paint. The foundation was adorned by a row of short shrubbery.

On the right was an adorable porch surrounded by a decorative railing. Julie's first thought was that it would be the perfect place for the porch swing she had wanted since she was a child.

The left side of the house featured a large window with quaint shutters painted a rusty color. The small front yard was divided into equal halves by a brick walkway leading to three steps which gave access to the front door. The door was painted in the same rusty color. At the top of the door were beveled windows giving the door a very grand appearance.

To each side of the driveway were the mighty oak trees Edie had spoken of. It was truly magnificent. Karen and Julie looked at each other in awe. Sure enough, there in the corner of the yard was a magnificent pine tree.

"Oh, mom it is perfect! This is really going to be our new home?"

Julie could only nod her agreement.

"That's the plan sweetheart. Say a prayer that they will let us have it!"

Karen struggled to believe this could actually be there new home.

"Mom, this is too much! Can we actually afford this? I mean look at it, it is so...gorgeous!"

Julie squeezed Karen's hand.

"Thanks to Robert we can sweetheart. Let's just hope they agree to rent it to us."

Karen looked at her mother with amazement.

"Oh wow, I never dreamed it would be this nice!"

The joy Karen's happiness brought Julie couldn't be measured. She thought back over the years of sadness and despair her daughter had to endure and how she so deserved this. She was now firmly resolved to do what ever it took to make this their home. Nothing was going to deprive her family of this happiness.

She was now truly a woman on a mission! Thinking further on her resolve she painfully admitted part of it was because she knew what it would mean to Robert.

There was a red pickup truck parked in the driveway telling her that Leonard had already arrived.

She turned to Karen and smiled.

"Okay, you ready for this?"

Karen just beamed.

"Oh yeah mom...let's do this! I can't wait to see my room!"

As they got out of the car they noticed the front door of the house opening. Emerging from inside was an older couple. She knew this had to have been Leonard and Edith.

She identified Edi immediately even though they had never met. She was just as she had envisioned her.

Julie had always enjoyed trying to visualize people on the phone and this time she was dead on.

Edi was short and heavy set. Her rounded face was framed by shoulder length silver blonde hair. She was busy jabbering to the man next to her, obviously Leonard who was doing nothing but passively listening.

They approached the couple and Edi saw them. She waved passionately and urged them forward.

Julie smile and glanced at Karen.

"Here we go!"

They approached the couple and Julie had to snicker. Leonard was the physical antithesis of his wife. While Edi was short and stout Leonard was tall and as skinny as a rail. They were the classic example of the old adage 'opposites attract'.

Edi brushed her husband aside and scurried down the steps to meet them. She spoke out even before Julie had a chance to extend her hand to shake hers.

"You must be Julie!"

Julie smiled.

"That I am and you must be Edith."

Edi returned the smile.

"Oh, honey now you call me Edi. This must be your daughter. Well, she's beautiful just like her mom. Hi Hon, I'm Edi it is a pleasure to meet you both."

They exchanged handshakes and Edi returned to the porch.

"This is my husband Leonard. He will be showing you the house and answering any questions you might have. If you stump him with anything don't worry, I'll be here."

They walked up to the porch and both shook Leonard's hand. Julie returned her attention to Edi. She decided now was a good time to start the charm.

"Well I am glad you decided to come along Edi I was looking forward to meeting you."

Edi glanced at her husband and then at Julie.

"Well doll I couldn't leave Leonard alone with such

a pretty and single lady such as you. I knew you were pretty I could tell by your voice on the phone. Leonard here sometimes forgets he is very old and very married!"

Leonard let out a loud grunt.

"Oh Edith just stop that nonsense! We've been married over thirty years now and..."

Edi boisterously interrupted him.

"Thirty-six years Leonard...thirty-six! Good gracious you can't even remember the actual number!"

She then winked at Julie and whispered.

"See what I told you about men! I just love bugging his goat like that. It gets him so riled up. I think it's what keeps our relationship fresh after all these years."

She walked over to Leonard and gave him a kiss on the cheek.

"Old Leonard here is a pretty good sport about it too. He knows I'm only ragging on him."

Julie couldn't help but laugh out loud at the exchange. She now knew she had won over Edi and was therefore becoming confident they just might get the house! Karen stood silently by her mother snickering.

Edi then turned her attention to Karen.

"Sweetheart what is your name and how old are you? You sure are a pretty one!"

Karen gave her mother a questionable glance before answering.

"I'm Karen and I am fifteen."

Edi gave Karen a pat on the back.

"Well I sure hope you and your mom decide to live here it would be wonderful having a nice family like you living here.

Now your mom told me if she takes the house you can have a kitten. Don't you let her weasel out of that one! In fact if I were you, I think you could talk her into getting you two!"

Karen's eyes lit up with joy.

Julie shook her head and laughed. Her heart was filled with happiness. She knew they had the place! She had to show her encouragement.

"We sure like what we have seen so far."

Edi nodded her approval.

"Well I have to admit at least part of my joy is selfish. I figure if the place were occupied maybe Leonard would spend a little more time at home where he belongs! Okay, enough of this small talk. Leonard dear, show these nice ladies the rest of the house."

Leonard opened the door and motioned for Julie and Karen to follow him inside while Edi remained on the porch.

They entered the house and were directed to the kitchen. Leonard smiled.

"You have to excuse my wife she can be a bit...well brash at times until you get to know her and her ways but she is a good woman. She has a wonderful heart, guess that's why I kept her around for so long and put up with her shenanigans. I can tell she likes you already."

Leonard showed her the kitchen first. She was amazed at the counter space. There was a nice refrigerator and stove and so many cabinets! She didn't think she had enough kitchen utensils to even fill them.

They then went to the living room which of course was void of any furniture. It had to have been twice the size of the one they were currently living in.

The carpet which was a deep burgundy looked brand new and the walls were freshly painted a very nice shade of coral.

Karen tugged at her mother's shirt sleeve with a huge smile on her face.

Leonard then showed them a small bathroom and they headed to the back room.

"Now you can use this room as a bedroom if you like, or anything else you might have in mind."

Julie turned to Karen.

"How would you like this for your room sweetheart?"

Karen's eyes were as big as saucers as she studied the room. Nice sapphire carpet graced the floor and the walls were a beautiful robin's egg blue.

"Oh mom this is awesome! I would love it. I have so much room!"

Leonard then led them upstairs where he showed them the two bedrooms and nice bathroom which was larger than the one downstairs.

I just redid all the plumbing so you will always have hot water for your bath or shower. The sink is new too I just replaced it."

Both Julie and Karen were simply over whelmed. Above the sink, which was a beautiful marble, was a huge decorative mirror with a row of lights affixed on top. Julie thought to herself she could actually see to put on her makeup!

Leonard spoke up.

"As you can hopefully tell we just repainted the whole place. My wife chose the colors and I just did most of the manual labor."

Julie and Karen just beamed.

"Oh it is beautiful, just perfect. This is even more than I had hoped for when Larry told me about it. You both did an incredible job it's just gorgeous!

This would be the nicest place either of us has ever lived in if you would allow us to have it!"

Leonard shrugged his shoulders.

"Well Edith seems to like you and she would have the final say. I don't have any problems with you having it. Edi has been nagging me for a year now to do something with this place and it would be nice to have her off my back so I am all in favor of you taking it; that is of course if you want it."

Julie was shaking with excitement. She glanced at Karen who was practically in hysteria.

"Oh most definably we want it!"

Leonard simply nodded his approval.

"Well I'm not really sure how people do this. I have never rented anything out before. I don't have any formal application and I'm not going to run a credit check anything crazy like that.

Edi and I are simple folk; if Larry vouches for you then I guess that is good enough for us. You seem like good people so let's just go with that."

They shook hands.

"Well now it's just a question of what you want to pay for it. You just give me an idea of what you can afford and we will run it by Edi and work something out. I sure ain't going to quarrel about money."

Julie was in a state of shock. This was going much easier than she had ever dreamed it would.

# 22

Before she had a chance to reply Edi entered the room.

"Well when are you folks moving in? I'm hoping my husband didn't scare you away!"

Leonard let out another grunt and addressed his wife.

"Edith everything is fine for crying out loud. They love the place now don't you go causing no big ado. I swear you can be such a horse's ass at times."

Julie and Karen both laughed out loud. Edith lovingly slapped her husband on the cheek.

"Isn't he just a hoot? Okay have we agreed on the rent? I've got things to do this afternoon and these wonderful ladies have to go home and start packing. Leonard and I really aren't concerned with it just throw out a figure and we can all go about our business. Now you make it something you are comfortable with honey."

Julie was totally perplexed with the offer. She had rented many apartments over the years and had never had a landlord ask her how much she could afford.

She remembered her father telling her that if something sounded too good to be true it usually was. She had to address her honest concerns with Edi.

"Edi I don't know quite what to say this is so unusual. I mean I am so grateful but..."

Edi sensed her uneasiness. She put her hand on Julie's shoulder and led her over to the corner of the room.

"Honey, let's talk. Leonard and I are...well doing very well if you know what I mean. He has a wonderful pension. He was a longshoreman for a big shipping company in

New York for almost thirty years. His union has given us a substantial pension.

Now I know you wouldn't know if from looking at me but my parents were very well off. Not only did I inherit this home from them but also quite a bit of money I must say.

Now Leonard and I live a very simple life. We have everything we need and then some. I am not about to take advantage of such a nice lady and her family to get money we quite frankly don't need. Now that just wouldn't be right, we are not that kind of people.

The biggest reward I want from this is to do something nice for nice people and I can tell you and your daughter are great people. You would be doing us a favor by taking the house and enjoying it."

Julie was touched beyond words. She tried to find a way to thank Edi and show her what her kindness meant to her.

"You and your husband have been a Godsend to my daughter and me. Your kindness has made our dream come true. This has been the miracle Karen and I have been waiting for and I can't thank you enough."

Edi wrapped her arms around Julie and gave her an unsolicited hug. Julie thought for a moment and had a question for her.

"Edi, do you have any children?"

Edi's expression turned to one of mournful thought. She sighed before answering. Her now serious expression seemed so out of place on her.

"No dear I do not. I guess that's the good Lord's way of saying he feels keeping an eye on Leonard is a big enough chore for me.

Oh we kicked the idea around a few times over the years but it just never happened. It has all turned out well thought. We have had the opportunity to do a lot of things we wanted to do and go a few places we wanted to go. These are things we might not have been able to do if we had had children.

I've thought about it now and again, I guess that's natural. You know; what kind of father Leonard would have been and what kind of mother I would have been for that matter.

I know there were a lot of joys we missed and I also know Leonard would have been an incredible father but the Lord knows what's best and we have both accepted it.

I am so blessed he gave me Leonard. You know we have been inseparable for the past thirty-six years! I can't imagine life without that old fool."

Julie took a moment to digest what Edi had just said. She was deeply moved by her admissions. She saw another side of Edi. She thought back to what Leonard has said earlier. Edi truly was a wonderful woman and she did indeed have a great heart.

Edi broke the uneasy silence with her usual charisma.

"So doll do you want the place?"

Julie could only smile.

"Oh yes Edi we really do!"

Edi's eyes lit up with joy.

"Well that's dandy! Let's get down to brass tacks. You just tell me what you want to pay for it and I will write you up a lease just to make things official and we will get the ball rolling and get you folks moved in!"

Julie hesitated before coming up with a figure. She didn't know how to respond. She wanted to come up with something fair but affordable to them. After giving it some thought she gave Edi a price and they agreed.

Julie was still in a state of bewilderment and amazement. She knew the figure they agreed upon was way below what the home would get on the market.

Edi shook her hand and continued.

"Well honey you sure aren't going to get a lot of boxes in that little car of yours. What's say we have Leonard help you with his truck. Now I won't take no for an answer so you get all your things packed and give him a call when you are ready and we will get you all squared away!

He will be a big help, he's always been a hard worker I'll give him that. Guess that's another thing men are good for, manual labor!"

Julie held back tears of joy. These people were angels!

They walked back to the Kitchen where Leonard had been waiting.

Edi walked over to her husband and smiled.

"Well we finally have this place rented Leonard and you are going to help them move."

Leonard let out another of his now famous grunts.

"You say what? Edith Parker every time you open your mouth it ends up giving me more work...oh alright. I swear woman I don't know why I keep you around!"

Edi was not about to let that slide.

"Because I'm the best thing that ever happened to you and we both know it... now hush!"

Leonard rolled his eyes and replied.

"Why do you always do that?"

Edi just shook her head.

"Because you would miss it if I didn't! We both know that too!"

Julie just loved this couple and adored their banter. Everyone shared a laugh as Julie and Karen left.

On the drive home Julie and Karen couldn't stop talking about how wonderful the new house was. Julie was telling Karen about how they would have to do some furniture shopping and stop on the way home at the grocery store to pick up some boxes.

Karen couldn't stop smiling.

"Oh mom this is so great! I've never been this excited in my life."

Hearing her daughter's words was the greatest gift she had ever received. She couldn't help but think back to just a year ago and how sad and disoriented Karen had been. She again silently thanked God and Robert for making this miracle a reality.

They picked up a lot of folded boxes from the grocery store and threw them in the trunk. Julie seized the moment.

"We are going out to lunch and celebrate!"

Karen nodded her head in agreement.

They stopped at their favorite Chinese buffet and had a wonderful lunch together. The conversation continued on ideas they had for the new home. Julie told Karen she was going to get a porch swing and Karen was buzzing with ideas for her new room.

Julie thought to herself that this was the happiest she had ever been in her life. They arrived home and stacked the boxes in the living room.

Julie scanned the apartment. This was going to be a major undertaking. She cursed herself for having collected so much junk over the years and what an effort it would be to get everything packed. But in the long run she knew the rewards would be worth it and she would have a very willing helper in Karen.

She fixed a pot of coffee and gathered her thoughts. She had enough boxes to at least get started. Remembering again the rent had been paid through the end of the month would give her enough time to get more if she needed them. She got packing tape and even remembered labels. Last time she moved she didn't label the boxes and it took forever to sort things out.

She would have to tell Larry at some point they had decided to take the house. This made her think about returning to work. As much as she loved her job she had to admit it was a nice change not having to go to it.

Her thoughts were interrupted by her cell phone chiming.

Julie's heart skipped a beat when she saw the caller ID. The call was coming from the hospital! With all her focus being on the new home she had almost forgotten her son was waiting to come home from the hospital!

She answered on the first ring almost panting from excitement.

"Hello?"

A woman responded.

"Is this Julie Wells?"

Her heart was now beating at a thousand miles per hour.

"Yes it is."

The woman spoke with enthusiasm.

"This is Nurse Ramsey from St. Thomas Hospital. I am calling with some good news for you Miss Wells. I just spoke with Dr. Hart and he asked me to call you. Your son is ready to come home. Could you come and pick him up?"

Julie smiled from ear to ear.

"Oh you bet I can. When can I get him?"

There was a pause and the woman continued.

"Well he is ready now so when ever you can make it will be fine. Now the doctor will not be here but we have prepared a going home package for your son.

Now it's my understanding that this has been a...well unusual situation in some ways."

Julie interrupted her.

"You could certainly say that."

The nurse continued.

"The reason I mention that is the doctor has prepared special instructions and some vitamin supplements for your son. He said he would like to get on a bi-weekly checkup program to monitor your son's progress. This is all explained in the instructions he has included in the take home package.

We have included a blanket, a cute jumper, his favorite stuffed animal and a number of baby necessities. So you will be coming in today of course?"

Julie confirmed and told the nurse they were on their way. The nurse concluded the conversation.

"I see this is your second child so you know the procedure. I must add that your son has been just a joy! He is so active and happy and rarely even cries; now that is unusual for a newborn because they tend to do that a lot. He has won over the hearts of everyone here. You've got quite a wonderful little boy Miss Wells. We're going to miss him. I look forward to seeing you soon."

Julie clicked off the phone and shouted out.

"Yes! Karen, get ready; we're going to pick up Robert!"

Karen came running out of her room.

"Robert is coming home...now?"

Julie ran over and hugged her daughter.

"Yes, the hospital just called. He is ready to come home. Now go get ready we're leaving now!"

Karen ran back to her room and changed clothes. Julie was in the kitchen running around in circles. She was trying to put coherent thoughts together.

She rethought all they had done to prepare Karen's room and was satisfied it was all ready for Robert.

She ran around frantically trying to remember where she had put her purse. She checked the kitchen without luck. She then ran into the living room again without success. She finally found it on the bathroom sink. Once she found it she was relieved to find her keys in it.

She took a brief second to laugh at her efforts. If it

took her this long to find it in this small apartment she will never find it in their huge new home.

Okay she had convinced herself she was all set. Now to make sure Karen gets moving.

"Karen hurry up let's go Robert wants to come home!"

There was a panicked voice coming from Karen's bedroom.

"I'm coming mom I just have to find my socks."

Julie growled to herself. Of all the times to lose your socks!

"Karen would you just grab another pair from the dresser for crying out loud we have to leave!"

Julie mumbled to herself in a moment of frustration only a parent could empathize with 'what did God have in mind when he created the teenage girl, did he think we missed the velociraptor?' Then she answered her own question...babysitting.

Karen finally came out of her bedroom. Julie studied her daughter and decided she looked presentable.

"You ready to bring your bother home?"

Karen beamed.

"Oh Hell yeah mom I can't wait!"

Karen immediately realized she had used a word she shouldn't have and looked at her mother in fear.

"Ahh, I'm sorry mom..."

Julie interrupted Karen's apology by giving her daughter an unexpected high five and a burst of joyful laughter.

"No worries I totally understand and I am just as excited...we'll discuss it later. Now let's go get Robert!"

They held hands as they went out to the car both smiling from ear to ear. Julie double checked the infant car seat secured in the back seat just to make sure everything was fastened tightly. Satisfied that it was properly in place they headed off to the hospital.

After a twenty minute ride filled with anticipative banter and laughter they arrived at the hospital. They took the elevator up to the maternity ward and checked in at the nurse's desk.

"I am Julie Wells; I was told I could take my son home today!"

The head nurse smiled and checked the computer.

"Yes indeed Miss Wells, how exciting! Doctor Hart was in this morning and did a thorough checkup on him. According to the charts your son is doing great and is all ready to go! I'm sure you are anxious to have him home! I'm so happy and excited for you! This is a big day!"

Julie nodded and smiled at Karen who was standing by her side. They were taken into a small room where Julie filled out mountains of paperwork. After completing the administrative requirements they were finally escorted to the nursery.

# 23

The nurse led them to the elevator and pushed the button for the floor of the maternity ward. She smiled as she looked at them sharing their excitement.

"Dr. Hart has prepared a coming home package for your son which you can pick up on your way out.

He has included instructions on the giving of the supplement vitamins and nutrients. This will be very simple as they are just added to his daily formula. There is a month's supply included getting you started.

He has also made up a chart for you to fill in keeping tabs of his growth and development. This will require you to measure and weigh him daily. Now this may seem a bit drastic but due to his unprecedented growth rate to this point Dr. Hart wants to continue monitoring this closely. He will review these at your checkups.

The doctor has made out a schedule of appointments. Initially, they will be every two weeks. Now I know this is probably more frequent than you went through with your daughter but I'm sure you understand due to the nature of his premature birth we want to keep close tabs on him.

Now the nature of these checkups is twofold. First and foremost, of course, is to check on the baby's health but secondly we want to closely monitor his growth due to the unusual maturation he has experienced up to this point."

Julie nodded attentively.

"Your son has really captured the attention of the entire medical community. The doctor will be checking all his vitals on each trip; these tests will again be more extensive than you would have gone through with your daughter due to the extraordinary circumstances."

Julie clenched Karen's hand and smiled in excitement. Karen beamed with delight.

"He's really coming home mom! I am so excited!"

Julie nodded as the nurse continued.

"The nurses on the ward added a little something as well. We got a card and all signed it, you know something you can show him when he gets older. We also included his favorite stuffed animal and blanket as well.

Your son has become quite a celebrity on the ward we all just love him. He has been the best-behaved baby we have had here in a long time. He rarely cries at all, he always seems so at peace. We're going to miss him!"

Karen and Julie just grinned from ear to ear as the elevator doors opened. The three walked down the long hallway to a set of double doors. Julie's heart was racing with anticipation and joy. To her left Karen was literally bouncing down the hall.

The nurse pushed a large green button on the wall and the doors swung open. The walked up to the desk and the nurse motioned for them to sit down while she completed the release procedures.

Julie and Karen looked across the reception area into the large glass enclosed adjoining room at all the babies tucked snugly into their respective cribs.

The nurse reappeared from behind the desk and smiled enthusiastically.

"Please excuse me for a moment while I bring out your son. I am so excited for you. I'll be just a moment."

Julie and Karen embraced each other in exultation. They smiled at each other in anxious anticipation.

Within minutes the nurse returned surprisingly accompanied by Dr. Hart. The nurse was carrying a small duffle bag but it was what was in Dr. Hart's arms that immediately caught their attention.

Dr. Hart was nestling a baby wrapped tightly in a

powder blue blanket. Both Julie's and Karen's hearts skipped a beat. There before them was Robert!

The doctor relished in their excitement.

"I have a little boy here that would love to go home Julie! I believe you two have already met."

Dr. Hart walked slowly over to Julie and gently handed her son to her. Julie took her son beaming with ecstasy.

She opened the blanket to get a better look at her son's face. She couldn't hold back tears of joy as she studied him.

He already had a beautiful head of light brown hair but it was his eyes that stood out to her. He undeniably had his father's eyes. The resemblance was uncanny. She closed her eyes for a brief second and she could see his father's face as clear as day.

Her tears now took on a different meaning. A tinge of sadness crossed over her. She so wished he could be there with them to share this beautiful moment.

Dr. Hart mercifully interrupted her train of thought.

"Nurse would you please give Karen here the going home package. Julie I am sure you were explained the contents. Everything you need to know is written in the instructions.

Allow me to congratulate you on a beautiful son. He has become quite popular here and we will all miss him but after all everyone has been through we are all so very happy he is finally going home!"

Karen took the duffle bag from the nurse and raced to her mother's side. Julie turned to allow Karen to see her brother.

"Oh mom he is so cool! Look at all his hair! I can't believe he is actually my baby brother!"

Julie chuckled.

"That he is big sister, now let's get him home!"

Julie addressed the doctor before leaving.

"Doctor I can't thank you enough for all you and your staff have done for us and especially for Robert. I know I wasn't always the easiest person to deal with at times but you all have been wonderful."

Dr. Hart put his arm around Julie.

"Julie you are more than welcome. It has been a pleasure. You have quite a little boy there. All babies are miracles but your son has raised the bar. He has the spirit of a lion!

Now call me if you have any questions and I will expect to see you in two weeks. Please be sure and keep up on the daily growth chart, I an anxious to see if this accelerated growth pattern continues. We will go over it when I see you. Now you three go home and get this little guy settled."

Julie, Karen and Robert left the nursery and started the walk to her car. Karen was so excited she tugged at her mother's arm every few steps to look at her brother until Julie's patience had had enough.

"Sweetheart, I know you're excited but he looks the same as he did a minute ago."

Upon reaching the car Julie secured Robert in the back seat car seat checking the belt and straps twice to make sure they were secure.

"Mom, can I sit in the back next to Robert?"

Julie smiled.

"I was just going to ask you if you would sweetheart; that would be perfect. You're going to be a wonderful big sister!"

Karen nodded.

"That's because he is going to be a wonderful little brother!"

Julie was happy beyond words. She said a silent prayer of thanks before starting the car. Almost involuntarily she found herself saying a few silent words to Robert. 'I love you so much, thank you for making this happen. I so wish you could be here with us to share this but you are with me in my heart.' She wiped the accompanying tears away before Karen noticed.

The drive home was a joyous one indeed. Karen wouldn't take her eyes off her baby brother adjusting his blanket every minute or so and continuously checking the security of his seat belt.

Arriving home Julie carefully unbuckled Robert's seatbelt. Before she even got him out of the car seat Karen piped up.

"Mom, can I carry him inside...please?"

Julie was so proud of her daughter. Karen was accepting her role as sister with such responsibility and enthusiasm.

"Of course you can sweetheart."

She lifted Robert out of his car seat and handed him to Karen instructing her on where to put her hands. Karen looked as if she had just won the lottery.

Julie grabbed the duffle bag and they entered the building where she noticed Larry tending bar. She turned to Karen.

"We have to introduce him to Larry."

Karen nodded in agreement and they walked over to the bar. Larry noticed them and literally ran over to them. Julie had to laugh as she spoke.

"Larry, I would like you to meet your new tenant, this is Robert Wells."

Larry's eyes grew as big as saucers and smiled from ear to ear. He bent down to get a close look.

"What do we have here, my goodness what a handsome young man! It is a pleasure to meet you Robert. It will be a joy having you here with us!"

Julie was glowing. She was so thankful Larry was being so understanding about the new addition.

"We just got back from the Hospital. I want to thank you again Larry for, well for everything."

Larry gently patted her on the shoulder and gave Karen thumbs up.

"Julie you have been a model tenant I would do anything to help you. I'm sure going to miss you all. Leonard tells me you really liked the place and all the details were worked out nicely.

Edi said you are excited about moving in! I'm really happy for you; this is quite an exciting time for you, a new baby and a new home all at once, wow that doesn't happen to a person every day!"

A moment of panic hit her. With those words Julie just remembered they were going to move. The excitement of Robert coming home had been the only thing on her mind. She had completely forgotten about them moving to the new home."

Larry continued to admire Robert.

"He is a beautiful baby Julie, I am thrilled for you! Do you have any idea when you will be moving? I'm sure you are anxious to get your family settled in the new home."

Julie turned to Karen and they mutually shrugged their shoulders.

"Well with all the excitement of Robert coming home we haven't even had a chance to start packing."

Larry smiled.

"Oh, I totally understand that! Well, let me know if there is anything I can do to help. Edie told me Leonard will help you with his truck when you are ready. I have a lot of boxes in the storage room that are yours for the taking. There is certainly no rush.

I know your rent is paid up through the first but let me add if you need more time next month is on me if you need an extra week or so! I know you have a lot going on and that's the least I can do."

Julie smiled and thanked him.

"That's so sweet of you Larry I can't begin to tell you how much I appreciate it. I also want you to know that once things settle down a bit I want to get back to work. I know what a strain it must be for you picking up all my shifts and I apologize for that."

Larry patted her on the shoulder.

"Oh don't you worry about that, you just take care of that baby. The bar will always be here and everyone will welcome your return."

Julie, Karen, and Robert headed upstairs to their apartment. Julie placed Robert in his crib. She kissed him on the forehead and tucked him in. She stood looking at him in complete joy. She was so happy he was finally home. Satisfied that he was sound asleep she then went to the kitchen for a much-needed cup of coffee.

Karen poured a glass of iced tea and joined her mother at the kitchen table. Julie closed her eyes for a brief moment of thought.

"We've got a lot of work to do sweetheart."

Karen nodded.

"We've got this mom...you've got me to help!"

Julie squeezed Karen's hand.

"When I go back to work I am going to depend on you a great deal. You are going to have to take care of Robert. I know that's going to be a lot of work for you in addition to school and all but we are both going to have to make some adjustments now that he is home."

Karen nodded as Julie took a sip of coffee.

"Well, the first thing is we are going to have to get all this stuff packed! Now Robert is asleep so let's seize the moment and get started!"

Julie took a deep breath, did a quick survey of the kitchen and tried not to get overwhelmed at the daunting task ahead of them. Karen noticed her mother's apprehension.

"Relax mom, we will just take one room at a time and before you know it we will be ready to go!"

Julie shook her head in complete amazement of the mature young lady her daughter had become.

"How did you get to be so mature and smart? It couldn't have come from me and I know it didn't come from your father."

Karen just giggled.

"Don't be silly mom; you're the smartest person I know except for maybe Robert."

In horror Karen immediately recognized what she had said and felt terrible. The last thing she wanted was her mother to start dwelling on Robert.

"Mom, I'm sorry I didn't ...."

Julie stopped her.

"Its okay sweetheart, it is. Don't worry about it I'm good. We just both have to accept that he's gone but will remain in our hearts forever. We can't be walking on eggshells worrying about mentioning him, it's going to happen. We can't just forget he was in our lives just be stronger for having that time with him.

Now what we need to do first is to take Larry up on his offer about those boxes since we only have a few now. I'll go down to the storage room and grab some more boxes.

Let's start in the living room. While I'm downstairs you start gathering all the small stuff. I have a bunch of old newspapers stacked in the closet in my bedroom, the boxes we have are in there too. Pack all the things in newspaper and start placing them in boxes, I'll be right back."

Julie went down to the storage room and scrounged

up boxes while Karen followed her instructions to the letter.

Julie returned and set the boxes in the living room where Karen was sitting on the floor surrounded by knick-knacks and boxes. Pleased that her daughter had taken her words to heart she checked on Robert.

She entered Karen's bedroom to find her son still sleeping peacefully. She returned to the living room to help Karen.

"These should get us a good start. You're doing great sweetheart!"

She made a quick trip to the kitchen to make another cup of coffee and refill Karen's iced tea. While in the kitchen she grabbed some masking tape and a felt tip pen.

Returning to the living room she joined Karen on the floor.

"Okay, be sure and label the boxes with what room they came from. One time I moved I failed to do this and it took me longer to organize things than it took me to pack them!"

Karen smiled and they enjoyed their drinks before returning to the business at hand.

They spent the rest of the day packing boxes. They made it fun, Julie put music on and they ordered pizza. By evening they had packed all the small items from the living room and both bedrooms.

Satisfied with their progress they stopped for the day. Julie then decided to go through the duffle bag they had brought home from the hospital.

In the bag she discovered a folder with instructions and the growth chart. There were two small bottles, one containing a vitamin supplement and the other a mixture of liquid proteins and nutrients. There was also a large container of powered organic formula.

At the bottom of the bag was a nice baby blanket,

three baby bottles, a nose syringe, a bag of diapers a large stuffed duck and the card that the nurse had promised containing many signatures.

Julie read the instructions and prepared Robert's first batch of formula. She and Karen went into the bedroom with the formula and found Robert lying in his crib awake but silent.

They just smiled and watched him as he lay there surveying his new surroundings peacefully.

"Oh mom he is so awesome!"

Julie nodded and gently picked up her son.

"He must be hungry it has had to have been a tiresome day for him!"

She brought Robert into the living room and they all sat on the couch. Karen studied every miniscule move he made as his mother gave him his bottle of formula. Karen gently held his head up as he drank it without any difficulty. This was a tremendous load off of Julie's mind.

They all sat together for a while and enjoyed their time together. Julie finally decided it was time to call it a day and returned Robert to his crib.

She tucked him in and gave his a soft kiss on the forehead. She couldn't stop looking at him. What a miracle he was. It wasn't enough that he was born three months early; he had already been through so much in his first few days of life. All the testing and scrutiny he has had to endure yet he seemed so at peace. She remembered what the doctor had said; he truly did possess the heart of a lion!

Julie and Karen sat on the couch and rehashed the day's events. Julie gave her daughter a hug and smile.

"Well, day one is in the books. He seems to be happy here, he ate well! Now we need to get some sleep so we can pick it up tomorrow.

Honey, you have been terrific! I can't thank you

enough for all your help. It is just so wonderful finally having our family finally home together!

This will begin a new chapter in our lives, a very happy and exciting one! Just think when we are all moved into our beautiful new home. Oh I am just so excited!

Now you get some sleep and we will pick up again tomorrow. This moving thing is going to be a piece of cake with us working like this together."

Julie and Karen enjoyed a long loving hug and each retired to their bedrooms.

# 24

The next two weeks flew by. Robert had a prodigious appetite. He thankfully took to the supplemented formula surprisingly well; he seemed to really enjoy it.

The only thing he did more than eat was sleep. He slept soundly, amazingly almost every night. During the night he would wake up only occasionally. This habit had Julie marveling and at times concerned for this was a feat rarely achieved by Karen at his age.

She would frequently check on him in the middle of the night out of habit not a necessity. She would stand by his crib in expectations of him waking up crying but he rarely did. In fact Robert rarely cried at all even when his diaper needed changed. He would most often just wait patiently until it was taken care of without complaining.

It was as if Robert knew he was going to be taken care of and refused to make an issue of it.

What truly held Julie awestruck was how attentive he was when he was held. When either she or Karen would pick him up he flashed a smile without fail, like even at that infant age he was showing appreciation for the attention.

Julie continued to blown away by his eyes. They grew more defined and expressive by the day. When she or Karen would hold him he would gaze directly into their face with such expression as if he were deep in thought studying them. She couldn't help but feel there was a lot of things going on in that tiny little mind that he were simply unable to express. It was adorable yet at the same time curious.

Julie had been gradually instructing Karen on the intricacies of childcare. First, she instructed her on the proper way to mix the formula, then how to hold him while feeding him. Karen picked this up like a trooper, even gently burping him afterward. She smiled with sisterly pride as Robert drank from the bottle in her arms.

The next lesson had Karen drain Robert's nose using the syringe, again Karen had no trouble with the task.

The final test was changing diapers. This one Karen had a problem with. Her face grimaced in terror as she watched her mother demonstrate the procedure.

"Mom, couldn't I just wait till you got home, this is really disgusting."

Julie took a long labored breath trying to hold in her frustration.

"No Karen Renee! This is something you need to do! His diaper needs to be changed or it could cause a very bad rash!

Now you want to be a big sister this comes with the territory. I had to do it with you and someday you will have to do it with your children so you had better learn to do it now! Robert and I are both depending on you!"

Karen just growled in displeasure with the wisdom that could only emanate from the mind of a fifteen-year-old girl.

"But mom really...no human being should be subjected to that!"

Julie didn't have to say a word in reply; her threatening expression said it all.

Karen had no other recourse than to comply.

"Oh all right, I'll do it."

Karen was a great help in keeping up on the growth chart. Julie had purchased an infant scale which she used to weigh Robert. Julie would weigh Robert and Karen's job was to write down the results.

Robert now weighed eight pounds one ounce; that

was a weight gain of nine ounces and he had grown an entire inch since he got home. The way he ate Julie was surprised he hadn't gained eight pounds! Karen diligently wrote down the totals on the chart.

After researching it Julie was satisfied that growth was in the normal range for an infant his age. Julie was greatly relieved at learning this for now maybe the unusually rapid growth rate had stopped and things could get back to normal again.

Her first appointment with Dr. Hart was tomorrow. She was anxious for his thoughts on Robert's progress. She got a cup of coffee and went into Karen's bedroom to check on her son.

He was wide awake and again smiling. She walked over to the window and couldn't help notice Robert's eyes following her around the room as he lay in his crib. He would laboriously move his tiny head intently following her motions around the room. He was certainly interested in and very much aware of his surroundings.

This surprised her because she wasn't sure if that was normal for a child his age. She remembered Karen would mostly just lay in her crib motionlessly seemingly indifferent to her environment at that age.

She walked over to his crib and his attention immediately focused on her. His eyes were glued to her face. She was somewhat taken back by his attentive nature, again not sure if this was normal. He seemed far more alert than Karen had been at his age.

She picked him up and looked into his eyes in wonder, 'Just what is going on in that mind of yours my dear son?' she thought to herself. Somehow she felt it was a lot more than she might realize.

Julie was more correct than she could ever have known. The benefactor of almost a million years of additional evolution over mankind, Robert's brain had developed far superior to that of a human brain.

Robert's system of neurons and synapses were much more complex and sophisticated than those found in a human.

Comparing Robert's brain to that of a human would be equivalent to comparing an abacus to a modern day computer. His capacity to learn and remember what he had learned was, by human standards, astonishing.

Robert had the ability to take full advantage of his mind power even at this infant stage. He was born with intelligence which didn't need developing, it was already genetically in place, and it needed only the opportunity and nurturing.

His brain was already absorbing absolutely every element it came in contact with. His mind was meticulously taking fastidious notes on his environment and interactions with his mother and sister and storing them in his infant memory. His ability to learn was second only to his thirst for knowledge.

She gently put him back in his crib and adjusted the blankets around him. She gave him a kiss on the forehead, she turned around as she reached the door and took one more look at her son; 'this is going to be interesting' she thought.

She slowly closed the bedroom door and went into the kitchen for a refill of coffee.

Karen was sitting at the kitchen table eating a sandwich and smiled as her mother poured her coffee.

"Are we going to do more packing today mom?"

Julie nodded her head in accord.

"We have to honey. We've got to get that done before the end of the month which isn't that far away! I'm going to take full advantage of you being home before school starts which is also not far away!"

Karen frowned.

"Yeah I know, don't remind me."

The two of them spent the afternoon packing. They worked on the bathroom and closets and made remarkable progress. A mountain of completed boxes now stood defiantly in the middle of the living room floor.

After dinner Karen reluctantly passed her first test of changing Robert's diaper. She immediately spent the next five minutes washing her hands before returning to Robert's crib side.

"The things I do for you little brother!"

Julie could only laugh and congratulate her on her arduous effort.

"See that wasn't so bad now was it?"

If looks could kill Karen would be making funeral arrangements for her mother.

Julie and Karen relaxed on the couch watching television and discussing the plans for finishing packing and getting ready for the move.

"Well, I think we have most of the small things packed now we have to figure out how to do the rest. We can't pack the things we use every day of course because I'm not exactly sure when we are actually going to move. I have to call Leonard and see when he can help us with the truck."

Karen replied with a quizzical look.

"Mom, we have to get furniture and stuff for the new place you know."

Without thinking Julie uttered a cry of dismay.

"Oh shit that's right. I had forgotten about there not being any there."

Julie immediately realized she could have chosen a better way of saying that. She glanced over at Karen with an embarrassing expression and chuckled.

"Oops; sorry sweetheart."

Karen just laughed.

"That's okay mom. Hey I bet we could get everything we need at the big consignment store downtown. Have you been in there? It's huge and they have furniture and everything! I bet they would be cheaper than a real furniture store too."

Julie thought for a moment and knew exactly the place Karen had in mind.

"That is a brilliant idea sweetheart! That would be the perfect place to go and I think they even have a delivery service that would take everything right to the new house! Thanks for mentioning that!"

Karen beamed with pride. Her mother got out a notebook and pen.

"Alright the first thing we need to do is compile a list of everything we need. I will call Leonard in the morning before I go to the doctor to see when he can help. We have to time this right."

The two combined heads and wrote a long list of all the furniture and things they would need. Julie was sure the consignment shop would have just about everything on the list. She wasn't going to be particular about the furniture, as long as it was comfortable and practical it would be fine. She just wanted to get the entire moving process over with and get her family settled in their beautiful new home.

Satisfied that their list was pretty comprehensive they retired for the night.

Julie set her alarm for eight-o-clock. Her appointment with Dr. Hart was at one-o-clock and she wanted to have time for breakfast, a shower, call Leonard and of course to get Robert ready. She set the coffee pot, turned off the television and gave Karen a big hug and kiss.

"Okay, get some sleep sweetheart we're going to have a busy day tomorrow. You're coming with me to the doctor's then we will all go out for lunch. I'm calling Leonard before we leave and we will have an idea when all this is going to happen.

If he wants to get this done soon then we might just hit the consignment shop in the afternoon and get moving on this!"

Karen's eyes lit up with excitement.

"Mom, when can I get my kitten?"

Julie laughed out loud. With all that is going on, all Karen can think of is getting her cat.

"Let's get moved first sweetheart. You'll get your kitten I promise now go to bed."

Karen and Julie walked into the bedroom and both checked on Robert who was sound asleep.

Julie then retired to her bedroom; she had a lot on her mind. The stress of moving was starting to get to her. She was tired, the dust hadn't settled from finally getting Robert home and now she has the burden of getting everything in order to move.

It's times like this that she really misses Robert's dad. He always had a way to calm her down, to settle her nerves and assure her that everything was going to work out fine.

She changed into her night clothes and settled in bed. No...she would not allow herself to start thinking about how much she missed him. As close as she came, she refused to cry. She took a deep breath and turned off the light curing herself for even allowing the thought to enter her mind. After about fifteen minutes of tossing and turning she finally managed to get to sleep.

The stillness of the morning was broken by the alarm going off. Startled by the unwelcome disturbance Julie jumped and wiped the sleep from her eyes after a restless night's sleep. It couldn't be eight-o-clock already she thought. The clock boldly declared otherwise.

She sat up in bed and sighed. She bit her lip as she was tried to assemble coherent thoughts. Her first mission was to check on Robert. He had slept through the night again without incident.

Running her fingers through her hair she managed to stand and walk into Karen's bedroom. Karen was still sound asleep, no surprise there. She turned to the crib in the corner and found Robert awake lying peacefully and surprisingly quiet. She studied him and discovered he was entranced looking at his mobile hanging overhead.

He was intently watching the stars and planets gently swaying above his head. Again she silently laughed at the irony of the theme of his mobile. Maybe he was homesick she whimsically thought.

She smiled and picked him up slowly. Julie took Robert into the kitchen and prepared his morning formula. She watched him as he ate and shook her head in amazement. 'You are one special little guy Robert' she thought to herself.

After the feeding Julie changed his diaper and returned him to his crib. She fixed a cup of coffee and plotted the day ahead. She would let Karen sleep for a while longer while she took her shower and got dressed.

She finished her coffee, took a long hot shower, got dressed and put on just enough makeup to look presentable. She decided Leonard should be up by now and it would be a good time to call him.

She got her cell phone out and clicked on Leonard's number. She refilled her coffee as she waited for him to answer. After three rings a woman answered, it was Edie.

"Hello?"

She smiled remembering what a character she was.

"Good morning Edie this is Julie Wells…"

That is as far as she got before Edie burst into the conversation with her usual boisterous enthusiasm.

"Well good morning doll! Gee it's good to hear from you! How are you-all doing over there?"

Julie couldn't help but chuckle.

"We're doing just fine thank you. We've pretty been busy with the baby home now. We have been packing and I was calling to see when Leonard would be available with the truck to help us."

Excited to hear the news about the baby, Edie's spirit rose even higher.

"Oh my goodness you got the little fella home? That's wonderful, how is he doing? Oh I just can't wait to see him!"

Julie sighed knowing that getting through this conversation could take days.

"He's just great Edie thank you. Now we have most everything packed do you know when your husband could lend a hand?"

Edie laughed.

"Well you just tell me when you want him and I will make sure his butt is over there! We're retired hon we can do this anytime you want."

Julie giggled but Edie wasn't through yet.

"He isn't doing nothing but just sittin' around the house getting on my nerves at times. Hell, I'll get him over this afternoon if you want, that is if I can get him off the couch.

I tell you I just can't figure that old geezer out. He was so ambitious and energetic when he was fixin up that house but now that it's done he has been about as useful around here as a pair of glasses to a blind man; so you just tell me when you're ready and we will be there."

Julie was touched with the offer.

"That is so nice of you; I really hate to trouble him with it."

Edie let out a loud laugh.

"Oh don't give it another thought sweetie. It will be good for him. It's about time he got off his butt and did something! He sure needs something to get his blood flowing again."

Julie thought for a moment.

"Well Edie, I have a doctor's appointment this afternoon. Today is the 23$^{rd}$ and I would like to be out by the end of the month so maybe we can set something up for next week. I'm not working at the moment so my schedule is pretty flexible."

Edie responded with her usual vigor.

"Well sweetie that sounds like a good plan to me. You just give him a call when you're ready, we'll be here. Now you take good care of that baby and I will look forward to seeing you soon."

Julie smiled and clicked off the phone. So far today is going perfectly. She hoped her good fortune would continue at the doctor's.

After a quick check on Robert she decided to pour another cup of coffee and relax while she could.

She sat on the couch staring at the momentous stack of boxes. She was pleased that the actual move could easily be done in one maybe two trips since all they were taking were the boxes, their clothes and other small miscellaneous items.

She did a mental checklist of where they stood at the moment in terms of preparations for the move.

They had packed everything they could and their help was in the wings waiting. So far so good she thought.

She had to at some point have the utilities transferred and make a trip to the post office to forward her mail. She would inform Larry when an actual date was set.

Furniture, yes they would also have to make that eventful trip to the consignment shop. The long list was intimidating. Once again the money Robert had left them would be a lifesaver.

She heard stirring coming from Karen's room telling her that her daughter was now awake.

Karen wandered into the kitchen and poured a glass of orange juice. She noticed her mother in the living room and joined her.

"Good morning mom."

Julie smiled and motioned for her daughter to join her on the couch.

"Good morning sweetheart. I just spoke with Edi; she said they were available to help us when ever we needed so we've got that covered.

With that in mind I figured we can go to the doctor, have lunch and then let's hit the consignment shop! The sooner we get all the furniture the sooner we can move. Are you up for this today?"

Karen nodded her head enthusiastically.

"Oh yeah, let's do this!"

It was now just past noon. They had enjoyed a quick breakfast and Karen showered and got dressed as Julie prepared Robert for the day ahead.

# 25

They arrived at the doctor's office at twelve forty-five, fifteen minutes before their scheduled appointment.

Julie checked in with the nurse at the front desk who phoned Dr. Hart letting him know they were there. She promised he would be out in a few minutes.

They sat down and both turned their attention to Robert, nestled comfortably in his mother's arms. He was very alert and again seemed to be enjoying their attention. His eyes switching constantly from his mother to his sister as they took turn tickling his face. Julie couldn't help but be astonished by his attentiveness and awareness.

He then slowly lifted his head as best he could to scan his new surroundings. Methodically he would look left, and then make the necessary adjustments to gradually turn his head to look right. There was no doubt he was making a conscious effort to familiarize himself with what was obviously a new world to him.

Julie's pleasure was gradually turning into concern. From what she had read a new born baby doesn't start holding his head up until six or seven weeks old, a milestone young Robert was still a few weeks away from.

Her relief that Robert's growing process was slowing down to normal was now again in question. If he had already developed such strong muscle control there could be no doubt that his unprecedented growth rate was continuing.

She took a deep breath and pondered the significance of this discovery. One the one hand she was of course very pleased that her son was strong and healthy but on the other hand she feared that this would lead to further scrutiny and testing once Dr. Hart noticed it and she was certain he would.

She heard her name called and noticed the receptionist waving her over. She handed Robert gently over to Karen and walked over to the desk.

"The doctor will see you now; he is in room three, you can go right in through these doors Miss Wells."

Julie smiled and motioned Karen to join her. Karen walked over and handed Robert back to his mother.

The three of them walked through the double doors and down the hall until they reached room three. Entering the room they found Dr. Hart smiling and motioning them in.

"Julie, so good to see you again, you are looking well. How has our young man been doing?"

Julie smiled and walked over to the doctor.

"He is doing just great doctor!"

Dr. Hart nodded his pleasure at the news and asked her to place Robert on the examining table. The doctor examined Robert who was lying on his back.

He got out his stethoscope and checked Robert's heartbeat jotting the findings in his folder.

He took out his ophthalmoscope and closely examined his eyes again making notes in his file. He then checked Robert's ears and mouth.

"He's looking good so far. Have you been keeping up on his growth chart Julie?"

Julie nodded and handed the doctor the chart. Dr. Hart studied the chart adding more notes to his folder.

"The growth here seems good and most importantly completely normal."

The doctor walked around the table and took note of Robert's reaction. Robert was painstakingly following the doctor's motion with his eyes, lifting his head ever so slightly to adjust his vision to the doctor's movements.

Dr. Hart took immediate notice of this. The doctor stopped and studied Robert whose attention was focused on the attending physician. The doctor turned to Julie with a puzzling expression.

"Did you see that?"

Julie was confused.

"Did I see what doctor?"

Dr. Hart kept his attention on Robert as he replied.

"The way he lifted his head and seemed to be following my motions was, well highly unusual. That takes an extraordinary amount of strength and muscle control. He is what...a month old?"

Julie's expression now turned to one of concern.

"Yes doctor, give or take a couple of days. Just what are you saying?"

The doctor thought for a moment.

"This type of strength and muscle control isn't commonly reached until between four and six months."

Julie turned to Karen who stood silently by her side. They shared a look of worry. Julie was at a loss for words. She had noticed the unusual behavior and feared it would raise questions.

"Is this something we should be concerned with doctor?"

Dr, Hart shook his head in confusion.

"Well, not so much concern but certainly intrigue, especially with him being three months premature. There is just no explaining how his muscles could have developed so quickly."

He took out his ophthalmoscope again and shined the light to the right of Robert's head. Robert's eyes adjusted and were glued on the object. The light was then moved to Robert's left and the infant slowly turned his head to follow it.

Dr. Hart was speechless. He made several notes in

his folder. The doctor leaned down and pressed lightly on various spots around Robert's neck. He then gently lifted Robert's head pressing lightly on his forehead and temples.

Julie scrutinized every facial expression the doctor made.

Dr. Hart's amazement was impossible to conceal. He rubbed his chin in thought as he continued to study Robert. He then, almost reluctantly, turned his attention to Julie. He knew she wouldn't like what he had to say.

"It seems the rapid development he was experiencing before birth is continuing. There is simply no medical explanation for this unusual phenomenon.

Now I don't mean to alarm you Julie, the baby is very healthy but just seems in a big hurry to grow up."

The doctor smiled and tickled Robert's chin in an effort to lighten the mood. He took a deep breath hesitantly continuing.

"This goes against everything they taught us in medical school but I'm leaning towards wanting to stunt his growth a bit.

We're going to stop those supplements and vitamins and go with just the straight formula until his next check up. We don't want to stimulate his system any more than it already is."

Julie nodded in agreement. She wanted to pursue the matter but wasn't sure of what questions to ask. She studied the doctor who was obviously in deep thought.

"So you can assure me there is nothing to worry about."

Dr. Hart thought for a moment before answering. He wanted to be careful how he approached his next idea.

"Well Julie, being totally honest with you, my thoughts now are now focusing on his brain development. It's important that his brain keep up with his body maturation. Every aspect of his growth needs to be in sync. I would be very curious as to what exactly is going on up there.

You have to understand all bodily functions originate from signals received from the brain and you must admit his body is getting some unusual premature signals. That tells me there must be an awful lot going on in that infant mind of his."

These words were upsetting to Julie for she knew what he was implying.

"Please doctor; tell me you are not suggesting more tests! Hasn't he been through enough already?"

Dr, Hart couldn't argue with that point. The poor child had already been run through the gamut. He had to convince her that he was only looking out for the best interest of the child.

It was times like this that he remembered his father advising against him going into the medical profession. 'Too many headaches and never any appreciation and if you screw up they sue you!' he used to say.

Perhaps that was good advice and he should have followed in his father's footsteps and become a teacher. The pay wouldn't have been as good but he would have slept better at night.

"I totally empathize with what you are saying Julie, he has indeed. But you must remember we are dealing with a very unique situation here.

Your son was born three months premature but rather than show a lack of development due to this handicap he has displayed remarkably the opposite. We are in uncharted territory here.

Up to this point he has shown no adverse effect but we can't be too careful because we simply have no idea what, if anything, this unprecedented maturation process could bring or just how long it will continue. I only want to insure your child's continued good health.

We want to know as much as possible about his physical and mental condition so we can best deal with what might lie ahead."

Julie knew the doctor was right and only doing his job but she couldn't help but pity her son having to be subjected to more poking and prodding.

She closed her eyes for a moment of silent reflection. Will this ever end she thought to herself. All she wanted was for Robert to live a normal healthy life.

Julie thought back to the years of mental health problems she had struggled through with Karen and how she had wished the same thing for her at the time. Robert was her second attempt and now this...why couldn't she just raise a normal child!

She then thought of the irony of the situation. While Robert senior had cured Karen's issues he was now the cause of Robert junior's problems.

Opening her eyes again she looked at her son lying peacefully on the examining table totally unaware of the dilemma...or was he...at this point she truly had her doubts.

She tried to formulate her thoughts into words the doctor would understand.

"I know that doctor; in my heart, I know you are only doing what you honestly feel is best for my son. But as his mother I so hate to see all he has to endure and the thought of further testing just breaks my heart. Just what do you feel we need to do?"

Dr. Hart cleared his throat unsure of how Julie would react to his proposal.

"I would suggest an MRI. This would clearly show us brain activity. As you know because you had one, it is unobtrusive and painless.

Julie, it would answer all our questions and only take a few minutes. I want to be sure his brain is functioning normally. With all that has been going on with his growth we can't ignore his most important organ, his brain.

If there is anything malignant going on in his brain we want to know as soon as possible so we can go forward with steps to correct it. This is not something you want to lallygag around with. In this case it is better safe than sorry.

Now of course I can't order this to be done I can only suggest it. You will make the final decision. Just understand we both want the same thing here."

Julie conceded that her frustration stemmed from her own personal annoyances and insecurities and not from the doctor's intentions.

She agreed to have the MRI done and they scheduled it for her next appointment in two weeks.

Dr. Hart's only closing words were for her to discontinue the use of the formula supplements, to continue to monitor his growth on the chart and to call if she had any other questions.

She picked up Robert, confirmed her next appointment at the front desk and the three of them walked to the car.

Karen, who had remained silent during the entire time, finally spoke up.

"Mom, just what is an MRI and why do they want Robert to have one?"

Julie sighed. She was so wrapped up in her own pity party she had neglected the stress that Karen must be under. She turned to her daughter and struggled to create a smile she knew Karen needed.

She tried to explain the procedure in terms her daughter would understand.

"An MRI is like an X-ray. They lay you on a table and you go through this tube that sends out rays that can see inside your body. It's not a big deal really, it doesn't hurt or anything."

Karen did her best to understand.

"Why does Robert have to have one? Do they think he is sick or something?"

Julie stopped walking and turned her complete attention to her daughter. The last thing she wanted was for Karen to worry about Robert's health when hopefully this was just a precautionary action."

"No sweetheart, that's not what they think at all. Robert is fine. Okay, how can I explain this....you know how Robert has been growing, I mean really fast, well they just want to make sure his brain is keeping up with it. There's nothing to worry about."

Karen wasn't totally convinced but accepted her mother's answer. She didn't know enough about it all to argue intelligently.

They reached the car, strapped Robert in and drove home. As she was driving Julie silently thought about what was next on the agenda.

She turned to Karen and spoke with determination.

"Well, Robert's next appointment is in two weeks and I have decided that we are going to be moved by then!"

Karen raised her eyebrows and smiled.

"Sounds like a good plan to me mom, let's do it!"

Resolved to her plan and pleased with her daughter's enthusiasm Julie put on some music and they spent the rest of the ride organizing their thoughts on the best way to accomplish their new mission.

She decided to get Karen and Robert home then make a trip to the consignment shop. Karen would be disappointed in not being able to go with her but it would be her job to baby-sit. She didn't want to carry Robert around for what could be hours at the consignment shop.

Once the furniture was purchased she would schedule

a delivery for next week and then explain everything to Larry.

She informed Karen of her plans and after a few minutes of disgruntled conversation Karen finally agreed after being reminded the sooner they get into their new home the sooner she would get her kitten.

They arrived home and Julie gave Robert his afternoon feeding remembering to omit the supplements. After changing his diaper she placed him in his crib and poured a cup of coffee collecting her thoughts before she left.

She told Karen that Robert was all taken care of and should be fine sleeping for a couple hours while she was gone. All she asked was for her to check on him every once in a while.

She then got out the list they had made and asked for Karen's input on various items taking notes on her thoughts.

Julie collected her purse and keys and took a quick glance in the mirror slightly adjusting her hair.

She promised Karen that if Robert was still alive and well when she got home they would get a pizza. Karen shook her head over her mother's exaggeration and insisted her mother take pictures of everything she bought so they could review them when she got home; her mother promised her she would. They both laughed and after a hug, Julie was off to the consignment store

As she was driving, Julie tried to recall the layout of their new home. She attempted to visualize the rooms, their size, and layout so she could get some idea of what furniture to purchase.

She again resolved herself to keeping the selection criteria to simply comfort and practicality and not so much worrying about lavish or stylish it might look.

Finally arriving at the consignment shop she got out

her list and prepared for the laborious task ahead. She was greeted at the door by a kindly older gentleman and after explaining her situation the two of them started the quest to furnish her new home.

"So basically, you are starting from scratch here?"

Julie meekly smiled and nodded. She handed the man the list and he examined it.

"Well I am sure we will have everything you need here, we have a huge selection. You've got quite a list here this is going to take some time but don't worry, I have all day and I will be happy to help you in any way I can."

He smiled at her and motioned for her to follow him to the first showroom. Julie was totally overwhelmed at the variety of furnishings the store offered. There were massive rooms filled with sofas, chairs, lamps and beds of all shapes, styles, and sizes.

Placed among them were decorative items such as paintings and house plants and other incidentals. In the next room were bookcases end tables and kitchen tables. It never ended she thought!

She took a deep breath and focused, vowing to get everything done in one trip however long it might take. She would attack the project one piece at a time.

Thankfully they had arranged the list by rooms so she could concentrate on one room at a time. She thought to herself; there is the rather large living room, the kitchen, three bedrooms, and two bathrooms.

She truly wished Karen could have joined her she would have been a great help. She gave that notion a second thought and conceded that maybe it was best she didn't for she was sure there would be major discussions involved in the selection of each item. This would only slow up the tedious task even further.

One by one she checked things off her list as she selected them, tabulating their cost and remembering to take pictures for Karen's approval later this evening. With each selection the salesman would place a small yellow "sold" tag on the item as he led her on to the next one.

She had to admit she was enjoying her time at the shop. It was like browsing through a museum of used furniture. She would get excited when she found a piece that appealed to her, imagining what it would look like in their new home. She was surprisingly pleased to notice all the furniture seemed to be in really good shape.

She found their prices to be very reasonable. Glancing at what was rapidly becoming a huge dollar amount she took a moment to silently thank Robert for taking the burden of how she would pay for all this out of the picture.

After an hour they took a break and the gentleman brought her a cup of coffee.

"I hope you are finding everything you need and like what you have selected."

Julie nodded her approval and thanked him for the unexpected, but much needed, cup of coffee.

She was on a roll now and actually found herself having a wonderful time. Exhilarated by her success and up to this point she checked her list for what was still remaining and spent the next hour and a half making her final selections.

Every entry on their list was scratched off and there had been many items added as she found things that were not on the list but simply too irresistible to pass up.

She was so excited at finding all the treasures and she couldn't wait to see them arranged in their new house. She was anxious to show Karen her selections.

Finally satisfied that she had everything they would need to get started in their new home Julie headed for the front counter where the man was waiting for her. She knew she had to leave or she would spend another hour just picking out even more treasures.

She paid the man who explained their delivery policy and asked her when and where she would like all this to be taken to.

Julie gave him the new address then thought about the delivery time. After plotting what still needed to be done before they could actually moved she chose a date five days ahead. This would give them enough time to contact Leonard and arrange a day for him to come over with the truck and for her to give Larry an actual date. This would also give her and Karen time to pack the remaining items and clean the apartment.

She knew everything wouldn't need to be unpacked at the new home when the furniture arrived so she felt comfortable with the date. She was sure they could at least have everything moved by then.

When she arrived back home Julie found Karen peacefully watching television. Checking on Robert she found him sound asleep in his crib. She returned to the living room smiling from ear to ear...Karen and Robert had both survived their first time alone together.

"Well big sister looks like you did a pretty good job babysitting. Did you have any problems?"

Karen shook her head.

"No mom, we were great. He slept most of the time. He started crying and I checked his diaper and changed it."

A look of shock came over Julie's face.

"You changed his diaper?"

Karen nodded with pride.

"Yeah I did mom, all by myself, how about that!"

Julie had to laugh and gave her daughter a huge hug.

"I am so proud of you Karen; see I knew you could do it! You certainly earned your pizza tonight!"

They enjoyed their pizza and were both relieved that

a date was finally set to move. This important step represented more than just a target date to both of them. What it represented was this was actually going to happen and they were about to embark on a wonderful new stage of their lives.

# 26

Julie called Leonard first thing in the morning and told him when the furniture would be delivered. He promised to be over early that morning to take all their belongings over and make sure they would be there when it arrived.

She finished her first cup of coffee and told Karen to keep an eye on Robert; she was going to go downstairs and inform Larry of their moving date.

She walked downstairs and noticed Larry behind the bar cleaning glasses. Looking up from his project Larry spotted her and smiled.

"Good morning Julie, how is everybody this morning? Let me grab us some coffee be right back."

Julie smiled and took a seat at the bar. Larry returned with two cups of coffee and grabbed a chair and sat across the bar from her.

"Everyone is doing just great Larry. I need to talk to you."

Larry nodded and took a sip of coffee.

"Okay now, what's up?"

Julie hesitated a moment trying to get the courage to tell Larry they had a moving date. It was a bittersweet moment for her. She was thrilled at finally moving into the dream house she had been wanting for so long, but on the other hand, she would miss Larry as a landlord. He had become not only a great landlord but a close friend to both her and Karen.

He had been so kind to them over the past seven years they had lived there. He had been the perfect landlord. When anything needed repair he was always there in a timely manner to fix it. He would give her rides when her car was down and even gave her a job.

Larry was so sweet to give her all the time off of work for her pregnancy, taking all her shifts himself.

He always understood the few times she had been late on her rent and had never raised the rent since they had moved in.

And finally he was responsible for making her dream come true for he had found them their new home. This was at the personal cost of knowing he would lose a tenant; his last one since he had already lost Robert and never filled the vacancy.

She took a sip of coffee and cleared her throat. She spoke with a heavy heart.

"Larry, this is hard for me, I have so enjoyed having you as a landlord, and it's been a pleasure being your tenant."

Larry noticed her struggle and anticipating where the conversation was going he jumped in and tried to help.

"Julie, we both knew this day would come sooner or later. I am sincerely happy for you. It's the best thing for you and Karen. I know you have been wishing you had a larger place and now with the baby it has become a necessity.

I was so glad when I learned Leonard and Edi had this place available. It will be perfect for you and your family. So, when's the big day?"

Julie giggled recognizing his effort.

"We're moving on Thursday Larry. It's all set up. I purchased all the furniture today, it's going to be delivered and Leonard is coming over with the truck Thursday morning to help."

Larry smiled and patted her hand.

"You're going to love the place I just know it and you will enjoy Leonard as a landlord, he's a good man. Edi will be a great help to you as well. She told me how much she thinks of you. I'm sure you will all be happy there."

Julie took a sip of coffee and giggled at the thought of Edi.

"Oh she is quite a lady that's for sure and Leonard was so kind to offer his truck and his help, Karen and I just think the world of both of them!

I can't thank you enough for making this dream of ours come true Larry. If you wouldn't have suggested Leonard's house this never would have happened.

Oh, Karen starts school in a couple of weeks and I would love to come back to work. I would have to work evenings after Karen came home from school so she could watch Robert while I am at work if that would be alright. I know you certainly deserve a break."

Larry grinned and nodded.

"I was hoping you would say that Julie. Evenings would be perfect for me as well, Claudia has hinted many times her displeasure at me being gone every evening working. She misses the days of us going out to dinner or a movie, she will be thrilled.

First things first, you get all settled in your new home and let me know when you can start, no hurry.

You're going to make a lot of customers happy seeing a pretty face behind the bar again; they are getting tired of looking at this old mug all the time."

Julie chuckled and thanked him again. She assured him she would keep in touch. She returned to her apartment and found Karen in the kitchen feeding Robert a bottle.

"Well just look at you big sister; I think you're getting the hang of this, great job sweetheart!"

Karen smiled with pride and handed Robert over to his mother.

"I just talked to Larry, he is so sweet. He is fine with Thursday being our moving date.

Now we still have a lot of work to do before we actually move. We have to pack everything that is still out and I want to get this place nice and clean for Larry, it's the least we can do."

Julie gently kissed Robert on the forehead and placed him in his crib.

For the next three days Julie and Karen worked in perfect unison. Julie proceeded to continue packing while Karen cleaned.

Karen was a ball of fire cleaning. She scrubbed all the baseboards, vacuumed and mopped all the floors, cleaned the kitchen and bathroom and even wiped down all the walls.

Julie enjoyed watching her daughter work; she could tell how excited she was about moving. It was a rare sight seeing Karen so motivated.

She wasn't sure if it was the prospect of living in a nice large home or the thought of getting her kitten that was motivating her but she was thankful something was.

Julie got more boxes and packed everything that didn't move. She cleared out the closets, bagged all their clothes and collected all the linens. She boxed everything in the kitchen save the coffee maker because she knew she was going to need that.

Having packed all their provisions the girls survived on pizza and sandwiches she got from the bar. A new mountain of boxes now dominated the now bare living room.

Exhausted, they collapsed on the sofa and surveyed the now barren apartment. They spent the evening enjoying the deluxe pizza Julie had ordered and watched television.

Moving day was tomorrow and in spite of their

weariness they were both too hyped up to sit still. Julie put her arm around Karen and smiled.

"Well, I think we are ready to move! Sweetheart you were an incredible help thank you! Tomorrow is the big day.

Leonard will be over somewhere around eight in the morning and we will get everything over there. Then all we have to do is wait for the furniture to arrive which they said will be between two and four. I can't believe we are really doing this!

We had better get to bed and try and get some sleep we've got a busy day tomorrow!"

Julie and Karen went into Karen's bedroom. They both checked on Robert who was sleeping soundly, unaware of the excitement.

Julie hugged her daughter and retired into her bedroom hoping she could somehow manage to get some sleep. She had set the alarm for six thirty, way too early for her liking but worth the inconvenience for the final reward it would bring them she thought.

She rethought everything they had done up to this point. She accessed a mental checklist and crossed off one task at a time. She retraced every step one by one.

Finally convincing herself that they had done everything they could she closed her eyes and prayed for sleep. She was anxious but it was a positive anxiousness.

Six thirty arrived hours before she had hoped it would. She slowly sat up in bed and closed and opened her eyes repeatedly hoping the action would send a signal to the brain that it was time to start functioning.

Taking a long determined deep breath she mustered the motivation to get out of bed and walk to Karen's room and first check on Robert then get her daughter awake and motivated.

Much to her surprise she found Karen sitting on her

bed holding her brother! He was nestled in her arms wide awake. He seemed totally content listening to his big sister talk to him softly.

Tears of joy flowed from Julie's eyes as she watched them in total bliss. She stood frozen at the door watching them in silence until Karen noticed her.

"Good morning mom!"

Still dumbfounded Julie found it hard to reply but finally managed to utter a response.

"Good morning sweetheart! Well look at you two! Is everything okay?"

Karen smiled and nodded that everything was just fine. She first addressed her brother.

"Hey little brother, your mommy is here, aren't you going to say good morning?"

Julie was actually fearful he might just do that. She walked over and took her son.

"Good morning handsome. Now just what are doing awake so early; just chatting with your sister? Let's get that diaper changed and get us all some breakfast!"

Karen grinned.

"I think he's excited about moving. I was half awake and heard him kind of gurgling so I thought I would pick him up and tell him about today!"

Julie shook her head in disbelief. She was so proud of her daughter. This was the perfect start for the day.

This innocent event was an undeniable symbol and cemented in her mind that their lives moving ahead were going to be just great.

She was now totally convinced that the move was truly a gift from heaven and that any doubts she might have had about Karen being a good sister were completely removed.

She changed Robert's diaper and fed him a bottle before laying him back in his crib.

All that remained unpacked in the way of breakfast food was cereal and milk so she and Karen made the best of that. Julie was so thankful she had the insight not to pack the coffee maker for she sure needed it now.

After breakfast they both showered and got dressed and Julie took one last look around the apartment for any stray items they had neglected to pack.

Pleased that she didn't find anything she got another cup of coffee and relaxed with Karen on the couch. She was going to let Robert sleep for as long as he could because there would be enough excitement for everyone later.

The clock was moving at a snail's pace. Julie clung to her cell phone waiting for Leonard's call. She then got up and walked through the apartment one last time, a sort of farewell tour. She casually walked into each room reliving the many memories she had with it.

Her heart was filled with nostalgia and many wonderful memories. She thought back on all the many moments, both good and bad, that she and Karen had there.

She again thought of how kind Larry had been to both of them over the years and how she would miss him. These thoughts were tempered by the knowledge of her continuing to work for him even after the move.

She glanced at Karen still sitting on the couch. She could see the excitement in her eyes. She then said a silent prayer to be shared by God and Robert thanking both of them for their part in making what had once been just a dream, a reality.

Julie's reflections were dramatically interrupted by her phone ringing. Startled but excited she answered it on the first ring in hopes it was Leonard. Looking on the screen her expectations were met.

"Hello Leonard I've been waiting for your call."

Her greeting was met with jovial laughter.

"Good morning Julie, I'm on my way. The misses is coming along for comic relief. We should be there in about ten minutes. Are you ready for us?"

Julie was all smiles. She had to laugh at his comment about Edi coming with him. She wished she could have been in the car with them because she knew Edi would have a few things to say to him about that remark.

"Oh you bet we are! I'll see you soon!"

Just before she clicked off the phone she could hear Edi in the background.

"You sit tight doll, me and the old fart will be right there! We'll have you moved in no time!"

She chuckled as she shut off her phone. This should be interesting she thought.

She alerted Karen to their pending arrival and poured a cup of coffee.

"Okay, get your shoes on and check your room just to make sure you didn't forget anything. I want this to go smoothly, and get Robert up. Change his diaper and gather all his things then bring him out to the kitchen."

Julie took her coffee and checked the living room just ensuring all the boxes were ready to go. She could hear Karen in her room grumbling about having to change the diaper.

Satisfied that everything seemed to be in order, Julie prepared a bottle for Robert. Karen brought Robert out assuring her mother she did indeed change his diaper.

Julie gave Robert his bottle and no sooner had they finished than her cell phone went off. She answered and was greeted by Edi.

"Hey doll, we're downstairs in the bar where are you? Leonard and Larry are chatting away and it will only be a matter of time before Larry offers him a whiskey and I want to get this started before he decides to indulge in one. Lord oh Mighty that would be the end of everything because I know he wouldn't stop at just one!

He's worthless when he's sober we wouldn't get anything done if he had a couple of shots. I know what would happen, those two would be gabbing all night and leave all the work to us womenfolk!"

Julie was laughing hysterically.

"We're just upstairs Edi; I'll be down in a second!"

Julie updated Karen with the latest and handed Robert to her as she raced downstairs.

Arriving at the bar she found Larry behind the bar chatting with Leonard both enjoying a beer as Edi was strolling through the bar obviously displeased at the morning's recent events.

Larry was the first to notice her arrival.

"Julie looks like your moving crew has arrived!"

Edi then noticed her and quickly walked over.

"Thank goodness you're here hon, just in the nick of time! My better half seems to have forgotten why we came over. My Lord it's only eight-o-clock and they are hitting it already! We better get moving fast!"

Julie gave Edi a warm hug and they both walked over to the bar. Just as Leonard was about to lift his glass Edi took it from him.

"Now you listen here, we've got work to do; we don't have time for this nonsense! This poor girl is depending on us. I'm surprised at you...but then again no I'm really not. And you Lawrence, don't you be encouraging him! I know how you two are when you get together.

Besides, it's eight in the morning; who in their right mind starts drinking at that hour...not that I would ever accuse you of being in your right mind you old geezer!"

Larry and Julie laughed in unison. Leonard got up from his seat at the bar and addressed his wife.

"Oh come on now woman can't a man enjoy a beer

with his brother in law? You know we don't get to see each other often anymore. We were just going to have one before we got started for crying out loud. And another thing, hell no I'm not in my right mind...I married you didn't I?"

Edi playfully slapped her husband on the shoulder.

"Oh don't you start with me and you have never had just one in your cotton picking life Leonard especially when you're with him. Guess that's what I get for marrying a man whose brother in law owns a bar. Now let's get this lady moved!"

Edi turned to Julie who was trying to remain composed through the exchange.

"Men, they're worthless I told you, see what I mean? That one there is going to be the death of me one of these days but I won't give him that satisfaction! He's not going to get rid of me that easy.

Oh I love that old fogy with all my heart, sometimes I can't understand why, but don't tell him that, it would go to his head and that's the last thing I need."

Julie couldn't let that remark go without answering.

"Edi, I think he already knows that."

Edi nodded.

"Yeah you're probably right or why else would I have stuck with him for all these years. Oh he's not stupid even though he acts that way sometimes. He has been smart enough to stay with me!"

Julie just shook her head and smiled. She had really grown fond of Edi. Leonard finally joined them.

"Alright Julie are you all packed? Guess we had better get this project started before the old girl has a conniption."

Edi couldn't let this comment pass without a retort.

"Oh you don't want to see one of my conniptions...old girl my butt!"

Julie tried to hold back further laughter and assured Leonard that she was all ready to go. She inwardly smiled at their banter. It was obvious the two of them were so in love and she so enjoyed their comical exchanges.

She found herself holding back a tear and replaced it with a melancholy sigh as she reflected on how she missed the whimsical banter she and Robert used to have. Forcing herself to regroup, she escorted them upstairs to her apartment.

Karen was sitting on the couch with Robert when they entered the apartment. Edi immediately took notice of them and walked quickly over to see the baby.

"Oh Leonard come over here and look at this beautiful baby!"

Leonard begrudgingly walked over to appease his wife. He glanced at Robert and then at his wife.

"Yep, that's a nice looking baby you have there Julie what is his name?"

Julie smiled.

"His name is Robert; he was named after his father."

Without asking Edi gently took Robert from Karen and just started talking to him.

"Oh aren't you just the cat's pajamas! Nice to meet you Robert I'm Edi and this here is my husband Leonard. You're going to be seeing a lot of us; it is a pleasure to meet you! You are just a living doll!

Your mommy is moving you all into a nice big house and you are going to be so happy there!"

Befuddled Karen just looked at her mother who silently gave her approval. Edi returned Robert to Karen and walked over to Julie.

"Now doll any time you need a baby sitter you just let me know! I'll take real good care of this little fella."

Leonard had to take the opportunity to get a jab in.

"Oh yeah, she's great with kids, it's just adults she struggles with."

Edi flashed her husband a belligerent look.

"Oh now you just hush! Let's get this happy family moved!"

Thinking about what Julie has just said Edi put curiosity ahead of tact and had to ask her something.

"Hon, you mentioned Robert was named after his father; I don't mean to pry but are you two still together? I can't remember you mentioning him."

Julie closed her eyes in sorrow; this was a subject she was hoping to avoid. She should have known it would come up at some point. She answered the question straight forwarded.

"No, we're not."

Edi shook her head in dismay.

"Oh doll, that's just not right...

Leonard interrupted his wife taking exception to the inquiry.

"Edith, would you mind your own business for once?' That's none of our concern."

Edi scowled at him.

"Leonard a young boy needs his father, its important!"

Julie just wanted to end this discussion.

"It's okay Leonard. Edi, his father passed away about a year ago. He never got to meet his son."

Edi lowered her head in sadness.

"Oh dear, I'm so sorry doll. I shouldn't have said anything. Sometimes I say things without thinking as I am sure you have noticed already."

Julie walked over to Edi to console her.

"No Edi, it's alright you didn't know."

Leonard scolded his wife.

"Now are you happy? Shame on you Edith; please

excuse my wife she doesn't know when to shut up at times."

Surprisingly, and completely out of character, there was no reply from Edi for the criticism; she knew, for once, her husband was right.

# 27

Leonard and Edi had all their belongings taken to their home in only an hour and a half; three trips in his truck did the job. They were both so helpful doing practically all the heavy lifting themselves. What wonderful people she thought. They were renewing her faith in the future, she was sure she would enjoy being their tenant.

Everyone was glad the distance between the two residences was short, cutting down on the time.

They stacked all the boxes neatly in the living room and Edi helped Julie sort out their clothes putting them in the correct bedrooms while Leonard sorted through the marked boxes placing them in the right rooms.

Leonard then made a quick trip to the connivance store bringing back doughnuts and refreshments for everyone while Edi helped Julie arrange things in the kitchen.

Karen rummaged through the boxes and found the diapers, changing Robert while Edi and Julie worked feverishly in the kitchen.

Taking a short break to enjoy the coffee and doughnuts Julie took the opportunity to give Robert a bottle. She studied her son as he was eating. He would take a few sips from his bottle then stop.

His eyes were wide open and alert. There was a strange intenseness about them. His expression was one of earnest if it were possible for such an infant mind to experience that.

He slowly turned his head in every which direction as if scanning his new environment with great interest. Julie couldn't help but feel he was absorbing everything, processing the information with keen awareness.

It was if she wasn't even there, his attention was completely focused on scrutinizing his new surroundings.

This wasn't the first time she felt this about her son. She had seen that intensity before. His father had a similar acuteness in his expression. The first time she actually took notice of it was when he saw their Christmas tree for the first time.

Anytime he ran across anything that he deemed odd or unusual, which was often, he would take a moment to study it, analyzing it with keen interest; she remembered thinking to herself at the time how she had never seen such intensity before or since...until now. Again she marveled at how closely Robert's eyes resembled his fathers.

This sensation gave Julie mixed emotions. She was very happy Robert appeared healthy and alert but she had to admit to herself there was also something rather unnerving, something inexplicitly unsettling about it as well.

She wished she could crawl inside his infant mind and understand exactly what was going on inside. She then remembered they had an MRI scheduled for next week and how she had initially balked at the idea. Giving the matter more thought she convinced herself that it might actually answer that very question.

Julie thanked Edi and Leonard for all they had done and told them the furniture delivery would be coming soon.

Edi said goodbye to Robert and Karen and then walked over to Julie.

"I just wanted to apologize if I had said anything earlier that upset you, Julie. I certainly didn't mean to. I know I talk too much at times; Leonard reminds me of that daily but I would never say or do anything to intentionally upset you.

I am so happy to have you living here and just remember Leonard and I are here to help you in any way we can."

Julie smiled and gave Edi a hug as she and Leonard left. She went into the kitchen and explored through the yet unpacked boxes for something easy to make for lunch.

Finally managing to find the bread and peanut butter she decided that would suffice for today. Karen and her sat down on the floor and enjoyed lunch.

She and Karen set up Robert's crib in his bedroom upstairs and she kissed him as she placed him down for a nap.

Returning downstairs she found Karen busy in her new bedroom unpacking boxes. The first thing she had unpacked was her CD player which she had already turned on and was enjoying her music as she sat in the middle of the floor. It was great to know the electricity had been turned on as promised.

Pleased that her daughter seemed amused for the time being she decided to let her continue with her project and she would set her sights on finding the coffee and coffee maker. She needed an energy boost before the furniture delivery people came.

She decided to take her coffee out to the front porch. Sitting on the steps she surveyed the area. She couldn't help but smile as she enjoyed the fresh air from the steps of her porch. She couldn't believe it was actually theirs!

She glanced to her left and thought that would be the perfect spot for the swing she had been wanting since she was a child. She beamed with joy watching the birds fly in and out of the beautiful pine tree in the corner of the lot. Edi was right; their songs filled the air with beautiful melodies.

She had always loved birds and thought back to how

she and her mother would enjoy all the birds that would flock to their birdfeeder as a child. She remembered Karen telling her many times about how she would love to have a bird feeder and vowed to get one so Karen and her could continue the tradition.

Finishing her coffee she elected to go and get one more cup. Just as she was standing up a large moving van slowed down in front of the house. A minute later it backed up and pulled into the yard. Two men in overalls got out of the cab and approached her.

"Excuse me, ma'am, are you Julie Wells?"

Excited that they had arrived Julie nodded. The man smiled and nodded to his partner.

"Oh, great, then we have the right place. I'm Dave and this is Jerry, we are from Williamson Consignment shop. We have a whole lot of furniture for you!"

Julie triumphantly raised her fist into the air. Her dream was coming true!

"Oh I am so happy to see you. I'm afraid it is only me and my daughter here so I don't think we will be of much help to you."

Dave smiled and shook his head.

"Don't worry about that ma'am. You just tell us where you want something and we will take care of all the work. It's all covered under your service contract, that's what we're here for."

For the next three hours, the men laboriously moved in all the furniture placing it exactly where Julie had directed. As the final chair was finally brought in Julie thanked the men with a glass of iced tea and bid them on their way.

Their new home was now totally furnished. All that remained to do was to gradually unpack the astounding number of boxes that lay scattered in every room.

Julie shook her head in amazement at all the junk

they had acquired over the years. Funny she thought; it didn't seem like that much before it was packed. This unpacking process could take years she thought! She was so thankful they had labeled the boxes to the appropriate rooms.

She marveled at the size of their new home thinking how crowded their old apartment was with all their junk and now she had more room than what she knew what to do with! She was confident that she and Karen would put it to good use eventually.

She ran upstairs to take care of Robert who, incredibly enough, had remained asleep during the entire process. She changed his diaper and took him downstairs to give him a bottle. Checking out each room as they progressed to the kitchen Julie spoke aloud to her son.

"Look, Robert, this is our new bathroom, isn't it nice, and this is my bedroom and we're going to go downstairs to our nice new kitchen."

Julie had to laugh as she caught herself chatting with him. She then thought she really needed to get out more.

The thought of returning to work was now more appealing than ever; not so much for the money it would bring them but for the social interaction she found herself desperately seeking.

Julie and Karen spent the next few days dutifully sorting through boxes putting things in their proper places. They found the excitement of being settled in their beautiful hew home was providing all the motivation and energy they needed to accomplish the task. They would work late into the night narrowing down the remaining boxes by the hour.

Karen had her bedroom all set up very nicely while Julie was pleased with her new kitchen and all the counter and cupboard space it gave her.

Both bathrooms were all squared away and all their clothes neatly hung in their respective closets.

Julie completed Robert's room by hanging his interstellar mobile above his crib. He took immediate notice of this. He lifted his head and looked upward studying its motions with seemingly great interest.

The day of Julie's next appointment with Dr. Hart finally arrived. It promised to be a very busy day. Karen starts school on Monday and she had to take her shopping. Buying school supplies would be the easy part, the difficulty would arise from the two- hour endurance test at the mall clothes shopping.

She knew she would be tortured with a constant bombardment of phrases such as 'Mom this looks stupid' 'Mom I'm not wearing this!' 'Mom; but all the girls are wearing these'. She laughed to herself thinking of all the joys of raising a teenage daughter.

She tried to remember if she were that crazy when she was that age and assured herself that she probably was.

After her third cup of coffee, she managed to shower and get dressed and even put on a touch of makeup just for effect.

She had told Karen to get Robert ready and surprisingly the two of them were in the kitchen waiting when she exited the shower.

Both were dressed and Karen had assured her she had changed Robert's diaper. After a quick verification, she was satisfied that was a true statement. Julie fed Robert a bottle and checked her purse to insure she had put Robert's growth chart in it.

Grabbing her purse and keys the three of them got in the car and headed for the doctor's office. Karen again sat in the back seat monitoring Robert in his car seat.

No sooner than he had been fastened in his car seat Robert began to fuss and fidget.

Karen took immediate notice of this strange behavior and tried to settle him down. She quipped jokingly.

"I don't think he wants to go to the doctor mom."

Julie turned her attention to her son. His usual smile was now replaced by what one could almost call a frown. He was obviously not happy.

She thought about what her daughter had just said. Could she actually be on to something? Could Robert really understand that he was going to the doctor for more testing?

She quickly dismissed that outrageous notion. Her rational mind tried to talk her out of that line of thought. Two-month-old babies simply do not have the ability to understand life to that degree yet. What bothered her was that Robert had already done a number of things normal two-month-old babies don't do.

As she drove she couldn't get that thought out of her mind. What scared her was she wasn't sure just what abilities her son might actually possess. She had to admit this behavior was most unusual for him.

She thought back to their morning. Robert's diaper had been changed and he was fed so neither of those could be the origin of his current displeasure. He seemed his usual happy self until they got into the car. She had Karen readjust the seat belt to ensure it wasn't too tight for him.

He continued to squirm in his seat as Karen softly talked to him trying to calm him down. Her consolation had no effect on him.

"He's sure upset about something mom, this isn't like him at all. Do you think he really knows he is going to the doctors? I mean, is that even possible?"

Julie just shook her head in bewilderment.

"I don't know sweetheart, I don't know what is possible anymore. Your little brother seems to have already taken the realm of possibility into the stratosphere, or should I say twelve light-years past it!"

Karen looked at Robert then at her mother in puzzlement.

"But how can a baby this young be so aware of things?"

Julie tried her best to answer that question intelligently.

"Well sweetheart, as much as we might like to try and forget about it, Robert is not a normal baby, you know as well as I do he is not entirely human.

He has genes that originate from a race of people that could be very far advanced from us not only intellectually but perhaps medically as well.

We both saw how quickly he grew even before he was born! I can't begin to even fathom what his genes might be capable of."

Karen again studied Robert as he fidgeted in his car seat.

"Mom, this is starting to freak me out. I understand all you said but the thought of my little brother being an alien is still rather creepy."

This talk infuriated Julie. Stopping at a red light she turned and glared at Karen. She couldn't have this kind of dissension, as innocent as it might be; she had to nip this in the bud before it got out of hand.

"Karen Renee, stop that right now! We are going to love and raise Robert just as if he were a normal human! You're being foolish and I won't have it!"

Karen retaliated.

"But mother, he isn't a normal human! Who knows what freaky things he might do as he gets older?"

Julie's patience had run out. She was abhorred at her daughter's thinking.

"You're not too big for me to take you over my knee right now so stop it! I will not tolerate you thinking like that!

He is your little brother, your flesh and blood and you will love him for who he is! Do I make myself clear? We will not have this discussion again young lady!"

Realizing she wasn't going to get anywhere pursuing this Karen had to mockingly reply to her mother's last statement.

"He may have some of my blood in him but he's got some pretty weird blood to go with it!"

The light turned green and Julie forced herself to ignore Karen's last barb. She didn't need anything else to worry about, there was already too much on her plate.

She now had to worry about how deeply seated these anxieties were in Karen's mind. She couldn't help but be concerned about what if any long term effects they might have.

Julie searched her soul, first for strength and then for common sense. She knew her daughter's heart and this wasn't like her.

She knew Karen loved her little brother and conceded that Karen's apprehension was nothing that she secretly wasn't harboring deep within herself as well. This was a difficult admission to make. She had always had an inward fear of the future and what unknowns it may hold but recent events have magnified that uneasiness.

How could she not ponder with uncertainty their future raising a child who is part alien? In reality, who really knew what he would be capable of? Of course, that would cause some concern especially in the mind of a fifteen-year-old.

She had to find a way to explain to Karen that she shared her apprehension in a way that it wouldn't be condoning it. She felt that maybe by admitting the same concerns it would lighten the burden for Karen and they could work together at overcoming them.

They pulled into the parking lot of the medical building

and Karen started to unfasten Robert's seatbelt. Julie turned off the ignition and stopped her.

"Sweetheart, listen to me for a moment please."

Still stinging from defeat, Karen reluctantly turned her attention to her mother while Julie tried to come up with the words she wanted her daughter to hear.

"I know you have a lot on your mind now, we both do. In fact, that is the very reason I want to talk to you. It's important I be honest with you. I'm going to be brutally honest with you and trust me this isn't easy to admit.

You have to know that everything you're feeling, everything you re fearing...well; I share every one of those feelings. Yeah, you heard me right.

I suppose that is something a mother should never feel about her own child and I do feel guilty about it but of course I have questions.

Neither of us knows what to expect in the future. Robert is different from us, it's true, and we have to face up to that but think about it this way. Robert senior was different from us as well, in the very same ways, and he was a warm, loving, compassionate man. He never gave us any reason to fear him; he loved us both very much. There is no reason to believe Robert junior will be any different.

It is natural to fear the unknown but remember we are both experiencing the very same thing with the very same apprehensions. You and I have always been a team, working together and this will be no different.

I'm sorry I blew up at you but you have to understand we can not approach this with that attitude. Robert is my son and your little brother. He can't help his genetic makeup. We need to love him and I promise you he will return that love.

We can't be afraid of the differences only cherish them as part of him. Give him a chance Karen that's all I'm asking you; don't judge him and for Heaven's sake don't fear him. Never forget that I share your apprehensions and anytime you need to talk about it I will be here. Now, are we okay with this?"

Karen was speechless, obviously stunned by her mother's openness. She thought for a moment.

"You really feel the same way mom?"

Julie was at least glad Karen had listened to her. She was hoping her honesty wasn't a mistake.

"Yeah, of course I'm a bit nervous about raising a child who, well, isn't all human. Raising a normal child is difficult enough neither of us knows what challenges may be ahead but we are in this together and we are going to make this work.

We're going to love that little boy with all our hearts and do what is necessary to create a very happy family."

Karen finally smiled.

"You are awesome mom. I know that it must have been hard for you to admit that to me and I want you to know it has given me such strength and encouragement. You know I love Robert and I didn't mean to say anything bad about him. I will do anything to make him happy."

Julie could finally breathe comfortably again. Karen released Robert's seatbelt and gave him a kiss. She handed Robert to his mother and smiled. Julie kissed her son then put her arm around Karen and gave her a hug. She was so proud of the mature young lady Karen had become. She looked down at Robert who was still fidgety in her arms.

"You've got quite a big sister little man. Now to find out what's bugging you?"

Karen chuckled and the three of them went into the office. Julie checked in with the receptionist and they waited to be called.

Within minutes Dr. Hart opened the door, peered out

and waved them over. The three of them walked over and were greeted by the doctor.

"Good morning Julie good to see you as always. How's the little guy this morning?"

Julie glanced quickly at her son and then turned her attention to the doctor.

"Well doctor, he's a little frigidity this morning. He doesn't seem to be in a very good mood. I can't understand it; this isn't like him at all. He's always so happy and content but not today.

His diaper has been changed and he ate a good breakfast but something is just bothering him."

Dr. Hart smiled and looked into Robert's eyes.

"We all just have those days when we are out of sorts, I'm sure it's nothing. Let's go back to the room and see if we can find out what's troubling him."

The four of them walked into the examining room and Julie placed Robert on the table where he immediately began to appear very antsy.

The doctor studied Robert's unusual behavior before starting his examination.

"He does seem a little jittery this morning."

He checked Robert's heart, eyes, ears, nose, and throat. He gently examined Robert's neck and head and hands. He jotted down a series of notes in Robert's folder.

He took particular notice of Robert's heart rate. A red flag popped up, Robert's heart was beating at an unusually high rate.

He was puzzled at this but based on Robert's other vitals there didn't appear to be any reason for concern at this point. The doctor took Robert's pulse and was satisfied it was normal. This finding added confusion as it didn't coincide with the normal effects a high heart rate should have; normally if a patient was experiencing a rapid heart rate that would be mirrored with a higher pulse. This wasn't the case.

What ever was the cause of the high heart rate was having no ill effect on Robert's system. His system seemed, on the surface, to be either adjusting to the high heart rate or accepting it completely. This went against everything he had ever learned in medical school.

He didn't want to alarm Julie just yet; he wanted the results of the MRI to see if they might add some insight to this anomaly. He sugar coated the results for now.

"Everything looks good so far. He's strong and appears very healthy. I can tell he's been growing. Do you have the growth chart? I would like to study it on a day by day basis."

Julie reached in her purse and handed the doctor the growth chart which she had continued to fill out daily.

Doctor Hart studied the chart with great interest.

"I'm pleased with his growth here, seems perfectly normal. I see you filled out his height and weight this morning so we won't have to do that."

Julie was relieved that everything seemed good so far. Her anxiety now focused on the pending MRI and what surprises the results might bring.

"Doctor, will he still be having the MRI today?"

Dr. Hart nodded as he continued to study Robert's eyes.

"Yes, I have everything all set up. Now the results usually take a couple of days but the radiologist who is doing the test is an old colleague of mine, we met at medical school and I asked him to push the results up as a favor to me. Oh he through a fit about it but promised he would have the results back to me by the end of the day; I'll call you when I get them."

This pleased Julie to no end. She hated waiting for

anything in general and was never very patient especially when her family was involved.

She knew the reason for the MRI was to check brain activity and she couldn't help but be nervous about what it may find. She totally empathized with Robert being jittery because she was just as jittery.

Her thoughts were interrupted by the nurse entering the room.

"We have everything ready for you doctor. It has been set to tesla 7 as you requested. Dr. Macut is ready for you."

Dr. Hart thanked her and gently picked up Robert.

"Okay Julie, we're going down and getting this taken care of. It will take about an hour so. I assure you Robert is in good hands, Dr. Macut is a wonderful man, like I said before, we go way back and may I add he is an incredible radiologist.

Why don't you and Karen go to the cafeteria and get a cup of coffee and something to eat. I would say come back up here in about an hour and we should be finished."

Julie nodded her head in reluctant agreement. As much as she wanted to be with her son during the test she knew that desire would be balked at. She gave her son a kiss and took Karen's hand and they took the elevator down to the cafeteria.

# 28

Walking into the cafeteria Julie immediately conceded to two things; first it was very busy. The room was crowded with doctors, nurses and she assumed visitors all scampering around in every which way hastily getting their lunches.

She hated crowds and was hoping for an hour of peaceful solitude with her daughter as they nervously awaited the results of Robert's test. They would just have to make the best of it. She scanned the room and was satisfied there were available tables to sit at.

Secondly, she accepted the fact that she wasn't really hungry. Her stomach was in knots, she was nervous about the test.

The nurse had used a term she wasn't familiar with, 'tesla'. At this point anything she didn't understand really concerned her. There have been too many intangibles already she didn't need any more confusion! She wanted to know exactly what that was and cursed herself silently for not asking Dr. Hart before they left. She decided to research the word on her phone once they got settled with their meals.

She squeezed Karen's hand and smiled the best she could as they approached the buffet line.

"What are you in the mood for sweetheart? It looks like they have quite a variety here!"

Karen sighed and took a deep breath.

"Oh I don't know mom, I'm not really hungry."

Julie totally empathized with her daughter for she was feeling the very same way.

"I understand sweetheart, I'm not really hungry either. I know we are both concerned about Robert's tests but we did skip breakfast so we should get something in our stomachs. He is in good hands, we can't do anything more for him so let's see what looks good."

They got trays and slowly walked down the buffet line. Julie finally talked Karen into getting a cheeseburger and fries while she decided on a small salad.

After paying for their selections they found a table in the corner as far from the maddening crowd as they could get and sat down.

Julie starred at her salad stirring it aimlessly with her fork trying to entice her appetite. Karen ogled her cheeseburger with no real interest. Karen broke the silence.

"Mom, just what are these tests Robert is having today?"

Julie took a deep breath trying to word an answer.

"Well sweetheart, Robert has been maturing so rapidly, both mentally and to some extent physically, that the doctors just want to be certain everything is alright.

Now you and I both know the reason for this rapid growth but you have to remember the doctors do not. So what they are doing today is checking his brain to make sure it is healthy."

Karen processed her mother's words and replied.

"So what are they going to do to his brain today? Why can't they just leave him alone...he's fine. He's healthy isn't he?"

Julie took Karen's hand and smiled.

"Yes, he's fine. They just are going to examine his brain with some kind of x-ray just to ensure that everything is as it should be. There is nothing to worry about. We all want to be sure Robert is progressing normally."

Karen wasn't satisfied with her mother's answer.

"But mom, you and I both know he isn't and we both

know why. Won't this show up in the test results and raise, well, difficult questions?"

Julie just shook her head in amazement over her daughter's insight.

"We'll deal with that if and when it arises, now eat your lunch!"

Karen slowly nodded her head and reluctantly took a small bite from her sandwich.

Julie finally forced herself to take a couple of bites of her salad before pushing it aside and concentrating on her iced tea. Her heart just wasn't into eating. She remembered she wanted to research the word 'tesla' the nurse had used.

She pulled out her phone and did an internet search. She discovered that the word 'tesla' is simply a measuring criterion for the magnitude of the impulses put out by the MRI machine.

She remembered the nurse specifying tesla 7. Thinking about it that seemed like it was probably a strong setting. They were really serious about finding out what was going on in Robert's head.

This realization disturbed her. If they delve too deeply into this they are bound to ask questions she would prefer not answering! She had to be prepared for a very unwelcome inquisition.

She had no doubt that Robert's brain activity would be, for lack of a better word, very alien to them. How would they attempt to explain that? She knew they would want an explanation and pursue it.

Her biggest fear is that they would suggest the finger be unknowingly, but correctly, pointed at his father. She knew how important DNA was in determining things like intelligence and if they were to do an intelligence test on her that the results would not justify the findings they would surely discover in Robert.

That would leave them only one source for the DNA which gave him the advanced brain activity, his father! What could she tell them about him if they asked? What story could she fabricate to throw them off the truth?

She had to laugh silently at that thought. They wouldn't believe the truth if she told them.

She took a long sip of her iced tea and decided it was out of her hands. She would wait for the findings and deal with the matter then. She said a silent prayer asking God to give her the words if necessary.

She stared blankly at her salad rearranging it with her fork but had no interest in finishing it. Karen noticed her mother's odd behavior.

"Mom, are you okay? You seem so far away."

Julie snapped out of her daze and forced a smile.

"Yes sweetheart I'm fine. I just drifted off into thought for a moment. Now you finish your sandwich."

Defiantly Karen replied.

"I will if you finish your salad!"

Julie nodded and conceded defeat.

"That's fair, you got a deal!"

Julie and Karen proceeded to slowly and unenthusiastically finish their respective lunches. They both silently respected each other's distance, mutually understanding its origin.

Julie couldn't help but pity Robert's short life up to this point. His first two months of life has been a constant ordeal of tests, prodding and probing his infant mind. This infuriated her. She was determined to put a stop to this and give her son a normal life.

She stopped for a moment to ponder that thought. Could he, or Karen and her for that matter, have a normal life? She had to accept the fact that Robert was indeed part alien and no one knew what the future might hold.

She chastised herself for allowing the same thoughts

she condemned Karen for expressing in the car to creep into her subconscious. She again asked God for guidance.

She dreaded the results of today's MRI fearing it would only lead to further analysis and subjecting him to a life of examinations and questions. She was not going to tolerate this!

Her motherly instincts took over. A mother always wants what is best for her child and fights with all her might to protect him.

The injustice of all of it rattled every nerve in her body. Poor Robert wasn't at fault for inheriting his father's genes. He never asked to be born with what ever super human DNA he might have received from his father. This only made her want to nurture him even more. She unconsciously pounded her fist on the table in frustration. Immediately recognizing her actions she glanced at Karen apologetically.

"I'm sorry sweetheart; I didn't mean to do that."

Karen smiled.

"I know mom, has it been an hour yet? I want to get out of here."

Julie checked her phone and discovered it had been about forty-five minutes since they had left.

"Yeah me too, it hasn't been an hour yet so let's go check out the gift shop for something to do."

Karen nodded in agreement and they got up and left the cafeteria. They followed the signs leading to the gift shop and finally arrived at their destination.

Walking into the small shop they were over whelmed with the collection of knickknacks, cards, flowers and stuffed animals. Karen immediately ran over to a large stuffed teddy bear holding a heart propped on a table alone in the corner.

The bear was about three feet tall, had fluffy light

brown fur and an adorable smile. It held a large red heart in its folded arms.

"Oh mom check this out, he's awesome!"

It was love at first sight. Julie adored him.

"What do you think mom, isn't he cool?"

Julie walked over to her daughter and took the bear.

"I think he's Robert's what do you think?"

Karen smiled from ear to ear.

"Oh yeah; you rock mom! Robert will love him!"

Julie just shook her head and took the prize to the cashier. She paid for the bear and they left the gift shop. Checking her phone again Julie discovered that it had been just about an hour since they left.

"Well, it's been about an hour let's head back up and see if they are finished."

Karen grabbed her mother's hand and they headed back to Dr. Hart's office. The trip to the gift shop was just what they needed. Spirits were again high and the melancholy moment at the cafeteria long forgotten.

She glanced at the bear she was carrying and thought for a moment. She smiled for she had decided that was divine intervention, they were meant to find him. She saw that as God's way of reassuring her to relax, things are going to be alright. Just as the bear was clutching his heart, God was clutching hers, telling her to clutch on to hope.

They entered Dr. Hart's office and Julie approached the receptionist.

"Hello, I'm Julie Wells; Dr. Hart took my son for an MRI and asked us to come back in an hour. Well it has been about an hour and I was wondering if they were finished."

The receptionist shook her head.

"I'm sorry Miss Wells but they haven't returned yet.

Please just have a seat and I am sure they will be back shortly."

Julie found nothing about this news to be reassuring. The doctor had to have had a pretty good idea of how long a normal MRI would last, why was Robert's taking longer?

Her mind started racing again. What did they find? She closed her eyes for a moment of silent contemplation. She was worried her darkest fears were about to come true. They had to have discovered something they were not happy about thus forcing a more detailed examination. This could lead to nothing good.

She took a deep breath and hesitantly acknowledged the receptionist. She instructed Karen to take a seat and then joined her.

"They are not back yet. I don't like this. I can't help but feel..."

Karen sensed her mother's concern.

"Relax mom, you know how hospitals can be, they can take forever on the simplest things."

Julie put her arm around her daughter and shed a tear. The pride she had in Karen had over taken the uncertainty of her worry.

"You're right sweetheart. I'm just an old worry wart. All we can do is sit here and wait. Have I told you I love you lately?"

Karen giggled.

"Not today mom."

They waited patiently, occupying their time by laughing at the articles in a Woman's World magazine they found on the table. The minutes ticked away. It had been another half hour since they had arrived back at the office and still no word.

Julie was now officially worried. There had to be something wrong, she felt it in her heart. Dr. Hart said it would take an hour and it was now approaching two hours! She tried her best to keep positive if only not to worry Karen.

Another twenty minutes passed and Julie looked up and noticed the receptionist motioning her over to her desk.

She anxiously approached the receptionist's desk.

"Miss Wells, Dr. Macut just called. He figured you would probably be wondering what was taking so long. He told me they just completed the scan and they will be up in a few minutes."

Julie was still quizzical about what took so long. She had been so used to worrying about one thing or another it had become second nature.

"Did he mention any problems or why it took longer than expected?"

The receptionist shook her head.

"No, I'm sorry he didn't mention anything. He will answer all your questions when they get here."

Her mind was involuntarily racing with possible scenarios. She wished she knew more about the MRI process.

"Are MRIs dangerous? I mean I really don't know anything about them."

The receptionist stopped her.

"No Miss Wells, it's not dangerous at all. An MRI is not like an X-ray or CT scan, there is absolutely no radiation involved so there is no danger to the patient at all. Now please just relax and I will let you know if I hear anything else. I'm sure they will be here shortly."

Julie scoffed at the woman's latest comment. Her voice was hinting at panic.

"Relax? That's easy for you to say this is my baby we're talking about!"

The receptionist slowly raised her hand in an effort to calm Julie down.

"I understand that Miss Wells and I assure you the doctors know what they are doing. Dr Macut is one of our best radiologists."

Julie could see that she was getting no where with the woman and reluctantly returned to her seat. She sat down deliberately and unwillingly grunted.

"Damn it, these people won't tell you anything! I'm just at the end of my rope with them!"

Taken back by her mother's outburst Karen tried to console her.

"Mom, calm down, it's alright, we can do this. What did she tell you?"

Julie put her hands to her forehead and just shook her head in disgust. She was tired, she was frustrated, she was worried and she was upset.

She sighed and felt guilty for upsetting Karen. She took a deep breath and thought to herself that she has got to get a better grip and handle things in a more adult manner. She tried to amend the situation.

"I'm sorry sweetheart that was uncalled for and I apologize. Again, sadly, you have taken the role of the mature adult and me that of the whimpering child."

Julie glanced at her daughter for her reaction then closed her eyes to regroup. Karen was obviously stunned and concerned. She owed her daughter an answer to her question. She bit her lip and replied softly.

"Oh all she said was that they had just completed the test and the doctors would be here shortly. I guess all we can do is wait for them to return, and then I'm sure we will have to wait even longer for the results!"

Karen knew there was nothing she could say that would ease her mother's troubled mind. She sat silently for a moment then just squeezed her mother's hand in support.

Within minutes Julie noticed the receptionist waving her back over. She walked over to the desk.

"Miss Wells, Dr. Hart has just returned. He and your son are in room 8 just down the hall, you can go back now."

Julie motioned to Karen to come over and the two of them went to room 8. Entering the room they noticed Robert lying on the examining table. They were greeted by Dr. Hart.

"Julie, Karen, come in please. I apologize for the long wait but everything went fine. Of course I really won't have anything to tell you until we get the findings back. Dr. Macut assured me we would have the results by the end of the day."

Julie picked up her son and hugged him.

"Just what took so long doctor?"

Dr. Hart managed a smile.

"Well, Robert just didn't want his picture taken today. He was a bit fussy and in order to get accurate results an MRI requires the patient to be as still as possible so we had to wait till he calmed down to get the test done.

The test itself went fine so now you all go home and I will call you when I hear from Dr. Macut. It should be sometime late this afternoon."

Julie sighed and looked at Karen who simply shrugged her shoulders.

"Alright doctor we will. Please call me as soon as you have the results, Karen and I will be at home on pins and needles."

Dr. Hart promised her he would. Karen picked up the teddy bear, which completely filled her arms, and Julie carried Robert and they left for the car.

Julie carefully strapped Robert into his car seat and

Karen took her seat next to him in the back seat. No sooner had Julie started the car but Karen whispered to her.

"Mom, he's asleep!"

Julie glanced back and smiled, sure enough, Robert was sound asleep in his car seat.

"Well, the little guy has had a rough day, I'm sure he must be exhausted. I'm glad he's finally getting some rest."

They arrived home and Julie put Robert in his crib. She strategically placed the teddy bear, which she had unofficially named 'hope,' at the end of the crib.

She smiled and whispered to the bear.

"Okay 'Hope,' I'd like you to meet your new best friend Robert. You watch over him until I get back."

She then went downstairs and heated a cup of this morning's coffee in the microwave. She was also exhausted; as much as an afternoon nap appealed to her she refused; wanting to stay awake in hopes that the call from Dr. Hart would be forthcoming soon.

# 29

Julie decided to take her coffee out to the porch. She still hadn't gotten used to having one. Karen got a glass of iced tea and joined her.

They sat together on the steps admiring their beautiful yard with their prize pine tree standing majestically in the far corner and the magnificent oak trees at the end of the driveway.

Julie watched the birds fly in and out of the tree and smiled.

"I still can't believe this is our home sweetheart! I just love it so! We still have some things to do to fix it up even nicer but I hope you are happy here."

Karen hugged her mother.

"Oh mom how could I not be! This place is perfect! It's so much nicer than that old apartment."

Julie stood up and surveyed the area.

"I want to get a swing and hook it up here, and we'll get a bird feeder so we can watch the birds like my mother and I did."

Karen smiled and added.

"The place needs some flowers mom. How about we plant a row of them along the porch?"

Julie nodded her approval.

"Excellent idea, I'll put you in charge of that!"

They enjoyed the sunny day for another few minutes then decided to go back inside.

Julie racked her brain to try and find something to pass the time and finally decided to challenge Karen to a game of monopoly which she agreed to; now to remember where they had put the game.

After playing for about an hour Julie was getting

frustrated that the diversion wasn't working. With her son's future on the line, putting a hotel on Park Place seemed rather trivial.

She kept staring at her cell phone in hopes that the attention would conjure up a call from Dr. Hart. The phone defiantly remained silent.

She went upstairs and checked on Robert who was still fast asleep. It was so wonderful to see him at rest after the troubling day he had.

She thought back to how restless he had been all day. Fidgeting in his car seat on the way to the doctor then fussing when Dr. Hart was trying to examine him. Then the doctor telling her how Robert had held up the procedure by being jittery.

Now he seemed so at peace being back home. Could he have been upset about the appointment? Could he have known about what was ahead?

She shook off that ridiculous notion and returned downstairs. She found Karen in her room with her headphones on listening to music in her room.

She heated up another cup of coffee and sat in the living room to wait. She tried to entertain herself with stupid game shows. The importance of her impending phone call made solving the puzzle on Wheel of Fortune meaningless. She accepted the fact that television wasn't going to take away her apprehension and turned it off.

She took a sip of her now cold coffee and pondered what Dr. Hart might have to say when he called. She was formulating different mental scripts for any possible scenario. She had to be prepared. Struggling with this attempt, she eventually realized nothing was coming to her that made any sense.

The one thing that did come to her was that she was exhausted, both physically and mentally and could no longer fight the need for some rest. Her mind and body simply couldn't take any more.

With the consoling knowledge of her son being peacefully asleep and Karen amused with her music, she decided to seize the rare opportunity to lie down on the couch and take a short nap. She placed the phone beside the pillow. She was sound asleep within a matter of minutes.

Robert softly caressed her hand as he tossed a pebble into the stream that was rippling by their feet. He turned to her and smiled.

"It's going to be alright my darling, you are going to get through this and everything will turn out fine in the end. Remember one thing, my love...I am with you, I have always been with you and I always will be."

She awoke suddenly in a cold sweat. Her body was shaking and sweat was pouring down her forehead. She sat up trembling trying to catch her breath. She closed her eyes and reopened them, desperately fearing the reality that would face her when she refocused.

He was gone. Dazed she frantically searched the room and there was no sign of him. It was now painfully obvious that how ever real or imagined her fantasy may have been; it was now cruelly terminated. Gasping for breath she cried out to him.

"Robert....Robert...don't leave me again! You were here, we were together. Oh God don't torture me by saying it was just a dream...no it was real, we were together! I felt it in my heart! I heard your voice; I felt your gentle touch. It was not a dream! God please tell me it was not a dream!"

She put her head in her hands and found herself weeping uncontrollably. She involuntarily let out a scream as the tears continued to flow.

Karen remained in her room, her music blasting in her headphones totally unaware of her mother's crisis.

Julie tried to compose herself. She rubbed her temples and finally got a good deep breath. At peace for the moment, she forced herself to attempt an introspection of the experience.

Her logical mind was insisting it was nothing more than a dream but her heart remained unconvinced. Her concentration was interrupted by Karen walking into the room, still innocently oblivious to her mother's plight.

"Mom, you have to hear this new song I found, it's..."

Karen stopped in mid-sentence. It was at this moment that Karen discovered that all was not well with her mom. Frantic with sudden worry about her mom Karen sat next to her.

"What's wrong mom, you look terrible!"

In spite of the trauma, she was experiencing Julie couldn't help but find humor in her daughter's statement and put her agony aside for a moment to respond.

"That's so sweet of you to say that. Let's just say I probably look a lot better than I feel at the moment."

Karen's face saddened.

"Mom, I didn't mean it like that..."

Julie embarrassingly wiped the tears from her eyes and placed two fingers over Karen's lips to silence her.

"I know sweetheart. Can I have a hug? I really need one right now."

Karen unconditionally wrapped her arms around her mother and held her tightly for a moment. She then released her grip and looked deeply into her mother's eyes. She could easily detect the tracks of tears in spite of her mother's attempt to conceal them.

She studied her mother's distraught expression and the tear soaked eyes and was frightened by the disturbing sight. She knew something was dramatically wrong.

"Mom, what's wrong? What happened?"

Julie took a deep breath trying to decide how to answer her daughter's question. She knew she would have to tell her something, her face gave away any chance of denial. She also knew Karen wouldn't believe the story she honestly wanted to tell her.

In her heart Julie wanted to share the truth with her daughter. She had always put a priority on telling Karen the truth about things.

Over the past year, since Karen's healing, they had developed, and remarkably managed to maintain, an honest and open relationship and she would never want to do or say anything to damage that.

She thought back to before Karen's miracle. It was impossible to have such a close relationship. Had it not been for Robert's intervention it could never have been possible.

She closed her eyes in an effort to rid her mind of these painful memories; she could not go down that road right now. She fought back the tears this memory was causing and thankfully was successful.

As much as she wanted to tell Karen the truth she was struggling because she wasn't sure herself just what exactly the truth was.

Composing herself she decided to throw caution to the wind and be totally honest with her daughter. She placed her hands on Karen's shoulders to get her undivided attention then looked straight into her eyes.

"Sweetheart, I know this is going to be difficult for you to grasp but I'm telling you the truth. I was with Robert!"

Karen pulled away from her mother and sat upright, frozen in thought. She was stunned and now very worried about her mom. Her young mind was trying to grasp for the right words to express both her love and concern for her mom at a time she knew her mother needed it.

She was inwardly hoping her mother meant she had spent time with her baby brother upstairs. Something in her heart feared this wasn't true.

"Well sure, he's asleep upstairs..."

Julie shook her head frantically.

"No, you don't understand. I was with his father!"

Karen's mouth dropped open. For a moment she was speechless.

"Mom, get a grip here; we both know that is impossible. You had a dream right?"

Julie shook her daughter.

"It wasn't a dream! It was more than that, it was real I swear to you!"

Karen shook her head in disbelief.

"It was just a dream mom, relax."

Julie continued to shake her head.

"Sweetheart, you know I never remember my dreams. I never had since I was a child. But he talked to me and I can remember every single word he said. That proves it wasn't just a dream. You have to believe me!"

Karen squeezed her mother's shoulder trying her best to come up with logical words that would calm her mother down.

"Mom, one of us has to get a handle on reality here and I'm really hoping it will be you, because you of all people know, based on my past, I'm not very good at it."

Julie clasped her hands in an effort to somehow gain strength and wisdom. She thought for a moment. She had to personally understand and totally accept what her heart was telling her before she could convince Karen of it.

"Sweetheart, listen to me, bear with me for just a moment as I try to explain this as best I can."

Karen hesitantly nodded in muddled confusion, more so in compliancy than actual consent.

"Dreams are cerebral; they originate in the mind and are really nothing but thoughts. What I just experienced didn't come from my mind, it came from my heart. I didn't think it...I felt it! Does that make any sense to you honey?"

Karen just slowly shook her head.

"No it doesn't mom, not at all, and it scares me!"

She took her mother's hand and tried to express her concern in a way that wouldn't upset her.

"We are doing so well now. Think about it mom, we have this beautiful house, Robert is alive and doing well. I start back to school next week and I'm really excited about that.

You're going back to work and I'm sure that will be a good thing for you. We have to look ahead. We can't change the past but we can work on having a wonderful future. Robert is gone and we have to accept that. He will always be with us in our hearts and that has to be good enough. Now does that make any sense?"

Karen offered her mother an encouraging smile and studied her mom's blank expression.

"It was just a dream mom, we both know that and it's okay, but please don't dwell on it. Robert wouldn't want you to, you know that."

Julie was speechless, totally overwhelmed Karen's lucid and insightful reasoning. She still had trouble at times recognizing Karen as the mature, intelligent, rational young lady she had become. The years of turmoil they experienced with her being a troubled, angry and defiant girl still lingered in the back of her mind.

To hear her talk like this was like talking to a stranger. Every syllable Karen just uttered was true and in her deepest mind she knew it. Her heart, on the other hand, still refused to comply. She knew she would never be able to explain, much less convince, Karen of what her soul was screaming at her.

After silently weighing her options, she decided to simply concede and leave her inner feelings to herself. She so admired Karen's efforts to console her and couldn't help but beam with motherly pride.

She thought to herself to get her priorities in order. She had to somehow make sense of what had just happened. She either had to totally convince herself that it was only a dream, or try and explain it another way.

She knew she would never convince herself of the former and that the latter would open up an even bigger can of worms. For now her top priority was to calm Karen down and assure her that she had nothing to worry about, her mom wasn't going crazy.

She held tightly on to her daughter's hand and smiled.

"Thank you sweetheart, those were beautiful words and so true. I am so blessed to have such a wonderful daughter.

I'm fine. You're right, it was just a dream but it seemed so real. I just over reacted I'm sorry for upsetting you."

Karen didn't buy a single word of her mother's reply.

"You don't believe that do you mom?"

Julie didn't know how to respond to that skepticism so she simply confessed the truth.

"No sweetheart, I don't. With God as my witness, Robert talked to me. He spoke kind words of love and encouragement.

Don't ask me to explain how, but he did. For that brief moment we were together, it was not a dream. I will go to my grave believing that.

Now I don't expect you to believe it but please don't condemn me for it, and don't worry about me either. I am fine with it."

Julie gave her daughter a hug. She rethought what

Karen had said and had to call her on something she found surprising, in an effort to change the subject if nothing else.

"You're really excited about going back to school?"

Karen managed a chuckle.

"Yeah mom, I miss my friends and I need to get out of the house. I've thought about it and I really want to have a good year at school."

Again Julie couldn't help but think back to the old Karen. That would have been the last thing she ever would have said. She hated school, but then again, she wasn't happy about anything.

Julie couldn't believe her ears. She had to laugh. She gave Karen a comical look.

"Have we met?"

Karen just grinned.

"Mom, you can be a real goof at times."

Julie nodded.

"So that's where you get it from."

They finally shared a much needed sincere smile. Her mind at ease, Karen went into the kitchen and got them both a glass of iced tea.

They took their drinks out to the porch and sat on the steps. Julie was sure to bring her cell phone which had remained silent through the entire ordeal. The dust having finally settled on her frantic incubus earlier, her attention now returned to the pending phone call from Dr. Hart.

They sat quietly enjoying the ambience of their front yard. Birds continued to fly in and out of the pine tree and a curious squirrel busily ran across the yard, stopping momentarily to check out the intruders then hurrying on his way.

Karen took a sip of her drink then turned to her mother.

"Mom, in this...well, dream you had, you say you remember what Robert said to you?"

Julie sighed and spoke solemnly.

"Yes I do, word for word."

Karen wasn't sure if she should pursue the matter or not but her curiosity got the best of her.

"What did he say mom, in your dream?"

Julie took her daughter's hand in an attempt to muster the strength to answer. As much as she wanted to let the matter die, at least for now, she wanted to keep the open communication with Karen going. She took a deep breath and replied honestly.

"He said things were going to work out fine in the end. Then he said 'I am with you, I have always been with you and I always will be'."

Karen was stupefied by her mother's words. She looked into her eyes and noticed a tear emerging from one of them. She then peered past her mother's eyes and directly into her heart. She had never seen her so mother so somber.

Whether it actually was a dream or not was no longer important to her; what was important was that her mother honestly believed it wasn't.

"Mom, I can't explain why, but I believe you."

Julie fought off feelings of remorse. She could tell her personal drama was taking an emotional toll on Karen and this was the last thing she wanted.

At the same time she felt so proud of her daughter who she could tell was being as loving and supporting as her young heart could. She brushed the hair out of Karen's eyes and reached out and gave her a hug.

"You have no idea how much your love and support mean to me sweetheart. I don't mean to be a pain as I know I can be at times. But thank you for being here and, well, thank you for just being you!"

Karen smirked and patted her mother's shoulder.

"Its okay mom, you're entitled, after all, I was a pain to you for, well years. I'll always be here for you mom, we're a team! We got this!"

Julie decided that maybe a shower would snap her back to normalcy. She got up and started walking to the door when her plan was abruptly interrupted by her phone ringing.

Her heart skipped a beat as she checked the caller ID; it was Dr. Hart's office.

# 30

Julie approached the call with mixed emotions. She was relieved that the doctor had finally called but was apprehensive about what he might have to say. She greeted the caller as calmly as she could.

"Miss Wells, this is Nurse Billinger from Dr. Hart's office."

Julie was immediately put off by the fact that a nurse was calling and not the doctor himself as he had promised.

"Yes, I have been expecting his call."

The nurse continued.

"Well the doctor has left for the day but he asked me to call you. He wanted me to tell you that the test results came back and that everything is fine.

He has set up a meeting with you for tomorrow morning at nine-o-clock to discuss the matter in further detail. Will this time be convenient for you?"

Julie didn't know what to think. Why couldn't he have just explained everything over the phone as he had promised? She thought for a moment, again fearing the worst.

If everything were fine she saw no reason for a special meeting. She knew she wouldn't get anything more from the nurse and let out a disgusted sigh.

"Well, why couldn't the doctor had told me this himself? I can hardly feel comfortable with the fact he wants all of us to come back in..."

Nurse Billinger interrupted Julie.

"Now Miss Wells I would look at this as an encouraging thing. If the doctor had found anything to be concerned about he would have called you himself."

Julie was beside herself.

"Encouraging...encouraging my ass!"

The nurse cleared her throat.

"There is no need for that tone Miss Wells. The doctor will clear everything up tomorrow for you. The Dr. Hart has also asked you to bring your son as well. Now is the time convenient for you?"

Now Julie was in a state of indignation rapidly approaching rage.

"Why does my son have to be there?"

The nurse replied.

"Dr. Hart didn't explain but did say it was important your son be there."

Julie realized arguing with the nurse wouldn't get her anywhere and reluctantly agreed to the time. She spoke harshly.

"We'll be there."

"Thank you Miss Wells I will let him know. Have a good day."

Julie thrust the phone back in her pocket and turned around in a total frenzy. She regretted not having an old fashioned phone, one that would have allowed her the satisfaction of slamming down the receiver because that was the mood she was in. A simple click on her cell phone just wasn't doing her anger justice.

She stormed back to the porch where Karen was still sitting quietly watching the birds.

Hearing that the doctor wanted Robert there could only mean one thing. It meant they had intended to do more testing on the poor child!

Julie mumbled angrily to herself, 'have a good day; yeah I'll have a great freaking day!'

She paced back and forth on the porch and finally let Karen in on the conversation.

"That was the doctor's office. They want all of us

to go in tomorrow morning for a meeting. The nurse specifically requested Robert to come with us. We both know what that means!"

Karen turned around and could see her mother was upset.

"You think they want to do more tests on him?"

Julie nodded.

"I can't think of any other reason he would want Robert to be there."

Karen sulked.

"That's nuts mom, hasn't he been through enough? Do you have to let them, I mean do you have a say in the matter?"

Julie shrugged her shoulders.

"I honestly don't know the legalities of it. I would certainly think I do. But, you have to trust the doctors to know what's best or why go to them?

At this point, I simply don't know what to do. I just hate the thought of him having to endure more tests. All we can do is go tomorrow and see what they have to say."

Karen walked over to her mother and gave her a hug. They went back inside and Julie went upstairs to check on Robert. He had been asleep since they got back and she felt it was time to wake him up, change him and get him something to eat.

After taking care of Robert Julie ordered Chinese for her and Karen and they spent the rest of the evening just watching television and eating egg rolls.

Julie calculated they would have to get up around six in the morning to get ready and be at the doctors by nine so she ordered Karen to bed. Karen had never been a morning person so her mother insisted she get s good night's sleep.

The challenge of getting her and Robert ready to go

added to the task of making herself presentable at that hour was going to be daunting.

Julie checked on Robert and after being satisfied he was asleep for the night she retired to her bedroom. Her head was swimming with conflicting thoughts as she tried to get her pillow fluffed just right.

She wanted what was best for her son of course but she dreaded the thought of him having to go through more tests.

She continued to fear that at some point she would be grilled about Robert's father. If the tests on his brain activity turned out as she anticipated they would have to be curious about him and his biological influence.

She took a brief moment to pity herself for being a single mother and how overwhelming her life seemed at times. She pondered all she had been through, just in the last year or so.

She reflected on the untimely loss of the man she loved so dearly, the years of raising an emotionally disturbed daughter and the fact that her son was half-alien. She sighed and thought there was the potential for a million-dollar blockbuster movie somewhere in there.

Her last waking thought was of her dream. She held back a tear as she drifted back to Robert's hand softly caressing hers and his tender words which were as clear as if he were in the room.

Was it a dream...or could it have perhaps been a vision? As much as she wanted to she wouldn't allow herself to think of it as any more than just a dream. This was nothing more than a defense mechanism, not her desire.

To look at it as a vision would require a hope her heart, and common sense, insisted on denying her. She resolved herself to the realization that she would never know. She tossed and turned for over an hour before finally falling peacefully asleep.

The morning went better than she could have hoped for. Karen was showered and dressed within twenty minutes and then surprisingly took charge of getting Robert ready.

She got him up, changed and dressed him and even gave him a bottle. This unexpected blessing gave Julie the time she needed to shower, get dressed, put her makeup on and even enjoy a much-needed cup of coffee on the front steps.

Karen and Robert joined her on the porch. Karen was holding Robert who was perfectly contented nestled in his sister's arms. She smiled with sisterly pride. She knew her mother could use some help and she was happy to jump in.

"We're all set mom, I even packed his bag."

Julie took a sip from her coffee and shook her head in amazement.

"Oh, sweetheart I can't thank you enough. You are a rock star and a wonderful big sister! I'm so proud of you."

Karen was smiling from ear to ear and sat down on the steps next to her mother. Julie took Robert and gave him a kiss.

"Well big guy, are we ready for another doctor's appointment? I know this is no fun for you but we are going to get through this together. Don't worry, mom and I have your back!"

Julie and Karen shared a smile and then got up to finalize their preparations for the trip.

Julie grabbed her purse and keys while Karen took Robert in one arm and his travel bag in the other. They headed for the car.

Karen secured Robert in his car seat and took her usual position sitting next to him in the back seat.

Unlike the last time, Robert was passive and offered no resistance. He seemed happy and content.

Julie started the car and did a quick check to the back seat making sure everyone was ready to go. Satisfied that the crew was all set she decided the trip needed some music.

She wanted to thank Karen for her help this morning so she put in one of her daughter's favorite CDs. It was some boy band who she could have done well without but tolerated it when she saw Karen beaming. She had to laugh to herself, 'the things we do for our kids' she thought.

As it worked out, their timing was perfect. Julie pulled into the parking lot at precisely eight-thirty. That would give her ample time to get everyone upstairs and check in with the receptionist before her appointment at nine.

She had to smile; maybe this was an omen that the rest of the day just might turn out better than she had thought. Up to this point everything had gone much smoother than she anticipated. She hoped this good fortune would last through the meeting. She clung to that thought in spite of her rational mind saying it was nothing more than wishful thinking.

They arrived at Dr. Hart's office and Karen took Robert and sat down as Julie checked in at the receptionist's desk.

"I'm Julie Wells; I have a nine-o-clock appointment with Dr. Hart."

The nurse checked her appointment calendar and smiled.

"Yes Miss Wells, the doctor is expecting you. I will let him know you are here, he will be out in a minute."

Julie sat down with Karen and Robert. Their wait was a short one as within a couple minutes Dr. Hart came out to greet them.

"Good morning Julie! It is always nice to see you. How is everyone this morning?"

Julie wasn't in the mood for small talk. She wanted to get down to the bottom of why this meeting was necessary.

"Everyone is fine thank you, now why are we here? Did you get the results of Robert's test? Why couldn't you have discussed this over the phone?"

Dr. Hart smiled cordially and extended his arm, pointing in the direction of the hallway.

"I have arranged a meeting with a couple colleagues and we will go over everything with you. Now Karen and Robert can wait here and we will..."

Julie defiantly interrupted him.

"My children will accompany me! Anything you say to me can be said to them as well. We handle things as a family!"

Karen silently beamed with pride as the doctor acknowledged Julie's demand.

"That's fine Julie. Will you all please follow me to the conference room?

The doctor started walking down the hall way and the three of them followed closely behind.

Julie found the doctor's suggestion rather disturbing. Why would they need to have a conference and why would he assist the help of other doctors? Her heart started racing as they entered a small conference room. She was now totally convinced something was wrong.

She remembered the nurses words yesterday saying that if anything were dramatically wrong the doctor would have called her himself. She couldn't argue with that reasoning but still they had to have discovered something they didn't like. Her heart had a pretty good idea what it might be.

They entered a small room dominated by a long table

with a number of chairs. Two of the chairs were already occupied. Dr. Hart motioned for them to sit down as he walked to one end of the table and sat down.

"Julie I have asked these gentlemen to join us this morning to add their professional insights.

First we have Dr. Benjamin Macut; he is the radiologist who preformed the MRI yesterday. He has over twenty years of experience in the radiology field. He and I attended medical school together and let me just say he is very good at what he does!"

A frail looking man obviously in his sixties smiled weakly and nodded. He was rather skinny. His narrow head featured salt and pepper hair which was thinning at the top. He donned wire rim glasses which gave him a nerdy look.

Dr. Hart continued.

"Seated next to him is Dr. Terrance Silverman, a neurologist from University hospital. Dr. Silverman is a leader in the field of neurobiology. He has had countless articles published in medical journals and has lectured on the topic all over the world. We are lucky to have him."

Dr. Silverman was the physical antitheses of Dr. Macut. He was muscular and appeared very fit for a man again obviously in his sixties. His chiseled face was highlighted by large, deeply set, dark brown eyes and thick eyelashes. He also had salt and pepper hair but it showed no signs of balding and was styled in the fashion a leading screen actor would be proud of.

Their attire also was dramatically different. Dr. Macut was wearing teal scrubs while Dr. Silverman was dressed in what was an obviously expensive, dark blue three piece suit.

Julie couldn't help but feel small and uncomfortably intimidated. She was a nervous wreck.

This did nothing to lessen the resentment she felt for

having to be a part of what she saw as an unnecessary inconvenience. Apprehension also played a role in her emotional state at the moment for her biggest concern was what they might have in mind for Robert. She knew they wouldn't have called this formal meeting simply to tell her everything was fine.

She studied the individual faces of the three doctors and found them all to be stoic, stern and uncompromised. This only reconfirmed her belief that they were about to tell her something she didn't want to hear.

She glanced to her right where Robert was silently cuddling in his sister's arms. She sighed, dwelling on his innocence. He didn't deserve this scrutiny. She then thought about what her reaction would be if the doctors were to tell her they are going to continue probing and testing him.

Does she have any recourse? Should she even try and interfere with what she hoped would be their best intentions for her son? Her head was spinning with confusion but her speculations were interrupted by Dr. Silverman.

"Allow me to begin Miss Wells. Dr. Hart called me yesterday and asked me to review the results of your son's MRI. He and Dr. Macut were somewhat taken back by their initial analysis saying the results were..."

The doctor paused in thought, and then continued.

"Inconclusive"

Julie and Karen looked at each other in confusion. Dr. Hart, seeing Julie's apprehension, interrupted his colleague.

"Doctor, if I may interject here. I have been Julie's physician for many years. I delivered this beautiful young lady sitting next to her to give you an idea of just how long."

Karen blushed as the doctor continued.

345

"We have always had a very open and honest relationship and I value that and want to continue it so with that in mind I must say inconclusive is not the proper adjective to use here. I am going to be up front with you Julie."

Julie sat silently intrigued by the doctor's words.

"We actually found the results of the first MRI quite startling."

Julie had to speak up after hearing this.

"You found them startling? Just what is that suppose to mean doctor?"

Dr. Hart cleared his throat.

"Well Julie, when I took Robert's vitals, before he went down for the test, I found his heart rate higher than we would expect. I didn't mention it at the time for two reasons. First of all I didn't want to alarm you before we found out more about what might be causing it.

Secondly, when a patient is experiencing a rapid heart rate the body normally reacts to it in a stressful way. The body finds itself having to deal with an excess flow of blood with no way of dispersing it in a healthy manner. I saw no signs of this in your son.

His other vitals were perfectly normal which told me his body was not struggling with the added blood flow the rapid heart rate was causing. Your son's body was totally at ease with this excess and showed no signs of stress."

Julie sat stunned, mouth gapping at this discourse. She wanted to question it but couldn't find the words. The Dr. Hart continued.

"The results of the first MRI gave us the answer, well on the surface. We found the results astonishing.""

Julie couldn't sit silent any longer.

"Just what were the findings and why did you find them so astonishing?"

Dr. Hart rubbed his forehead in thought. He was at a crossroad. He wanted to give Julie an accurate assessment but not alarm her. He chose his words carefully.

"As you know, we did the MRI to check Robert's brain activity. Well what we discovered completely surprised us. Robert's heart was pumping fast to supply his brain with the blood it was requiring.

Blood stimulates brain activity by supplying the brain with oxygen and nutrients. At Robert's age brain activity is present of course but still very limited to things such as distinguishing colors, shapes, movements and just elementary things."

Julie was bewildered as she tried to digest what the doctor was saying and more importantly where he was going with it.

"Your son's brain is trying to do a lot more than that. It wouldn't be an over statement to say his brain activity was simply off the charts and like nothing we had ever seen from a child his age."

Dr. Macut had sat silently through his colleague's dialog but now spoke up.

"Miss Wells, you have an extraordinary child. The MRI does not lie; it shows us very clearly that your son's mind is vastly advanced as compared to that of a normal two month old baby. Now where we go from here is of course entirely up to you."

Julie found herself dumbfounded. She wasn't sure where they were going with this line of thought but she knew she had to find out.

"Just what are you suggesting? Doctor my only concern is with the health of my child!"

Dr. Hart spoke up.

"Julie your son is in very good health; that is not the issue here at all. We are simply saying he is displaying abnormally high brain activity."

Karen couldn't hold her silence for any longer.

"So you're saying my little brother is some kind of genius or something?"

Dr. Silverman shook his head and addressed the question.

"No, that is not what we are saying here at all."

Julie was at the end of her wits and cried out loudly.

"Then just what the hell are you saying?"

Dr. Silverman clasped his hands together and thought for a moment before continuing.

"You must first understand that an MRI is not for measuring intelligence. At this young age there is no way of actually calculating intelligence. The MRI is simply telling us that there is an incredible high level of brain activity."

Julie shook her head in confusion.

"I don't understand what you are telling me here and what it means to my son. You insist he is healthy then what is this all about?

Is this about determining his intelligence? Isn't he a little young to be worried about something like that? You admitted yourself that there is no way of determining that at his age, then why subject him to all of this?"

Dr. Silverman replied.

"Miss Wells, we are looking at his growth potential here. No, we can't determine his actual intelligence at this age. His actual knowledge is of course very limited now.

Let me explain it this way. When you first build a library it has no books, no knowledge or resources but what it does have is countless shelves which in time will hold those books. The books are where the knowledge comes from but they of course need shelf space.

Your son's brain is indicating it has a lot of shelves, more than would normally be expected in a child his age. There is a lot of room in that tiny brain for knowledge and based on the flow of blood it is receiving, it's got the capacity."

Julie and Karen stared at each other quizzically as the doctor continued.

"I reviewed your son's charts and I noticed there was also a very high level of white blood cells in his blood, yet his body was acting totally normal to this anomaly which is highly unusual.

Now Miss Wells there is a lot going on with your son's physiology that we simply don't understand. What makes this so puzzling is that your son is indeed very healthy and is showing no signs of any distress over any of this as you would normally expect it to.

Summing it up, I have to say from what we have gathered so far your son has unprecedented potential. If his brain continues to develop in this fashion this gift would present him with infinitesimal possibilities.

As a mother, I would think you would be interesting in its origins, we certainly are."

# 31

Now that was the final straw! How dare he question her concerns as a mother!

"Doctor, my only concern is with the health of my son and you have assured me is fine. I will not sit here and listen to you question my morals as a mother!"

Dr. Hart jumped in.

"Julie, by no means is anyone questioning that. Dr. Silverman was just saying that we are all interested in Robert's health and best interests and he was simply pointing out that your son is exceptional and this gift might be something we want to learn more about."

Julie glared at Dr. Hart with disdain.

"Just what are you suggesting now?"

Dr. Silverman picked up the conversation.

"We have set up an electroencephalograph which would help us understand just how his brain cells are communicating."

Julie pounded her fists on the table.

"Not without my consent you haven't! I will absolutely not approve that under any circumstances! I will not have Robert turned into a science experiment for the advancement of medical research! You tell me Robert is healthy and that is all I want to hear."

Dr. Hart glanced at Dr. Silverman and then addressed Julie.

"Julie, if indeed Robert has been blessed in this way we owe it to him to explore its origins so we can better understand it and help him nurture and develop this gift in the future. This is all for his benefit."

Julie scowled at the doctor. She dreaded hearing the

word 'origins' knowing where that would lead. Her fears were about to be realized as Dr. Silverman continued.

"There could be a number of factors that cause abnormal brain activity. Trauma or injury, drug abuse during pregnancy but I think in this case the most likely source of the genes that would initiate such unusual development would be DNA. Intelligence is much like musical talent; it is generally inherited from the parents. If you would permit me to ask you a few questions we could get a better grasp of where you son might have inherited this gift."

Julie closed her eyes in a moment of mental agony..... here it comes. She glanced to her right to see Karen looking at her fully aware of the situation. She patted her daughter's hand in an effort to assure her she was alright.

She was thinking if she placed the emphasis on herself, answering questions, however impossible they may be to answer, it would take the attention off Robert which was her top priority.

"I will not allow my son to endure any more testing; he's had enough of that. If you want to ask me questions I will answer them to the best of my ability. I just want my son left out of it!"

Dr. Silverman nodded and opened up a folder which was in front of him.

"Dr. Hart has assured me that drugs, be it illicit or prescription, are not an issue with you; would you confirm that Miss Wells?"

Julie glanced at Dr. Hart who gave her a reassuring smile.

"No doctor, I have never taken any illegal drugs; that was something that I was just never into, even when I was younger. I have even shied away from taking prescriptions; I simply have never felt comfortable with drugs of any kind."

Dr. Silverman wrote on his yellow legal pad and continued.

"I see, what about alcohol? Did you ever have a problem with it and did you drink during your pregnancy?"

Julie shook her head in disgust.

"I have never been a heavy drinker. I'll have a glass of wine now and again but I have never had a problem with it and I did not drink anything during my pregnancy. Working in a bar as I do I have seen what excessive alcohol abuse can do to a person so I have avoided it!"

Dr. Silverman again jotted notes on his legal pad.

"Has your son suffered any head injuries at all?"

Julie simply shook her head. Dr. Silverman rubbed his chin in thought and proceeded.

"Well this leaves us with the DNA factor. Parental genes play a huge factor in child development. They influence everything from eye color to height and body structure. They also influence intellectual capacity. I have no other choice but to believe this is what we are dealing with here."

Julie rubbed her forehead to try and avert a rapidly developing headache. She saw this coming and knew exactly where the conversation would end up.

"What is your highest level of education Miss Wells?"

She closed her eyes and answered with a tinge of embarrassment.

"I graduated from high school, and that in itself was a struggle for me."

Dr. Silverman nodded.

"Have you ever had your IQ tested?"

She was repulsed at having to answer this line of questions.

"Now why would I have done that? Doctor, I am no

Einstein and I know it. No I have never had my IQ tested! I am not the source of these genes you refer to!"

Julie gasped at the realization of what she had just said. She was appalled at herself for saying such a stupid thing.

Not only did she volunteer that she wasn't the source for the superhuman genes but she paved the road to their inquiry into the father! She silently screamed every expletive that came to her mind.

Dr. Silverman glanced at Dr. Hart in a moment of contemplation. Dr. Hart returned his glance with a subtle nod, giving the doctor his consent to continue his line of questioning.

"Parental genes are very competitive. The maternal genes and paternal genes battle for dominance. Sometimes the maternal genes dominate, sometimes the paternal genes dominate and sometimes they just meet in the middle. I would be very interested in the father's genetic makeup."

Julie took a deep breath and silently thought to herself 'I bet you would' you would be more than just interested if you knew the truth!' She knew that was something she could never share.

She had to quickly formulate just how she was going to answer the uncomfortable questions she knew were forthcoming.

Dr. Silverman paused; taking a deep breath before asking what he knew would be a painful question.

"Dr. Hart informed me that the father passed away before your son was born, I'm very sorry. What was the cause of death?"

Julie sighed, in spite of expecting the question she was still overcome with having to answer it.

"He died suddenly of a heart attack."

Dr. Silverman nodded respectfully.

"How long had you two been together?"

Holding back the tears Julie answered unemotionally.

"We were together for one year doctor."

The doctor jotted notes on his legal pad.

"Did he have any health issues that you were aware of?"

Julie simply shook her head continuing to refrain from bursting out in tears.

"He was in very good health as far as I knew, it was totally unexpected."

Dr. Silverman continued.

"What did he do for a living Miss Wells?"

Panic overtook her. This was one question she wasn't expecting. Why was he asking this and more importantly how could she answer? She thought quickly and blurted out the first thing that came to her.

"Well, he wasn't working when I knew him. His parents were quite wealthy and left him a large sum of money when they passed so he was surviving on his inheritance."

Julie sighed deeply with relief when she saw the doctor writing on his notepad, apparently accepting her fabricated response without questioning.

"What was his highest level of education? Would you say he was a man of high intelligence?"

Karen glanced at her mother with empathy. She knew the torture these questions were causing. Robert remained silently cuddling in his sister's arm totally unawares of the goings on.

Again Julie had to quickly concoct a believable answer. Should she make up a college and degree for him; would they research it? She didn't know what to do and knew she had little time to decide.

"He was the most intelligent man I had ever met."

She left the thought dangling hoping they wouldn't pursue it.

Dr. Hart could easily notice the agony Julie was experiencing and mercifully decided to end the inquisition. He had grown to appreciate Julie as more than a just a patient but looked at her as a close friend. He wanted to put an end to her suffering seeing nothing to gain from further interrogation.

"Terrence, I think we have gotten everything we needed here. Julie I know this has been hard on you and I offer you my sincere apologies for any inconvenience.

I hope you understand that this gives us a better awareness of your son and this gift he has appeared to have inherited. We all want what is best for him.

Now what we do from here is entirely your call. There are many avenues we can explore concerning Robert's potential. You have plenty of time to decide what is best for him since he is only two months old. I'm glad we discovered this at such a young age.

As his doctor I naturally would hope to keep a close eye on his progress and monitor any changes as he grows.

For now your son is perfectly healthy and that of course is our first interest. Any further testing would be entirely up to your discretion Julie."

Dr. Silverman had been tapping his fingers lightly on the table and spoke up.

"I'm afraid I must take exception to Dr. Hart's evaluation. I honestly don't feel complacency is the best route to take here.

I see your son was three months premature. Now his growth, both physically and intellectually is remarkable even for a full term baby at his age.

I won't argue the point that he is indeed very healthy at the moment but what concerns me is if this metabolic growth continues that it might lead to something malignant down the road. I simply can't say.

I don't understand this unprecedented growth and that is why my recommendation would be to continue testing until we can get our fingers on what is causing it. It is best to address it before it becomes a health hazard."

Julie was devastated to hear this. She looked at Karen who shared her dread. She then glanced at Dr. Hart and was surprised to see him shaking his head in disagreement.

Dr. Hart gave her a reassuring nod and spoke.

"Terrance my friend, I'm afraid you have been staring into microscopes too long. What we have here is a healthy two month old baby whose rapid development could be explained by a number of things none of which I find alarming.

I have examined him a number of times during his young life and find his vitals are normal, his respiratory, circulatory, digestive and excretory systems are all functioning perfectly normal.

His muscles are exceptionally strong and functioning fine, he is responsive, alert and I simply find nothing to support your fear of any of them leading into any health problems.

Do I find his condition unusual, of course I do but I would not call it threatening."

Julie and Karen shared an unexpected smile, they hadn't seen that coming! They both knew exactly what the other was thinking. Dr. Hart continued.

"Now if Julie wants further testing done that is fine and good and we can comply, but if she is satisfied with her son's health then I see no reason to continue this obtrusive and, in my opinion unnecessary, testing.

I will of course be continuing his bi weekly exams keeping an eye open for any problems or changes."

Julie wanted to jump out of her chair and hug Dr.

Hart. She had always liked him but was still surprised by his unbridled and unexpected support.

Dr. Silverman put up his hands in a mock gesture of defeat and leaned back in his chair.

Dr. Hart stood up and walked over to Julie. He smiled and gently patted Robert on the head.

"Julie, we have your next appointment scheduled in two weeks. I'll have my receptionist call you a few days in advance to remind you. I see no reason why you can't take your family home now."

Karen smiled and raised her fist in victory. She knew what the doctor's words had to have meant to her mother. Julie stood up and squeezed Dr. Hart's arm in a show of thanks.

They left the room and walked to the car. As usual, Karen secured Robert in his car seat and took the seat next to him in the back seat.

Julie started the car and turned and faced Karen.

"By Jove, I think we won that one!"

Karen nodded and smiled ear to ear.

"He was so cool mom!"

Julie winked and started to drive home. She chuckled as she replied.

"Well, now that we have your little brother all squared away it's time to work on you! You know you start school on Monday, are you ready?"

Karen acknowledged her.

"Yeah I'm ready mom, I have my outfit all picked out!"

Julie grinned, she was hoping for a different response. She tried to keep her sarcasm in check while replying.

"Oh thank goodness, that's been weighing heavily on my mind."

Putting that aside for a moment Julie couldn't help but smile. She was so relieved that the meeting went as well as it did, in fact better than she could have hoped for.

She could now stop worrying about any further, unsolicited, testing on Robert and was so thankful to have Dr. Hart's full understanding and support in her desires to end it.

Even the questioning went better than she had feared it would. While the subject of Robert's father was brought up, as she expected, thankfully it was not pursued, as she feared it would be. That in itself was a huge blessing.

Her mind then drifted off in another direction. She had vowed to herself that once Karen returned to school that she would return to work. She found herself pondering that decision.

She silently tossed around the pros and cons of returning to work. At the current time they didn't need the money. They still had a substantial amount of the money Robert had left them. She calculated approximately what they had drawn from it and about what they had left. She was satisfied they could live comfortably for at least a year on what was left.

Then there was the issue of what to do about Robert. Her initial intentions were to work at night as she had been before. Karen could watch Robert when she got home from school. The more she thought about it she was feeling that wouldn't be fair to her daughter.

Poor Karen would be toiling all day at school then asked to baby-sit at night. This school year was very important to both her and Karen. This would be the first full year of school that Karen could relish as mature, rational young lady.

She had struggled so much with school because of her mental disabilities in the past that she never had the chance to really enjoy the experience and get the full educational value out of it. This year would be different.

She already knew Karen was sincerely looking forward

to returning to school and she was sure her new mental outlook was a dominant factor in her eagerness.

The old Karen dreaded everything about school. She had no interest in her education what so ever and had made no real friends. Julie didn't want anything interfering with her optimistic outlook for the coming year.

With Karen's new mindset and enthusiasm her possibilities would be endless. Julie had spent so many countless, sleepless nights dreaming of Karen reaching this point that she didn't want to do anything to detour her from it. Karen so deserved this and she was going to do everything she could to encourage and support her.

Taking all of this into consideration she now pondered the possibility of working days. This of course would require a baby sitter. She wasn't very keen on that idea.

Apprehension crept into her already cluttered mind. But her apprehension extended further than a normal mother's worry about leaving their infant son with a baby sitter. Her fears included the genetic makeup of her son and how, in all seriousness, she didn't know what Robert might be capable of doing and when he might do it.

Her imagination took over for a moment. How would she explain Robert levitating his teddy bear to a naive baby sitter? That possibility, as small as it may be, was simply one she wanted to avoid at all cost.

She had one last passing thought about working. One benefit for her personally would be social interaction, something she desperately missed. At times she would just go stir crazy just being in the house alone, or even with Karen.

While she was working she would so enjoy the interactions with her customers. It gave her a chance to meet many interesting people which she found to be a delight. Was considering this aspect being selfish? She didn't have an answer for that.

While she was with Robert he would provide her with such pleasing and gratifying company in so many ways. This companionship was sorely lacking in her life now.

She thought back to words her mother had told her many times. 'In order to make others happy you have to make yourself happy first'. Those words never seemed more poignant than they did now.

She couldn't make a determination now, her mind was too cloudy. She decided she would call Larry and, first of all, get his take one the idea and discuss what openings he might have. It was an idea she refused to give up on for the time being and would base her decision on what Larry had to say.

# 32

They arrived home and the first thing Julie did was change Robert's diaper. It was painfully apparent the task needed done immediately. She then gave him a bottle and put him in his crib.

She decided to heat up a cup of the morning's coffee and went outside to sit at her favorite spot, the porch steps. She kicked off her shoes, took a sip of her coffee and enjoyed the cool breeze. It was so peaceful and quiet. One of the best selling points for their new home was its location.

The house was far off the beaten trail, a far cry from their old apartment which was smack dab in the middle of downtown and surprisingly only a fifteen minute drive away. But what a difference that fifteen minutes made, it was like being on another planet.

There was a narrow access road leading past their home and their closest neighbor, other than birds, squirrels, chipmunks and an occasional rabbit, was at least a mile down that road. The road was paved only with dirt and was barely two lanes wide.

The road was bordered on both sides by beautiful tall trees of many varieties whose branches extended over the road providing a natural canopy. Each tree was adorned with its own unique leaves and shades of green.

This provided a very tranquil, secluded front yard. She adored the isolation their home provided them. Karen would now be taking a school bus to school but after researching it Julie found the bus went right down their road.

Their front yard was also fenced in by a line of trees, broken only by the driveway. The pride and joy of the botanical collection was the majestic pine tree in the corner which towered over the other smaller trees. Even the air smelled better out here.

The morning meeting was all of a sudden coming back to haunt her. She reflected on Dr. Silverman's inquiry about Robert. She surveyed the front yard and thought about how wonderful it would be to have Robert's arm around her as they watched the birds and squirrels. She smiled thinking about how he would have enjoyed that and would have asked countless questions about them. He always had so many wonderful questions about everything.

She had always thought it quaint that here she was a high school educated woman teaching a man whose intelligence was vastly superior to anything she could even imagine.

Her mind then involuntarily drifted off to a place she had sworn she wouldn't return to, how much she missed him.

She thought about all the things they never got to do and the many things he never had the opportunity to enjoy with her. First, she reflected on the little things, like walking in the rain or having a snowball fight. Then her heart turned really cruel and stabbed her with the big things, like taking their wedding vows and raising their son together.

She thought about what a wonderful father Robert would have made. He had such kindness and compassion in his heart. She knew he would have worshiped his son.

She then thought about how little he actually knew about their world and because of that how very childlike he was in his wonder of it. That would have made for some interesting situations with his son as the two of them would both be asking the same questions and learning together.

She snapped herself out of her moment of weakness. She would not allow herself to go down that path again. She took a moment to collect her thoughts. She thought about how blessed she was and all of the things she had to be thankful for.

She thanked God for giving them this beautiful home; she thanked him for giving Karen a chance at a wonderful school year and a beautiful future. She thanked him for bringing Robert senior into her life and finally she thanked him for taking away the fear of further testing on her son.

She thought about how her life was just over a year ago. Karen was an emotional wreck, she lived in a shabby apartment in the heart of the city living from paycheck to paycheck, and she didn't have Robert, either one of them. What a difference a year can make.

Yes, she was truly blessed and she knew it. She vowed herself from this day forward to look ahead and not back. She knew how difficult this would be but she also knew she had no other choice.

She took another sip of coffee and her mind went back to the job dilemma. She found herself really wanting to go back to work. She knew the money Robert had left them would only last so long and she would have to return to work eventually. She also couldn't deny she was lonely. She pondered that last notion. Yes, she was lonely but not for romance but simply for social interaction.

Romance in her eyes was now a thing of the past. She had always of the opinion that a person has one soul mate and she had already found, and sadly lost, hers. She firmly believed that God doesn't give second chances in that department and she wasn't interested in one if he did. No, romance wasn't a factor. She had absolutely no intent or any interest at all in finding anyone else.

What she found most devastating about this realization

was as much as her heart had been fighting it for over a year; she now totally believed and accepted it. This admission would give her peace of mind at the mere expense of a part of her heart; a part she knew she would never get back.

Her stomach was all of a sudden feeling queasy. She got chills and all of a sudden felt very uneasy. Something was wrong, she could sense it, but she couldn't put her finger on it. Her motherly instinct told her to check on Robert.

She ran upstairs and found Robert peacefully sleeping in his crib. Relived, she returned downstairs and poured another cup of coffee. Her thoughts inexplicitly turned to the movie 'Star War's' and Obi-Wan's fear of pending doom. She truly sensed 'a disturbance in the force'.

Karen peeked out the front door window and noticed her mother sitting on the porch steps and then went out to join her.

"I just checked on Robert, he's still sound asleep. How are you doing?"

Julie smiled and motioned for her daughter to sit down next to her.

"Thank you sweetheart, you are such a great big sister, I'm so proud of you!"

She put her arm around Karen.

"I don't really know how I am doing at the moment. Something is bothering me but I can't figure out what it is."

Karen responded with a sullen expression.

"Gee mom; I can't imagine what it would be. Everything is pretty good as I see it."

Julie squeezed Karen's arm and just shrugged her shoulders.

"Oh it's nothing. You know me I am always worrying about every silly thing. It just feels like something is out of place, I can't explain it. Call it mother's intuition I guess, we're always looking for something to go wrong without any reasoning behind it."

Karen just nodded her head.

"Well, I'm here for you if you need me."

Julie took a minute for introspection. Robert was fine; Karen was fine...what could be troubling her? She was very pleased with their trip to the doctor's this morning so it wasn't that.

She tried to ignore the feeling but the queasiness in her stomach just wouldn't go away. Again her thoughts paralleled Obi-Wan's...he wasn't sure why he felt the disturbance either but it turned out he was right. What bothered her most was she had these feelings many times before and usually she was correct as well.

Karen tried to be as consoling as she could.

"Well mom, we've been through a lot and it would be only natural for you to worry about things but I think everything is going really well now. I guess worrying is a tough habit to break."

Julie shook her head in amazement over her daughter's insight. The more she thought about it the more she felt Karen had hit the nail on the head. She just wasn't used to not having anything to worry about.

Maybe her mind was going out of its way to try and find something to stress over. She wanted to believe that. Karen was right; things were going very well lately so she put her troubled mind aside.

She wrapped her arms around her daughter and smiled.

"You are my rock of Gibraltar sweetheart! I just get so befuddled at times she can't see the forest from the trees, thankfully you can. Thank you for your beautiful insight!"

Julie stood up and went upstairs to wake up Robert.

She wanted to give him a bath and a fresh diaper then give him a bottle.

Karen was assigned to come up with something for their dinner while she did all of that.

Julie entered Robert's room to discover him wide awake. She noticed him staring at the foot of his crib. Upon closer inspection she discovered his gaze was intently studying 'hope' the teddy bear who was sitting quietly in the corner of the crib. It was obvious this was the first time he had noticed his crib mate.

He would slowly sway his head back and forth but his eyes never left the bear. She chuckled softly as she watched him.

"That's 'Hope' sweetheart, I hope you like him. Your sister and I thought he could keep you company. You both are about the same size."

He slowly turned his head to face his mother and just cooed contently. Julie took this as a sign he approved of his new friend.

She gave him his bath and changed him then fed him a bottle which he accepted vivaciously. She then returned him to his crib, kissed his forehead and put his blanket over him.

Returning downstairs she was anxious to see what Karen had come up with for dinner.

On the kitchen table were two plates each containing a large portion of macaroni and cheese and a hotdog bursting with every condiment known to man!

"Oh this looks good sweetheart! Thank you so much for doing this for us. I can't begin to tell you how much your help means to me!'

Karen beamed with pride and they enjoyed their dinner. Karen put her hand to her chin and Julie knew she had something on her mind.

"Mom, I was thinking about you returning to work. I

know you want to and I really think it would be good for you. If you worked during the day we could still spend our evenings together, what do you think?"

Julie got up and put their plates in the sink.

"If I worked during the day Robert would need a sitter..."

Karen interrupted her.

"I know, and what I was thinking was that Edi could sit with him. Remember she had told you she would love to baby sit for him?"

Julie had forgotten all about Edi and what she had proclaimed but thinking about it Karen was right. She had told them she would do anything she could for them and would dearly love to baby sit.

Perhaps that would be the answer. Karen was also correct saying that if she worked days they could still have their evenings together. The more she thought about it the more she liked that idea.

She really liked Edi. Edi was a wonderful woman, a little brusque on the outside perhaps but she could tell she had a very compassionate and loving heart on the inside. She knew Edi adored all of them and she would have no qualms trusting her with Robert.

What an ingenious idea! Again, she found her daughter's insight and wisdom simply amazing. Now all she had to do was to get Edi's approval of the idea; oh yes, and to see if Larry had an opening.

"I really like that idea. I would never have thought of her! I think Edi would make a wonderful baby sitter! I know she isn't doing anything during the day because she and Leonard are both retired. She really adored Robert too. How do you come up with these great ideas?"

Karen laughed and replied with a glimmer in her eye.

"I pay attention mom. Come on now, you don't have all the brains in the family."

Julie gently punched Karen's arm and winked.

"That would be perfect. I could work during the day while you're in school and we could hang out together in the evening. I love it! I'm going to call Larry right now and see if he has an opening for the days."

Karen gave thumbs up.

"You go mom!"

Julie got her cell phone out and clicked on Larry's number. Her heart was racing. This would be a big step and require some adjusting. It had been a while since she was working but it was something she wanted to do.

The phone rang several times before Larry finally answered.

"Julie; this is quite a nice surprise! It seems so long since we talked. How are you?"

Julie nodded at Karen and replied.

"Everyone here is great Larry; how have you been?"

She could hear a lot of noise in the background.

"Oh I am doing fantastic. Things here have been bustling. I got a couple large flat screen televisions and installed them behind the bar so now everyone comes in to watch the football games.

Business has really been great. It's all I can do to keep up but I'm not complaining. I don't know why I didn't do that before.

I set up a buffet table for the games and have special prices for drinks. It has really made a world of difference. Oh we still have the regular crowd during the week but on the weekends we get all the football fans!

Claudia isn't happy with it of course because I have been working a lot of additional hours but I know she's happy about it in her own way.

Hey, are you still interested in coming back to work? I sure could use you; I'm too old to be working all these double shifts! I don't want to push my luck too far with Claudia; her patience will only go so far with me I know!"

This was music to her ears. Her question about an opening had already been answered! How perfect she thought. She turned to Karen and smiled from ear to ear.

"Well Larry, it's funny you should ask that because that was the very reason I was calling. Yes I am very interested in coming back. So you are looking for someone to cover the weekends?"

"No, actually I enjoy working the games. What I would hope for is someone to help me during the week so I could spend a little time at home."

This was too good to be true. Julie was hoping to have the weekends off so she and Karen could do things together. Her smile kept getting bigger.

"That would be perfect for me Larry. Now did you want someone for the days or evenings?"

"Well Julie, I just hired a very nice young man who can only work nights so would you be available during the days? I know you are used to being on nights and Karen will be in school and you need to think of your son..."

Julie couldn't believe her luck. She stopped him in mid sentence.

"That is actually what I was hoping for Larry. I wanted to spend the evenings with Karen. I was thinking about asking Edi to baby sit Robert, do you think she would do it?"

Larry laughed joyfully.

"Oh she would love that I'm sure! She has spoken about him many times and it would give her something to do, yes I think that is a marvelous idea! She is really good with children, it's a shame she and Leonard couldn't have any of their own. I'm sure that would mean a lot to her."

Julie was inspired by his encouragement.

"I'm going to call her as soon as we get off the phone and I will let you know what she says."

"Well it sounds like we just may have an arrangement that will work out for everyone then. You will enjoy the weekdays because like I said the usual group still comes in and I am sure everyone will be thrilled to see you back. I know Claudia will be thrilled, she thinks I am getting too old for all of this. When can you start?"

Julie wanted to jump right in so she gave him the best answer she could.

"Karen starts school Monday so if I can arrange my baby sitter I could start then. I will give her a call and get back to you."

They chatted for a few minutes, Larry caught her up with all the changes he had made to the bar and she filled him in on the latest on Karen and Robert. They mutually agreed on how wonderful it was to get back in touch and how excited they both were about her returning to work then hung up.

She filled Karen in with the details of their conversation and then heated up a cup of coffee. She then clicked on Edi's number.

Edi checked her caller ID then greeted the surprise caller with her usual warm outgoing personality.

"Well I'll be, Julie, what a joy it is to hear that sweet voice of yours again. How are y'all doing doll?"

Julie giggled. She so enjoyed talking to her.

"Edi it is a pleasure hearing yours as well. We are all doing fantastic! How are things with you and Leonard?"

Edi didn't skip a beat.

"Oh let me tell you about that old fart. Do you know what he did? Since he doesn't have your house to pitter around in any more he went out and bought a new car! Well, it's hardly new; it must be thirty years old. It's a piece of shit if you ask me. A dang sports car, the damn thing only has two seats!

What the hell does an old geezer like him need a sports car for? It's going to take more than that for him to impress anyone!

Not only that, but he insists on taking us for rides practically every day, usually right through town where everyone we know can see us! Do you know how ridiculous we look riding around in that stupid teenager car? Hell I can hardly fit in the damn thing!"

Julie was now laughing hysterically.

"Well Edi, I guess he could have done a lot worse things. I hear all men his age have a mid life crisis I think you're getting off pretty easy actually. It's been known for some men to do a lot worse things."

Edi let out a loud grunt.

"Well if you are referring to him possibly having an affair I'm not worried about that at all. He knows I'd slice him up like a cucumber before he even got his pants off! Besides, there isn't another woman on this planet that would want him!"

Julie was laughing almost to the point of tears as Edi continued.

"So doll, what brought you to pick up the phone?"

Julie tried to compose herself.

"Edi, I'm going back to work at Larry's. Now he wants me to work days which of course is when Karen would be in school so, in a nutshell, I need a baby sitter for Robert and you were the first person I thought of. Would you be interested?"

Edi replied without hesitation.

"Oh glory be, yes I would love to! Oh honey that would mean the world to me. You know I love that little guy and that would get me away from that crazy man I live with; might extend his life. Then he could go joy riding in his jalopy all he wants and make a fool of himself alone. I would love to baby sit for you, when can I start?"

Julie shook her head in disbelief.

"Well we need to discuss your salary Edi."

Edi laughed.

"Discuss my salary? Oh hell you don't need to pay me, I would enjoy it. Leonard and I don't need any money; I would love to do it, like I said; just to get out of this dang house. That would be all the payment I would need."

Julie was beside herself with joy. Everything was falling into place so nicely. She was returning to work, Karen was excited about the new school year, Robert wouldn't be forced to take anymore testing and now she has a baby sitter who isn't even charging her!

She told Edi she would be starting Monday. They set a time for Edi to be there and she thanked her over and over again.

Julie updated Karen then called Larry back and they agreed she would start work Monday morning.

# 33

Dr. Silverman decided to pay an unexpected visit to Dr. Hart's office. Something was gnawing at him that his professional mind wouldn't let go of. He knocked on his door and was invited in.

"Well this is a surprise Terrance, what are you doing in this neighborhood?"

Dr. Silverman sat in the chair facing Dr. Hart's desk.

"John, I can't get the Well's child out of my head. I went over his charts again and reviewed his test results and it just doesn't add up."

Dr. Hart rubbed his forehead in thought.

"What's troubling you Terrance?"

Terrance shook his head in confusion.

"John, you have seen the same things I have. You know what's troubling me! My God, the kid's brain development is through the roof! I've never seen anything like it and I know you haven't either!

Not only were his MRI results practically unbelievable but the records you have about his blood composition, well they don't make any sense!

You have to feel the same way, there's no other way of looking at it. How can you explain his white cell count? That alone should be a red flag; it could an immune system disorder, a bone marrow problem or even a prelude to leukemia!"

Dr. Hart remained silent as Dr. Silverman continued.

"John, the child was three months premature yet shows no sign of it. His growth and development have skyrocketed and would be exaggerated even in a full term baby. Doesn't this alarm you in any way, or at least pique your interest?"

Dr. Hart reached into his bottom left desk drawer and pulled out a bottle of Crown Royal and two shot glasses. He poured the shots and slid one over to his colleague.

"Terrance, let's have a drink. Do the results pique my interest, of course they do. Do I find anything to be concerned about, no I do not.

It's our job as doctors to ensure our patients are healthy and I an completely satisfied that young Robert here is very healthy so I can sleep well at night knowing I am doing a pretty good job with this patient. Now where does your problem lie?"

The doctor picked up his shot and stared into it before returning his glance to Dr. Hart.

"Let me ask you this, don't we also have an obligation to the furthering of medical science? John, what we have here could be a mutation that could give us incredible new knowledge into human development!

If we can break down what is causing this the end results could be mind-boggling! It could present us with inconceivable breakthroughs, can't you see that? We have a gold mine here!

And his blood, well it's nothing short of a medical miracle! If we could break it down and somehow synthesize it, do you realize how many lives we might save?""

Dr. Hart chugged his shot then poured another. He pointed to Terrance's shot and encouraged him to do the same.

"Terrance, I didn't become a doctor to advance medical science. I became a doctor to help people and I do that by making sure my patients are healthy which is exactly what I have done in this case.

Now just what can I do to calm your jets here?"

Dr. Silverman finally drank his shot and pushed his empty glass towards John in a silent request for a refill. He thought for a moment.

"Okay John, I can appreciate your desire not to further inconvenience your patient, I will respect that. I also concur that the patient is indeed healthy at the moment so no further testing is required to ensure that.

I think I have an answer that will solve both my curiosity and your wishes for your patient."

Dr. Hart finished his second shot and nodded slowly.

"Alright doctor, what might that suggestion be?"

Dr. Silverman drank his shot and then addressed his friend.

"Do you have any blood samples from the child?"

John nodded.

"Of course I do, why?"

Dr. Silverman cleared his throat.

"May I have one? I know of an excellent hematologist, a leader in the field. He is at the Antwerp Hematology Research Center in Belgium so you wouldn't have to worry about him coming over and pursuing it any further. He has won the ASH award twice, he's good!

I would dearly love for him to take a look at it and see just what he has to say about it. I promise you I will not contact your patient or even suggest any further testing be done on him. Appease me here John please."

Putting his humanitarian heart aside for just one moment, Dr. Hart drew from his professional mind. In the very back of that mind were the very same curiosities. Robert did have the most intriguing physiology he had ever encountered and there were a lot of unanswered questions. As a medical doctor how could he deny them? He knew Dr. Silverman had a valid point.

"Terrance, I can't believe I am agreeing to this. It goes against my better judgment and I'm not even sure how legal it is but if this is what it is going to take to get you off my back I will give you the sample. Before I do give me your solemn word as a gentleman no further investigation will follow this.

Yes, of course, as a professional I share your inquisitiveness but I want no additional stress put on the family. Do we completely understand each other?"

Dr. Silverman extended his arm for a handshake.

"We do indeed doctor. I will agree to those terms."

Dr. Hart made the necessary phone call to arrange the sample transfer and poured another shot for both of them. He said a silent prayer that he hadn't just opened up Pandora's Box.

"John, I have no desire or intention of bringing your patient into this. My inquiry will be simply to reach out and see if we have anything we can learn from here. We just might be on the doorstep to some incredible discovery that will benefit the medical community as a whole. I will share the results of his diagnosis when I get them with you."

Dr. Hart nodded in hesitant agreement and Dr. Silverman left to go to the lab and get the blood sample.

The next day Dr. Silverman had packaged the sample and was ready to send it off to Belgium. He thought about how he wanted to present the project to his foreign colleague and decided a simple phone call would suffice to explain the delivery and request that went along with it.

He wanted a completely unbiased and unprejudiced evaluation so he decided to avert giving the doctor any information what so ever about the origin of the sample. He was intentionally vague, never mentioning it was from a child or a patient or why he found the sample to be so worthy of such an unusual request.

He deliberately avoided mentioning any background about it or where it came from stating only that it was an unusual sample he wanted a thorough examination and professional evaluation of.

After quickly discovering any further questioning was pointless, Dr. Guillaume Mertens cordially agreed and said he would look forward to receiving it. Dr. Mertens promised to give it his top priority and have results for him as quickly as possible.

A week had passed before Dr. Silverman finally got the call he had been sitting on pins and needles waiting for. His phone rang and checking the caller ID he was ecstatic to see it was Dr. Mertens.

"Dr. Mertens, it is so good to hear from you! I have been anxiously awaiting your call."

Guillaume cleared his throat before answering.

"After studying the blood sample you sent me I have no doubt that you have. It has been the talk of our entire department for the past week I must say."

Dr. Silverman quickly got out his legal pad and pen and proceeded.

"So you have analyzed the sample?"

Dr. Mertens replied enthusiastically.

"Oh yes indeed, after an initial examination of it I have had my entire team do nothing but analyze it! When you first mentioned you had an unusual blood sample you wanted my thoughts on I found it strange. I said to myself, with all the excellent physicians you have access to there why would you need my opinion.

Well, I now have a complete understanding of why you would solicit our help. You have a lot of people over here shaking their heads and I am one of them!"

Dr. Silverman rubbed his eyes fearing that this might actually lead to more questions than answers.

"Well then will you tell me your conclusions doctor?"

Dr. Mertens ran his fingers through his hair trying to sound intelligent with his reply.

"That's just it, I'm afraid we don't have any, well none that make any sense. I have never encountered any blood like this in my entire career. Before I go further you have to tell me what type of creature did you draw this sample from?"

Dr. Silverman thought the wordage of that reply very odd and had to question him on it.

"Doctor; that was what I was hoping you could tell me."

Guillaume sighed trying to formulate the correct words that wouldn't have his medical license revoked.

"Well, you gave me no information to start off with. I had no idea what we were dealing with here. I didn't know if it were animal, vegetable or mineral but after examining it and collecting the informed opinions of my department heads I can assure you of one thing....it's not human!"

Dr. Silverman had to take a deep breath. He anticipated an interesting testimony but nothing like this.

"That's absurd doctor. Just what are you saying?"

Dr. Mertens took a moment and lit a cigarette.

"Terrance, the sample you sent me was unlike any blood I have ever seen. I had of course initially assumed it was from one of your patients so I studied it with that in mind.

The first thing we tried to do was to type it, to get an idea of what we were dealing with. We preformed the standard ABO typing test. Well the first alarm went off when we discovered it wouldn't allow us to categorize it. The blood cells were not reacting normally.

This of course threw us off a bit so my first thought was that it might be from an animal. This notion didn't last long. While the cells wouldn't stick together as was expected they did display some human characteristics.

We then skipped that step and proceeded. First of all the white blood cell count was surprisingly high, I'm sure you were already aware of that.

We then moved on to the red cells which were taking

in an extraordinary about of oxygen, the levels of which I have never seen. I couldn't imagine a human circulatory system capable of managing that amount of oxygen to the brain.

The same can be said about the plasma. The plasma was carrying unheard of amounts of protein and nutrients, some of which we couldn't even identify! I can say with every ounce of certainty that this was not human blood, at least not of any human we know of!

Now will you please tell me where this sample came from?"

Dr. Silverman was at a total loss for words. He meekly replied.

"It came from a two-month-old child."

Dr. Mertens replied boisterously.

"That would be impossible doctor. No two-month-old child could survive with this flowing through his veins! This blood is the most remarkable concoction I have ever run across. You don't realize what we are dealing with here.

The white cells would give the creature almost complete immunity to any invading pathogens that nature could conjure up. The extraordinary level of oxygen could only end up in the brain and God knows what capacity that would provide and the proteins and nutrients would provide incredible stamina and strength to any tissue they would encounter.

What ever creature is enjoying this life force must be one tough son of a bitch is all I can say. But I can say with certainty it isn't human and most definitely not a two-month-old child!"

Dr. Silverman needed final confirmation before continuing.

"You're absolutely certain on that?"

Dr. Mertens replied without hesitation.

"There is no doubt about that."

Terrence flew himself against the back of his chair. He closed his eyes and folded his hands on his lap in dismay. He wished he had another shot of that Crown Royal right now; this simply wasn't making any sense. What he initially thought of as only an enigma was rapidly turning into a major conundrum.

Dr. Mertens was a leader in the field of hematology; he wouldn't go off half cocked like this unless he had a pretty good reason. He had no thoughts what so ever on this interpretation. He was in a state of shock. Just how was he supposed to respond to such an outrageous statement? He simply thanked the doctor for his time and efforts and hung up.

He sat back in his chair deep in thought. He had no other recourse than to totally believe and respect what he had just heard considering its source; now how to process that information and more importantly who to share it with.

He was at a moral and ethical crossroads. He had promised his good friend Dr. Hart not to pursue it but if what he had just heard was actually true he owed it to the medical community to follow up on it.

Never in his wildest dreams had he anticipated such an astonishing finding. Would the gravity of this discovery negate his promise to his colleague? He remembered he had promised Dr. Hart to share the results once he got them so he thought calling him would be the next logical step.

He kept repeating the words 'it's not human' in his mind. What could that really mean? He saw the child himself; it certainly looked human to him. If it's not human then what the hell is it? Just what were the implications of this discovery?

Initially he had feared the condition to be a threat

only to the child, but now he was beginning to wonder if it might be a risk to the entire general population!

He was glad he had the insight to make Dr. Mertens promise confidentiality before he gave him the sample. Dr. Mertens was a respected member of the medical community and a long time friend, he trusted him to keep that promise.

Now the only way this would leak out would be by either Dr. Hart or himself. Dr. Mertens said he would fax him a complete report. He had requested this because he knew when he presented Dr. Hart with the findings he would demand proof.

Just how was he supposed to explain this to Dr. Hart? He was very anxious for his reaction. He knew how protective the doctor was of his patient but how could he just let something like this go? There would be only one way of answering that question.

He had to convince him to research this further! They were now dealing with something that could be a lot larger than either of them had ever anticipated. He was certain of three things. First there was something wrong with the child's blood that no one understood. Second it had to be taken seriously because until they figured out exactly what it was it had to be considered an epidemic threat and thirdly he would have to be the one to initiate any further study because he knew Dr. Hart would refuse.

His first concern was to prevent an epidemic. If the child was indeed carrying some form of viral infection or mutation he would have to be quarantined to prevent any possibility of a propagated epidemic. Until they totally understood this abnormality the risk couldn't be denied. Even Dr. Hart, once he learned the truth, couldn't argue this.

Secondly they would have to contact the appropriate

authorities to ensure they got the help they needed to figure this out. He had never dealt with anything like this before and he wasn't sure just who to contact.

The first thing he wanted to do was to share this with Dr. Hart. He had promised he would give him the results once he got them and he was sure they would get the doctor's attention.

He called John's cell phone. Dr. Hart answered on the second ring and after checking his caller ID greeted the caller with enthusiasm.

"Terrance, how are you?"

Dr. Silverman wasted no time emphasizing this was not a social call.

"John, we have to talk!"

Dr. Hart was taken back by the caller's tone of voice.

"Okay, I've got a few minutes, what's up?"

"No, we have to discuss this in person. I'm going to be in town tomorrow you have any free time?"

John was confused by his colleague's urgency.

"Well, I was actually going to take tomorrow off. The wife is out of town for a few days and I was going out to Clearwater point to do some fishing, I hear the bass are really hitting and I had hopes of getting a few."

Dr. Silverman cleared his throat.

"Put away your rod and reel John, you may already be sitting on the biggest catch of your life! Now I owe you a drink, can you meet me at Fennecci's about three?"

Dr. Hart took a minute to think. There was something about Terrance's articulation that bothered him immediately. He had a bad feeling he knew what this concerned.

"Alright Terrance, I could be there. Will you tell me what this is all about? Is this about the Well's child?"

Dr. Silverman replied honestly.

"You know it is John. This is something that has to be addressed."

Dr. Hart slammed his fist on his desk.

"You promised me you wouldn't pursue this!"

"You will feel differently once I tell you what I have found out. You're not going to believe this! This is big John, really big! I will explain everything tomorrow. I will see you at three."

Dr. Silverman pulled into Fennecci's parking lot and grabbed his satchel. He entered the crowded restaurant and quickly found Dr. Hart already at the bar.

He took the seat next to him they exchanged nods and shook hands. John took a sip of his bourbon and coke and addressed his friend.

"Okay Terrance, I don't know what you are trying to pull here, I told you not to pursue anything about the Well's child and you agreed so why are we here?"

Dr. Silverman ordered a double shot of scotch and lit a cigarette. He opened his satchel and paged through the many papers inside until he came to the hematology report. He handed the two page fax to Dr. Hart.

"Just take a couple minutes John and read this."

Dr. Hart took the papers then ordered another drink. His stare turned to his colleague.

"Terrance, I don't want to see this."

Dr, Silverman glared back.

"Oh you need to see this! Keep in mind it comes from one of the most respected hematologists in the world."

John took a drink then reluctantly read the report. He put his hand to his forehead deep in thought. The words on the document were piercing and couldn't be refuted. He was totally shocked. Dumbfounded, he gave Dr. Silverman a puzzled look.

"I don't know what to make of this; it simply doesn't make any sense. Not human? Be serious, you saw the child we both know he is as human as you and I! How could they have come up with such an absurd conclusion?"

Dr. Silverman finished his shot and put out his cigarette, quickly lighting another one. He then requested another shot from the bartender who happened to be passing by. He scowled at his friend.

"Is he?" Do we know that for sure? If that's the case John then explain these findings! Why would a renowned doctor with his reputation at stake even imply such a thing? I'm telling you, there is more here than meets the eye and we have to find out what it is.

We took an oath as doctors to do what is best for the health of our patients and the general population and we have to remember that! I know you like the family but you have to admit we might have a problem here!

I don't want to go over your head John but this state has laws requiring physicians to report possible health risks to the CDC. We need to find out just what is going on with that child!"

Dr. Hart slammed his fist on the bar.

"This child is no health risk! He is showing no signs of any illness or distress. You are way out of line here!"

Dr. Silverman shook his head in disagreement.

"I understand that but he could be a carrier and show no ill effects. John we don't have any idea what we might be dealing with here and we have to find out before it becomes a real problem!

The child's growth and development are frightening and simply cannot be explained. We as physicians have to take this abnormality seriously! We don't know if this might be some malignancy or prelude to some infectious outbreak. Are you willing to take that chance?"

Dr. Hart rubbed his temples in frustration and gulped the remainder of his drink. He flagged down the bartender and ordered another. There were many points of Dr. Silverman's argument he couldn't deny. Robert's growth was indeed alarming and unexplained and the state did have such laws but was he really a health risk?

In all his years as a doctor he had never run across anything like this. There has to be something causing Robert's rapid development but was it a health risk?

He knew Dr. Silverman could go over his head and not be questioned. He also knew if the CDC became involved he would have to relinquish all of Robert's medical records and that would certainly open some eyes and lead to extensive additional testing on the poor child and incredible stress to her mother.

Finally he admitted that while he personally saw no threat, if indeed there turned out to be one and he resisted further inquiry, it would be the end of his career. Dr. Silverman seemed determined to pursue this and there was little he could do to stop him.

He gulped down his fresh drink and replied.

"Terrance, you saw the child, you saw the test results, and do you really believe him to be a possible health threat?"

Dr. Silverman just shrugged his shoulders.

"John, we simply can't say. But in this case it is better safe than sorry. We need to get to the bottom of this! I hope I'm wrong, I really do. But if this thing turns out ugly and you go against it you know your ass will be in a sling. You won't be able to get a job as a paramedic!"

Dr. Hart folded his hands in thought and stared at his drink. He and Terrance had been friends for years and had developed a deep respect for each other. This is why he had called for his opinion in the first place.

It was now time for him to draw upon that friendship and mutual respect again.

"Terrance, I come to you now as a close friend and

not a colleague. I honestly see no threat to public safety in this at all. The child appears to be in perfect health which is my first concern.

Julie is a good Christian lady who has been through a hell of a lot already. She has had to raise an emotionally disabled daughter all by herself.

She has lost her significant other to a sudden and unforeseen heart attack. She is struggling financially simply to make ends meet. If you were to pursue this it would cause incredible and probably irreparable additional suffering to her and her daughter.

I have to say neither of these good people need or deserve such additional turmoil in their lives, especially over this witch hunt you have concocted based on nothing but speculation.

If I had any professional concerns over this issue of course I would allow you to pursue it but I can truthfully say I do not. A crucial element in being a doctor is the ability to show compassion; now would be a good time to practice that!

So Terrance, I have known you for many years as both a respected colleague and trusted friend, you're a good man, and I am asking you not to persist this investigation; as a personal favor to me."

Dr. Silverman stirred his drink for no other reason than to buy him a minute to respond. He took a deep breath and bit his lip as he replied in earnest.

"This means that much to you John?"

Dr. Hart nodded.

"Yes Terrance, it does."

Dr. Silverman rubbed his forehead.

"John, if this thing blows up you have to know that it will be all on you. Are you willing to risk your career on this? I'm completely washing my hands of it."

Dr. Hart finished his drink and looked sternly at his friend.

"I am and I am confident that this child places no threat to anyone."

Terrance took a deep breath.

"Alright John, consider the issue dropped. I hope this doesn't come back and bite us on the ass. This is a huge gamble you're taking and I will not go down with you, as long as you know and accept that."

The two men shook hands.

# 34

The past year had been amazing. Julie was loving being back at work. She marveled at the improvements Larry had made in the bar and rejoiced in being reacquainted with many of the same patrons she remembered from before and had grown to call friends.

The social interaction was allowing her to regain some lost self respect she was suffering from in her time away. It also was a wonderful cure for the loneliness and depression she would occasionally find herself reluctantly wallowing in.

Karen was excelling in school. She had earned a 3.0 GPA and had been named the captain of the debate team. Julie had found both parental pride and humor in this accomplishment. She thought back to all the years of arguing the two of them had endured and how accomplished Karen had become at it.

She was glad it had finally paid a dividend for her daughter and she was using that skill for a good purpose. Julie was also thrilled that Karen had made many new friends, good kids, who she would invite home on occasion.

Robert continued to grow and mature at an alarming rate. They had been continuing their bi-weekly checkups and Dr. Hart habitually mentioned this. With every visit he would first assure her that he was very healthy but continued to be amazed at his growth.

Robert was crawling at three months, and his first attempts at walking came only a couple months later. According to Dr. Hart both of these milestones were way ahead of schedule.

He had grown a remarkable head of dark brown hair

which matched his deep brown eyes. He looked more like his father with each passing day. Even his developing facial expressions reminded her of his dad. The curiosity, inquisitiveness and wonder in his eyes mirrored that of his father's.

The doctor remained amazed at Robert's alertness, commenting that the child always seemed fascinated and very much aware of his surroundings. He found this most unusual for a child his age. Julie could only wonder about what surprises might lay in the future as he continues to grow and mature.

Edi had been a wonderful baby sitter. She would always arrive early and almost always bearing gifts. One day she would bring bags of groceries and then another day a box of blankets or children's clothes. While there, her complete attention never wavered from Robert. She would get on the floor and play with him for hours. The two of them created an incredible bond.

Julie would enjoy watching them interact when she got home from work. She would thoroughly revel in watching Edi, on her hands and knees, talking to Robert. Robert would listen intently and study his new and most interesting friend as if he were just humoring her.

She chuckled to herself that such a brash woman on the outside could be so awesome with children. She then reflected on how Edi had sadly confessed she couldn't have any children of her own and thought it a shame, for she would have made an incredible mother.

Everything was going so well. In the evenings when she came home from work she and Karen would go over her homework together then, after dinner, either watch television or play a game.

Julie cherished her time with her daughter and things were working out where it allowed her a great deal of time with her. Robert was always there on the floor right beside them. He seemed to take great interest in the family's activities. He was always reaching out as if he wanted to be more of a part of them.

August 12th was a very special day at the Well's residence; it was Robert's first birthday! Julie found it hard to believe it had been a year since Robert was born.

She and Karen had organized a festive party to celebrate the occasion. Julie had baked a beautiful chocolate layer cake with whipped cream icing. As much as she wanted to put an alien face on the top she wisely settled for a clown holding balloons after Karen reminded her not everyone in attendance would be wise to their little secret and that would be difficult to explain.

The event was held on their front porch which Julie had elaborately decorated with colorful bunting and a multitude of balloons. She ignored repeated reminders by her daughter that little Robert would be too young to actually appreciate her intentions.

She couldn't help but harbor thoughts that just maybe he wasn't and he would indeed recognize and hopefully appreciate her efforts.

Larry had catered the event with food from the bar. He grilled a couple dozen of his famous cheeseburgers and added a few pizzas he made himself. He supplied chips, dips and pretzels and brought cases of beverages courtesy of the bar's supplies.

Larry and Claudia were the first to arrive. Julie smiled with joy as Larry unpacked countless boxes filled with food and drink from the back of his truck. Claudia helped arrange everything on the porch, setting up a nice buffet table as Julie thanked them numerous times.

Minutes later a red pick up truck pulled in the driveway behind Larry's truck and Julie knew Edi and Leonard had arrived.

Edi bounced out of the cab and motioned Julie to come over.

"Come over here doll, I brought something for us!"

Julie continued to enjoy Edi's unique personality and was anxious to see what she had brought.

Edie gave Julie a hug. She walked to the bed of the truck.

"Do you-all have a punch bowl?"

Julie gave her friend a quizzical look.

"Do I have a punch bowl? I think I have an old one somewhere why?"

Edi grabbed a large plastic jug from the bed of the truck and handed it to Julie.

"Well this is a special occasion so I brought something for us. Its a little concoction I make for special occasions I call Edi's elixir. It's guaranteed to cure what ails you and make you feel real good while doing it!

Now you fetch that punch bowl and set it somewhere inside. We've got to keep the youngins away from this because this is only for us adults."

Julie could only shake her head and laugh as the two of them carried the punch into the kitchen.

After rummaging through the kitchen counters Julie finally unearthed the punch bowl and after washing it out she placed it on the kitchen table.

Edie quickly grabbed the jug and poured the red liquid into the bowl.

"Okay sweetie, now get us some glasses or straws or something, we don't want to let this stuff just sit out too long here it might explode and we have a party to get started here!"

Julie chuckled as she got them two small glasses. Edi immediately filled them with her punch and handed one to Julie.

"Bottoms up woman, we have to celebrate this little fellow's big day!"

Julie sniffed the punch and could tell it was high octane. She was never much of a hard liquor drinker and was hesitant about just how powerful this drink might be.

Edie and Julie touched glasses in a toast and both consumed the punch.

It burned going down her throat and Julie gasped.

"Wow, I think this was the stuff they used to get to the moon! What is in this?"

Edie laughed out loud and grabbed Julie's glass refilling it.

"Oh this is an old family recipe my daddy used to make. Let me just say you won't find it in any store! Now this is an auspicious occasion so let's start it off right!"

Julie reluctantly took the glass and then a deep breath. She hesitated before drinking it. She was never very good at handling her liquor which is largely why she had avoided it over the years.

"C'mon woman, you're a big girl. You deserve this; a toast to a happy birthday for little Robert!"

They again touched glasses and Julie downed the drink. Julie put her hands to her head as if to calm it down. She was thinking she drank too quickly because she could already start to feel the effects of the alcohol.

Edi was not finished yet. She poured a third drink and handed Julie the glass.

Julie waved it off.

"Oh I shouldn't, I have to keep my wits here I have a party to supervise."

Edi just laughed.

"Oh doll I have your back don't worry about a thing. Now you enjoy yourself."

Julie hesitantly sipped the drink before finally gaining

the courage to finish it. She placed her glass in the sink to prevent Edi from filling it again.

Edi got the hint and they both walked out to the porch to rejoin the party which was growing rapidly.

A number of Karen's school friends had arrived and she noticed Dr. Hart walking up the driveway bearing a gift. She was shocked to see him never expecting him to come even though she had invited him. She never thought he would take time out of his busy schedule to attend.

Her head was spinning. She wasn't used to having this much hard liquor so she stopped at the doorway to regain her senses.

Julie's first priority was to track down her son. She scanned the yard and was relieved he hadn't wandered off unattended. She then glanced at the porch which was buzzing with activity.

Edi, Leonard, Claudia and Larry were attending the buffet table and there were a number of teenagers mingling about. She noticed little Robert waddling amongst the kids. He was forced to endure constant pats on the head from each of them as he strolled by.

It was obvious Robert was taking center stage as he would awkwardly try and walk amongst the guests, having to constantly be interrupted by annoying pats on the head. He seemed to be tolerating, rather than actually enjoying, all the adoration. He would occasional let out a coo or a giggle, obviously intrigued with all the unusual attention.

She was pleased to see Karen attentive to him as he tolerated the endless stream of adulation. She then took another deep breath, with the knowledge that Robert was in good hands she now had to deal with the ordeal of greeting Dr. Hart.

She would have to conceal, as best she could, the fact

that, as much as she tried to deny it, she was very close to being totally intoxicated. This was an area in which she had little experience.

Julie slowly and courageously made it down the porch steps to the yard where the doctor was rapidly approaching. She walked deliberately, yet cautiously, towards him. She discovered she had to make a conscious effort to avoid swaying which embarrassed her. She knew she had to limit her words for she wasn't sure how impaired her speech might be.

She finally reached him and they shook hands.

"Dr. Hart what a surprise, I mean it is such a pleasure to see you, it really is doctor I mean it. I'm so glad you could come! It's really great that you came."

She cringed at her awkward wording as the doctor smiled and handed her a gift.

"I really wanted to be here Julie. You, Karen and Robert have become like family to me over the years. I brought a little something for him."

She took the gift and thanked him as they walked to the porch. Karen and Robert were sitting on the steps as they approached.

The doctor leaned down and patted Robert on the head.

"There's the birthday boy! Karen, it's good to see you how have you been?"

Karen smiled.

"I've been good thanks. It's really cool you came!"

The doctor continued on to the porch and Julie sat down next to her family.

Robert nestled in his mother's lap as Karen spoke.

"This party really turned out great mom. It looks like everyone is having a great time."

Julie smiled and clutched her son tightly as much for fear of dropping him as a sign of affection.

"Yes it has. I only wish his dad could be here to enjoy this with us, he would have loved it."

Robert listened carefully to the words his mother had spoken, meticulously analyzing every syllable. He raised his head to look directly in his mother's eyes with a curious stare.

"Da?"

Julie's mouth dropped to the floor. Karen's eyes grew as big as saucers. This was the first sound Robert had ever made that could be construed as an attempt to speak a word.

Karen and her mother looked at each other in unison and in shock. Julie finally managed to speak.

"Did you just hear that?"

Karen nodded.

"Mom, it sounded like he tried to say dad!"

Julie grabbed her daughter's shoulder.

"I think that's exactly what he was trying to say! I mean what else did it sound like huh? How about that! That's really, well it's really something."

While his mother and sister tried to come to grips with the situation, Robert fought his mother's grip and crawled out of her lap and down the steps. He then stood up and walked slowly and clumsily out to the grass in the front yard where he dropped to the ground.

Karen turned her attention to her mother.

"Mom, are you okay, you look funny, and you're talking funny too."

Julie was alarmed at her daughter's statement. She wondered to herself if her intoxication was that noticeable. She spoke slowly but unbeknownst to her, with a distinctive slur.

"I'm just fine sweetheart! Isn't this a wonderful party? Look at all the people, wow."

Karen was now certain of her mother's condition.

"Mother, have you been drinking?"

Julie was totally distraught over her daughter's observation. Her secret was out. She had to calm the situation. She wanted to continue her history of always being totally honest with Karen while at the same time downplay the severity.

"Oh Edi and I just had a little one. I'm fine sweetheart. I'm so proud of you watching over your brother like you are!"

She told herself to just shut up and relax. Karen just scowled her displeasure and returned her attention to Robert who was now nestled in the grass.

Dr. Hart excused himself to the ladies who were still sitting on the steps. He walked past them and strolled out on to the lawn and lit a cigarette. He was about ten feet from Robert who was now standing gazing up at the sky.

The child extended his arm and pointed to the heavens.

"Dah....dah"

Karen, who had been watching her brother, took immediate notice of his actions. An expression of complete shock crossed her face.

"Mom, did you hear that?"

Dr. Hart also noticed the child's behavior and in puzzlement walked over to him.

Julie shared their amazement. Karen jumped up in excitement.

"He talked, he actually talked mom! He tried to say dad again!"

Julie put her hands to her head in an effort to gather her thoughts.

"It certainly sounded that way didn't it? Yep it sure did."

Karen studied her brother in the yard. He was still pointing to the sky. Her mind was struggling with confusing thoughts.

"He's pointing to the sky looking and saying daddy....
he knows....mom, somehow he knows!"

Julie was wrestling with her intoxicated state. She
tried to come up with a reply that would put an end to
that train of thought. Her words were notably slurred.

"Oh that's just ridiculous. He's only one year old he
couldn't know anything, at least I don't think he could...
could he? Hell, who knows what he can do."

The alcohol was now clearly inhibiting her rational
thoughts. She closed her eyes knowing this was going
to be an ordeal getting through the party. She cursed
herself for succumbing to Edi's pressure to drink more
than she should.

Dr. Hart motioned Julie to join him next to Robert.
As much as she dearly wanted to remain sitting and
motionless she slowly stood up and walked gingerly
over to them. The world was spinning around making
navigating the short walk precarious. She could only
hope her staggering wouldn't be noticed.

She finally met up with Dr. Hart and smiled. The
doctor pointed to Robert.

"Did you hear him Julie, he said 'daddy' were these
his first words?"

Julie was not in the mood for questions. She sighed
and spoke slowly.

"Yes they certainly were! He has never said a word
before this."

Dr. Hart looked at Robert then at Julie.

"Well that's wonderful you must be pretty excited
having him say his first words on his birthday."

At the present moment, in her inebriated state, she
wasn't excited about anything and just nodded as the
doctor continued.

"I think it was adorable how he pointed to heaven and
said 'daddy'. Did you tell him his father was in heaven?"

Julie was totally confused by the unexpected question. She answered without thinking.

"Huh? No I didn't tell him anything like that."

Dr. Hart was surprised by her answer. He could tell from her broken speech and her swaying that she had been drinking but didn't address his observation.

"Well, if that's the case don't you find it rather odd that he's pointing to the sky and saying daddy? I wonder where his mindset is."

Julie uttered a drunken laugh. Her reply was slurred and spontaneous.

"You haven't heard odd yet. I could tell you some really odd stuff. Oh his daddy is up there alright, but he's not in heaven!"

Dr. Hart was now concerned about Julie's drunken state.

"Julie, we both know you have been drinking but just what are you trying to say?"

She tried to maintain her balance which was becoming a challenging task. She blurted out her next statement with no preconceived thought.

"I'm trying to tell you his father is an alien, you know from space. I guess I should have mentioned that to you before, but anyways…he's from another planet…Mars or Jupiter or someplace, I don't know all the damn planets and besides, he never told me the exact one so I don't really know where he's from."

Dr. Hart shook his head and sighed. He felt pity for Julie's condition and wasn't sure how to handle this. He knew she was intoxicated but none the less this was quite a story.

"Julie, we both know this is the alcohol talking and…"

She interrupted him.

"No, no, no it's not doctor, I'm telling you the truth I

really am. He's a freaking alien. I didn't believe it at first either."

The doctor bit his lip before speaking.

"Julie, I think you should go inside and lay down for a bit, maybe have some coffee."

Julie put up her hands and shook her head.

"I know you don't believe me but I can prove it...I can! You'll see and then you will believe me! Come inside with me doctor, you're going to love this; if I remember where I put the stuff that is."

Dr. Hart felt bad for Julie and the last thing he wanted to do was argue. He knew it was the alcohol talking so he just humored her.

# 35

On a distant planet twelve light years from Earth, a man lay frozen, dormant, in a complete state of hibernation, in cubicle 4, in the preservation wing of the Cryonics Laboratory. The lab was contained in the basement of the correctional facility. The man had no consciousness, no pain and was totally unawares of his surroundings as if in a deep sleep.

His body functions were being keenly monitored by a medley of assorted electronic instruments. Tubes ran in and out of the coffin-like tube which contained his body.

Computer graphs kept close track of his vitals ensuring they allow the body to remain in its current state. While appearing dead to the casual observer, he was very much alive.

Julie took the doctor's hand and leaned softly against him for balance. She led him towards the house. Her swaying gave the doctor reason for concern. He silently walked besides her allowing her to lean on him with an unspoken understanding.

They walked past Karen and Julie turned to her daughter.

"Karen, keep an eye on the little guy for a few minutes I have to show the good doctor here something. Just watch him okay?"

Karen first looked at her mother with disgruntled disapproval then at the doctor who returned her glance with a blank stare of confusion. They walked through the kitchen and Julie ignored the doctor's suggestion of getting a cup of coffee.

Julie led him into her bedroom where she instructed Dr. Hart to sit on the floor. He looked at her in total confusion and Julie just motioned with her arms. Her speech was slurred.

"Just sit on the floor and get comfortable I have got to find something, it will only take a minute, or maybe two, I hope, I don't know where the damn this is actually."

The doctor wanted to avoid any confrontation and thought it would be best for the moment to simply appease her. He sat Indian style on the floor and studied her as she opened the closet door.

Julie fumbled in the closet searching for Robert's suitcase. The doctor could hear sounds of boxes falling off the top shelf and resisted the urge to jump up to see if she was alright.

Moments later Julie emerged from the closet dragging a suitcase on the floor behind her. She slowly walked over to the doctor who had remained sitting on the floor and slid the suitcase over to him.

"I found it! I knew it was in there somewhere. Okay doc, this is where the fun begins; open it."

Doctor Hart looked at the satchel then at Julie who stood swaying before him.

"Julie, seriously what are we doing here? You better sit down before you fall down. I really think you should get a cup of coffee and..."

Julie interrupted him.

"Oh you will see in a minute and boy will you be surprised! Now I want you to open the suitcase okay? Go ahead, open it if you can."

She slowly and precariously lowered herself on to the floor next to the doctor who pulled the suitcase close to him and examined it.

Julie couldn't stop rambling in her impeded speech as the doctor studied the suitcase.

"Oh this is going to be so much fun. You're going to

totally freak out doc, you will, but then you will believe what I told you! You'll see!"

Dr. Hart lifted the suitcase and scrutinized it closely. It was unlike any suitcase he had ever seen before.

"This is a very nice satchel Julie, most unusual, is it yours?"

Julie shook her head in an exaggerated motion.

"Oh no, it was Robert's, he left it here."

The doctor nodded, avoiding for the moment at least, questioning the comment. He continued to examine it with increasing interest.

"I have never seen one like this before. It looks, maybe, European perhaps?"

Julie again shook her head.

"Well, it's from out of the country all right but it sure isn't from Europe I can tell you that! You just open it, take your time."

He checked every inch of the suitcase and gave Julie a puzzled expression.

"I don't see any way of opening it Julie. There are no latches I can't even determine a seam separating the top from the bottom anywhere. Just how do you open this thing?"

Julie laughed out loud and took the suitcase. She lifted the handle and found the red rectangle. She thought for a moment, trying to remember how Karen had done it and then placed her thumb over the rectangle. The suitcase slowly opened. Julie smiled with smug pride and winked at the doctor.

"You gotta have the touch doc. Now admit it, you won't find this at the local department store and don't even waste your time looking for it on the internet because you ain't gonna find it there either!"

Dr. Hart jumped back in amazement. He remained silent as Julie opened the top of the suitcase and peered inside. The doctor, now keenly interested in the item, watched her every move. He couldn't help but ponder the unusualness of the suitcase and how she opened it.

Julie knew exactly what she was looking for, the medical bag. She knew this would be of the most interest to the doctor and provide her with the best chance of proving her story.

She tossed aside the clothes which were on top and picked up the black leather pouch. Julie lifted it out of the suitcase and placed it between them.

Opening it in the same manner as she did the satchel she first grabbed a small leather pouch which contained the medical instrument and attachments that had been successfully used on Karen. Doctor Hart sat in quiet astonishment as she held the gold metallic object. She smiled and handed the instrument to the doctor.

"Now be real careful with this thing, we don't know what all it can do!"

Dr, Hart hesitantly took the object and gingerly examined it. He could tell immediately that this was no toy. It seemed masterly crafted in quality materials. He questioned the metal it was constructed with. It was too heavy to be titanium or platinum yet it didn't have the feel of steel. It had a hefty weight for its size so he could instantly recognize it as an instrument of some kind. He marveled at the glistening gold finish to the object.

He noticed a handle, and a row of very small buttons on the side each with a minuscule symbol below each one. He studied the symbols and couldn't make heads or tails of them; they were totally unfamiliar to him.

He then noticed four small circles which appeared to be lights. No, this was no toy; a lot of work had been put into the construction of this intricate thing. Now to determine exactly what it was.

He then examined the other end, the barrel end. He

noticed a thin tube which narrowed as it reached its end. At the very end of the tube was a slot and below that a tiny prong.

He placed it carefully on the floor and glanced at the small bag Julie had had handed him with the instrument. The bag contained what appeared to be attachments for the main part. Noticing the ends of the attachments he matched them up to the needle and prong at the end of the instrument. They were indeed components of the main part.

He had never seen anything like this in his life. He gave Julie a look of total awe as she sat silently smiling, enjoying his reaction.

Returning his attention to the device he pressed the first button. A laser shot out a needle thin beam of blue light from the tip of the instrument. The ray hit the wall and instantly burned into the wood paneling.

The doctor threw down the device and jumped back in alarm.

"What the hell is this thing, a light saber?"

Julie's eyes exploded in surprise.

"Wow, I didn't know it could do that! I told you to be careful with it. Far out...that was really cool!"

Dr. Hart looked at the instrument which now sat harmlessly on the floor next to him. He didn't know what to say.

"Julie, what the hell is this thing? Where did you get it from, I have never seen anything like this in my life! What is it used for?"

Julie shrugged her shoulders.

"It's some kind of medical thing; I thought you would know what it was you're the doctor. But wait, that's right you wouldn't. You would have no way of knowing what it is because we haven't invented it yet, that's what Robert said."

Dr. Hart was beyond confused. Still jittery from the shock of the instrument and the unexpected laser beam he thought about Julie's last sentence. He glanced at her in hopes she could answer some of the many questions he had.

"Julie, you said Robert had left it here I'm assuming you mean Robert's father?"

Julie nodded.

"Doc, of course I meant his father silly."

Dr. Hart was trying to assemble the pieces of what is turning out to be a very complex puzzle.

"You told me his father had passed away."

Julie put up her hands in embarrassment.

"Well, that isn't exactly accurate. I may have changed the story a bit because I didn't think you would believe the truth okay?"

The doctor was trying to make sense of the picture.

"You want me to believe the truth is he is from another planet is that right Julie?"

Julie smiled and nodded as the doctor tried to digest all of this.

"I'm sure you know how outlandish this story is Julie."

Julie pointed to the instrument sitting on the floor.

"Well doc; that's why we are sitting here now, so I can prove it to you. So you're still not convinced?"

The doctor shook his head.

"Julie, while I will admit this is a most unusual instrument it in no way proves Robert's father is, well who you claim him to be.

Let's just forget where you got it from for now, just what is this instrument used for Julie?"

She sighed. How was she supposed to explain that to him? Being in the inebriated state she was in, she found the truth just spilling from her lips without much effort.

"That was what he used to heal Karen. You said

yourself you couldn't explain how her miracle cure happened; well now you can! Make sense now?"

Dr. Hart placed his hand to his forehead in frustration. He thought about what she had just said and gently picked up the instrument again. He remembered the total bewilderment he and his colleagues struggled with after seeing Karen's miraculous healing.

He studied the device again being careful not to accidentally touch any of the buttons this time. Julie was correct; there simply was no rational medical explanation for what had happened in Karen's brain.

Could this...this thing have had anything to actually do with it? He certainly couldn't prove it didn't because he wasn't even sure what it was.

He cleared his mind for a second not happy with the direction his thoughts were going. There was no way he would ever be convinced this contraption came from another planet, another country perhaps but certainly not another planet that was just ridiculous.

He curtailed that thought as he knew the international medical community was a tight knit group. They didn't harbor secrets from one another. When a breakthrough is discovered it is shared internationally. No, this thing wasn't from France or Sweden or he would have found out about it. His train of thought was mercifully interrupted.

"So you still don't believe me? You still don't believe Robert was from, well up there somewhere?"

Dr. Hart shook his head.

"Julie there is no way I can believe such a strange thing like that. I'm not sure what this thing is or where it came from but I can bet my paycheck it didn't come from Mars now come on."

Trying to hide her disappointment Julie rubbed her fingers on her chin in thought. The perfect solution came to her in a flash; the salve...how it instantly heals a cut or burn. She knew that would blow him away. She knew he would never have seen anything like that. She smiled and decided a demonstration was in order; that had to convince him!

The doctor wanted to get back to the subject of Robert. Julie had said something earlier that was bothering him for a number of reasons.

First he had never seen anything like that instrument before and he made a conscious effort to keep up on the latest medical advancements from around the world.

Secondly he could see the power it had, just creating that laser was quite an impressive display, who knew what else it might be capable of.

That took him back to the miracle curing of Karen. It would have taken nothing less than such an unorthodox procedure to accomplish what had happened with Karen.

He still wasn't ready to concede the device was from another world but he certainly couldn't place it in this one...yet. He tried to collect his thoughts, an endeavor he was struggling with at the moment. He wanted to touch back on something Julie had said before he lost his train of thought.

"Julie, you had mentioned earlier that Robert said 'we hadn't invented it yet', just what did you mean by that?"

She hadn't remembered saying that and was regretting she must have. She reminded herself this is why she shied away from alcohol.

"Well, what he meant was they were a lot farther advanced than us and we hadn't invented it yet, simple as that doc."

Dr. Hart shook his head.

"You're really clinging on to that crazy story aren't you Julie. I mean really now, you expect me to believe that! You have to know how unbelievable it is."

Julie ran her fingers through her hair.

"Yes I do know, I didn't believe it at first either but I know how to convince you now. Give me a minute you'll see."

Julie reached in the medical bag and pulled out the tube of salve. Now she knew the doctor wouldn't believe her simply by looking at the tube, an actual demonstration would be needed. The aspect of this idea that was bothering her was she also knew some self inflicted pain would be involved.

She searched the medical bag and found a small scalpel. She cringed at the sight of it and the thought of what she was going to have to do to prove her point. As much as she hated pain, and even wondered if she would have the guts to actually do it, she was determined to get Dr. Hart to believe her.

Dr. Hart's eyes bugged out of his head as he saw her take the scalpel out.

"Julie, stop...what are you doing with that!"

Julie gave him a nervous smile.

"Just relax doc, it's all in the name of science you'll see. I promise you that you will believe me after this, if for no other reason than the great lengths I am going through to convince you!"

She knew she would have to do this quickly before she talked herself out of it. She took the scalpel and drew it close to her thumb.

Dr. Hart shouted out in panic.

"My God Julie stop for just a minute...what are you doing? Julie, stop and just hear me out. I don't understand why you are doing this or what you are trying to prove.

Maybe this is your way of denying the pain of losing him but it's not healthy. There are better ways of dealing with loss than making up cockamamie stories about him being an alien. There simply is no evidence of life on other planets so let's look at this rationally."

Julie winked at the doctor. She opened the tube of salve and again placed the scalpel to her thumb.

"Doctor, I am about to show you evidence!"

She closed her eyes and took a deep breath. She cringed trying to prepare for the pain she knew was imminent.

Without further thought she took the scalpel and methodically cut into the meaty part of her thumb. Blood immediately spurted out and she screamed in pain.

"Oh damn that hurt! Damn, damn, damn!"

Dr. Hart jumped up.

"Let me get you a band aid Julie. That was really stupid!"

Julie smiled through the pain.

"Oh that won't be necessary doctor, watch this. You are about to be amazed."

The doctor stopped and nervously watched her put the salve on the wound. Within seconds the clear ointment had changed to a milky white which now covered the cut.

Julie took another apprehensive deep breath and wiped the substance off. There was no trace of the wound.

Dr. Hart's mouth dropped to the floor and his eyes gapped in awe. He took Julie's hand and closely examined where the cut had been just seconds before. There was no indication that the thumb had ever been damaged. He pressed on the area with no inkling from Julie of any pain.

Their eyes met. The doctor was speechless. Julie spoke up.

"Well doc, can you explain this one?"

The doctor was struggling with words. He had just witnessed the medically impossible. All of his years of schooling and training had taught him this was inconceivable. There was nothing that could speed up the healing process to this degree, it just didn't exist and for that matter, couldn't even have been dreamt of. It was physically impossible for the body to heal that fast.

The only thing he was convinced of was that there were no smoke and mirrors, no trickery or deception... this had actually happened right before his eyes!

He saw the wound, he saw the blood and now he sees a perfectly normal, totally uninjured thumb. His mind was racing, he could feel his blood pressure rising. He was beyond shock. This just didn't make any sense but yet he couldn't deny he saw it.

"I didn't just see this!"

Julie couldn't help but smile.

"Oh yes you did doctor!"

Dr. Hart again took Julie's hand and closely examined her thumb. There was no denying it.

"Julie, what did I just witness?"

Julie found the weight of the mood sobering her up quickly. She put her hand on the doctor's shoulder.

"What did you just witness you ask...evidence perhaps? Doctor, I'm not making this up, this is not a defense mechanism...Robert is from another planet. The things you see here are things he brought here with him.

Now if you can explain it any other way I am open for your arguments but we both know you can't. We simply do not have this technology and you know it. His people are way advanced of ours. I didn't believe it when he first told me either but now neither of us can deny it. Go ahead doctor, explain it another way."

# 36

Over his thirty-five years in the medical profession, he had seen many healings. Some of them he took personal responsibility for. There was always a logical cause and effect. He performed some techniques that saved the patient and it made sense.

But then there have been a few that couldn't be explained by just the use of his professional prowess.

He had always been a spiritual man, a man who truly believes in God and to some extent miracles. When healing took place that he felt went beyond his efforts he sincerely believed that God may have indeed played a role in the process. The feeling gave him strength and encouragement. He was comfortable with that.

A doctor has a difficult, challenging and sometimes impossible job so he looked for assistance in any direction it might come from, including divine intervention.

What he had just witnessed was not a miracle, it was not any type of spiritual healing; this was science. There had been something in that salve that completely healed the wound instantly; that could not be denied, that much he had to accept. That narrowed the options.

It was now time to define just what those options were. He picked up the tube of salve and studied it. It appeared in size and shape like that of a tube of toothpaste, right down to the normal looking screw on top. That is where the similarities ended.

Scrolled across the tube was a series of hieroglyphic like characters. This was obviously a language of some kind but one he did not recognize. While not familiar with the writing characters of Egypt or any other country for that matter, the characters of this language were strangely alien to him. He cringed at his mind for coming up with that exact word but it fit.

He set the tube down and turned to Julie.

"Just where did you get this from....no, wait, I know, you're going to say he brought it with him."

Julie nodded.

"Yes he did, it was in this medical bag which of course was in the suitcase."

The doctor nodded in defeat. This was getting nowhere. His mind then suddenly went in an entirely different direction. He thought again about what he had just seen and how it could not be denied.

He tried to explain to himself where this miracle salve might have come from and why he hadn't heard about it. If such an incredible salve did indeed exist why wasn't it being used? Why hadn't he even been aware of it?

He then thought about what it might mean to the medical community if its extraordinary attributes were available to the medical world. This would be the greatest breakthrough since the discovery of penicillin!

This would be a great asset in surgery to close up the wound. It would be a tremendous benefit to soldiers in combat who would need their wounds repaired quickly. Police, fire and first responders could carry this to heal their wounds when proper medical treatment wasn't immediately available. There would be so many uses and benefits for such a miracle salve.

His initial thoughts were of a humanitarian nature. What this salve could bring to doctors around the world, the many millions of people it would help.

Then all of a sudden, his mind went a different direction; he now thought of its commercial potential... it would be astronomical. Again he cursed his mind for its choice of words.

As much as he initially hated to admit it, he found his thoughts straying from the charitable ramifications.

He was now contemplating the possible financial aspects of being the one to introduce this to the world. What price tag could you possibly place on such an incredible breakthrough?

He was very familiar with the incredible amount of money involved with the introduction of new drugs and procedures. He often spoke against the system and it's priorities of making a dollar.

In the past he had cursed the pharmaceutical companies for their practice of profit over affordability. He always believed he was part of the solution and not part of the problem.

He questioned himself for even thinking about the money that might become available if he were to somehow be able to introduce this salve. He calmed this feeling with the knowledge that his intentions were by no means narcisstic; he had nobler intentions in mind.

His thoughts then turned to Brandon and the promise he had made him before he passed away. Brandon was his younger brother who had sadly succumbed to cancer at the young age of only twenty-seven.

Brandon first learned of his illness at age twenty-four while attending medical school at the University of North Carolina. He was in his third year and had dreams of becoming a pediatrician.

He loved children and wanted more than anything to become a doctor who could help children in need. He would give his brother, who was eight years older and already a physician, all the credit for guiding him into a profession that would enable him to do just that.

John was very close to his brother. While eight years his senior they shared so many things in common. Growing up they were inseparable. John would take his younger brother fishing and they would talk about their dreams and ambitions.

Brandon so admired his brother when he ventured off to medical school and later when he graduated and became a doctor. It was his admiration for his brother that inspired him to follow in his footsteps.

Brandon was forced to drop out of medical school as treatment for his ailment became a full-time burden. Chemotherapy was taking its toll on his body. He was constantly fatigued and the sickness that accompanied the treatment became inhumane.

His doctors contemplated surgery but held off on that with hopes the chemo would eventually help, it wasn't.

The pain was shared by John. He was ravished at seeing his brother in so much agony and the thought of Brandon's dream vanishing was devastating to him.

He visited his brother at the hospital two days before he died. Holding back the tears he made a promise to him. He promised him his dream would survive. He gave his brother a solemn oath that someday, somehow, he would do something to help children who were suffering from the same horrible infliction.

He had never totally forgotten that pledge. He had shelved it in the back of his mind with sincere intentions of fulfilling it when time and finances allowed.

While he had the time and the intentions, what was holding him back was his modest income as a general practitioner. Oh, he was living comfortably but he never had the extra money to do anything noteworthy.

The thought of the windfall this salve might provide threw him into a tailspin. This could provide him with the financial resources needed to complete his brother's dream.

He had connections in the pharmaceutical industry, he knew researchers who could take this and develop and market the salve. It would be a win-win situation. He would be giving the world an incredible medical breakthrough while at the same time finally getting the resources to make his brother's dream of helping children come true.

He thought about the insane amount of money a development like this could bring. He would feel no guilt about being a part of it. He was doing a good thing and would be using the money for a very good cause.

With that kind of money, he might be able to open a pediatric cancer center. He knew that would bring his brother such joy and satisfaction. He had already decided he would call the clinic 'The Brandon Hart Memorial Children's Cancer Clinic'.

Even though it had been many years ago, he could still see his brother's forsaken eyes as he lay hours from his death. This could be his golden ticket to finally be able to fulfill his brother's dream.

Those eyes would haunt him occasionally over the years. He would think of his brother's dream of helping children in need and how he was stricken before he could fulfill those dreams.

Many times he had pondered what he could do to at least keep his brother's dream alive. All of a sudden he couldn't help but think this might be the opportunity he had been waiting for.

Establishing a clinic would take a lot of money he knew, but he also knew the kind of money introducing such an astonishing breakthrough like this salve might bring.

He took a deep breath and tried to come up with a plan. If he could only get a sample of the salve he could get the wheels in motion. He had an old golfing partner who now works for Tamlin pharmaceutical. He would be the perfect partner to get this thing started.

He couldn't remember exactly what position Jeremy held but he knew it was in upper management and he would have the influence to have their lab analyze the substance and get his company to get it in production.

He was sure they would be as enthusiastic about the discovery as he was. What pharmaceutical company wouldn't want to be in on the ground floor of such an amazing find?

This would mean millions to the company not to mention the prestige that would come with introducing and patenting such an astounding breakthrough. He would only ask for what would be needed to start work on the clinic. Once his project was started he was sure he could get additional backing to complete it.

He would want nothing for himself; this was all about Brandon and his dream. He was sure they could work out a deal for the financial arrangements.

It would then only be a matter of getting it tested and approved by the FDA which he didn't see as a problem. How could anyone hold back such a groundbreaking discovery!

It would only take a small amount of salve to give the lab people an opportunity to break it down and produce it in large quantities.

Now the trick would be to get Julie to allow him to take a sample. He inwardly felt that might be quite a challenge. He knew he would need some kind of leverage to convince her to give him a sample.

Julie tapped him on the shoulder.

"Well, are you convinced yet?"

He took a deep breath and paused before answering. A million thoughts came rushing into his already crowded mind.

He thought back to how bewildered everyone was over

the miracle curing of Karen, how it simply made no sense and there was no medical explanation for it.

He thought about Julie's amazingly short pregnancy and Robert's rapid and unexplained accelerated growth.

He then reflected on the meeting with Dr. Silverman after he had shared Robert's blood sample with the Belgium hematologist, much to his chagrin.

He remembered reading the report on the blood sample and the conclusion that it 'wasn't even human'. He pondered his shock over the wording coming from a world renowned hematologist. At the time he couldn't rationalize such a dramatic statement.

His thoughts then reluctantly turned to Julie's outrageous claim that Robert's father was an alien.

He was well aware of Julie's state of intoxication and initially attributed the alcohol to her outlandish claim. Then, an old adage came to mind. He remembered hearing once that there are only two kinds of people that tell the truth, drunks and children. Could there be something to that?

Why was everything pointing to the fact that Julie might possibly be telling the truth? No...he couldn't possibly accept that, so he asked himself to find another solution. He cursed himself for even entertaining the notion about how that would explain everything.

"Julie, be serious, I can't begin to believe that."

Julie studied the doctor's eyes. She could detect a tinge of doubt in them.

"You're thinking about it aren't you doctor?"

Dr. Hart rubbed his forehead as a headache was rapidly developing. He had no idea how to answer Julie's question. Was he really thinking about it? Was he actually putting any credence into that outrageous claim?

As a man of science could he take such an idea seriously? What scared him most at the moment was that he wasn't sure. What he couldn't deny was that would certainly explain a lot of anomalies he has been struggling with which can't be explained in any rational way.

He knew he had to reply because Julie surely wasn't going to simply let it go. He threw caution to the wind and came up with the best reply he could think of.

"Julie, okay, just for one second let's suppose I believed you. Now I'm not saying I do, but let's just take that thought to the next level.

You're an intelligent woman so think this out. You say Robert's father is from another planet. Going as far out on a limb as I can let me ask you this...why would someone from another planet come all the way to Earth and decide to come to only you? Now does that make any sense?

No offense intended, but wouldn't you think there would be higher priorities for him? Wouldn't you think he would want to see the president or speak with The United Nations or something?

I mean he has come a long way just to meet a single mother. That is taking a very far fetched idea even further. Do you have a reasonable explanation for why an extraterrestrial would do that?"

Julie had to admit he had a valid point but was pleased he was even considering it. She really didn't have an answer to that one either other than what Robert had told her about his situation. Now the question was just how much information to offer the doctor.

Encouraged by his response she offered a meek answer.

"I will answer that question as best I can but it would require some explanation."

As he awaited her story he kept running three words over and over in his head...'it's not human'. What, just supposing, it wasn't! The more he thought about it, the closer he was coming to actually believing it.

Where would Julie possibly have come up with such a crazy idea if it weren't true? He had known Julie for almost twenty years and knew she was a very intelligent, rational woman. She had never shown any tendencies to any mental disorders or delusions.

He knew, as her doctor, she had never done drugs or ever had any drinking problems. Where would she come up with such a story? That wasn't like her at all.

Then, for just a moment, he thought about the distant possibility that it was indeed true. It would certainly explain all the strange unexplainable medical events that have taken place in the last year.

Dr. Mertens was an internationally known and respected hematologist and if he said he had never seen blood like Robert's before that had to carry some weight. If Julie's story were true, this would be the most historically significant development in human history!

Man has been contemplating the existence of life on other planets for centuries. Astronomers, philosophers, theologians have pondered the significance of finding life elsewhere in the universe without success. It would change the world and it's thinking beyond comprehension if such a discovery would ever be made. Could he be sitting on that discovery? He found himself shaking at the possibility.

Just how would he explain the salve if Julie were indeed to allow him to take a sample? Where could he say he got it?

Julie cleared her throat. She at least had somehow managed to regain her sobriety.

"Well, doctor, he told me why he was here. Now you're going to have to promise me you will listen to this because, well, it's going to sound pretty far fetched...and yes I know it already does, but please bear with me. Will you listen to me doctor?"

Dr. Hart hesitantly nodded.

"You have my undivided attention Julie, I owe you that."

Julie smiled as she tried to figure out a way of explaining this rather odd story in a manner that wouldn't end up getting her committed. She wasn't totally sure of the doctor's sincerity but knew she couldn't change that.

She thought about all the events since Robert first came into her life and tried to formulate them into a sequence that was accurate and hopefully, at least somewhat, believable.

Where and how to begin...she started by telling the doctor how they first met. Robert had come into the bar and was as far as she knew, just another customer. She recalled how distant and almost angry he was. He was evasive to any questions she asked him and she initially thought he was just rude.

She went on to say he mentioned he needed a place to live for exactly one year. She introduced him to Larry and he rented him the apartment across the hall from her. She told the doctor how they had eventually became friends and would see each other occasionally.

She hesitated because now she had gotten to the part where Robert 'heals' Karen. She had no idea how to explain this. She glanced to the floor and took notice of the device. With the confidence that Dr. Hart had already examined it and was witness to its unusual power, she continued.

She explained how she didn't actually see this but from what Karen had told her that Robert had somehow used this instrument on her and, well the results were known to all.

Dr. Hart held up his hand to pause her. He picked up

the instrument with keen interest. "You're saying that Robert, well his father, used this...thing, whatever it is, on Karen and this was what caused the dramatic change in her?"

Julie nodded her head.

"Did she mention exactly what he did with it? Did she tell you how he used it?" Their conversation was interrupted by Karen appearing at the door ranting like a typical teenager.

# 37

"Mom, where have you been? Everyone is asking about you! Robert is really getting cranky, he needs...."

She stopped in mid-sentence as she glanced around the room. She saw her mother and Dr. Hart sitting on the floor. She also saw Robert's suitcase sitting between them with its contents spread around them. Her mouth dropped in horror.

"Oh my God mother, what are you doing?"

Julie glanced at her daughter then at Dr. Hart who remained silent. She noticed the panicked expression on Karen's face and the reality of the situation hit her like a ton of bricks.

In her drunken state she hadn't thought things out. She didn't take into consideration the ramifications of what she was doing. She attempted a reply.

"I was showing Dr. Hart..."

Karen stopped her in a fit of rage.

"I can see that! Do you realize what this means if anyone else knows the truth about him? They will take him mom, you have to know that!

They will poke and test and put him under every microscope in the world! Mom, they will take him from us and God knows what they will do with us! They will put him on display like some kind of circus freak! You can't let that happen!"

Silently John was absorbing the exchange. Based on Karen's reaction his heart was all of a sudden telling him that Julie might just be telling the truth. While Julie's story might be attributed to her alcohol, Karen's reaction could not.

He studied her shock and disapproval. He took note of

the anger in her tone of voice and her forthright approach to what she was seeing. She really felt she had a good reason to fly into the rage she was currently displaying.

He knew Karen all her life and she was not one to fly off the handle for no reason, at least not after her miracle cure. That more than anything reinforced his believe that Julie was telling the truth.

In his excitement over the possibility of finally having the financial resources to start the clinic, he had forgotten what the consequences for Julie and her family might be.

He knew Karen was right. If evidence comes out that Robert is indeed an extraterrestrial none of their lives would ever be the same.

Julie processed her daughter's words. That was an aspect she hadn't thought of. She knew Karen was totally correct and suddenly felt panic stricken. The cat was out of the bag, there was now no way of putting him back in. Dr. Hart was now fully aware of the truth. Would he believe it? If he did, would he go to the authorities?

How could she have been so stupid! She cursed herself for drinking Edi's punch for she knew in her heart that was the culprit. Had she been sober she would never do anything to hurt her family. All she could hope for was compassion from Dr. Hart.

She said a silent prayer. She first asked God to forgive her for drinking and then asked him for a miracle. She asked him to somehow prevent Dr. Hart from telling the world the incredible truth and ruining all their lives in the process.

Dr. Hart continued to sit silently taking everything in. He had a lot on his mind. Was he indeed witnessing the most incredible event in human history, the proof of life elsewhere in the universe? What would it mean to be the man who finally presents evidence to that mystery that has been baffling mankind for centuries?

One thing he knew for sure was that if he did, Julie's, Karen's and Robert's life would never be the same. They would certainly take Robert into custody and turn him into a massive science project. Julie and Karen would be abused by the media for years to come and neither deserved that type of life shattering scrutiny.

He had known Julie for almost twenty years and Karen all her life for he had delivered her. They were more than patients to him; he looked at them as almost family. He would never want to do anything to cause them any harm. He knew if he exposed Robert their lives would be more than harmed, they would be destroyed.

His thoughts then returned to Brandon. If he could somehow market that salve it would provide him with the funds to get that clinic started. This became his priority.

He wasn't interested in fame or notoriety. Those had never been important to him. When he decided to become a doctor he approached it with old fashioned values. His goals were only to help people and feel like he was making a difference in people's lives.

This could provide the leverage he felt he would need to talk Julie into giving him that sample. He would offer her a proposition, one that would benefit both sides.

He glanced at Julie and could see the stress mounting on her face. She would glance at him and then at her daughter and back again. He couldn't help but empathize with her dilemma. He wanted to find a way of reducing that stress, not adding to it.

Julie put her hand to her forehead in thought. She knew the issue had to be addressed before something tragic happened. She wasn't sure if he believed their story or not but this is something she couldn't be too careful about.

She looked at her daughter, who stood obviously mortified, next to her expecting a response. She then looked at Dr. Hart who simply looked perplexed. She studied his face trying to get an idea of what was going on inside his mind.

She couldn't read anything in his eyes that satisfied her but she knew she would have to break this uncomfortable silence with some kind of statement. She looked at Karen again, her face was all too easy to decipher.

Knowing nothing she could say to her daughter would change her disposition she directed her comments to Dr. Hart.

Did he believe them and more importantly, if he did would he talk? She had to find out now before it was too late. She thought about her options before speaking. How could she get him to promise secrecy? Her contemplation was interrupted by Dr. Hart.

His head was now swimming with nonsensical thoughts.

"Before you say anything Julie, I would like to ask Karen a question if I may."

A look of shock came across both Julie and Karen's face. Realizing she wasn't in much of a position to bargain she nodded her head. She glanced at her daughter and gave her an expression of consent.

Dr. Hart picked up the instrument Julie had claimed cured her daughter. He examined it briefly then turned his attention to Karen.

"Karen, have you seen this instrument before?"

Karen looked at her mother with confusion. Julie gave her daughter a weak smile of approval.

"It's okay sweetheart. Be honest with him."

Karen cleared her throat.

"Yes sir."

The doctor set the device back on the floor and tried to look as calm as he could.

"Your mother claims this was the apparatus that cured you. Can you verify that?"

Karen took a deep breath. She looked down at the floor and spoke softly.

"Yes sir; that was what he used."

"Just how did he do that Karen?"

Karen shook her head.

"I don't really know; he put me to sleep before he actually did anything."

The doctor replied with a stoic thank you. He was inwardly hoping for another answer but couldn't deny the sincerity of Karen's response. Something inside his gut was telling him she was speaking the truth. He was wrestling with that.

Julie closed her eyes in deep thought. She was realizing the size of the hole they had dug for themselves. She said a silent prayer that God might have the mercy to somehow make this turn out alright.

Dr. Hart took a moment to digest this latest bit of information. The story was continuing to get more and more obscure. What concerned him even more; was that it was getting more believable. With Karen's testimony he once again concentrated on the device.

He was convinced it was some kind of professionally crafted contraption and had a brief demonstration of its powers. If it were indeed a medical instrument and if indeed it had done what Julie and Karen say, it certainly wasn't built on this planet. Medical science wasn't even close to coming up with something like this.

Julie collected her thoughts and broke the unnerving silence.

"Doctor, just hear me out for a moment please. I have made a terrible mistake today. I can blame the alcohol but that wouldn't fix anything. What is done is done.

I don't know what is going on inside your head right

now. I don't know if you are on the verge of believing us or just having us committed but I do know one thing. If word of this comes out they will take my son. If scientists don't, children's services surely will."

The look of distress on her face almost brought the doctor to tears. He had to put an end to her suffering. He again thought of Brandon and came up with an idea that might solve the problem. It was now his turn to hope that Julie would believe him.

"Julie, I would never let that happen. What I believe is irrelevant. Let me offer you a proposal that would help both of us."

Julie took a deep breath in anticipation.

"I'm listening doctor, I have no other choice. We are totally at your mercy."

Dr. Hart chose his words carefully.

"I would never do anything to harm you or your beautiful family. Do I believe your incredible story...I honestly don't know myself. You are presenting a very convincing argument but that's not what is at issue here.

I think I have a solution that would benefit both of us and put the anguish this has caused to an end.

Would you allow me to take a sample of the salve? If you were to agree to that you would have my solemn oath nothing that has happened in this room today will leave this room."

Karen's mouth dropped to the floor. She shouted at her mother.

"Oh sure, give you the salve so you can make a million dollars off of it, that's just great! How would we know you would keep your word? See mom he is just looking out for himself!"

Julie scorned her daughter.

"Karen Renee that is not necessary! That is not a very nice thing to say..."

Dr. Hart interrupted her.

"No, Julie it's alright. Karen is absolutely correct."

Julie and Karen shared a glance that combined stupefaction with confusion as the doctor continued.

"I'm going to be totally honest with you. The benefits this salve could bring to mankind are of course a factor but the money that could be made from this is my underlying motivation.

Now before you think of me poorly for this let me assure you it's not what you think.

The money would go to a very worthy cause."

Karen was still unconvinced.

"Worthy cause I bet, like yachts and European vacations I'm sure!"

Dr. Hart stood up and walked slowly around the room in thought. He hadn't intended on sharing his plan with them but now it looked as if it might be a necessity.

"No Karen; that is where you are wrong. I know how this must sound but please allow me to explain.

Some twenty years my brother, Brandon, passed away from cancer. He was in medical school to become a pediatrician. His dream was to help children and sadly he died before he could fulfill that dream. Nothing could be done to save him but I felt responsible for at least keeping his dream alive.

Since that day I had vowed to someday, somehow I would honor his memory by doing something to at least keep his dream alive. I have never been in the position to follow up on that vow until now.

With the money this breakthrough would bring I could start a cancer clinic for children and name it after him. That is what I would do with the money Karen."

Julie took a moment to digest what she had just heard. Initially it sounded too good to be true but, giving it a second thought, she contemplated the history they had with John over the past twenty years.

He had been good to them. He had delivered Karen and now Robert. He always had their best interest in mind. He had never given her any reason to doubt his words today. She knew convincing Karen might not be as easy.

She glanced at the doctor then at her daughter who continued to stand defiantly beside her.

"Sweetheart, I believe him. We are kind of backed into a corner here and really don't have any other choice. I don't have a problem with giving him a sample of the salve but I need your input. We are a family and we make decisions together."

Karen took a deep breath and thought about what her mother had said. She liked the doctor, she always had. He had always been kind and understanding to her, even during the difficult years. She hadn't recognized it at the time but in retrospect she had to be honest about it.

She had to agree with one thing her mother said, they were indeed in a pickle. She knew the doctor would leave with the truth regardless of what they decided and in that case perhaps it might be best to give him some incentive to keep it to himself.

"Okay mom, I will agree with whatever you decide. Like you said, I guess we really don't have a choice."

She glanced at her mother who smiled and then at the doctor who remained stoic.

Julie accepted her reply and turned to the doctor.

"I just have one question; if I did agree to give you a sample and you presented it, where would you say it came from?"

Dr. Hart thought for a moment. He wanted to give her a good, but honest answer.

"I have a lot of close friends in the pharmaceutical

industry, some of which I actually have known since college. They are aware of my interest in chemistry and my constant hope and search for new and improved drugs.

I would simply explain this was something I have been working on. They would know I have always had an acute interest in chemistry and would have access to the resources I would need to pursue it. I can assure you they wouldn't question it. Once they saw what it could do, its origin would be the least of their concerns.

I promise you, your name would never be mentioned or any suspicions come up. I would even be willing, in fact I would insist upon, sharing the profits with you. I just want enough to start the cancer center my brother had dreamed of."

Julie again glanced at Karen and was reassured by her expression she would have her support. She sighed and finally gave the doctor her agreement with the deal.

Dr. Hart got his pack of cigarettes from his shirt pocket and took off the cellophane wrapper. He handed it to Julie who opened the tube of salve and squeezed an inch or so of it into the wrapper. She twisted it closed and returned it to him.

She hesitated before letting go of the wrapper.

"Doctor, our lives are now in your hands."

Dr. Hart solemnly placed the wrapper back in his shirt pocket and smiled.

"You have my word Julie, you and your family will never face any repercussions from this but will actually benefit from it. You have done a wonderful thing not only for me and my brother but for the world as well."

Julie nodded her approval and Karen spoke up.

"Mom, we should get back to the party. Robert was getting cranky and I think he needs a nap. Edi is watching him but I think you should get back."

Julie stood up and acknowledged her. Dr. Hart also stood up.

"Julie, you and Karen get back to your celebration I really need to get going."

Dr. Hart gave her a reassuring smile and walked towards the door. Julie walked with him to his car then returned to the party.

Karen was in the yard catching up with her friends and Julie found her son comfortably nestled in Edi's lap in the corner of the porch. Walking over to them she caught Edi's eye.

"Doll where have you been, you're missing all the fun. This little guy has been keeping me company; lord knows where my beloved husband ran off to. I think you might want to lay him down for a nap he's getting a bit fussy."

Edi stood up and handed Julie her son. Julie took him upstairs to his room and set him in his crib.

As the afternoon progressed the guests gradually left, eventually leaving only Julie, Karen, Edi and Leonard whom Edi finally found in the living room watching a baseball game.

Julie, Edi and Karen cleaned up the remnants of the party from the porch as Robert slept peacefully in his crib upstairs. They all laughed as Leonard supervised the operation. Edi threw in her three cents.

"The operation would go much quicker if you would chip in and stop just standing there making a dang fool of yourself!"

Finally conceding to his wife's complaint, Leonard reluctantly assisted in the cleanup and the entire porch was finally cleared.

Julie and Edi went into the kitchen to start on the dishes and put away the leftovers.

Edi glared at her husband who was standing by the door.

"Well, are you going to help us you old goat?"

Leonard just motioned with his arm.

"Oh now that there is woman's work, you don't need me."

Edi just shook her head and Leonard returned to his baseball game. Edie winked at Julie.

"I've said it before; if it weren't for their necessity in making babies I would have no use for men at all! They sure ain't good for nothing else!"

Julie broke out in laughter. They finished everything in the kitchen and Edi decided it was time for them to go home.

"Well doll, I think we have everything all squared away. I think it's time for me to gather that old geezer and get home. I sure enjoyed the party! You be sure and kiss the birthday boy goodbye for me. He is such a sweetie!

Now if there is ever anything me or the old coot can do for you don't hesitate to call."

Edi gave Julie a hug and retrieved her husband from the living room and the two of them left.

Julie poured a cup of coffee and reflected back on the past few hours. It had been a great party. Everyone seemed to have a good time. She was so thankful for all the wonderful food Larry had brought and the help and comic relief Edi gave her.

This led her thoughts in another direction. She then drifted to her indiscretion about the drinking and its aftermath. She cursed Edi for bringing the punch and herself for indulging in it. How could she have allowed herself to have that happen?

She knew without question, that had she not chose to drink the punch they would not find themselves in the situation they do now. Her indiscretions had put her family in harm's way. This was a mother's worst nightmare.

She was nervous about the incident with Dr. Hart. He held their lives in his hands now. She trusted him but still the doubts remained, the stakes were so high. She said a silent prayer asking for forgiveness and mercy at the same time. God has been kind to her but she realized she was asking him for a big favor this time. She finished her coffee and her train of thought.

She poured another cup of coffee and a glass of iced tea and called Karen down from her room. They played a game of scrabble and had another piece of birthday cake.

The mood during the game was solemn, a far cry from the jovial banter they usually enjoyed while playing a game together. Neither one of them were much in the mood for conversation.

They would occasionally mention the party and how it appeared everyone had enjoyed it, but there was an unspoken, mutually shared and understood apprehension. The comments were more to break the uncomfortable silence than to relive the joy of the moment. There was a dark cloud silently hanging over both of them.

This originated from their confrontation with Dr. Hart. They both knew the gravity of the situation and the possible horrific consequences it could bring. While neither of them came out and specified the cause of their unrest, they both knew it was one they shared.

At the end of the game Julie gave her daughter a reassuring hug, one they both needed, and they both went to bed.

# 38

The next six years flew by quickly but not uneventfully. Life was indeed interesting having a little alien running around. Raising any infant presents daily challenges but in this case the challenges were a bit more uncertain.

As human as her son appeared on the outside, Julie knew there were extenuating circumstances involved here. She was fully aware that half of the blood that was flowing in her son's veins was not of Earth origin. What she wasn't aware of is just what that bonus DNA might mean or what unearthly abilities they might give him.

She didn't know if that one morning she might find him levitating the furniture or turning on the television by pointing with his finger! The possibilities were endless and a bit unnerving. She literally didn't know what those 'people' were capable of!

While she refused to go to the point of fearing her son, she had to admit she was keeping a sharp eye on him. As much as she tried, she could never fully rid herself of the image of Gort from 'The day the Earth stood still'.

She noticed nothing out of the ordinary for the first two years. As an infant, Robert had no interest in trivial things that normally amuse a toddler, like stuffed animals or rattles. He would literally throw them out of his crib as if in protest of having to share his bed with them.

He would become fascinated by anything that he found a challenge. He received a set of building blocks for his first birthday and immediately took to creating fascinating structures with them, some of the designs seemingly defying gravity.

Robert would soon become interested in jigsaw puzzles,

quickly catching on to the objective and completing them in only a matter of minutes. It soon got to the point where even they no longer presented him with a challenge.

Having seen his ability to master children's jigsaw puzzles Karen bought him a fifty piece puzzle...that one took him ten minutes.

He would get bored easily. It was if he required an objective to be met for every activity he attempted, which is why he found the simplicity of stuffed animals pointless. It was clear to see his mind was always active. Now as far as active with what, only he had the answer to.

He appreciated an activity center which Karen had bought him for his second birthday. This allowed him to spin wheels and dials with various pictures changing which he studied each time they came up. He would ask his mother for further information on them as he would point to the picture and then to her. She was astounded by his constant thirst for knowledge.

Much to Julie's bewilderment he was fascinated with television and would plant himself directly in front of it any time his mother or sister had it on. He studied the images on the screen taking everything in, never taking his eyes off them as long as the set remained on.

His mother and sister would watch him in amazement as they wondered just how much of it he really understood. From his intense facial expressions, they had a hunch he was absorbing more than they realized.

Robert starting connecting words shortly after his second birthday and shortly after could speak in fragmented sentences. He seemed to have a knack for picking up words. He spoke his first word "dah" on his first birthday.

His efforts to speak intensified every day afterwards. He would attempt to mimic words his mother or sister spoke and, after practicing, actually got quite proficient at it. He was speaking in complete sentences by the age of five.

Initially Julie just looked at this practice as parrot like…mimicking the words without really understanding their meaning but as the months progressed she was beginning to get the impression he understood them as well.

With both Karen and Julie's help, he was reading children's books at age three. He loved the many books Julie had bought him. Reading seemed to be an elementary task for him. Mastering the simple sentences, he would always scrutinize the accompanying pictures; not just glancing at them but intensely ruminating over each image.

His accelerated rate of growth continued. This was something that started the moment he was conceived. He had now developed a full head of thick, dark brown hair and his dark brown eyes had become tantalizing. He was becoming the spitting image of his father. His physique was slender but strong and firm, once again exactly like his father.

His physical checkups had all gone well. Dr. Hart continued to be amazed at his growth rate. At age six, he was currently four feet tall and weighed sixty-two pounds. While the doctor did admit there were in the upper percentile for his age he assured them it was in the healthy range.

His heart and respiratory systems were perfect. Dr. Hart would always be outwardly impressed each time he gave Robert a sight or hearing test. Many times he commented on Robert's acute hearing and eyesight.

Each time the doctor withheld his inner most astonishment when he would silently recall Robert's early checkups and his bewilderment at his growth rate, not to mention his most unusual blood. He remembered wondering whether this pattern would continue or was simply an unusual birth trait...he questions had now been answered. He never mentioned any concerns to Julie for his only interest was that his patient was healthy and indeed he was.

Julie had decided against enrolling him in day care or kindergarten. She wasn't comfortable with that. She wanted to observe him as he matured for as long as she could at home just in the event he might have some surprises in store.

She wasn't ready to release him into the world, not just yet. She would laugh to herself when she thought of it, not being sure if that line of thinking was for the benefit of her son, or the world.

She was satisfied Robert was getting a very good preschool education right at home. Both she and Karen were very active and attentive on a daily basis keeping up with his curriculum. They would read with him, help him with words and watched countless educations programs on television with him.

This was, of course, in addition to teaching him good health habits and manners. They would talk to him, continually teaching him social customs and techniques.

Edi continued to watch him during the days while Karen was at school and Julie was at work.

Karen and Robert gradually created an incredible bond. She was a wonderful big sister who adored her little brother. She would spend countless hours with him reading or helping him in what ever way she could. They would play games together, read together and he would talk to her as best he could.

She never protested over doing anything that was required to make sure he was healthy and safe. This included bathing, changing and feeding him when he was younger. Julie continued to be amazed at her daughter's diligence, commitment and devotion to her brother. She couldn't help but think back to a day in their past when things would have been different.

It was obvious the feeling was mutual. Robert would ogle her as she sat with him and always seemed to enjoy her company. He was always very attentive any time she spoke. They would laugh and hug all the time.

They became inseparable when they were both home. She would get the biggest kick out of him calling her name when ever she would get up and momentarily leave for a moment. Julie was so happy, and relieved it had worked out that way.

There was an alluring incident with a game of scrabble when Robert was just over four years old. Julie and Karen were on the floor playing the game when a curious Robert joined them.

He sat next to Karen and studied her latest move with great interest. She had just played the word 'cent'. She smiled at her mother in victory. Her brother glanced at her then at her letter collection. He slowly picked out the letters 'u', 'r', and 'y' changing her word to century, adding 12 points to her score.

Karen's mouth dropped to the floor. She looked over to her mother who was equally astonished. Robert just sat silently smiling.

A curious incident occurred while the family was at a department store. Having completed their shopping the three of them strolled down to the toy aisle. Karen wanted to buy something new for Robert.

She noticed a set of toy army men and thought every little boy loves army toys. She noticed Robert standing by a display and showed it to him. He shook his head and picked up a box of outer space themed action figures. There were astronauts and aliens and even a little flying saucer.

He smiled and took the set of army men from his sister and replaced it with the set he had picked out. Karen looked at her mother and shared a common, silent, but mutually unsettling thought. Julie couldn't help but wonder if the decision was simply because the item caught his eye or perhaps there was more going on in that mind of his than they knew.

Among the many lavish gifts Robert received for his fourth birthday was a model of the solar system his mother had gotten him. Julie had noticed his keen interest in science and especially astronomy.

Inwardly wondering how much of this interest was created by his general quest for knowledge or, as far fetched as it might seem, a mysterious influence of his father, she encouraged it.

After the party Julie had collected all the gifts and placed them on the living room floor. Robert hastily joined her to explore all his new treasures.

She sat on the floor with him and first pulled over the box with the solar system model in it. She wanted to be a part of his enjoyment so she opened the box and started assembling it for him.

Never being a person fond of following or even reading instructions, Julie just proceeded to put the tiny planets on the rings which comprised the base of the model paying no attention to the order.

She proudly handed the completed model to her son. Robert studied the model for a moment. He gave his mother a look of total puzzlement and proceeded to take apart the model, quickly reassembling it with the planets all in the correct order then calmly handed it back to his mother.

Julie was speechless and could think of no other reaction other than just smile at her amazing son.

As his reading aptitude increased so did his desire. He

became obsessed with reading. Julie made regular trips to the library to satisfy his passion. He didn't care for story books but preferred educational books. His mother would bring him text books, many of which were written for high school students.

His face would always light up when she came back from her latest library trip. He would go through the selection and chose one that caught his eye.

Not only was his reading level way above the norm for his age so was the speed with which he read. He would normally finish a book within a day or two.

Julie continued to marvel at his incredible learning curve and would always encourage it. She wondered if it were too early to order brochures from Harvard.

What amazed her even further was not only was he reading the materials but he also understood them. This became apparent when after he finished a particularly challenging book, say one on high school chemistry; he would always discuss it with her. What she found embarrassing about that was that she usually had no idea what he was talking about.

She found her ego unwillingly being bruised. It was startling to realize her five year old son was more intelligent than she was. This was something she had always considered a possibility in the back of her mind considering the factors involved, but now it was being thrown blatantly in her face!

He never did it in a malicious way; he honestly expected her to be able to keep up with him and never considered the possibility that his intellect level was that far superior to hers.

Robert had grown and matured to be an incredible young man. He was always polite and respectful to everyone he encountered. He adored his sister and cherished his mother.

He faithfully paid attention during his home school lessons and continued his passion for reading and ardent interest in television. He seemed especially enamored with the news. He appeared to find what's happening in the world fascinating. Julie wasn't sure of the nature of this interest but found nothing harmful about it.

After it was over he would question his mother on certain events. Julie was thankful to have Karen assist her in these questions as she seemed more informed on the world's events than she did.

Julie was so proud of her little alien. She was very pleased with how wonderful he had turned out. She was never sure of just how much of this could be attributed to her genes and to what extent his father's genes might be playing a major role.

His father was a very kind and compassionate man. He was also a very intelligent one. Julie had only a high school education so she gave his father all the credit for Robert's intellectual capacity.

After giving it some honest thought, she also conceded that his good looks came from his father. The more she thought about it, she pretty much resigned herself to the fact that most of Robert's wonderful qualities came from his father.

She knew that first grade was approaching soon. She would lay awake at night wondering, pondering, just what she was about to unleash on the world.

She wasn't concerned at all about the academic aspect. Robert had already proven his intelligence and thirst for knowledge; no, he would excel in that respect she was certain.

What was starting to worry her was the social aspect. Her son had been displaying indications that, for what ever reasoning he used, he was different, special. He surely picked up that he was more intelligent than his sister or even his mother. She was sure he was well aware of that.

She would occasionally see an odd expression in his eyes that only further heightened her suspicions. He would give them a quizzical expression as in question of why she or Karen didn't understand what he was trying to say or do. Like he was surprised they weren't right in line with his thinking.

She avoided the urge to go back to the library and get books on child psychology because she was sure no parent or psychiatrist had ever run into this one before so therefore they would be of no help. No, she knew she would be alone on this one.

She couldn't really get much consolation from Karen because she knew her daughter would respond by saying it was nothing more than unnecessary worrying.

Perhaps Karen would be right. Perhaps she was over thinking it, but something in her protective mother's instincts told her there might be an issue here.

Trying to think ahead, anticipating problems, she took the idea a bit further. She was sure Robert would excel in school. She wouldn't be surprised at him making the honor roll or what ever academic award they give to grade school students.

What was concerning her now is how the other children would react once they discovered the unsettling truth she recently had, that Robert was far more intelligent than any of them could ever hope to be.

This combined with the notion that Robert already knew he was somehow special or different from them could cause problems. Children can be very resentful and cruel and she wasn't sure how a gentle soul like her son would react to such treatment and possible abuse.

Every logical neuron in her head kept telling her it was going to be just fine, she was just being an overly protective mother, and then the reality of it kicked and reminded her that her son was indeed half alien.

What troubled her most was that she honestly didn't know what he could be capable of. He had already displayed his mental superiority and exhibited signs that he was aware that he was 'different' but to this point that those were the only things separating him from a normal child.

She then remembered his alarming growth pattern and his blood which specialists have claimed was nothing like they had ever seen. She remembered he was three months premature and yet suffered no ill effects from it. Just how does a mother calm her nerves with all this on her mind?

Karen was now twenty-one, she had graduated from high school with honors and even received a special certificate for both her academic achievements and her involvement with extracurricular activates.

While attending the commencement ceremony Julie broke down in tears. Her mind drifted back to the troubled young teenager who hated her life and everyone in it. She thought about the sad future her daughter was facing and how she was helpless to do anything about it. She then thought of Robert and how he had rescued both of them.

Karen had received partial scholarships from three universalities but had declined them. She decided instead to get a job as a waitress at a local restaurant and remain at home to help her mother with Robert.

Julie was initially distraught by this decision. She had silently cursed herself for being in a position where her daughter felt the need to sacrifice her own life because her mother needed help.

Julie cursed herself for not having a man around the house to alleviate the guilt Karen might feel but then she remembered....she had one. It wasn't her fault that he was no longer there.

She thought about God, and how he has helped her through so many trying times in her past. How he gave her strength and guidance to endure the pain and heartache of raising an emotionally disturbed child. She pondered on how he had always provided for her whenever she needed it.

She then thought about how he had finally given her the soul mate she had always dreamed of, the most incredible man she had ever met. He showed her the beautiful future she had always dreamed of.

She smiled as she knew God had arranged their meeting and them falling in love. God had even given her the greatest gift of all, their son.

She then thought about how he had cruelly taken him from her. How all her dreams and aspirations had been stripped away in an instant and how now she finds herself in a position where her daughter feels the need to give up her dreams to help her mother?

# 39

Miss Benning stood in front of her first-grade class and smiled.

"Good morning everyone and welcome to the first grade; I am Miss Benning and I will be your teacher. This is going to be an exciting year and I am looking forward to getting to know all of you. We're going to be learning so much and I hope we can have some fun too.

Now I know this is a new experience for all of you so before we go any further does anyone have any questions for me?"

Robert immediately raised his hand. Miss Benning pointed her finger at him.

"Yes, Robert, what is your question?"

Robert smiled.

"Are we going to learn about astronomy?"

Miss Benning chuckled.

"Well Robert, we will be including a little bit of all the sciences and yes, we can touch on astronomy and learn about the nine planets we have in our solar system."

Robert's eyes grew big and immediately responded.

"Actually there are only eight planets in our solar system Miss Benning, Pluto has been changed to a dwarf planet and is no longer counted."

All the children in the room turned their eyes to him and Miss Benning just stood in silent embarrassment.

She had never encountered such a quizzical child before. Most first graders enter school with a clean slate but it appeared his blackboard was pretty full already.

The classroom environment exposed another of Robert's, up to now hidden, personality traits, he was very outgoing. Up to this point he had never had much of an opportunity to showcase this for the majority of his life he had been sequestered by only his mother and sister.

Throughout the course of his first day in school Robert would ask many more questions, never taking anything at face value, he had to know the who, the how or the why of everything. This immediately drew the attention of his teacher and classmates, many of whom introduced themselves to him after class. Miss Benning could already see she was going to have her hands full with this inquisitive student. She looked forward to the challenge.

Julie picked up her son from school and leaned over and gave him a big hug when he entered the car.

"How was your first day of school big guy?"

Robert hunched his shoulders.

"Oh, it was okay I guess. I don't think our teacher is very bright though."

Julie gave him a surprised expression.

"What would make you say that?"

Robert took a deep breath and answered honestly.

"Well, she thought Pluto was a planet."

His mother looked confused.

"And it's not?"

Robert shook his head.

"No mom, Mike Brown, a Caltech astronomer changed it to a dwarf planet in 2006. I tried to explain that to her but she said she didn't even know who he was, can you believe that?"

Julie wasn't sure how to respond to this unexpected conversation. She tried to keep her sarcasm to a minimum but was finding it difficult.

"Imagine that, so they are teaching astronomy in first grade now?"

Robert again shook his head.

"No, I brought it up."

Julie giggled.

"How did I just know that?"

It was starting already, her premonitions were coming true. Her little extraterrestrial had only been out in the world for one day and was already making his presence felt.

She could only wonder what would come next. Raising this child was surely going to be an adventure. She glanced in the rearview mirror checking for gray hairs.

As the school year progressed Robert continued to excel academically. He would bring home his simple tests and exams and Julie couldn't remember seeing any that were not 100%. This came as little surprise to Julie.

He would go every day with pep and enthusiasm and a bounce in his steps. It appeared obvious to her he was enjoying the experience.

What Julie didn't know was the origin of his excitement. This was a secret Robert kept to himself. She had assumed it was from his active involvement in an opportunity to further his education. She concluded it had to come from him being able to finally put his thirst for knowledge to good use in a place where it was encouraged. What she didn't know was that she couldn't be further from the truth.

Inwardly, Robert was becoming terribly bored. He found nothing Miss Benning offered challenging or stimulating in the least way. He felt himself trapped in an environment that not only did nothing to further his education but was actually inhibiting it. In his eyes first grade was doing nothing but holding him back and a total waste of time.

He would attend class daily, listening, trying to absorb everything his teacher was saying hoping she could enlighten him with something he didn't already know.

Each day he would come home disappointed. He felt his mind was being hampered by being forced to sit through such elementary lessons. He found the mentality of his classmates and even his teacher almost insulting. He was shocked by their intellectual level.

No, it wasn't the educational challenge that was fueling his enthusiasm; it was the verification that he was indeed special. He had been getting an inkling of this before but by spending time with other children his age his feeling of superiority was now confirmed.

He found this boost to his ego very satisfying and relished in the environment taking every chance he could to flaunt it to those around him.

His initial confidence had gradually evolved to the point of actually approaching arrogance. He eventually got to the point of secretly resented being forced to attend classes which were obviously beneath him. Again, the only satisfaction he was getting from first grade was to reinforce his feeling of intellectual superiority, which he fed on.

Julie's misconceptions would rise to the surface during the midterm parent-teacher conference. She walked into Miss Benning's office and they shook hands.

"It's such a pleasure to finally meet you Miss Wells, please have a seat."

Julie sat down and took a deep breath. She was nervous about what the woman might have to say. She wasn't worried about Robert's grades; she knew they had to be near perfect. She couldn't put her finger on the source of her apprehension but she would soon find out.

"Miss Wells, you truly have an exceptional son, it has been such a joy having him in my class. You must be very proud of him."

Julie involuntarily let out a snicker, thinking to herself if only you knew just how 'exceptional' he really was. As much as she was getting tired of hearing how exceptional her son was she still managed to thank Miss Benning for her kind words and the teacher continued.

"I must say I have never met such a, well, gifted child. I have been teaching first grade for six years now and I have never had a more inquisitive student. His eagerness to learn is like nothing I have ever witnessed before. He is always asking questions and..."

Julie interrupted her.

"Just how is he doing academically Miss Benning?"

Miss Benning opened up a folder she had in front of her.

"The only word that comes to mind is simply amazing. We have a quiz every Friday on the materials we covered during that week. We are in the tenth week now and, well up to this point, Robert has not missed a single question on any of the quizzes. I have never had a student before that could claim that."

Julie studied the teacher's face. There was something in her eyes that was telling her there was more to come. While obviously pleased with her son's test scores it appeared the woman had something more on her mind.

"Let me first address his progress academically. As I just said, he has not missed a single question on any of our quizzes; this goes beyond being highly unusual but is totally unprecedented. He is always the first to complete them too. Initially I just thought he was a very bright child but as this trend continued I began to wonder."

Julie tried to hold a gasp in...oh boy here it comes she thought. Miss Benning continued.

"Based on his quiz results and the acuity of the questions he asks daily I have to ask you, have you considered having his intelligence tested? Miss Wells you may have a truly gifted child here. I can't help but feel we might actually be holding him back."

This conversation was surely taking a direction she hadn't anticipated. How could she explain she knew she had an incredibly gifted child without telling her half his genes were from another planet?

Miss Benning continued sparing her from answering for the moment.

"Tell me more about Robert if you will. What does he do at home? What are his interests? Have you noticed his thought patterns or behavior well, different than what might be expected of a six year old?"

Julie was starting to feel really uncomfortable. Her first thought was that Dr. Hart may no longer be her biggest concern. It appears that Miss Benning had obviously noticed Robert's uniqueness and her curiosity may cause more trouble than the doctor's. She knew she had to answer the questions.

She felt the walls closing in on her, now there were two outside factors she had to contend with. She was sure more would follow. She should have known it would be only a matter of time before her son's 'gift' would raise eyebrows.

For the time being she had to play the game as coolly and subtlety as she could.

"Robert loves to read. He has an incredible thirst for knowledge. He enjoys things that challenge him, that make him think."

Miss Benning nodded her head, seemingly approving of her response.

"Well I can tell you that all that reading has certainly paid off. Robert not only questions everything but seems to deeply analyze my answers. I've never encountered a child with such a keen interest in things.

This is why I asked about having him tested. There are many programs out there geared at gifted students and steering them in a direction that would be the most beneficial to them.

I just want to make sure he gets the opportunity to make the most of this incredible mind he has. I really think you might want to pursue this Miss Wells."

Julie wasn't sure what she thought of that idea. She wasn't surprised at all with what Miss Benning had said so far about his intellect. He had already proven that at home. Miss Benning continued.

"Now Miss Wells; one thing that has struck me as being rather unusual is his interaction with the other children. While most children that age are anxious to mingle he seems hesitant to make friends.

When any of his classmates approach him he seems, well, hesitant to interact with them. He rarely even speaks to any of the other children as if he had no interest in making friends. He pretty much keeps to himself. Does he have any brothers or sisters?"

Miss Benning now had her undivided attention. She wasn't expecting this. Robert had always been outgoing with Karen and her and never shy about meeting the few people he has had a chance to meet.

"He has a sister, Karen, she is twenty-one. They are very close."

The teacher nodded her head in thought.

"You say they are close, does he talk to her a lot? Is he open with her?"

Julie smiled.

"Oh yes he is. They are practically inseparable. They play games together and do a number of things. When he reads he always discusses the book with her. Yes I would say he is very open with her."

Miss Benning rubbed her chin.

"How interesting; I wonder why he is so shy with his classmates. What I found especially strange about this behavior was that the first week or so he did seem so outgoing. He would chat with other children but in the weeks afterwards he has gone to being very withdrawn.

Don't be alarmed Miss Wells, I assure you he is by no means rude or disrespectful, he just keeps to himself.

Well, that's about all I have for you. Summing it up I'm very pleased with Robert's overall performance and class participation.

Like I said he always asks questions and contributes to class discussion and his grades speak for themselves. He is well behaved and has very pleasing manners.

You have done a wonderful job Miss Wells. I just want to reemphasize my feelings on perhaps getting him tested. His contributions to class discussion seem so mature for his age. I would really put some thought into checking out having his IQ tested. Your son could have unlimited potential."

Julie rehashed a number of things Miss Benning had said during her drive home. The grades came as no surprise to her. She would have expected nothing less. Her current train of thought centered on Robert being unsocial. Why would he initially be open and friendly then become shy and withdrawn? This was an enigma to her.

She then thought about the teacher's suggestion about having his intelligence tested. No, that would not be a good idea, what if they discovered it was off the charts? How would she explain that one? Something told her that if she did have him tested that would be exactly what the findings would be. No, that is not something she could take a chance on doing.

She wondered if the school could, at some point, actually require her to do that. What if these trends of never missing a question and coming up with all these off the wall discussion topics continued or got worse? She had to research the legalities of this. She wanted to be prepared if that day ever came up.

Julie decided to have a talk with Robert when she got home to see if she could discover the reason for his behavior with the other children.

She arrived home and found Karen busy in the kitchen getting out plates. A large take home box sat on the kitchen table

"Hi mom, I brought us dinner from work! How did the meeting go?

She beamed with motherly pride.

"Oh sweetheart, that was so nice of you thanks!"

Karen smiled from ear to ear.

"Well don't get too excited, it's just chicken and French fries. Robert is in his room doing something, I don't know, probably building a nuclear reactor or something. He sure spends a lot of time up there I don't know what he does. How was your meeting at school?"

Julie set her purse and keys down on the table and got a glass of iced tea. She checked out the contents of the box and snatched a French fry.

"Has Robert eaten?"

Karen nodded.

"Yeah, he grabbed a plate and went to his room. Now are you going to tell me about the meeting?"

Julie took a plate and put a piece of chicken and a mound of French fries on it. She walked into the living room and motioned Karen to join her.

She spent the next half hour explaining everything Miss Benning had said in detail.

Karen grilled her mother on every point before concluding the conversation.

"Mom, I think you had better talk to him. You don't know how this story will end."

Julie had to laugh but agreed.

"That's exactly what I intend on doing."

Karen just stared at her mother.

"Okay daughter, I'm going up now!"

Julie finished her plate and returned it to the kitchen. She wasn't sure how she was going to approach this. She wished she had a glass of wine to give her a little courage. She immediately rethought that. The last time she had alcohol things didn't turn out very well. She settled for a cup of coffee.

She took a couple of minutes trying to formulate just what she wanted to talk about with him. She would of course praise him for his exceptional grades. She would also thank him for being so cooperative about going every day never putting up any kind of fuss.

Now would come the tough part. She wanted to address why he was having difficulty making friends, or at least seemingly reluctant to try. This concerned her.

He was a very handsome young man so his appearance certainly wouldn't lead him to be shy. She thought he had a sparkling personality so that wouldn't be a factor. He was likable, kind and from what she could tell at least somewhat outgoing. No, none of these could be the problem.

She then thought about how intelligent he was, initially concluding that wouldn't inhibit him. She stopped for a second, or could it? Her mind drifted to her early school days and how none of the kids liked the ones who were really smart. They resented them if for no other reason than they would raise the grading curve. She was guilty of that very thing.

She was never the most intelligent kid and when she ran across someone who was she couldn't help but feel inferior. These feelings would evolve into resentment and she wouldn't associate with them. Perhaps this is the problem. She was certain the other children would pick up on his intelligence and maybe avoid him.

She all of a sudden thought she may have come up with the answer. She had to find out whether he was rejecting the other children or they were rejecting him.

Now the question would be how to bring this up to Robert. She had to be careful about how she presented it to him. She didn't want to make him feel uncomfortable; she needed him to be completely open and honest.

She was beginning to think she wished she had some wine after all.

# 40

Julie was trying to remember the last moment in her life when she wasn't apprehensive about something, this wouldn't be it.

She gathered her determination and headed upstairs to Robert's room. She noticed his bedroom door closed and gently knocked on it.

After being invited in she opened the door to find Robert sitting on his bed immersed on his laptop.

"Hi mom, you should check this out. Did you know Yellowstone National Park sits right on top of a huge magma lake?"

She had to remind herself that he was only six years old. Don't six-year-old boys play with trucks and action figures? Why is hers studying geology on a computer? She already knew the answer to that.

"No, I wasn't aware of that."

Robert encouraged her to sit with him.

"Yeah, it's fascinating! They say here it could erupt any time and cause a worldwide disaster!"

Julie simply nodded and sat next to him on the bed. That wasn't the disaster she currently had on her mind.

"Well that's really interesting but put that aside for now, I want to talk to you about something else."

He complied, closing the computer and turned to face his mother.

"Okay, mom, what's up?"

She found his childlike smile so adorable. Okay she thought, no time to be a wimp; she needed some straight forward information from him and tried to get into mother mode.

"Bobby, I want to talk about school. I just got back

from the parent-teacher conference. I met your teacher, Miss Benning; she seems really nice."

Robert gave her a look of complacency.

"Yeah, she is alright I guess."

Julie put her arm around his shoulders.

"I am so proud of you! Your grades are outstanding!"

Robert simply shrugged his shoulders.

"That really wasn't difficult mom."

Julie sighed. She could see where this was going.

"Well that be what it may, I am still proud of you. You get up and go everyday without giving me any problems. You are the best son in the world."

Robert interrupted her.

"The way I see it I really don't have a choice do I?"

Julie shook her head in frustration.

"That's not the point, you do it voluntarily and that just makes things so much easier. I'm just trying to show my appreciation for your efforts."

Robert smiled meekly.

"No problem mom."

Now for the difficult part she thought. Just how was she going to address his...social issues? She decided to work her way into it slowly.

"Do you enjoy school Bobby?"

Robert now looked confused. He thought for a moment before answering.

"I really don't find much to enjoy there mom, it's really boring if you want to know the truth. I feel my time could be much better spent studying at home actually. That way I could choose my own studies, you know; more practical and useful things rather than the nonsense they cover in school."

This was the perfect statement to dive into his problems making friends.

"But even if that were an option you wouldn't have

the opportunity to meet new friends and get to know them and…"

Again, Robert interrupted her.

"Oh mom let's be serious."

She was taken back by the outburst.

"I am being serious. School gives you the opportunity to get to know other children and become friends."

Robert shook his head.

"There is no one there I would want to be friends with. These kids are, well, just stupid. You can't talk to them much less have any interest in being friends with them!"

Julie shook her head.

"Oh I can't believe that."

Robert put his hand on his mother's shoulder.

"Okay, you don't believe me? All they guys want to talk about is sports or super hero movies. I mean, really?

Let me give you an example. This morning I was talking to this kid named Taylor. I asked him what he thought about Bill Gates, you want to know what he said? He asked me what team he played for! Now just how am I supposed to carry on a conversation with someone like that? Mom, he didn't know who Bill Gates was!"

She was now totally perplexed. She totally understood his dilemma and she also had one advantage over him… she knew why he was struggling with this and sadly he did not.

She was at a crossroads. Her son was struggling with something he didn't have the full story on. He had obviously discovered his intellectual superiority over other children his age, and, for that matter, most adults, but he was assuming it was due to their intelligence level and not his own. He knew he was smarter than they were but had no clue as to why and it was confusing him. His frustration over not being able to relate to his peers would only increase as he got older. She knew that with certainty.

She had to decide, and decide quickly just what, and how much, she should tell him. She sighed, realizing that even if she had the courage to tell him the entire truth, he wouldn't believe her.

How she would ever get him to believe and accept the truth was at the moment beyond her. Her next question was should she try at all? That became a mute point because she knew if she didn't bring it up, he would eventually.

She knew this day would come sooner or later. She was fully aware at some point he would wonder about his father. Up to this point, much to her surprise, he had never mentioned him. Just how do you tell a child his father is from another planet? She was certain Dr. Spock never ran across this one.

She glanced at her son, innocent, naïve, kind and sweet little boy he was, with a mind Einstein would envy. She pitied the conversational attempts he must have had to endure at school.

Little Johnny was thrilled at the way the Raiders were playing and he was contemplating the theories of Galileo. No wonder he wasn't enjoying the classroom environment. He must feel so isolated and alone. The kids in his class couldn't even spell Galileo much less know who he was; but her son sure did.

She was determined to address this issue now before it continued unchecked and caused irreversible psychological damage. Her son was in danger, danger of growing up with a complex he would never be able to rid himself of.

While over the past six years she had contemplated many aspects of the problems of raising a half alien child that she might encounter, this was one thing she hadn't thought of. Here she had been worrying about the effects it might have on the world, she had neglected to think about the inner problems it might cause him.

Then her thoughts went in the opposite direction. Supposing she did convince him of the truth, just how would a six-year-old child handle knowing his father was from another planet? What kind of psychological damage could that cause him! This was rapidly turning into a no win situation.

Robert sensed his mother was wrestling with something. He smiled reassuringly.

"I'm sorry mom; I can see this is troubling you. It's just that the lessons are so elementary, so boring. As far as making friends, I just don't see anyone that interests me. I try and talk to them and they just look at me funny, in fact even Miss Benning looks at me funny sometimes.

The other kids are just stupid mom, it's true. You can't talk to them about anything."

Julie pulled her son close to her and gave him a hug.

"Sweetheart, the kids are not stupid, they are just ordinary six year old children."

Robert gave her a puzzled look. He thought about what she had just said.

"Well, if they are just ordinary, what does that make me? I am certainly not at their level."

Julie bowed her head and sighed, dismayed. 'Oh boy' she thought, here it comes. There would be no way of avoiding the conversation now.

"No Bobby, you are not."

Robert's expression changed to one of total confusion.

"I don't get it mom, if you're telling me they are not stupid and are just normal, then why am I so much smarter than they are? Just what makes me so special?"

Julie's mind was churning nervously. She had truly opened Pandora's Box now. She confessed to herself that she would have no other recourse than to tell him the entire truth; there would be no other way of explaining it.

There was no turning back now, he wants answers and she was determined to give them to him. Her concern now was not that she wouldn't have to courage to tell him, but what his reaction would be.

She sighed and again wished she had that glass of wine. She studied her son's eyes. He was reaching out to her for help. They looked so innocent and trusting and deeply wanting answers. She all of a sudden felt so small. She said a short, silent prayer asking for divine intervention.

She gently brushed the hair out of her son's eyes.

"I'm getting to that Bobby."

She took a deep breath and threw caution to the wind. Her son was pleading for help and for divine guidance. She knew she didn't have the words to properly explain things and she put her faith in God to guide her down this difficult road. Her thoughts were interrupted by her son.

"So explain to me mom, what makes me so different than everyone else? I mean, I know I am special but I don't understand why."

She was determined to uphold her responsibility as a mother and give him the answers he so desperately needed. She just didn't have a clue as to how she was going to do it.

"Well sweetheart, as much as I would like to take credit for it I can't. I think it's time we had a talk about your father."

Robert's eyes grew as big as saucers at the unexpected mention of his father. He had never given him much thought. He had obviously never met him and his mother never mentioned him. He was totally taken back by the reference. It was now his turn to think and digest what was being said.

"My dad...you have never talked about him. Why would you bring him up now mom?"

Julie couldn't resist giving her son a tight hug. This was as much for her comfort as it was for his.

"Well Bobby; I mention him because you are asking me questions that can only be answered by telling you about your father."

Robert now gave his mother a serious expression.

"Just where is my father and why isn't he here with us? Why haven't you mentioned before now? Mom, why did you pick now to have this conversation?"

Julie put her hand to her forehead. She ran her fingers through her hair in thought. This wasn't going to be easy.

"Slow down now Bobby, one thing at a time. I will answer all your questions but you have to listen with an open mind. This is going to be difficult for both of us. What I am about to tell you will be hard to hear and believe me it's equally hard for me to say it."

So far so good she thought. She definitely had her son's undivided attention. She clutched her son's hands tightly and looked directly into his eyes. She knew she would have to start off with the most painful part. She now prayed silently for strength.

"You have a right to know this and I am sorry for not telling you sooner but I wanted to wait until I thought you were old enough to understand, well most of it.

There is no easy way to tell you this so I will just come right out and say it. Bobby, your father died before you were born. The reason I am telling you this now is because he holds the all answers to your questions sweetheart."

A tear came to her eye and she clenched her son's

hands even tighter. She immediately studied his eyes to see what reaction they might give away.

Robert was devastated. He looked like a deer in front of the headlights. He broke lose from his mother's grip and stood up. He franticly paced around the room in a state of shock before finally turning and facing his mother who had remained seated on the bed.

"My father is dead?"

Julie fought the tears back and replied solemnly.

"Yes sweetheart, I'm afraid so. He passed away a few months before you were born. I'm so sorry."

Robert returned to sitting on the bed and took his mother's hand. Julie was relieved that the moment was over. She took a deep breath then began struggling with another thought, what if he asked her how he died?

She cursed herself for not thoroughly thinking the conversation entirely through before hand. She should have been prepared for any question he might ask but she was so apprehensive about it she hadn't thought it all out.

Robert thought for a moment. He was finding it hard to mourn for a person he had never met, even though it was his father. He knew nothing about him because his mother had never mentioned him. He had never given his father any thought as if he didn't exist. His logical mind was prohibiting him from feeling a great sense of loss.

His thoughts now turned to how his mother was claiming that the answers to his questions lie with his father. How could someone who died before he was born carry so much influence in his life now? He found that thought very intriguing and had to find out more.

"Mom, you said the only way of explaining my situation was by telling me about him, what did you mean by that? How can he be so important if he isn't here? How can he affect me because I never even met him?"

Julie again focused on her son's eyes. They seemed to show no signs of remorse or sadness but instead cried out for answers. She was a bit taken back by this lack of compassion but, after giving it some thought, realized she should have expected nothing less.

Robert indeed never met his father, had no memories of him and because of her avoiding the subject up to this point, had no knowledge of who his father was as a person.

She knew this was something she had to rectify.

"Sweetheart, you asked me why you were special, why you were different, well the answer is your father was special and he was, well, very different."

Robert stood up and again paced around his room. He walked over to the model of the solar system he had on his desk and studied it for a moment simply to give him time to digest and absorb everything he was hearing. He spun the miniature Earth around while deep in thought.

"Okay mom, explain to me how my father is responsible for me being so smart. Was he really smart? I read about genes and DNA and all so please level with me. Is that what you are trying to say? I'm smart because I inherited it from his genes?"

Julie had to remind herself that she was talking to a six year old. She kept thinking a six year old boy should be talking about Spiderman or baseball, not about genetics. This defied everything in the parenting manual.

She had to laugh for a second, she had thrown out that manual the day Robert was born. She chuckled when she thought she could rewrite the parenting manual but then there wouldn't be a big demand for her version.

Good Lord she thought, she would have to deal with this for at least another twelve years and it will only get worse.

She had always felt a parent had to talk down to a six

year old in order to communicate effectively but in this case the tables were clearly reversed. She couldn't help but feel it was the six year old who was talking down to her for that very reason.

"Yes Bobby, your father was a brilliant man. He was so much smarter than I am."

Robert accepted that answer.

"Well, I guess that makes sense then. Do you really think that is why I am smarter than the other kids?"

Julie knew her tribulations were far from over. The most challenging part of the confession was yet to come. There was an awkward moment of silence between them as she pondered how to put her thoughts into words.

Suddenly Robert gently placed his hand on her forehead and closed his eyes. This took Julie by surprise. She sat motionless for a moment or two as Robert continued to press his hand against her forehead. He reopened his eyes keeping his scrupulous stare into her eyes.

"Mom, I'm getting really freaked out here. I can't explain it, I..."

Julie could see the expression on her son's face change from one of an inquisitive nature to a look of total distress. She immediately went into protective mother mode.

"Sweetheart, what's wrong?"

Robert withdrew his hand from his mother's forehead and looked at it in confusion.

"This is really strange mom; I have never felt anything like this before. I'm really freaking out here!"

Julie gave her son a tight hug trying to calm him down. She was now getting very concerned. This conversation had taken a turn she wasn't anticipating. She could tell something was seriously bothering her son, something that just came out of nowhere suddenly.

"What is it Bobby? What are you feeling?"

Robert clasped his hands together and took a deep breath. Julie noticed him actually shaking. She was now beyond worry. Her motherly instinct now told her that her son was in peril. She had no clue as to what was the cause of this abrupt change in behavior.

Why would Robert place his hand on her forehead? That just didn't make any sense. Her son was visibly shaken. She took his hand and squeezed it tightly.

"Sweetheart, talk to me. What is wrong?"

Robert shook his head. He pulled his hand back and placed both palms up sending the signal that he didn't want to be touched at this moment. His eyes now showed what could only be construed as nothing but fear. He continued to shake.

He stood up and nervously paced the room. His breathing was obviously labored and his eyes now vacant. It was apparent that something had frightened him. Julie knew it was her job to find out exactly what that was.

"Bobby, sit down and talk to me. I want to help, you what is wrong, what is upsetting you honey?"

Robert shook his head defiantly and continued to pace the room. He finally stopped and put his hands to his temples.

"Mom, I don't know what is going on! I don't know how to explain this but it's really freaking me out. You're not going to believe me I know it."

Julie stood up and walked over to her son in an effort to try and calm him down. Initially he withdrew her approach then conceded to her hug. Julie was mortified to see her son in this condition.

"Bobby, I am here for you. You can tell me anything. I need to know what is troubling you in order to help you sweetheart now please sit down and talk to me!"

# 41

Robert sat back down on the bed and remained silent, motionless in his own world.

Julie sat down beside him and put her arm around him.

"Bobby, it's okay, I am here for you; but we need to finish this talk, about your father."

Robert shook his head lethargically. He stared at his mother with a distant, blank expression.

"No we don't mom, it's already finished."

Julie looked totally perplexed.

"What are you talking about? I'm afraid it is not. You don't know what I have to tell you! There is more I need to explain to you about him that will..."

Her son interrupted her. He stared at her for a moment in silence before speaking.

"You are going to tell me my father isn't human, that he is from another planet. Isn't that what you were going to say?

But you're scared and you don't know how to tell me. You're afraid I won't believe you. Isn't that right mom?"

Julie jumped back in astonishment. A chill ran down her spine. She suddenly lost all sense of reality and spoke without thinking.

"How in the name of Jesus did you know that?"

Robert sighed and stared at the floor for a moment. He then looked at her with the blank expression of a zombie, as if he were looking right through her.

"I read your mind, I don't know how, but all of a sudden, it just happened. Your thoughts became crystal clear, as if they were my own."

Julie's eyes were about to pop out of her head and her mouth dropped to the floor. She felt cold and frightened.

She was totally speechless. She tried to formulate words but her mind wouldn't cooperate. In all her nightmares about possible scenarios, this wasn't one of them. Robert sensed her uneasiness.

"Mom, I'm really scared...I didn't know I could do that. I wasn't trying, it just happened. I know it's scaring you too, I could feel that."

Jumping into protective mother mode again Julie hugged her son. Robert broke away from the embrace and stared blankly at his mother.

"It's true isn't it?"

Lacking the ability to come up with a more appropriate response, Julie just bowed her head and nodded.

"Yes sweetheart, it is true. I didn't know how to tell you in a manner you would understand or believe."

Robert closed his eyes and sighed.

"I know you didn't. It's okay mom, I...I just sense it now. It's as if he told me himself. It's like I feel him with me all of a sudden, like a presence or something. I can't explain it. Now I know that isn't normal! Mom, what's wrong with me?"

Julie was totally dumbfounded. She hadn't seen this coming. Not only was her son super intelligent but now she discovers he can read minds. Good Lord she thought; what next! She was feeling a total nervous breakdown on the horizon.

She quickly said a silent prayer for strength which, at the moment, she desperately needed. She tried to collect her thoughts. She tried to look at it from the perspective that now he knows the truth about his father. This was supposed to be the hard part but what she was struggling with now was; how he found out!

She studied her son as they looked into each other's eyes. She was struggling with two vastly opposite trains of thought.

Her primary focus was on his innocence. He was her son, he was scared and overwhelmed and naive about what was happening to him. He was looking towards her for comfort and reassurance. He was simply a normal little six-year-old boy.

It was the other train of thought that was troubling her. She knew he wasn't just a normal six-year-old boy. He was anything but normal. He already had the intellect of a Harvard professor and now she discovers he can read minds!

What other surprises might he harbor in the future? If he is all of this at only age six, what will he be capable of in the years ahead? She had to switch gears. Her son needed her and needed her now.

Just how was she going to approach calming her son down? She started to worry about a total nervous breakdown on his horizon as well. She had to find a way to continue the conversation in a relaxed manner. Her mind wasn't convinced that would be possible now.

"Okay sweetheart, first of all, nothing is wrong with you. We are just dealing with an extraordinary situation here."

Julie thought back to what he had just said. Something was troubling her. Perhaps it was just ramblings of a six-year-old but she had to call him on it.

"Sweetheart, okay, how can I say this...you say you can read my mind. I really can't dispute that because there would have been no other way for you to know what you do. That was exactly what I was trying to tell you but you resolved that without me saying a word. Enough of that for now, we'll come back to that."

He son had just confessed he felt his father's presence in his mind. She couldn't help but think back to her experience in the hospital when she experienced the same thing. She had to find out more about what he was feeling if for no other reason than to add to the validity of her experience.

"Something else you said just struck me. You said it was like he was with you, like he told you himself. What made you think that?"

Robert thought for a moment before answering. He took his mother's hand and did his best to attempt a smile.

"I don't know mom, I don't know how to explain it. It felt like he was inside my head telling me what to think."

Beyond that mom, there are so many questions I would like to ask you about him. They are all coming to me at once but I have to ask you this one first. I don't know why, but it's important. Are you certain he is dead? I mean, were you two together when he died?"

Tears started flowing from her eyes. She wasn't prepared for this conversation. She wasn't planning on having to relive that moment. She owed him as honest an answer as she could come up with.

"Well Bobby, yes we were together but I wasn't with him when it happened. That's the best answer I can give you."

Robert digested her words and it brought about another question. Another question she wasn't prepared for.

"If you were not with him then how do you know he died? I mean, did you have a funeral or anything?"

This wasn't getting any easier. With every memory came more tears.

"Bobby, since you have accepted the truth about your father I can explain. If you hadn't it wouldn't make any sense. No, there was no funeral.

You're not going to like this but you deserve the truth. Your father really didn't share much with me about his past; we never really talked about it.

He did tell me that he was a criminal on his planet.

He never really came out and said what he actually did but he did tell me he was facing the death sentence. They sent him to Earth until they could, well carry out the sentence. Once again, he really didn't go into detail as to why it was handled this way. He was here for one year.

At the end of the year he was taken back, I had to assume to be executed. I'm so sorry to have to tell you this. So to answer your question, I wasn't with him but I can only conclude it was carried out."

Julie put her hand on his shoulder, rubbing it softly.

"So tell me what made you think he was with you. You have never met him and that was just an odd thing to say sweetheart."

Robert stood up and again started pacing.

"Mom, I will try and explain. I didn't know I could read minds and I couldn't, until I placed my hand on your forehead. How did I know to do that? Mom, something, or maybe someone, told me I needed to do that. I certainly didn't come up with that on my own!"

Julie had no answer to that but had to admit it was a rather provocative point. How would he have known? A million thoughts suddenly entered her already crowded mind.

Could his father have somehow sent him that knowledge from beyond the grave? Did they have that power as well? Dear Lord, just how advanced are they? Then another, even more disturbing; thought interrupted...could he still be alive?

If these people can read minds how can she be sure they couldn't communicate telepathically, even from across great distances. Lord knows what they might be capable of! This thought did nothing to ease her mind about her son.

She shook her head to try and clear out the cobwebs. She had never given any thought of the possibility of him being still alive but now she found herself actually questioning it. She reluctantly thought about how her son might have come up with a valid point...she never actually saw him die.

Her heart was screaming at her to stop that line of thinking. It was cruel and pointless. Even if he were alive he was twelve light year away from her and never coming back.

She was wondering if that was only wishful thinking or perhaps, just perhaps, her son may have stumbled on something dramatic. She wished she knew more about science and paranormal activity to give her a notion if the idea really merited further consideration. For now she had to put that idea aside and deal with her son.

"That's a question I can't answer sweetheart. I have gone these past six years with the acceptance of him having passed. From what he had told me I had no reason to believe otherwise.

Right after he left I felt such anguish in my heart at the thought of him actually having died. I had no other recourse than to accept it. I had nightmares of actually seeing him executed, they became so real."

Robert gave her a puzzled look.

"But you can't be sure can you mom? I mean, you have no proof of it. How was he taken back? Were you with him?"

Julie could no longer hold back the tears. Reliving that last afternoon together was opening wounds that had never properly healed in the first place. She was crucifying herself with torturous memories.

She had tried to bury any thoughts of that last day together but now was being forced to relive them. Defying her aching heart, she tried to explain their last moments together.

"We were sitting on the sofa having coffee. I knew he

would be taken soon so I went to the bathroom to get tissues for the tears I knew were coming. I was only gone for less than a minute but when I returned to the living room; he was simply gone."

Robert could instinctively sense his mother's pain. He again placed his hand on her forehead.

"Mom, I think this will be easier for you."

Julie immediately picked up on his intentions. He was trying to help her avoid the pain of having to verbally explain everything and would gather all the information he required by simply reading her thoughts.

She couldn't decide if she was relieved by this or troubled even more. As much as she admired her son's unforeseen compassion she was frightened about what thoughts might actually be in her mind.

Just how deeply could he probe into her brain? She was sure there were thoughts that would be better kept from him. She knew she harbored fears of what he might become and this was the last thing he needed to be aware of!

She all of a sudden felt wary of him reading her inner most thoughts and, after a moment or two, withdrew his hand from her forehead. She would rather endure the pain of telling him than to risk his discovery of her fears.

She looked at her son and her instinct told her Robert was even more upset than he was before. His eyes said it all. He appeared taken back, almost surprised. Her deepest fears were about to come true.

Robert took a deep breath and spoke without hesitation.

"You're afraid of me aren't you mom?"

Her apprehensions were now clearly becoming the disturbing truth. Robert had the ability to delve not only into her conscious thoughts but also into her deepest kept secrets. This thought was terrifying her.

She had to keep this unsettling ability of his in check and not allow him such access to her mind in the future. Now she had to get herself out of the hole she was currently finding herself in.

As much as she wanted to, she knew she couldn't deny her thoughts to him. He had already become painfully aware of their existence in a manner she couldn't contradict. She now had to somehow soften them. She couldn't stand the thought of her son feeling she actually feared him. She was sure his ego was already damaged and also knew she would be his sole source of support.

She then thought what was already on his young mind. The poor child was already feeling confused about his alienation from his peers and now, knowing the reason behind it, could only bring him more distress. He certainly didn't need to feel his mother feared him!

He looked at her with unsettling eyes. She now wished she had the ability to read his mind, she knew there had to be some horrific thoughts within it; thoughts that would be unraveling to an adult much less a poor little six-year-old child.

She so pitied him at the moment. She saw all the innocence in his eyes suddenly vanish. She had to come up with words that would reassure him that the uneasiness he detected in her thoughts had no bearing on the love she had for him and the support she would promise him.

"Sweetheart, foremost you have to know, I love you with all my heart and I will always be here for you. I am not afraid of you, I'm just a little nervous, well let's say uneasy, about what abilities you might have.

Irregardless I will support and encourage you in any way I can. This will not come between us in any way!

I know you have been given a lot to think about this morning. I can't imagine what it would feel like to have to deal with what has been thrown at you but I am your mother and I will get us through this together!"

Robert placed his hands to his temples and lowered his head. The poor child had the weight of the world on his young shoulders. Julie couldn't help but feel how unfair it was. First he had to deal with the fact that he wasn't totally human, now he feels his only support group, his mother, is terrified of him! Just how does someone deal with that?

She was glad he wasn't reading her thoughts at the moment for she was dreading the remainder of the conversation.

"Mom, why are you afraid of me? I would never hurt you."

The tears were flowing uncontrollably from her reddened eyes. She was now in damage control. She had to come up with something to calm him down, it was obvious he wasn't doing well emotionally at the moment and she felt she was a major contributor to his current unrest.

"Bobby, listen to me. Sometimes a parent just overreacts when they see their children struggling with things."

Robert shook his head defiantly.

"No mom, it goes beyond that, you really fear me. You are afraid of what I might be able to do. These are your thoughts, not mine. I feel like some kind of circus freak!"

Julie closed her eyes for a moment of private thought. She was devastated hearing this coming from her son. She had no precedence to follow for guidance. She knew no parent in human history ever had to deal with this issue before.

Not only was her son far more intelligent than she was but he also knew her inner most thoughts. Honesty was her only option.

"Okay Bobby, since you already know what I am thinking, let me at least explain myself. Yes, I am apprehensive about what all you might be able to do. We simply don't know what you are capable of sweetheart. That is not a bad thing, just a situation that would naturally cause some, well, uneasiness. Please don't mistake that for outright fear, there is a big difference."

Robert nodded his head slowly. Julie looked at this as a good sign, a sign that he was at least accepting her honest reply.

His words continued to echo in her mind causing her extreme despair.

"Bobby I don't want you to ever think that! You are not a freak sweetheart. You just have to deal with an unusual gene pool. Now you need to look at this as a gift. You have already proven your intelligence which is a wonderful thing!

It's true we don't know just what you are capable of but you are an incredible young man. As time goes by we will discover many wonderful new things together and we will deal with each one as a family.

You have your sister and me as your support group. We both love you and will be by your side through what ever the future may bring."

Robert stood up and returned to the model of the solar system on his desk. He studied it. It all of a sudden carried much more significance than it had before. His mind was traveling silently at a million miles a second. He turned and faced his mother, still seated on the bed.

"Mom, did dad tell you where he was from? I mean; what planet?"

It amazed Julie how calmly he had accepted this startling realization. She wondered how she would have handled the news. Robert was so matter of fact about the whole thing.

She tried to rationalize his line of thinking and could only come up with perhaps their minds were so superior to hers that they may be able to deal with things with a totally different perspective. Maybe their brains just work differently than ours; perhaps they have lessened the emphasis of emotion and replaced it with logic.

She concluded that she would have been a total basket case had her mother told her what she had just told her son. Robert was apparently unfazed by it at all. She then remembered he had asked her a question.

"No sweetheart, he never mentioned exactly where he was from. He only mentioned that it was about twelve light years away, what ever that meant."

Robert shook his head in obvious disgust over his mother's unfamiliarity over what he saw as a very basic astronomical term. He had calmed down, seemingly totally accepting and amazingly at peace, with the fact that he was half extraterrestrial. He spun the miniature Earth and watched it spin. Julie watched him ever so wishing she could read his thoughts.

"Well, I guess that explains why I am so smart. They must be pretty smart on that planet where ever it is. They must obviously be able to read minds as well because I don't think many people here can. I wonder what else they can do mom? Do you think I'm going to grow up to be some kind of monster or something?"

Julie jumped up and raced to her son. She gave him a big hug and held him tightly.

"Oh Bobby stop that nonsense this minute! No, you are not going to become anything of the sort! Your father was an incredible man and by no means a monster!"

Robert simply shook his head compliantly.

"Okay mom, I'm sorry, I just have a lot to deal with at the moment. It's not every kid that has to accept he is part alien. It's strange now that I think about it. It really didn't shock me like I guess it should have. I mean, I knew I was different than the other kids but I wasn't sure why.

Now that I know, it kind of all makes sense. It's like I almost felt it somehow you know? It's hard to explain but it was like something inside was preparing me for this conversation, really weird!"

# 42

Julie was slowly, and totally against her will, being convinced that there was a presence of his father in Robert beyond his inherited genes. What really unnerved her was, based on her experience at the hospital; it appeared he might have a connection with both of them! She couldn't put her finger on the exact nature of the connection but she was sure there was something there. Robert's argument simply made that conclusion inevitable.

She was growing very uncomfortable with that knowledge but from a personal standpoint. For a moment she actually envied her son for having that relationship, as vague as it may be, wishing she shared it as strongly as he seemed to. She would give anything to have any kind of connection with him.

She was pleased that her son seemed to be taking it all in stride and wanted to encourage that demeanor. This was making her job much easier than initially anticipated. She was curious just how intimate this connection might be and what the implications of it might be in the future. She again wondered just what powers or abilities those people might have.

She wanted the conversation to continue, seizing the moment of his compliance to tell him more about the father he sadly never got to know. She felt that now that her son accepted his fate she could use this opportunity to tell him more about his father; she knew that was important, to both of them.

She and her parents were very close growing up. She couldn't imagine what it would be like to not have a father and she wanted to do everything she could to lessen the burden on her son.

While she knew they could never actually meet, she wanted her son to have a better understanding about the kind of man his father was. If he were going to be forced to endure the genetics he at least had the right to know more about their origin.

Robert managed a weak smile and sat attentively as his mother spent the next hour sharing stories about his father. She told him how they first met, how they eventually fell in love and became inseparable. She smiled as she recalled his wonderful sense of humor and how innocently naïve he was about the ways of humans.

She explained the ordeal she had trying to get his father to understand the ways of people on Earth. They actually laughed and she managed to hold back the tears that were accompanying the memories.

She made a point of telling him how compassionate and empathetic his father was as well as how brilliant he was. She was hoping her son would emulate not only his father's intelligence but his kindness as well.

She then explained how he was born three months premature and how amazed the doctors were with his rapid physical development. She figured that would help him come to grips about his intellectual development as well.

She told him their concern over his unique blood but emphasized the doctors, as one, all confirmed his overall good health. He listened intently with great fascination, never once showing any signs of unrest.

Robert would frequently ask probing questions about his father which were always answered honestly. As the conversation continued, Julie became more comfortable reliving the memories. She no longer felt a sense of loss but rather a sense of joy that he had given her so many wonderful recollections. As long as they remained in her heart, so would he.

It was getting late and Julie could see her son's eye lids starting to get heavy. She was very satisfied and pleased that the talk went as well as it did. They had covered a lot of ground. Robert now had a solid foundation on the father he would never truly know.

Julie decided to stop for now and gave her son a hug which, for the first time during their time together tonight, was returned sincerely.

"Well sweetheart, I think it's time we call it a night. I have so enjoyed this talk and I can only hope it has given you an understanding of what a wonderful man your father was. I see so much of him in you already.

You are a wonderful son Bobby. Your sister and I both love you so much and we are so proud of you!

I'm going down and getting a cup of coffee, would you like to join me for something to drink before you go to sleep?"

He nodded his head and smiled. Robert followed his mother downstairs and she poured him a glass of iced tea and herself a cup of coffee. He took a drink then walked out the front door and stood on the porch. His mind was racing after their conversation.

The cloudless evening sky was a beautiful shade of indigo blue and the heavens were littered with countless numbers of stars twinkling brightly. Robert took his drink and sat out in the front yard. He stared into the sky wondering, as silly as he knew the notion was, if his father might, just by chance, be somewhere up there staring back.

He had already known he was different than the other children but tonight's explanation of the reasoning behind that difference was a bit overwhelming.

He was now feeling so alone. His six-year-old mind

was now inundated with a weight that would be difficult to deal with even if he were an adult. He realized this feeling would never go away, that he would always be different. He fully understood that this alienation would continue for the rest of his life.

Up to this point he had never given much time to anything emotional. His logical mind prohibited him from wasting mental energy on, what to him, seemed a senseless waste of thought power.

Even at school, with the frustrations of not being able to make friends, he never let it bother him emotionally. Making friends had not been a priority. But suddenly, the facts behind it opened up a door he wasn't expecting. He was, without warning, now feeling so detached from everything.

His mind refused to allow him to be only six-years-old. His intellect was now betraying him. He knew as he grew older his estrangement would only increase.

For a brief second he even wished he was normal, like other children. His analytical mind refused to allow him to continue that thought and reminded him of how he almost pitied the other kids for their lack of intelligence. Still, the thought of never having any friends nagged at him.

He thought about his father, if only he were here with him he wouldn't feel so isolated, he wouldn't be the only one who was different. He would have someone he could confide in who would understand.

As much as he loved his mother and his sister he knew they would never be able to totally empathize with his dilemma but rather just add sympathy. He knew their intentions would be good, and that he could rely on them for encouragement and support, he would never have a sense of comradely with them. He reminded himself that he was only half human and there would be no way for them to ever totally understand how he felt.

His mind unfortunately far surpassed his young age. In his mind he knew he was the only person on the entire planet whose father was an extraterrestrial. He knew what that meant. His efforts to make friends with his classmates had ended unsuccessfully and he knew that trend would only continue.

He was well aware of the fact that as he grew older his intellect would continue to increase making the bridges between him and his peers even more impassable. He felt so alone.

He continued to stare up at the heavens deep in thought. He wondered just where his father came from and, more importantly, whether he might really still be alive. He then realized that if what his mother had told him were true, that dad said he was from twelve light years away, it really wouldn't matter if he were alive or not.

Then another thought struck him. If his father managed to get here once, what would prevent him from getting back a second time. Twelve light years wasn't really that prohibitively far in astronomical terms, especially to a race of people who have already proven they can conquer it.

Julie discovered him sitting in the front yard and just watched him staring at the sky for a moment. She could only wonder what was going through his mind. She was relieved at having that difficult discussion over with but saddened at the burden she knew he was now carrying. She pondered the long term effect the revelation would have on him.

Just what would it be like to know your father was from another planet and that no matter how hard you tried to fit in, there would always be that separation from every living soul on the planet? She shed a single tear, but this time, not out of pity for herself but for her son. She couldn't help but feel in her heart the terrible sense of isolation her son must be feeling now.

She let out a long, labored sigh. She knew in his heart he would have to deal with an affliction no other living person could ever totally understand. She took a deep breath and tried to calm herself down as she called him back inside. She kissed him and he went to bed.

Julie placed her empty cup in the sink and reflected on the one thing she didn't tell him. She had intentionally omitted any reference to his father curing Karen. She wasn't sure if that was something he really needed to know while also respecting Karen's privacy. She resolved herself to the notion if that was something his sister wanted him to know she could tell him herself.

The days flew by and quickly turned to weeks, which, in turn, became months. The ending of Robert's first year in school was rapidly drawing near.

He would continue to attend daily without complaints although it was clear to see his heart wasn't in it. When he would come home at the end of the day he was lackadaisical. He rarely said anything about how his day went and answered any questions his mother or sister would ask lethargically.

It was obvious he was getting nothing from attending school and was starting to look at the process as nothing more than an unnecessary obligation if not a burden.

His listless attitude was not reflected in his grades. He continued to get perfect scores on every quiz and test he took. His report card was a line of 100% test results. He had earned an 'A' in every subject.

At the bottom of the card was a hand written note from Miss Benning. 'Robert's grades are the best of any student I have ever had but he needs to work on his social skills. He is very withdrawn and seems uninterested in making friends.'

Her year end parent-teacher conference was rather unsettling. Miss Benning spent the first twenty minutes raving about his academic achievements and emphasizing his perfect test scores.

She recalled an incident where she had given the students a mathematical word problem to solve on the board. It had involved a child with so many apples and a child with so many oranges. She asked the students a question and Robert volunteered to put the answer on the board. He proceeded to write an algebraic formula which answered the question perfectly. What concerned her was the students wouldn't be exposed to algebra for another seven years!

She stressed this was not an isolated incident but that Robert would frequently answer questions with knowledge and insight the typical first grader would have no way of acquiring.

She again brought up the subject of having his IQ tested and the possibility of enrolling him in a program geared at students with exceptionally high IQs. She proclaimed she felt that her class might actually be inhibiting his education and that he would excel in that program.

Julie listened with trepidation. She was getting nervous. Miss Benning's comments were beginning to wreak an aura of what could only be construed as suspicion. She couldn't be too careful about this and wanted to nip these conjectures in the bud before they became a problem. She couldn't have Miss Benning take this any further.

While she couldn't deny that she herself would be very interested in those results she couldn't encourage it any further, not at the possible costs that might be involved.

If word got out just how intelligent he really was she was sure there would be follow up questions and tests and they had been through enough of those already. She paid Miss Benning lip service and promised her it would be something she would consider.

Miss Benning then dwelled on his inability to make friends and lack of effort to even try. She said Robert didn't give any attempts at making friends and seemed uninterested in his classmates.

This news came as no surprise to Julie for she got that information straight from Robert. She promised she would talk to him about it and try and get to the root of the problem.

The remainder of the meeting was cordial and consisted mostly of small talk. Miss Benning again quizzed her on Robert's behavior at home and Julie skirted the questions as best she could. The teacher concluded the meeting with her praise of Robert and her best wishes for him in the second grade.

Summer arrived and Julie was looking forward to spending more time with her son. They would spend the days together while Karen worked and when his sister got home she would then go to work at the bar. Larry had once again been kind enough to put her back on nights once she explained Karen would be working days and was able to sit with Robert at night.

She still enjoyed working for Larry and the social value of mixing with all the customers. She needed that break.

On Karen's days off the three of them would always find family activates to enjoy. They would go out to eat, or see a movie. Robert was fascinated with movies because they gave him a glimpse of ways of live he would otherwise never be exposed to. He would always question her about certain things in the movie afterwards. Some questions were easier to answer than others but Julie enjoyed his inquisitiveness.

There was just so much he didn't understand about the world. She had to remind herself that was natural because after all he was only six years old but that didn't totally answer the curiosity her son showed. He had such a thirst for knowledge.

If they had happened to see a war movie his questions were broad, 'why are there wars?' If they had just seen a romantic scene he would ponder why love was so important.

Just how does a mother answer these questions? Karen, on the other hand, as a child, was the direct opposite. She just pretty much took everything in stride and never seemed overly concerned with anything. Julie then had to remind herself that her daughter was dealing with an emotional disorder during that time that Robert couldn't begin to comprehend.

One afternoon Karen suggested they teach Robert how to fish. She thought that was a wonderful idea and bought them all fishing equipment. Robert picked up on the sport immediately and really enjoyed it.

Julie thought it was strange how her son would always insist on returning any fish he caught back to the water. She once tried to explain to him that they all enjoy eating fish and it would make a good dinner. He simply replied that they already had plenty of food at home and he saw no reason to kill an innocent animal for such a ridiculous reason.

Julie couldn't help but look at that as a young child imprisoned by a highly analytical mind. He was looking at the situation from a purely logical point of view. He was looking at it from the point of view that they already had food and there was simply no reason to kill the animal.

Many times she would silently pity him for this cerebral incarceration. His mind simply wouldn't allow him to let go, to be a child.

Every thought had to be painfully deduced, thought out and be filtered down to the logic contained within it. To him, releasing the fish was simply the most logical thing to do. If nothing else, it did ease her mind that her son was indeed inheriting his father's compassion.

Karen continued to be wonderful with her brother. They would spend time together while Julie was at work in the evenings. She would watch television with him and even taught him a little about cooking since she was responsible for their dinner.

They would read together and play games. He sincerely enjoyed his time with his sister. They developed an incredible bond. Karen would always listen to him and help him with his problems. He would confide in her and relished the closeness they had nurtured.

Julie continued to enjoy her job at the bar. She so enjoyed the social interaction with the guests, many of whom had been coming in for years and she considered them more than customers but good friends.

While she had no interest in getting back into any type of romantic relationship, she did miss companionship. These frequent and casual conversations provided her with all she required.

Larry had been so kind to her. He always allowed her input on her schedule and even gave her a substantial raise, knowing she could use it. He would occasionally bring them up pizzas or cheeseburgers or a case of soda.

He was having some health problems and Julie returned his kindness by working extra shifts when she could to give him more time off. She was worried about him. He insisted it was nothing serious but his behavior hinted otherwise.

He had lost that bounce in his step and just seemed to be generally slowing down. She knew he was getting up in the years but he had always appeared so healthy for his age.

She just had a sense that something wasn't right and there may be more to it than what he cared to share. She didn't want to press him further on the issue but took a mental note to ask Claudia about exactly what was going on next time she saw her.

Robert had discovered a new game which he took to immediately, chess. He said he first became aware of it in a movie they watched. Julie had never played chess in her life but bought him a chess board.

Knowing he would have no one to play with she volunteered and he indulged her by explaining how the game is played. She never fully knew how he learned himself but she had a feeling Google might have played a role in it.

He was obviously the chess master of the house finding little challenge in beating his mother or his sister, never having lost a game to either of them.

He was fascinating to watch during a game. He studied each move with meticulous precision, often taking five minutes to decide on the best maneuver. Julie could tell he had finally found something to stimulate that incredible mind of his, she only wished she were able to provide him with more competition.

After a month the game became too simple and unchallenging for him and that, combined with the lack of available competition, forced him to lose all interest in it completely. He resumed to his passion of reading.

Julie would make weekly trips to the library fulfilling his requirements for new reading material. While he would occasionally use the internet for research on a particular subject, for some unknown reason, he always preferred reading an actual book. He once told his mother the physical presence of a book in his hand made him feel more connected with the knowledge contained within its pages.

He was fascinated with all kinds of books, preferring nonfiction or textbooks over novels. This allure came to an alarming crescendo one afternoon while Julie was cleaning out her bedroom closet.

Robert was sitting on his mother's bedroom floor playing a game on his laptop while she cleaned out her closet. He would occasionally glance at her as she pulled things out of the closet with little interest.

She came across Robert senior's suitcase and placed it innocently outside the closet. This of course immediately caught her son's attention. Being totally absorbed in her project she gave no thought to the significance of the valise and had practically forgotten her son was sitting just a few feet behind her.

Robert stood up and walked over to the suitcase. He studied it for a moment then turned to his mother who had her back turned buried in the walk in closet unawares.

"Mom, what is this?"

Julie turned around and panicked. Her heart skipped a beat. 'Oh Hell!' she thought silently to herself. She had instantly realized she had opened a can of worms the size of Mt. Rushmore.

She racked her brains trying to quickly recall just what exactly was in the suitcase. She had to prepare herself for what she knew would be inevitable. Robert, once he found out what the object was, would demand to see its contents.

The first thing that came to her mind was the medical bag. This of course included the miraculous instrument his father had used to cure his sister. She then remembered how she had intentionally avoided evening mentioning that event to Robert during their conversation.

How was she going to explain that and how would she explain not evening bringing it up to him before? She closed her eyes for a second trying to remember what else was in there.

She knew there were his clothes which would be of little interest to him. There was the manila folder containing his father's legal documents. She couldn't even read those so she hoped she could just bypass them for at least the moment.

She remembered a number of personal items were also in the suitcase. She reflected seeing his deodorant, cologne, the bottle she had gotten him for Christmas, his after shave, an electric razor, which she had to explain to him how to work, and a couple bars of soap. Julie felt none of these items would be of the least of interest to her son.

No, the big issue would be the medical bag. If she could just keep his interest away from that bag she thought she could deal with anything else. She was wrong. There was one item that had escaped her.

# 43

"That was your father's suitcase, Bobby. He had to leave it here."

Robert gaped at the object and went over to it and laid it on its side.

"Oh wow, this thing is really cool! Check it out! So this actually came from another planet? Mom, you have to open it I want to see what's inside!"

Julie sighed. She knew with his interest in space, let alone the fact that it was his father's, there would be no way of talking him out of it but she wanted to at least try.

"Bobby, I'm trying to get this closet organized can we do this another time?"

Robert gave her a look of disappointment.

"He was my father, I really think I have the right to see it, mom, please?"

Julie knew she had lost the battle. She looked into her son's eyes and could tell it was important to him. She reluctantly conceded he was correct, it was his father's and he did have a right to see it. She knew if the tables were reversed she would feel the same way. Sometimes it was so hard being a fair parent.

She turned around and pulled the suitcase over to her. She then decided to try an experiment. Pushing the suitcase directly in front of her son smiled.

"Okay Bobby, why don't you open it?"

Julie remembered being perplexed as to how it opened and had to have Karen eventually figure it out. She was just curious as to whether he would struggle with it as well. She fully expected him to simply hand it back to her.

Robert studied the case for a moment. The wheels in

his mind were spinning a hundred miles an hour. Julie could tell he was enjoying the challenge.

A moment later, he lifted up the handle and ran his thumb across the red square without any assistance as if he knew instinctively how it opened. Smiling he pushed the case back over to his mother.

"That was easy."

She just shook her head. She should have known. She closed her eyes and held her breath and slowly lifted the top up.

Robert sat silently beside her in anticipation, his eyes glued to the inside of the case. Julie first took out all the clothes which were on top and gently placed them in a pile beside her. She saw the black medical bag nestled in the corner. She had to find a way of taking it out before her son questioned her on it.

Robert was curiously going through the pile of clothes and Julie heeded the moment to nonchalantly pick out the bag and stealthily placed it behind her. She was thankful her son was too preoccupied with the clothes to even notice the action.

Her son picked out a black button down-shirt with a number stitched in white above the left breast pocket. He studied the shirt with great interest.

"Mom, why is there a number on his shirt?"

This was a conversation Julie was hoping to avoid but at this point. she was thankful for anything that would keep her son's mind off the medical bag. She remembered she had already explained about his father being a prisoner so this shouldn't be too difficult.

"That was your father's prison uniform sweetheart."

Seemingly satisfied with his mother's answer, Robert placed the shirt back in the pile without questioning her further on it.

Julie then grabbed the bag of personal items and

placed it aside. She explained its contents to her son. Robert was still going through the stack of clothes and expressed no interest in the contents of the bag. Julie then continued searching through the suitcase.

Robert pulled out the Beatles tee-shirt she had bought him after learning he actually enjoyed their music.

"This was my father's?"

Julie shed a tear as the tee-shirt brought back some very painful memories. That was the shirt he was wearing the last time they made love.

"Yes sweetheart it was, I bought that for him. He actually liked their music."

Robert looked at the shirt then at his mother.

"Now that is really strange mom."

Julie's tears were now broken by the smile her son's comment had given her. She returned her concentration to the contents of the suitcase. She pulled out the manila envelope and placed it behind the case with the medical bag. She didn't need Robert questioning her on that.

Robert, now bored with the pile of clothes, looked into the case. Among the few items left inside was his book of poetry which Julie had forgotten all about. This, due to his fascination with books, immediately caught her son's attention.

"Mom, check this out, he had a book? Oh, this has got to be awesome! I wonder what kind of things he liked to read about!"

Julie wasn't sure how to react to the most recent discovery. She knew exactly what it was and wasn't really concerned because she knew there would be no way for Robert to actually read it.

Robert grabbed the book before his mother even had a chance to explain to him what it was. He looked at the cover and scrutinized the lettering. He then opened it and paged through it. Julie watched him with great interest. He came to a page and stopped; studying it keenly. After a moment he set the book down and turned to his mother.

"This was my father's?"

Julie smiled and nodded as Robert picked the book up again and reexamined the page.

"This is very nice, so dad enjoyed poetry?"

Julie's mouth dropped to the floor. She was stunned at what her son had just said. How could he have known? Could he actually read it? That would be impossible.

"You can read that sweetheart?"

Robert smiled.

"Of course I can mom; they are just a derivative of elementary hieroglyphics. The symbols used are really basic. The figures many times actually depict the word they are meant to covey. It's very easy. This is a nice poem; did dad ever read them to you?"

A tear once again appeared in Julie's eye. The shock of his ability to actually read it was put temporality on hold as the memory of how his father would read her poetry dominated her thoughts.

She was so touched by these moments, it showed her a more tender side of him, one that she so missed.

"Yes he did Bobby. He said the poems relaxed him and he would read them to me all the time. I can't believe you can actually read it!"

Robert just smiled.

"It was really pretty easy mom. Some of the words were a bit strange, I mean the phrasing was a little different but I figured it out. I assume this is the language they use?"

Julie didn't know how to respond. She found it amazing that he could decipher their writing. She wasn't sure how he could but just attributed it to his vastly advanced mind. Her son's intellect continued to amaze her and she could only wonder what the future would bring.

"Yes sweetheart, it was written in their language. I obviously couldn't read it."

Robert continued to read then smiled at his mother.

"I don't really understand it mom. I just look at the page and see words, just like a normal book. It really doesn't require any extra effort. I would really like to learn their language. I don't imagine there would be any books in our library about it would there be."

Julie just shook her head.

"No Bobby, I would think that would be highly unlikely."

He paused and reflected for a moment looking up towards the ceiling. There was obviously something on his mind.

"Reading it was so easy mom; do you think maybe dad is helping me with this one too?"

His words sent a chill down Julie's spine. She wondered if there might indeed be some kind of psychic connection between the two of them. She wasn't sure if he was soliciting a response or simply asking a rhetorical question. She felt an obligation to at least acknowledge the statement.

"I really can't say Bobby. I suppose there is that possibility. Your father could do some amazing things, this would hardly surprise me.

I know he remains in my heart and sometimes I can almost hear his voice. I try not to dwell on it because I know he's gone but he will always remain in my heart.

Maybe with you it might be even more. Maybe with both your advanced minds there could actually be a connection. I honestly don't know what you and your father are capable of.

I really don't know anything about all that paranormal

stuff. I've never had any reason to look into it but something tells me I might have one now."

Robert gave her a puzzling expression.

"Well, it's not like he is talking to me or anything, I mean, I cant hear his voice, but I get ideas that just come out of nowhere, ideas I don't remember coming up with myself. It's kind of spooky actually."

Julie gave her son an extended hug. She didn't want to let go. She couldn't help but hope that by hugging her son, if there were a connection with his father, perhaps he might feel it too.

They had emptied the suitcase and while Robert was in the bathroom Julie took the opportunity to return everything, including the medical bag and folder with the legal papers, back in before he had a chance to question her on them.

As enlightening as their recent time together had been, she wasn't ready for his query on these items just yet. She closed it up and returned it to the closet.

The three of them had a wonderful evening together. Karen had brought sub sandwiches home for everyone from work and they all played a game of scrabble, which of course, Robert won.

He was so cute, always trying to suggest better moves for both his mother and sister and Karen kept trying to get him to stop, saying the object was to win the game not help your opponents.

It was moments like this that made Julie look at her son in a different light. She had been so preoccupied with seeing him as a young genius she inadvertently overlooked the other elements of his personality.

He was kind, polite and respectful to anyone he met. He was obedient and never gave her or Karen any problems. He always volunteered to help around the house in any way he could.

Julie would smile at the thought that he did inherit more from his father than just intelligence; he had indeed inherited his father's compassion.

Julie just silently enjoyed the friendship her two children had developed between them. They truly adored each other. She was so blessed to have such wonderful children.

Karen so relished her role as big sister. She spoiled her bother every chance she got. She brought home a brownie from work every night just for him because he really liked them.

They so enjoyed just spending time together. They would work together to fix dinner on nights Julie worked and he always helped her clean up afterwards. They would watch movies together and Karen was always so patient answering all his questions afterwards.

When she found herself getting stressed over Robert's questionable future she would draw from these thoughts to regain her sanity, they were so comforting to her.

Robert's next five years of grade school went pretty much as expected. He continued to attend every day without making much of a fuss over it. He continued to be bored to tears. He would confront his mother almost daily reiterating how he wasn't learning anything and how pointless this whole thing was. He also continued his streak of perfect test scores.

If Julie could have a dollar for every time either his teacher or the principle called her suggesting an IQ test and a more appropriate school she could retire. They hounded her almost weekly for the next five years and she continued to promise them she would consider it. Many times she actually did.

She considered the pros and cons of having him tested and put into a special school where his advanced intelligence might turn from a curse to a blessing. Was she responsible for actually holding him back? Would a special school benefit him? She knew how ever special the school would be he would still stand out.

She was stuck between a rock and a hard place. She knew he wasn't getting anything educational out of his current situation and the reasoning to keep him there to make friends was no longer a factor; that simply wasn't going to happen. Robert continued to show no interest in socializing with his classmates and she totally understood the reasons behind it.

Perhaps if he were in an environment where the children were at least closer to his intellect might change that. At some point in his life he would have to make friends. She knew it would be a big enough burden going through life as super intelligent without the added anxiety of dealing with it as a recluse.

But then she was hit with the thought of what the results of any IQ test would be. She knew they would surely be off the charts, that was a given. She also knew that would raise eyebrows and she feared what the repercussions could be.

Would they enroll him at Princeton? Would they fly him out to Stanford to be put under a microscope? She didn't want to take any chances. She didn't need an IQ test to tell her how intellectually advanced her son was, she already knew that. She therefore saw nothing to gain from them and there for no motivation to get him one, nothing good could happen as a result of it.

At age twelve, while in sixth grade, Robert took an interest in music for the first time. It was an affection initiated more by curiosity than any intrinsic enthusiasm for music.

The school had a piano in the gymnasium and one day after gym class he took notice of it. He had seen the piano countless times before, never paying it any mind, but that day, for some reason, something made him sit on the stool and see exactly what it could do.

He gently pressed down on a key then slowly went up the scale. He found it most interesting, and surprisingly pleasing. He thought about the change in tones as he progressed up the scale.

He noted how the increment of pitch raised as he went from one key to the next. He then flattened a note and was intrigued at the alluring result.

He played the scale again but this time adding a couple flats and sharps. He was tickled at the quaint results. He immediately found it fascinating how he could change the complete sound of the scale simply by exerting these simple alterations.

He realized this was nothing more than mathematics. In math, if you took one, and added one, it became two; the same principle applied to the piano. If you took one note then went to the next one the tone went up one pitch. He marveled at the simplicity of the concept wondering why everyone can't play beautiful piano.

He then experimented with creating basic chords and attempted a simple melody. He quickly discovered which notes sounded good together and which didn't, again using simple mathematics.

It all came so surprisingly easy to him. He fell in love with the piano instantly. It enabled him to make use of his love of math, while at the same time, creating music. He had to have one of these! He would have to talk mom into getting them a piano!

After about a month of constant badgering Robert finally got his piano. Julie had bought him a nice electronic keyboard as an early Christmas gift and the boy and his instrument became inseparable.

One afternoon after work Karen stopped at a music store and bought him a book of music. She briefly explained the concept of how it was intended to enable him to play music he otherwise wouldn't know.

He was delighted at the gift and, never having seen sheet music before, took right too the challenge of deciphering the mysterious symbols on the pages.

Without any further help or instruction, he figured it on his own in a matter of hours and was playing incredible classical pieces shortly afterwards, simply by following along with the music his sister had bought him.

Julie and Karen were mutually in awe of his musical prowess and would enjoy listing to him play for hours. They also enjoy the smile on his face as he was playing relishing in the fact that Robert was truly enjoying the time he spent at the keyboard.

They would frequently ask him how he learned to be so good so quickly and he just brushed it off repeating his insistence that it was just using basic math. Julie remembered her days in high school band struggling trying to master the clarinet. No amount of math could have helped that hopeless cause.

She wasn't sure if Robert senior had any musical talent. He had never mentioned any musical ability and hardly mentioned music at all other than the times they would listen to the radio and he would offer comments on the various artists. She could be certain of one thing; Robert's musical gift surely didn't come from her because she quit the clarinet in frustration after one disastrous year.

Robert's passion for the piano continued into middle school. His music books were getting more complicated and he continued to swim right through them without the slightest difficulty.

He showed an especial admiration for Bach, many times commending his complex counterpoint melodies and arrangements. Julie would snicker when he would say Johann must have been good at math as well.

The principle heard him play one afternoon and invited him to join the band but he respectfully declined. That would require him to socialize with his peers who have already proven their inferiority intellectually and, having heard the band before; they had also proven their inferiority musically. Attempting to play with them would be as frustrating to him as it had been simply trying to carry on an intelligent conversation with them.

He continued to play at home giving occasional recitals for his mother and sister. He was accumulating quite a repertoire having amassed a collection of music books ranging from Classic rock to Beethoven sonatas.

Music, while providing a source of enjoyment for him, by no means replaced his quest for general knowledge. He continued to read every text book he could get his hands on and furthered his research on the computer. His thirst for knowledge continued to expand experientially; the more he learned; the more doors it opened to inquire about even a broader range of topics.

His grades continued to be perfect. He was soon to complete his seventh consecutive academic year and had yet to miss a single question on any test, quiz or exam. His teacher continued to suggest alternate educational opportunities for him and Julie continued to promise to consider them. His principle was adamant about having his IQ tested. Julie paid him lip service and maintained her determination to avoid that at any cost.

Robert's days in middle school had ended. The three of them proudly attended a very nice graduation ceremony and were thrilled when the principle presented Robert with an academic achievement award. Julie was sure there would be more of those in his future.

Her son was so adorable standing up on stage

shaking the principle's hand, smiling from ear to ear, actually appearing to enjoy the adulation. He lifted the small plaque over his head with pride to the captivated audience.

Julie was beyond proud she was, to a degree, relieved at Robert's enthusiastic response to the citation. She saw that as very encouraging. Perhaps this will give him the motivation to continue with his education with a positive attitude in spite of the difficulties he has relating to his peers. She was sure finally being recognized for his achievements would fuel his desire to move forward with high school.

Julie and Karen had prepared a surprise party back at the house to celebrate Robert's graduation. She had given Edi complete authority over the organization of it and made a point of telling her not to bring any punch this time.

Edi had been conspiring with Leonard, Claudia and Larry to have everything set up while the family was at the ceremony. Larry had again catered the event with a mountain of his famous cheeseburgers, fries and a couple of pizzas as well as a case of pop.

Edi and Leonard decorated the living room with Crepe paper and bunting and she had made a very nice and decorative cake.

The party was a huge success. Robert was thrilled and even entertained the guests with some piano playing. Karen and Julie each gave a little speech proclaiming how proud they were of Robert and Edi gave him a Star Wars tee-shirt which he put on immediately.

The guests all left and the three of them teamed up to clean the place up. Robert took down all the decorations and put everything back in its place while she and Karen took care of the dishes and put away the leftover food. Everyone slept very soundly and peacefully.

For the moment, life was good. Julie could honestly attest to feeling no stress or worry for the first time in ages. Robert was very happy, Karen was doing well at her job and everyone was getting along wonderfully.

Julie was looking forward to a nice summer spending as much time with her children as possible and getting Robert ready for high school. She didn't anticipate any problems in that area for from what she could see Robert was ready for college.

She reflected on her life over the past twenty years. She thought of the turmoil and trials and tribulations over Robert and his future, the drama she had endured with Karen during her early years, and the devastation she felt over losing Robert senior. Now she felt like everything was falling into place. The dream she once thought was unachievable was coming true, they were finally a happy family.

# 44

Chancellor Elihu sat at his desk and glanced at the mountain of folders and paperwork that cluttered the desktop. The man pondered all the events of the past year. He put his hand on his forehead, massaging it gently, as he took a deep breath.

Exhaling, he closed his eyes for a brief moment. The Chancellor was enjoying the peace and quiet of his office, a quiet he had longed for and waited for over a year to enjoy. There were no sounds of small arms fire, no explosions in the distance, all that was mercifully over, it was finally quiet. The madness had ended and with it can come the hope of a new dawn.

His one-hundred-five year old body was aching. His mind was weary. It had been an exhausting campaign. He shed one tear of remorse for all the lives that were lost, it was the least he could do. He felt he owed them that much. He denied himself too much penance because he knew causalities in war were inevitable and he had the solace of knowing their deaths would not be in vain.

Now the people can sleep in peace without fear. They would no longer have the dread of heinous invasions of their privacy and obstruction and total denial of their rights. The tyranny was over. The madmen responsible for it had been removed from office and his evil accomplices taken care of.

It would take a lot of work to totally restructure the government but he knew he and his staff would be up to the challenge

The past year had been a torturous ordeal for everyone. So many casualties, so many innocent lives lost; there had been such unparalleled destruction. It would take years to recover and rebuild. But, alas, it was finally over.

He consoled himself with the knowledge that had that administration not been overrun, the loss of life would have, in the long run, been much greater than the results of the revolution.

Revolutions are never a pleasant way to settle a dispute but in this case there was no other way. The current administration was pompous, arrogant and not about to change on its own so change would have to be forced on it. The coercion and torture of the people had to be put to a stop.

. After a year of failed negotiations an alternative plan had to be initiated. A full military overthrow was implemented. Victory had been achieved; the regime had fallen to defeat. The tyrant had been executed and all his corrupt legislators imprisoned. He didn't have the luxury to lament the casualties; there was much work to be done.

He already had the infrastructure in place. He had been working on the details long before the actual coup had even begun. He had organized and recruited committees to deal with every issue. These were all in place before the first shot was even fired.

Today would mark a new beginning, a new government, a fair government. Gone are the days of tyranny, the days of ruthless bloodthirsty oppression. He had promised his followers a fair, just government and he would deliver just that. The question on his mind was now where to begin.

His primary role would be the legislative end of things. A new constitution would have to be written with the best interests of the people, not the administration, as had been the case, in mind.

His first priority was to totally revamp and update the penal system. This had been a pet peeve of his since he was a senator many years ago. He had heard too many horror stories of abuse and corruption in the prison system to allow that to continue.

Prisoners were being desecrated and mistreated and the prisons were antiquated and in total shambles. They were over crowded to the point of having to exile prisoners to another planet until their sentences could be carried out due to lack of cell space.

He had a task force already in motion to review policies and offer suggestions for improvements. This was the origin of the mass of paperwork he currently found in front of him.

Ambassador Kreia had been placed in charge of this. He was a progressive thinker and had a reputation for creative solutions. The Ambassador was also a compassionate man who always had the best intentions of his constituents in mind. He got action and was the perfect man to head up the reform of the penal system. He had already submitted a number of suggestions and means of implementing them.

The Chancellor's thoughts were interrupted by a beep from the intercom. He woke from his daze and answered the call.

"Yes?"

His secretary spoke.

"Sir, Ambassador Kreia has arrived."

He managed a weak smile.

"Very good, send him in please."

Chancellor Elihu walked over to the door to greet his visitor. Upon entering the room the Ambassador and Chancellor heartily shook hands.

"Do sit down Ayohod it's good to see you my friend. You are looking good."

The Ambassador smiled.

"Thank you sir, you are as well. I am sure these are trying times for you."

The two sat down and the Ambassador opened a folder he had brought.

"I know you are a busy man and our time together is short so may I get straight to business?"

Chancellor Elihu nodded his approval.

"That is one of the many reasons you were selected for this job Ayohod, you are a no nonsense man, please proceed."

Ambassador Kreia handed the folder to his superior.

"I have started touring the facilities on your list sir. I have just spent three days at the detention center in Teludia. I must say the conditions were deplorable!

The plumbing was antiquated, the electrical system sorely outdated and there was hardly any heat. The entire building is in dire need of repair, or to simply be torn down completely. It is not a proper place to house anyone, even prisoners!"

The Chancellor sadly nodded his head.

"This is exactly what I had suspected.

The ambassador continued.

"The men that I spoke with who are incarcerated there are border lining on a complete revolt. I can foresee a problem there in the future."

Chancellor Elihu fingered his chin in thought.

"You have done well Ayohod. What facility are you planning of seeing next?"

Ambassador Kreia cleared his throat and hesitated before replying.

"Well sir, before we continue there is something I think I should bring to your attention, if I may."

Elihu gave his colleague a puzzled expression.

"Of course, just what might that be Ayohod?"

Ayohod shuffled through his papers until he found

the one he was looking for. He studied the page a moment before continuing.

"Well, before I started the tour I met with the warden. I asked for a list of the current inmates. I wanted to talk to a few of them at some point to get a feel for what life was like for them there.

After reading a few profiles, one stuck out for some reason. This man had been convicted of murder but there seemed to be some insinuating circumstances behind it.

What really struck me as odd was it appeared he was given a hurried trial. It seemed the judge wanted to get it out of court quickly. This of course was unusual and heightened my interest.

After what had to have been a mockery of a trial he was sentenced to death so I doubted he would actually be there to talk to but he was still on the list of current inmates. I wanted to ask the warden if he had remembered him.

I had to hear the warden's explanation for how a man who should have been executed many years ago still appears on the current inmate list.

I asked about him and the warden explained he was no longer in the general population."

Chancellor Elihu was very intrigued by this.

"You're telling me a man who was scheduled to be executed years ago, as you say, was still incarcerated? Was there any mention of a reprieve or a stay of execution in his file?"

Ayohod shook his head.

"None, that was my first thought. I read the entire file twice looking for that very thing but there was no mention of it."

The Chancellor was now beyond interested. He valued justice and couldn't help but wonder what exactly was going on.

"You say he is no longer in the general population but he is still on the current inmate list. Do you even know if he's still alive? I mean, if he is, where the hell is he?"

Ayohod grinned.

"Now this is where it gets really strange."

Elihu nodded, biting at the chomp to hear more.

"I'm listening. First of all, do you even know if he's still alive? I mean, if he is, where the hell is he?"

Ayohod took a deep breath knowing what he was about to tell the Chancellor would require explaining.

"Yes sir, he is still very much alive."

Ambassador Kreia was correct in his assessment.

"So you're telling me a man, sentenced to death many years ago, is still alive but not in the general population? So then where would he be?"

Ayohod nodded.

"According to the warden, he is currently in the Cryonics ward."

The Chancellor threw himself against the back of his chair.

"The Cryonics ward, are you sure? Now that is just ridiculous! We haven't used that procedure in I don't know how many years. It was only intended to be used in cases where there would be an extended delay in the legal proceedings because it was less expensive than keeping a prisoner in custody and due to lack of available cells.

Another thing, it had only been used in cases where the delay would be a year or at the longest, two. We weren't even sure we could keep a body alive for longer than that, it had never been tested for prolonged use beyond that.

I didn't think anyone was still in hibernation, I actually thought the program was discontinued"

The ambassador nodded.

"Apparently not, but he appears to be the only one who still is sir."

Perplexed, the Chancellor had one more question he had to ask.

"That's incredible! Just when was this man put into hibernation?"

The Ambassador shook his head in bewilderment.

"According to his file, he has been under for about fifteen years!"

The Chancellor was shocked.

"Fifteen years? That's simply unbelievable! You are sure he is still alive?"

Ayohod nodded.

"Yes sir, after questioning the warden he admitted there was a staff insuring that very thing. I know that's hard to believe, but they have been monitoring him daily, even after all these years. Yeah, they keep an eye on him, he's alive."

Elihu shook his head in disbelief. It just didn't make any sense to him. Why would they have sentenced a prisoner to death, then reverse the decision and put him in deep freeze for over fifteen years without an official reprieve. No one had ever been put in a cryonic state for anything close to that time before.

He scanned the man's file for any additional information that might explain this unusual situation. He was concerned over Ayohod mentioning the trial seemed rushed.

The file stated the man was arrested for murder and the defendant had pleaded self defense.

He then took notice that the date of execution was only a month after the date of the arrest. Now that was indeed strange. A murder trial can linger on for months if not a year. Why was the administration so concerned to get this over with in a hurry?

Then, after the sentence was issued, it was, for what ever reason, revoked and the decision was made to simply take this man out of circulation without killing him. Things were just not adding up. Could the courts be trying to hide something?

Elihu thought for a moment. He knew he was dealing with a corrupt system, one that had no tolerance for anything deviant or possibly harmful to the administration. Just why is this man still alive? At this point he trusted no one. The only way he could get to the truth would be to talk to the man himself.

He returned his attention to the Ambassador.

"Alright, the first thing we need to do is to thaw this guy out. I want to talk to him. I want you to go back to Teludia and get this man released into my custody. If they give you any problems have them call me, I do run the show now!

I want you to hold off on inspecting any other facilities for now and get right on that; I want him here as soon as possible! I have to talk to him; this just doesn't make any sense."

Ayohod stood up and they shook hands again.

"I'll go back this afternoon sir. I'll get him for you, after all, I'm an Ambassador, and I think that outranks a warden."

Elihu smiled.

"You've done a great job and have uncovered yet another of the travesties committed by those hoodlums, hopefully one we can get to the bottom of and correct. There can be no rational explanation for something like this to happen.

I can't imagine the adversity this man must have experienced and the shock and hardship he will have to endure when he awakens. I can only pray he is still in good health.

I thank you and the people thank you. There will be a commendation in this for you after this is straightened out my friend. Now let's get moving on it. I want this man out of deep freeze immediately; he has been subjected to that long enough! Something about this whole thing just doesn't smell right."

Ayohod left and the Chancellor returned to his seat, again deep in thought. This case was bugging him. The legalities for a murder case are simple...if found guilty the perpetrator is executed, if found innocent he is simply released. There is no middle ground.

If you see the case will be delayed for an extended period it would have been the normal thing back then to freeze him until the proceedings can continue. This would be for a year, maybe two but under no circumstances for fifteen!

Even under a corrupt system like the one that had been in place, would there be any reason for this course of action. It wouldn't make any sense or be of any benefit to the administration...unless they were trying to cover it up and just get him out of the way.

Knowing the previous regime as well as he did, he knew they would have a lot they would want covered up. Perhaps they felt removing him from society would be a form of saving face, where as if they had executed him, and the truth ever come out, it might give them a black eye.

He rubbed his eyes. He reread the man's dossier; he wanted to know as much as he could before he actually met with him. The file stated that the man had been a repeated offender.

He had been arrested a number of times on issues ranging from disturbing the peace to assault and battery. There were a couple robberies and even a drug charge mixed in but he was basically slapped on the wrist and released after short prison stays.

This time it was for murder in the first degree and the punishment couldn't be quite so lenient. He stabbed a man to death in a bar room scuffle in front of a number of witness's. There was of course the additional resisting arrest and even coercive behavior.

Then something startling caught his eye. The victim was the director of finance for the state! Now this was a horse of a different color. This was no random killing or arbitrary drunken bar fight. He had no doubt the man knew who the victim was! You don't just haphazardly get into a bar fight with the director of finance, no, he was targeted!

Now the question remains, why would an ordinary criminal decide to murder a public official, in full view of witness's, knowing he would be caught and undoubtedly executed? He would have to have had a pretty good reason.

What bothered the Chancellor most was that he knew there were probably many good reasons a number of people would want to kill him. He then connected this with the speedy trial. He was now sure of two things, first he did have a good reason and secondly that the administration was indeed trying to slip this one under the rug quickly before any details could seep out.

He closed the folder and sighed. He was beginning to look at this from a different perspective. He was really looking forward to meeting this man. He wanted the man's side of the story, his explanation.

He was certain of one more thing. He knew of the corruption contained within the previous administration. He pretty much conceded that would be what the man would be telling him. Somehow this guy knew too much and reached the point where he deemed it necessary to play vigilante, even at the cost of his own life.

He was beginning to actually pity the man and almost admire him. One thing was for certain, the man had paid for his crime with fifteen years of his life and, if the crime was as justified as he thought it might be; that would be enough punishment.

Something was telling him he had a pretty good reason for the act, one that he would totally sympathize with. He was well aware of the atrocities being committed and wouldn't need convinced of them. Obviously the perpetrator knew of them as well. The speedy trial was now making perfect sense to him.

He would listen to the man's story with a totally open mind and, if satisfied with what he heard, he would revise the charge to justifiable homicide, clear his name, and give him a complete pardon. Hell, by the time he was through with him he might have a statue erected for him in the park.

Elihu was actually thinking this might be beneficial to both of them. On the one hand it would be giving a man deserving of his freedom just that, and, on the other hand, what better way of showing the public the fairness, the just intentions of the new administration than by freeing an oppressed hostage of the previous corrupt one?

The hours passed and the Chancellor was finally making some headway on that mountain of paperwork. His endeavor was interrupted by a beeping from the intercom.

He pressed the button.

"Yes?"

His secretary responded.

"Ambassador Kreia is here, he has the prisoner with him sir."

# 45

The chancellor thought for a moment before replying over the intercom.

"Would you please send in Ambassador Kreia alone please? Ask the prisoner to have a seat and tell him we will be with him shortly, thank you."

Within seconds the Ambassador walked through the door and smiled.

"Everything went well sir."

Chancellor Elihu returned the smile and motioned for the Ambassador to have a seat. He opened the top folder in front of him and studied it, occasionally glancing up at his guest.

"They didn't give you any problems with releasing him?"

The Ambassador shook his head.

"Quite the contrary sir, they were happy to get rid of him. The warden said with him being the only inmate in that department they were now free to close it down completely and he could assign his staff to what he referred to as more important matters.

It was just a matter of filling out the proper paperwork and having him go through the exit procedures. None the less he is with me."

Elihu was pleased. He continued to read the file, scrutinizing each detail.

"You did a great job; I knew I could count on you.

So Ayohod, tell me a little about this man, I mean from what you have observed in the short time you have been together."

Ayohod rubbed his chin in thought and grinned.

"Well, of course he is still very groggy and somewhat sedated. They allowed him time to clean up, you know, he had a shower and shaved and they gave him a clean uniform. They gave him a couple prescriptions but he's still really out of it.

He was very corporative. I would go as far as saying he was quite polite and respectful. He must have thanked me a dozen times for what I was doing.

I wasn't sure what you wanted me to tell him about his, well, his hiatus, so I didn't mention anything at all."

Chancellor Elihu nodded.

"He didn't ask you anything about it?"

Ayohod shook his head.

"No sir, like I said, he is very woozy and I'm sure confused. The ride over here was pretty much silent. He spent the majority of the trip with his eyes closed more or less meditating. He didn't press me for any information.

I wasn't surprised at all, after all the man has been through quite an ordeal, I'm sure its going to take a while to get reoriented. He's been on one hell of a long trip."

The Chancellor agreed.

"Yes, no one can imagine what that would have been like. I've heard you have no concept of time, it's just like a long night's sleep but fifteen years, that's unimaginable! The body was never meant to be dormant for that period of time. It's inhumane if you think about it. I can't fathom what physical consequences he might be suffering from."

Ambassador Kreia politely interrupted.

"Sir, I don't think it's the physical ramifications we need to be concerned with. He appears to be a strong, healthy individual. I am sure, with time; he will fully recover from whatever physical hardships he is currently experiencing; but what about the emotional trauma he will experience when you tell him how long he was under?"

The Chancellor sighed.

"So you didn't even mention that?"

Ayohod shook his head.

"No sir, nothing about anything related to his chasm was mentioned at all. No one at the center mentioned it to him either; I was with him the entire time. Sir, he has no idea how long he has been out."

The Chancellor ran his fingers through his balding scalp trying to grasp the gravity of what he was about to have to tell the prisoner. How do you tell someone they have been asleep for fifteen years?

At the moment he was dealing with a diverse collection of thoughts. He had to straighten them out before meeting with the prisoner. He wanted to approach the meeting with a clear, logical and fair mind.

He couldn't deny that the man in question was a repeat offender, a habitual criminal with a number of charges in his past, not the least of which was the murder of a prominent elected government official.

This, of course led him to the knowledge that said official was a member of a corrupt administration and was probably deserving of the fate. He had not had the opportunity, as of yet, to review the individual members of the previous administration to determine their personal involvements with the atrocities being committed.

Also to be taken into consideration was the fact that the man had served a fifteen year sentence already. He had already paid a harsh debt to society, if indeed he owed one at all.

Something continued to tell him that the assassination, if that was actually what it was, might have literally been a benefit to the people.

He also factored in the report from Ambassador Kreia. Ayohod had told him the prisoner was cordial, polite and respectful.

Elihu stood up and walked over to the Ambassador. He put his hand on Ayohod's shoulder.

"I need your input on this one Ayohod. You're a good judge of character, that's why you make such a great Ambassador; what are your gut feelings on this one? You think we should give this guy a chance?"

Ayohod turned and faced the Chancellor.

"Well, in all honesty it's a tough call sir. I've only known him for a couple hours and during that time he was pretty doped up. You want my gut feeling; I say he seems like a decent person. I know it might just be an act but for some reason I don't think so. He seems sincere.

I realize he has a long track record of offenses but that being said, he's done fifteen years and from the sounds of it never got a fair trial. Maybe it's time he caught a break.

Based on our brief time together I say talk to him, you get a drift on the kind of person he is and go with your gut feeling sir. He seems okay to me, if it were my call I would go with the pardon, he's been through enough already."

Elihu patted him on the shoulder and thanked him. He returned to his desk and spoke into the intercom.

"You can have the prisoner come in now thank you."

The two men shared a hesitant glance and then turned their attention to the door as the prisoner walked in.

Elihu stood up and walked over to the prisoner. He placed one hand on his shoulder for support, as the man was swaying, and shook his hand with the other.

"Hello Kmyviks, it's a pleasure to meet you. Would you please have a seat?"

Kmyviks took the seat next to the Ambassador across from Elihu's desk. The Chancellor studied the man with great interest. He wanted to determine as much as he could about his current state before he started the interview.

The prisoner's discomfort was obvious. It was plain to see he had been through quite an ordeal. He was pale and his face was sunken. He appeared weak and frail. His eyes were cloudy and disoriented. He slouched in his chair. He struggled to keep his head up.

The Chancellor empathized with the prisoner. He almost pitied him.

"Is there anything I can get for you?"

Kmyviks shook his head and spoke for the first time.

"No sir, but thank you, I'm fine. Forgive my appearance..."

Elihu stopped him.

"Son, you have nothing to apologize for. Now try and relax. I am Chancellor Elihu. I am in charge now. We have a lot to go over and I'm sure you will have a lot of questions which we will address shortly."

Kmyviks nodded slowly. He was trying to focus, his eyes weren't cooperating. Everything was blurry and he did his best to try and disguise his condition. He was having trouble even understanding the Chancellor's words.

The room was spinning and it reminded him of his drug days when this would be a daily occurrence. His mind was a blank; he knew he hadn't done any drugs in years and couldn't, at the moment, comprehend the reason for him feeling as he did. He struggled to speak but felt he owed the Chancellor some explanation for what must seem like very odd behavior.

"Sir, I must apologize and ask for your understanding. I am feeling really out of it and I know you must think I am high but I assure you I am not. I can't explain this."

The Chancellor and Ambassador shared a look of alarm. They were both thinking the same thing. It wasn't Kmyviks behavior that was disturbing them; it was they both mutually realized he had absolutely no recollection of the entire ordeal.

Elihu took a deep breath now realizing the task in front

of him would be even daunting than he had anticipated. He wanted to first assert the last memory Kmyviks had. He asked a question and dreaded the answer.

"Kmyviks, just what is the last thing you remember?"

The prisoner rubbed his eyebrows and closed his eyes. He racked his brain for any memories.

"Sir, I'm sorry but I really can't remember much of anything right now. I'm not even sure of my own name."

Elihu shook his head.

"Try son, try real hard; now think; it's important. What is the last thing you remember? What is the last thing you are sure of?"

Kmyviks lowered his head and again closed his eyes. His breathing was labored. It was obvious he was deep in thought. After a few minutes he finally managed a reply.

"I was...I was in a cell...yeah in a cell. I was being held there and I seem to remember they were...I think they were going to... take me somewhere. That's honestly all I remember."

The Chancellor shook his head in total disbelief.

"You are sure you can't remember anything after that?"

Kmyviks simply shook his head in defeat.

"No sir, it's all black after that. Can you help me with this?"

The Chancellor and Ambassador shared a brief look of anguish.

"Yes, Kmyviks I will help you with it but it's not going to be an easy road to travel."

Elihu didn't know where to start. He knew he would have to explain about the revolution and the new administration. He also knew he would have to explain about how he was in hibernation for fifteen years. This would be especially difficult considering he didn't even remember being put into hibernation at all!

He started off with the easy part. For the next hour he detailed how the government was overthrown and a new administration was now in place. He explained how he was now in charge and his plans for the new dawn. He promised Kmyviks he intended to right all the wrongs of the previous government and he was starting with the penal system.

He told him he intended on reviewing all the correctional facilities and bringing them up to date. He then explained how he planned on reassessing each inmate and whether or not they should remain in custody. He told him this was the reason he brought him here.

Kmyviks welcomed this news with open arms. He was very receptive to everything the Chancellor was spelling out to him. He asked many questions, all of which were answered honestly.

The prisoner would frequently comment on the old regime and his personal repulsion over it. He would offer snide remarks on the former president and his officials. The Chancellor absorbed every detail with keen interest and took every opportunity he could find to agree with him. It became apparent that, at least in this respect, the two men were on the same side.

The more he heard the prisoner talk about the insides of the corruption in the old government the more he was led to believe that Kmyviks did know more than the average citizen.

This confirmed two things. The first was the probable justification in his killing the man he did. He must have known what the victim was involved with and acted accordingly.

The second was he would obviously have been dangerous to the regime. He knew too much and there for had to be dealt with in a quick and stealthy manner.

This in turn would explain the hasty trial. Everything was starting to add up.

The two of them were beginning to form a rapport. They exchanged stories and the Chancellor brought in lunch for everyone. Kmyviks was slowly regaining some sort of grip on reality but there was still much he didn't know. The most difficult leg of the journey still lay ahead.

Elihu rubbed the back of his neck and cleared his throat. He was going to have to make this up as he went along. He had no way of knowing how Kmyviks would react. He wondered how he would react if he were the one being told what he was about to tell the prisoner.

"Kmyviks, there is going to be no easy way of telling you this, I'm sorry. What memories you do have are correct. You were in a cell and they did indeed take you somewhere.

Now stop me anytime you have any questions, this is going to be difficult to hear. We're here for you. You were taken to the cryonics ward."

The Chancellor paused for a moment to catch his reaction. At the moment there was simply a look of puzzlement on his face. He was sure as the conversation continued, that would change.

"The details of your trial are sketchy at best but it appears from what I can make out from reading your file, that you were exiled for a year then returned. Upon your return, the sentence was never carried out obviously but I see no explanation as to why. Instead, you were then taken to the cryonics ward and, well, put in a state of artificially preserved hibernation.

You say you have no recollection of any of this?"

Kmyviks shook his head.

"No sir, I can't remember anything about that."

The Chancellor nodded and scanned the prisoner's file

in hopes of finding the answer to a question he wanted to avoid asking. He found nothing.

"So, Kmyviks, you there for would have no idea why the sentence wasn't carried out?"

Again, Kmyviks shook his head. Elihu was bewildered.

"You do realize you were sentenced to death don't you? You do remember that don't you?"

This time Kmyviks took a deep breath and nodded reluctantly.

"Yes sir, I remember the sentence and I remember being exiled; I remember every detail of that, but nothing much after I returned.

I remember being returned, being thrown into a cell and the fear of my imminent death. I can remember waiting, and then they came with the intentions of taking me somewhere, I assumed to be executed, that's pretty much it."

"So you do remember being exiled?"

Kmyviks took a deep breath and managed to nod.

"Yes sir, I remember every moment of it."

A tear surprisingly came to Kmyviks eye. Both the Chancellor and Ambassador took notice of the unexpected display of emotion. They glanced at each other to insure each had noticed it.

Elihu took a mental note to question him about it later but wanted to get this difficult conversation out of the way first.

Kmyviks motioned to the Chancellor seemingly eliciting the opportunity to say something.

The Chancellor acknowledged the request.

"Kmyviks, feel free to speak anytime you want, this is not an inquisition. Do you have a question?"

The prisoner nodded.

"Just how long was I....asleep?"

This was the question he feared. He knew of no other

way around it rather than just come out and to tell him honest truth, then deal with the repercussions as they came. There was simply no way to sugar coat such a traumatic confession. He immediately went into damage control.

"Son, I realize this is going to be hard for you to hear, I'm sorry."

He sighed and hesitated as he tried to come up with a humane way of telling him.

"You have been in hibernation for over fifteen years."

Kmyviks threw himself against the back of his chair in shock. It seemed like just yesterday he was in the cell. It couldn't have been fifteen years ago!

He turned as white as a ghost. His eyes bulged out of his head and his mouth dropped to the floor. He started to shake.

Ambassador Kreia jumped out of his chair and put his hand on the prisoner's shoulder to attempt to comfort him.

"Son, take a deep breath, I know that's quite a shock but you're going to get through this. We are going to help you; we're on your side. Is there anything we can get you?"

Kmyviks brushed the hand aside and continued to tremble.

"That's impossible! That's simply impossible; you don't expect me to believe that!"

Elihu looked straight down at his desk top; he couldn't address the man looking into his eyes.

"I'm afraid it is true. According to the date on your file the process was initiated slightly over fifteen years ago. Now I know it may seem like only a day to you, but we can't deny the truth, we have to come to grips with it and go on from here.

The important thing here is you were well looked

after. The center had a staff whose sole purpose was to keep you alive and they did a great job. You are alive and seemingly healthy. We can deal with everything else."

Kmyviks was in a total state of denial. His mind couldn't fathom what he was being told. He shot back at the Chancellor in anger.

"We can deal with everything else? How can I deal with losing fifteen years of my life?"

Elihu motioned for him to calm down.

"That's just it Kmyviks, you haven't lost a day of your life. You haven't aged more than a day. You have your whole life ahead of you."

Kmyviks gave him a disgruntled expression.

"That is of little consolation Chancellor."

Elihu continued, ignoring the reaction.

"Now if we could move on for just a moment, I want to discuss something I think will be very important to you.

I have thoroughly examined the details of your case. I feel a great injustice has been made. I reviewed all the details of your crime, your trial and sentencing. I am well aware of the atrocities that were committed by the previous administration on a number of levels and that leads me to the conclusion that your act was entirely justified.

I have come to the conclusion that you may well have actually done society a favor by ridding it of one of the hoodlums responsible. Sadly because of that, you were deemed a threat to the government and had to be silenced. The previous government was nothing short of tyrannical; I can promise you this one will not be!

With that in mind, in addition to the fact that your trial; and I hesitate to even call it a trial, was tainted, unfair and was merely a formality to justify the sentence which had already been decided on, I have made a decision."

Kmyviks had clamed down and was listening intently as the Chancellor continued.

"I have reduced your crime to justifiable homicide, cleared your name of any wrong doings, and hereby announce I have awarded you a complete and unconditional pardon. Kmyviks, as of today you are a free man!

I can only hope that this will take at least some of the sting away from your wrongful incarceration and heinous sentence."

Kmyviks was stunned. He had too much to digest at one time. First he was told he had been frozen for fifteen years, and now he is being told he is a free man. He put his hands to his head and massaged his temples in an attempt to squeeze out the severe headache he had suddenly been stricken with.

He leaned back in his chair and closed his eyes deep in thought. He was wishing this was all a bad dream. He cursed his memory for betraying him of any recollections of even being put in cryonics.

On the one hand he was elated at the Chancellor's decision but, on the other, he was trying to digest exactly what it meant to be a free man and what would lie ahead.

# 46

Karen's thirtieth birthday brought a mixture of joy and sadness. Julie threw a nice party for her at the house. In attendance were Julie and Robert, Edi and Leonard, Claudia, and Karen and her boyfriend Rick, along with a number of their friends.

It wasn't the elements that were present that brought the sadness, but it was those that were absent that brought heartbreak. There were no deluxe burgers; no home made pizza, no cases of pop, staples of every party they had ever thrown. Larry had passed away a month before.

Unbeknownst to anyone, he had been battling pancreatic cancer. It had been a well kept secret which Larry insisted on. Only he was privileged to the complete story. He was never one to elicit sympathy from anyone.

Julie knew he had been ill but was unaware of the severity. She suspected something when he had embarrassingly asked her to work extra shifts. He just claimed he was tired and wanted to spend more time with Claudia. She accepted his reasoning but there was something about his tone of voice that disturbed her. She never questioned him on it.

She started to really worry when she noticed Leonard at the bar nightly, not drinking, but behind the bar, with Larry always close by his side. She thought this was odd, she had never seen this before. Oh Leonard would come in and have a couple beers but he was never behind the bar. Larry never once hinted at the real reason behind these unusual visits.

Larry had been training him to take over but was very subtle about it. He would joke with her saying Leonard had been begging him for a job. He told her Leonard had claimed to have way too much free time and just had to get out of the house.

Leonard played right along with it saying he could only take so much of Edi. She would simply laugh, totally understanding. Just how much Leonard actually knew during all this she wasn't sure of but they were convincing and naively she believed them.

Julie discovered the news of his passing from Leonard. It was a Saturday morning and she went down to work. She found Leonard sitting at a bar stool with his head in his hands. It was apparent he had been crying.

She approached him and he wrapped his arms around her without saying a word. She suspected the worse and she got it. Leonard released his hug and spoke.

"I am so sorry to have to say this, but it looks like I am your boss and landlord now, Larry passed away this morning."

They spent the next twenty minutes crying. Larry had not only been her boss and landlord but a close family friend. He would personally cater every party they ever threw free of charge and he would frequently loan her money until pay day. He never missed a holiday or birthday without showering them with wonderful gifts.

He would always work with her whenever she needed a particular day off or even allowed her to take time off when ever she needed it. He was always tolerant when she told him her rent would be late. She owed him everything. He had given her not only a home, but a job to pay for it.

She remembered how kind he was when she told him she was pregnant. He gave her extra time off and even helped her with the crib and changing table. She couldn't imagine where her life would be had she not known him.

His funeral was quite an occasion. Over a hundred

of his regular customers were there as well as a number of his old army buddies, a few of whom had come from out of state, to pay their respects. Larry was loved by everyone.

The reception was held at the bar with Leonard solemnly tending bar. Edi helped him as she could and Karen had brought trays of sandwiches from work.

Claudia was holding up as best she could. Julie and Karen had become very close to her and provided what support and encouragement they could on those days when she would come over and just cry.

There was sadness for Julie on another front. Karen had been promoted to assistant manager and with it came a very nice pay raise. Julie was so proud of her. She had been dating a wonderful young man named Rick for almost a year now.

Rick was a salesman at the local Ford dealership and was making a very nice living. He was a true gentleman. He always dressed nicely, was very respectful to Julie and treated Karen like a queen. He was always taking her out to eat or to a movie and frequently had flowers sent.

He really liked Robert. They shared a fascination with astronomy and the two of them would spend hours talking about their passion. Robert adored him because he was the only person in his life that not only shared his interest but could discuss it intelligently.

Rick even took Robert to the planetarium and reported back to Julie that her son had corrected the tour guide on a number of occasions.

Julie was very fond of Rick and was so happy that Karen had found such a nice young man. She thought back to her teenage years and the struggles they had endured and how she never thought this day would come for her. They were truly a very happy couple.

It was a Thursday evening when they dropped the bomb. Rick had picked up Karen from work and the two of them stopped by afterwards.

It was past midnight and Robert was in bed. Julie was watching television when they arrived. Karen and her mother enjoyed a hug at the door and she cheerfully shook Rick's hand as she invited them both inside. Rick and Karen sat on the sofa and Julie sat on the chair beside it.

"How was your night at work sweetheart? Are you getting the hang of being a manager yet? I'm sure that must be quite an adjustment for you."

Karen smiled.

"Oh it's coming along really good mom. It's really easy and everyone has been so helpful, I really like it."

Julie nodded.

"So Rick, how are things going at the dealership? Sell any cars today?"

Rick glanced at Karen and then at her mother.

"Oh it's going fantastic Mrs. Wells and as a matter of fact I did close on one this afternoon!"

Julie gave them joyful thumbs up.

"Oh I am so happy for both of you!"

Karen nudged her boyfriend and he nodded.

"Mom, we have something to tell you and I don't know for sure how you are going to respond. Oh mom this is so exciting!"

Julie gave her daughter a puzzled expression. After giving her daughter's statement further thought, the look of puzzlement was quickly replaced by a mother's look of concern. A million and one things were suddenly going through her mind.

She hoped her daughter's definition of 'exciting' was similar to her own. She tried to prepare herself in the event it wasn't.

"Sweetheart, you can tell me anything you should know that by now. I mean my goodness, after all we have been through together you shouldn't be afraid to tell me anything. Now what is this exciting news you have for me?"

Karen couldn't argue with that and smiled. She again glanced at Rick for encouragement which he gave her by means of a kiss on the cheek.

He whispered in her ear.

"Tell her Karen, we are going to do this!"

Karen cleared her throat and took a deep breath.

"Well, I guess I will come right out and tell you mom. Rick and I are getting an apartment."

Julie immediately let out a sigh of relief. She said a quick thank you to God without going into detail with him, she was sure he would already know.

There were some things she could handle and others she would struggle with. Thankfully this was one she thought she could deal with.

"So... you're getting an apartment? Well this is sudden."

Rick looked at Karen with consternation.

"Well, actually Mrs. Wells, we have been thinking about it for some time. We have put a lot of thought into this and mutually decided it was what we both wanted.

With Karie's promotion and what I'm making, that would give us financial stability and we can finally afford it without worries. We so want your approval Mrs. Wells, it's very important to both of us."

Julie looked at her daughter who was sitting silently in apprehension.

"Sweetheart, you know all I want is for you to be happy. You are an adult and I certainly can't tell you what to do and you certainly don't need my approval."

Karen looked at Rick, again for reassurance which this time he gave her with a smile.

"Well mom, you know I wanted to stay here and help you with Bobby while he was little but he's all grown up now and I think he can take care of himself. I second Rick's feelings that your approval is important mom."

Julie nodded.

"I can't argue with that sweetheart. You were a tremendous help, I couldn't have made it without you. You are correct; he can most assuredly take care of himself now."

Karen reached over and held her mother's hand.

"It's not like we're moving to the moon, we will only be twenty minutes away. We found this incredible apartment over on Blaine Ave., you know, on the north side. Oh mom you would love it!

It has an adorable little kitchen with beautiful cabinets and a new refrigerator and stove and even a dishwasher! Can you imagine that...a dishwasher! The living room is huge and the entire place has new carpeting!"

Julie was enjoying her daughter's excitement. It was so good to see her sincerely happy.

"It sounds really nice sweetheart."

Karen smiled and continued.

"It has air conditioning and a beautiful bathroom. Oh, and it has a really nice front yard with a really cool cobblestone walkway to the front door. Mom you will love it, I can't wait for you to see it!"

Julie could tell Karen really wanted this. She couldn't help but notice over the months how happy she has been with Rick. He treats her very well and they are both so happy when they are together.

She knew Rick was a responsible young man with a good income and he treated her daughter like a queen. She liked him and trusted him with Karen. This made the news a lot easier to handle. She knew her daughter was in good hands

She certainly didn't have any complaints against him, she could have done a lot worse. Now she had to weigh her mixed emotions.

Of course she wants her daughter to be happy, and there is no doubt she is happy with him. Now, the other side of the coin, the selfish side; if she moved out, there would be a vacancy not only in the home but in her heart.

It was reassuring, to a point, that they would only be twenty minutes away but it wasn't the mileage that was bothering her.

She remembered when she first moved out of her parent's home she only moved about twenty minutes away. Once she got out of their house and into her own place, visiting mom and dad was not her first priority.

Oh she would call now and again but she was young and too wrapped up in enjoying her new found independence to be concerned with mom and dad missing her.

She totally trusted Karen. Her daughter was intelligent, responsible and had a lot of common sense. No, this wasn't about Karen, it was totally about her. She knew she still had Robert at home but that was different.

She loved her son with all her heart but nothing could approach the drama, the problems and turmoil that she and Karen endured for so many years. These kinds of things create a tremendous bond between a mother and her child. Those difficult days and her miraculous recovery had cemented her daughter a very special place in her heart.

Having survived and triumphed over those impossible times together had just given Karen a very deeply ingrained place in her heart, the intensity of which a normal relationship couldn't come close to.

She knew Karen would only be a short drive away but

it would never be the same as having her in the home with her, seeing her every day.

She also realized this was being totally selfish. Karen was an adult and had every right to move on and live her own life. Julie realized the sacrifice Karen had made by putting off this move as long as she had. She would never deny her that but her heart would suffer as a result.

Julie sat and thought about how unreasonable her mind was currently being. She knew this was a natural thing for any young person to desire and my goodness Karen had stayed with her until she was thirty! That was above and beyond any normal sacrifice any child should make to their parents.

She smiled and vowed her total support.

"Sweetheart, I am very happy for you and you both have my complete support. Rick, you are a wonderful young man and I am so glad Karen found someone nice like you."

Karen stood up and gave her mother a big hug. She then turned to the couch and gave Rick the same, only this time adding a quick kiss for good measure.

"Oh mom, I can't tell you what that means to me and Rick."

Surprisingly, Rick stood up and also gave Julie a hug.

"You know Karie will be fine with me Mrs. Wells. I will take good care of her. I was thinking; the place has two bedrooms and maybe once we are settled in Robert would like to come over for a weekend and we could do things together, we'd love to have him. That would also give you some time to, well, do something you might like to do without worrying about him. It was just a thought."

Julie was now beaming with joy. What a nice offer.

"So when is all of this going to take place sweetheart?"

Karen looked at Rick as if to determine who was going to answer the question. Rick quickly volunteered.

"We were planning on signing the lease next week and moving, well, whenever we can get the boxes and everything together."

Julie nodded and offered her help in collecting boxes for them. She resigned herself that this was going to be a good thing for everyone. She was going to be alright as long as she knew Karen was happy.

The following week was busy for everyone. Karen and Rick had been over daily organizing all her things and Robert was enthusiastic about assisting them. Robert was taking the news of his sister moving very well.

A large part of that was due to the fact that he had a new best friend in Rick and was happy he was going to remain around.

Julie spent the next few days running all over town finding boxes and buying supplies to help in the move. Everyone was working as a team towards the common goal. She found herself actually getting excited about the move largely because she could see how thrilled Karen was with it.

She couldn't help but think back to those dark teenage years for Karen and how her life has completely turned around. Whenever she finds herself recalling those days her mind automatically goes back to Robert senior and how none of this would be possible today without his intervention. She continued to miss him every day.

While the moving project was going very well, one area where Julie found herself struggling was with work. She found it so difficult to go to work with Larry gone.

She adored Leonard and he was very good to her and easy to work for but she missed Larry every time she put her apron on. She missed his adorable sense of humor and his soft gentle nature.

It was a pain that simply wouldn't go away and having to continue to work in the same environment without him forced too many daily reminders to make forgetting him impossible. The place just wasn't the same without him.

Leonard had made very little changes around the bar with the exception of the menu. He knew he could never recreate the incredible customized cheeseburgers that had been a specialty of Larry and any attempt would be inadvertently compared to the original. He replaced the cheeseburger with a selection of sub sandwiches.

He also contracted a pizza shop to come in and take over the pizza role since he could never hope to match Larry's homemade pizza.

One change in the drink selection was the addition of a new, very potent, specialty drink that Edi had created and he affectionately named 'Larry's Legend'. This was a concoction of two kinds of bourbon, a shot of spiced rum, honey, a bit of sugar, bitters and was garnished with a slice of orange.

He knew Larry loved his bourbon and wanted to honor him in a way he thought his friend would appreciate. It proved to be a very popular selection with the regulars.

As an additional tribute, he donated a dollar from each 'Larry's Legend' sold to the humane society which Larry was a long time supporter of, that was also Edi's suggestion.

The only noticeable change to the appearance of the bar was a very nice, ten by twelve, picture of Larry and Claudia which he hung up respectfully right above the cash register

After two weeks of frantic preparation, moving day for Karen finally arrived. Julie had rented a moving van which Leonard volunteered to drive. Rick had a few of his friends come over and do all the heavy lifting and after about three hours all of Karen's belongings were relocated to their new apartment.

When the task was completed, the couple had a house

warming party. Julie and Robert were there as were Claudia, Leonard and Edi and a few of Rick and Karen's friends.

Julie and Robert were given the grand tour and both were highly impressed. It was a beautiful apartment. Rick made a point of inviting Robert over any time he wanted to come and he promised he would take him up on the offer.

Karen had again catered the affair with trays of sandwiches from work and Leonard chipped in with a keg of beer and a case of pop.

As the party was winding down, Julie found herself silently dreading going home. It would be her first night without Karen being in the home. She knew this was foolish but couldn't help feeling like there would be a huge vacancy when they returned. She would have to come up with a way of dealing with this void because it was one she would have to learn to live with.

Everyone said their goodbyes and she enjoyed a hug from both members of the happy couple. After arriving at home Julie immediately forced herself to go straight into Karen's old room. It was something she knew she had to do and wanted to get it over with. She knew how she would feel and she wanted to face her demons head on.

The bed, the dresser with its beautiful mirror and her television set and stereo were of course all gone. The walls, once adorned with her many posters of kittens, puppies and fairies were now bare.

The windows were now sans of curtains. She had loved her pink curtains with cats on them and was insistent on taking them with her, they matched her bedspread.

The room was completely empty with the exception of memories. The smell of her perfume still lingered. A tear came to Julie's eye. Her little girl had indeed grown up.

# 47

The chancellor had refreshments brought in for everyone. The mood was much more tranquil now. He studied Kmyviks and noticed him to be more relaxed. His breathing was calmer and his eyes more alert. He was now sitting upright and seemed more attentive, more at ease.

He was pleased at the improvement and wanted to take advantage of it, there was much more he wanted to know about him.

"Kmyviks, please allow me to ask you a question. I don't mean to embarrass you, but I noticed something extremely interesting and I simply want to ask you about it if you don't mind."

Kmyviks took a sip from his drink and nodded.

"Yes sir, you can ask me anything."

Elihu thought for a minute, he wanted to make sure he worded this correctly.

"You say you remember your year in exile?"

Again, Kmyviks nodded.

"I remember every minute, every detail sir."

The chancellor pondered his reply.

"Good, well when I first mentioned it, I noticed a tear come to your eye. I found this reaction quite curious. Was your time there that painful?"

Kmyviks put his hand on his forehead, his discomfort with the question very noticeable. He took a deep breath and replied softly.

"No sir, quite the opposite. It was the most wonderful year of my life."

The Chancellor was completely taken back by his answer. An exile was meant as a continuation of the sentence, not a vacation. That is why the program was created in the first place, to free up jail space and at the same time transport the prisoner to a totally alien world where his time there was meant to be miserable.

Over the years he had heard many horrific stories by prisoners returning from exile; many claiming it to be the most horrible experience of their lives. Some compared it to a year of solitary confinement, no familiar faces, no familiarity with any of the customs, being so far from home, a total feeling of isolation, as it was meant to be.

So how could he was it was the most wonderful year of his life? This simply made no sense. He had to question him further on it.

"I must question you on that Kmyviks, and again, no offense intended, I just find that hard to believe.

You were exiled to a foreign planet, alone, with no friends or even anyone else of your kind. You were given just enough to survive on and had no contact with us here. How can you tell me that was a pleasurable experience?"

The Chancellor couldn't help but notice another tear forming in the prisoner's eye. His disposition had changed instantly. Besides obviously being in deep thought, he all of a sudden appeared stricken, distant, and alone. A look of sadness now appeared on his face which had changed completely. His eyes closed tightly as if in an attempt to block further tears. The change was dramatic and very observable.

"Are you alright Kmyviks? What is upsetting you?"

Kmyviks raised his hand in an effort to assure the Chancellor that he was fine.

"I'll be alright sir. This is just very difficult for me. I thought that was all in my past. I thought when I was returned here, I would be executed and not have to relive this again.

I wasn't expecting this line of questioning sir. I am sorry but I was hoping not to have to remember certain things again."

Elihu glanced at the Ambassador still sitting silently besides the prisoner. Kreia was equally bewildered and simply shrugged his shoulders. He sensed the Chancellor wanted his involvement so he asked the prisoner a question.

"Kmyviks, are you trying to tell us you actually enjoyed your year of exile in this strange place?"

The prisoner turned and faced the Ambassador. He spoke softly and solemnly.

"More than I have ever enjoyed anything in my life sir."

Kmyviks pondered the experience and finally felt comfortable enough to share his thoughts on it.

"I don't know how familiar you are with the place I was sent. I couldn't even tell you where it was, they never told me. Can you believe that? Of course it wasn't important enough to me to ask. It didn't really matter, at the time, where it was really.

All I knew was it was some distant rock, so many light years from home. It was just a convenient way to get me out of society and watch me slowly die a little bit each day, until they could return me here and finish the job in a more humane manner. That's really all it was to me, at first.

My first thoughts were that I hoped I would die during the transfer and save me a year of misery. I had no idea what to expect but I knew it wouldn't be anything pleasant. I mean, I knew my death was eminent and unavoidable, I knew I was to be executed upon my return so why prolong the inevitable?

The whole exile concept is inhumane. You are torturing a man already sentenced to death, to a prequel of a year of isolation, just to free up a jail cell.

It seemed to me that was equivalent to pulling the wings off a butterfly and then sadistically enjoy watching it walk around helpless until it died, a fate I'm sure the creature was well aware of, just as the man exiled is aware of his. What kind of society gains pleasure from such actions? Isn't the execution enough of a price to pay?

I had lost all my fight, my hope or any desire to even continue living. Did I dread the coming year, most definitely. I didn't want to be there and I didn't even want to be alive. I just wanted the whole damn nightmare to be over. I had finally accepted my fate and actually longed for it. I was in the frame of mind where it couldn't come soon enough."

The Chancellor and Ambassador were stunned. They stared at each other in total perplexity until finally Elihu broke the tension.

"Excuse me Kmyviks now I am totally confused. If this is how you felt initially, yet you now say it was the most wonderful year of your life, what caused your change of view? What could have possibly happened to turn that around son? I think we should discuss this."

It was clear Kmyviks was contentious about continuing this conversation. He gave the Chancellor an antagonistic look and sighed. He hadn't planned on having to discuss any of this. He wanted any memory of that year to be erased. He saw no reason to torture him with having to relive it.

He had been given his unconditional release from custody, why must the Chancellor now add conditions.

He knew he wouldn't get away with his desire of simply not giving any response at all so he was honest.

"Sir, with all due respect, is it really necessary to go into that? It's over, I'm trying to get past it and move on and with your kindness today it is making that a possibility. I sincerely appreciate what you are doing for me and I would just like to leave the past where it is, in the past."

Elihu grunted. He wasn't satisfied with that answer.

"I am trying to get to know more about you Kmyviks. We have established new programs that could be a real benefit to your rehabilitation but in order to implement the ones that would help you the most we need to get to know you better.

Now obviously something happened while you were there that totally changed your perspective on the experience, I am only asking you to explain to us what it might have been.

Kmyviks, I am doing you a huge favor here, I am under no legal obligation to release you; that was entirely my decision. Now all I ask in return is your honesty."

Kmyviks heart was silently breaking at the thought of being forced into this discussion. He remembered everything, in great detail and had even reached the point of accepting it was over but now to have to relive it was heart wrenching.

Why couldn't they just leave it alone and let him leave? What good could come of him explaining the details? He finally conceded, reluctantly, to talking.

"Well, I met a woman while I was there. She was different than any woman I had ever known; here. She was very kind to me."

The Chancellor and Ambassador shared a look of astonishment. They were both speechless until Kreia finally managed a question.

"You met a woman, and you say she was kind to you. Are you now telling us this kindness developed into a relationship?"

Kmyviks nodded.

"Yes sir, it did. I would even go as far as saying we

were totally in love with each other. This was certainly not something I had anticipated or solicited, it just happened.

I had never experienced love before. I had never cared about anyone as much as I did her. For the first time in my life, I actually felt alive. I felt life was worth living, ironically at a time when I knew that wouldn't mean much."

Elihu lit up his pipe and studied the smoke arising from it. He then turned his attention to Kmyviks.

"I would never have even dreamed such a thing was possible. You mean to tell me, in full knowledge of her being an entirely different species, you somehow managed to fall in love with her?

Just what was it about her that made you feel this way Kmyviks, this is simply mind boggling!"

Kmyviks sighed; the memories were too painful to bear.

"Sir, all my life I have never been loved by anyone, not even my parents. I used women; I must sadly admit that I did. I'm not proud of that now but it's the truth. I then simply discarded them without ever getting emotionally involved. No one ever cared about me or believed in me like she did.

She showed me what it was like to be loved and needed. We respected each other and truly cared about each other. I have never been so happy in my life.

I had waited all my life with hopes of someday feeling like that but had given up on any hope of it actually happening long ago. I mean face it; I wasn't an easy person to love. I knew this inside and perhaps I just never gave anyone a chance

I went through my wretched life trying to convince myself that it really wasn't important to me but she somehow showed me I was only fooling myself. Somewhere deep in a part of my heart I didn't even know existed, she touched me, like I had never been touched before."

Kreia shook his head in disbelief.

"And she felt the same way about you?"

Kmyviks managed a weak smile.

"Amazingly she did."

Elihu was thoroughly enthralled by this unexpected story. He continued to shake his head in bewilderment.

"Allow me to ask you this Kmyvoks; did she know who you really were?"

He answered respectfully.

"Not at first, but circumstances presented themselves where I had to confide in her and tell her the truth."

Kreia looked at him with amazement.

"And she continues to love you even after knowing all the facts?"

Kmyviks nodded.

"Eventually she knew everything. I, of course, told her where I was from and that led me to telling her about my past and the reason I was there.

She eventually accepted everything. Of course she was skeptical at first, but I provided enough proof to finally convince her. Yes, she still loved me after I told her."

Elihu put his head in his hands.

"That has to be the most remarkable thing I have ever heard Kmyviks. I don't know what to say at this point. I thank you and admire your honesty. If all of what you say is true this confession had to be difficult for you and I respect that."

The meeting was now approaching three hours and everyone was getting noticeably tired. Elihu had heard everything he needed to hear. He looked at Kreia and acknowledged him. He then addressed Kmyviks.

"It has been a long meeting and I think we are all getting tired. I am totally satisfied with the results and

I have heard enough here. May I ask you to go into the lobby for a few minutes while the Ambassador and I wrap up the final details of your release?"

Kmyviks stood up and silently walked out the door. Elihu stood up and paced the room. He turned to his colleague.

"Well Ayohod, what are your thoughts?"

The Ambassador simply shook his head.

"That was quite a story he gave us."

Elihu agreed.

"The question we have here is do you believe it?"

Ayohod shrugged his shoulders.

"My question to you is, as unbelievable as it may sound, why would he lie about it? What would he have to gain?"

Elihu continued to pace and put his hand on his chin pondering the question.

"That's a very good point my friend. So let's go with it as fact. Now, what are we going to do with him?"

Ayohod raised his hands in compliance.

"That is your call sir."

Elihu was impressed with the candor of Kmyviks testimony. He could see the pain that was involved with recounting the story and that only added to its sincerity. He had no doubt that, in spite of its outlandish claim, that it was indeed the truth.

He liked Kmyviks, he found him to be a good man despite his rough exterior and tainted past. He wanted to help him; he truly felt the man had suffered enough. With the additional anguish that his latest confession brought to the equation he was going to do something for him.

He put his hand on the Ambassador's shoulder.

"You know, we could send him back."

Kreia was taken back by the suggestion.

"Are you serious? Do you think that would be what he would want?"

Elihu thought for a moment.

"Well, think about it. He certainly didn't have anything here. Even without the threat of execution what does the man have here? Okay, we simply release him, what does he do?

He's been asleep for fifteen years, if he did have any friends they would have long since forgotten about him, and I'm sure they would not be the best influence on him if they did remember him.

His past was nothing more than a string of arrests and there is always the chance of his desperation leading him back into drugs. He deserves better than that."

The Ambassador had to agree.

"You do present a strong case sir. I really don't see a bright future here for him. He has no job skills, no friends, no home or income, and you are correct, if things don't go well for him there is a good chance he would return to his old ways."

Elihu patted his colleague on the back in agreement.

"The emotion he displayed when talking about that woman was touching. He sounded like he had finally found happiness. After all we have put him through I certainly think he deserves that."

The Ambassador smiled.

"I think you would be doing a good thing sir. I think that would make him happy. He has no reason to stay here and, like you said, after all he's been through I think he deserves something good to happen to him. I would certainly support that decision."

Elihu nodded in agreement and returned to his desk. He pushed a button on the intercom.

"Send the prisoner back in if you would please."

The Ambassador returned to his chair and the two of them watched the door as Kmyviks returned.

The Chancellor pointed to the vacant seat.

"Sit down Kmyviks; I want to talk to you."

Kmyviks sat down and first glanced at the Ambassador seated next to him and then at the Chancellor. He appeared nervous.

"Yes sir?"

Elihu and Ayohod gave each other a silent nod of understanding and agreement as the Chancellor began.

"Kmyviks; let me begin by saying, as Chancellor of the new order, allow me to offer my sincere apologies for what the previous ministry had done to you.

I find their treatment of you appalling and inexcusable. I can assure you those days are over!

I realize no amount of remorse can undo the damage they caused you but I can make an effort of atonement."

The Chancellor had Kmyviks undivided attention.

"As you know, I have pardoned you; you are now a free man. As noble as this gesture may be I still feel we owe you more. An apology is by no means enough. I want you to think about this, what can we do to give you a jumpstart to your new life?"

Kmyviks was startled by the Chancellor's offer. He wasn't expecting this. He honestly didn't have a reply. To him, his freedom was the greatest reward they could have offered him and he already had that.

"Sir, I appreciate your sentiments. Giving me my release is all the thanks I would need from you. You have not wronged me and you personally don't owe me anything."

Elihu looked at Kreia for support. The Ambassador smiled.

"Kmyviks; let me ask you one thing. You say your year of exile was the happiest year of your life."

The prisoner nodded.

"Yes sir, I never realized what happiness was before."

The Chancellor smiled.

"And this woman you met, she was the reason for this elation?"

At a loss for words, Kmyviks simply nodded. He closed his eyes as embarrassing tears started to pour from his eyes.

The Chancellor couldn't help but notice and be touched by the unexpected emotional response. He took a deep breath. This only added to his resolution that his offer would be a good thing and the best for Kmyviks.

"How would you like to return to her?"

Kmyviks was overwhelmed to the point of astonishment by the Chancellor's offer. This was the last thing he ever expected to hear. He closed his eyes and thought about the ramifications of the statement.

Was he serious? If this was some kind of joke it was the cruelest one anyone had ever played on him. He thought further on it and realized the Chancellor would have no motivation to do anything like that.

If this were possible it would be the greatest gift he ever had. This was beyond his wildest dreams. He tried to form an intelligent response. His body was literally shaking from anticipation. He wiped his tears and his voice trembled as he replied.

"Is that even possible?"

The Chancellor and Ambassador both smiled as one.

"Kmyviks, I am the Chancellor, I can make anything possible!"

This was surreal. This wasn't a dream come true, it was beyond that. He could never have even dreamed this would be a possibility. Getting his freedom was the most he could have hoped for.

To actually see Julie again, to embrace her and feel

her lips against his again would be more than he could have ever hoped for. He never even entertained the hope of that ever happening.

He was in shock. He couldn't even think. He again closed his eyes and a vision of Julie came to him. He missed her so much. He had just accepted the fact that he would never see her again.

He thought about the pain she must have endured when he was taken back and how that thought upset him even more than the thought of his eminent death.

Tired of waiting for a response, the Chancellor spoke.

"So tell me Kmyviks, would this make you happy? Would this somehow atone for the wrong that has been done to you?"

Kmyviks was trembling.

"Yes sir, this would be the greatest thing that ever happened to me."

# 48

Chancellor Elihu clicked on the intercom.

"Zellai, could you please prepare and send in forms CR 85 and EE 21 please, thank you."

He clicked off the intercom and addressed Kmyviks.

"Well Kmyviks, if you are sure this is what you want; I see no reason to delay it any further. We can get the wheels in motion right away.

I have requested your release forms and the form to initiate the exile. Once the release forms are completed we fill out the exile papers and you will be on your way."

Kmyviks finally managed a smile.

"Oh I am sure this is what I want sir. I have nothing here, no future at all. To be able to go back and be with Julie would mean the world to me!"

Elihu sighed. He thought about the reason Kmyviks was so excited about going back. There was a girl there. A tinge of sadness crossed his mind. There was something he wanted to make sure the man understood.

"Very well, this time I'm pleased to say your exile is entirely your decision, and it's for your happiness and not to free up a jail cell. I in no way want to influence that decision but there is one thing I have to remind you of.

In spite of what it may like to seem to you, fifteen years have passed. They have passed here and they have also passed there. Things will not be the same as when you left. You realize a lot can happen in fifteen years.

I know the reason you are excited to go back and I just want you to be aware of, well what you might find when you get there."

Kmyviks took a deep breath, the words briefly startled him. In the excitement of the moment he had temporarily forgotten that. He thought about how long fifteen years really was and how a person's life can change in even less of an amount of time.

He pondered the many scenarios he might face upon his return, all of them revolving around Julie and of them were bad.

He knew Julie would think he was dead; and even if she somehow she thought he might still be alive she would never expect him to return. She would have no other choice but to move on. He had to come to grips with the fact that it would very likely she may be with someone else. After an absence of fifteen years he certainly couldn't blame her.

He weighed his options. He was certain of his future here. In time, he would fall back into his old lifestyle. He would either die on the streets or once again be arrested. No, staying here wasn't an option. He would return. If Julie had indeed moved on, he would deal with it, if and when it came to that.

The people there were different than they were here. They knew kindness and compassion. He had never gotten respect from anyone in this world but he was showered with it on theirs. He would somehow find a way to survive. At least there he would have a chance; here he wouldn't have any chance at all, his fate would be sealed.

He loved her that much. Julie had become his life and only reason to continue. She had taken him from the depths of despair and given him a reason to live. That woman single handedly made him more of a man than he ever dreamed possible.

She broke through what he thought was an inapproachable heart and showed him love for the first time in his life. She was worth taking a risk on. He owed her that much. Even a chance at getting her back was worth any risks involved.

He knew if he stayed here there would be no chance of ever seeing her again but if he did go back there would at least be a chance. He announced his decision.

"I realize going back is a gamble, I know I am taking a chance. I totally understand that a lot can indeed happen in fifteen years but to remain here would be anything but a gamble.

I have nothing to keep me here. No, it wouldn't be a gamble it would be a done deal. I know myself too well. I have a pretty good idea what would happen if I decided to stay. I am willing to take my chances, I have nothing to lose.

You know my past; if I were to remain here I am certain you and I would be having a very different conversation in the near future, one that wouldn't be quite so pleasant. I am prepared to face what ever awaits me there. It would certainly be better than what would await me here."

Elihu nodded solemnly as his secretary came in carrying two folders. One folder contained the release papers, the other containing the exile papers.

"Here are the forms you requested sir."

The chancellor smiled and thanked her as she left the room. He set the folders on his desk and smiled.

"Kmyviks, here is all the paperwork we need to return you. You must be pretty excited; I know I am excited for you."

That statement was only half true. The Chancellor was sure Kmyviks would be excited but he personally was very apprehensive about what he might find when he got there and even more importantly, how he would react.

Elihu started filling out the paperwork as the Ambassador spoke.

"One thing the Chancellor failed to mention, which is very important, is that we need for you to know, before you go, this is a one way trip. Once you are there; you will not be able to return.

You will not have the tracking device they put in you on your previous trip. What this means is there will be no way for us to know where you are. I just want you to be aware of that before you make your final decision. This will be a permanent move."

The Ambassador's words were of little consequence to him, he had no intentions of coming back. If Julie were indeed available he would have no reason to want to come back, if, on the other hand, she wasn't, he would have nothing to come back to anyways.

No, he was planning on staying one way or the other. He continued to think about the possible scenarios as the Chancellor completed the paperwork. He nodded his acceptance of those terms.

Finally, Elihu looked up from his work.

"Kmyviks everything is completed. All I need are is your signature in a couple places here and we can get moving along."

The Chancellor motioned for him over and handed him a pen. He signed all the documents without even reading them. He saw no reason to read them, he knew what they would say and wanted to get the formality over with. Regardless of what they might have said it would in no way effect his decision.

The anticipation was mounting. He found himself getting nervous and wanted to go as quickly as possible. He didn't need any more time to think about it, he simply needed to do it.

Elihu glanced at all the papers and, after being satisfied that they had been signed in all the appropriate places clicked on the intercom.

"Zellai, the papers are ready to be filed could you come in for a moment."

Within minutes his secretary walked through the door.

"Yes sir?"

Elihu handed her the folders.

"Please get these processed as quickly as possible. Kmyviks is going to need a few things for his trip. I want you to get him a nice set of clothes and please fix up the usual exile provision case for him. Put a little extra of everything in it and check his file, include about five thousand of their dollars. He's going back to the same place so please forward the coordinates to the deportation center so they can have everything ready when he arrives. We want to properly take care of this gentleman."

The secretary nodded and assured him she would have everything within in the hour.

Kmyviks was shocked at the offering.

"Sir, I appreciate your offer but I can't take any money."

The Canceller just chuckled.

"Of course you can, just consider it a bounty on the hoodlum you took care of for us. Besides, it's not my money; in fact it's not anyone's money. We simply verify the planet you are going to, check their currency and print it up at the lab as needed."

Elihu had lunch brought in for the three of them as they awaited the secretary's return.

Kreia had to know more about this woman that Kmyviks was so stricken with.

"So tell me more about this woman. I still find this situation most unusual and highly unexpected.

I am very curious about what makes this woman so exceptional. What could be so special about her that you would be willing to give up everything you have ever know to live on a strange alien world simply to be with her, please enlighten me."

Kmyviks thoughts now drifted to Julie. How could he possibly describe her and what she meant to him? He was sure anything he would say would sound strange coming from a man they would know only from his criminal background folder

He pondered how they had not only fallen in love, but how she had completely changed him. He was no longer the same man whose life story is documented on a criminal record file; that man no longer exists.

He glanced at the clock whose hands were moving way too slow for his liking. He knew the Ambassador would demand an answer. The more he thought about it the less he cared about what answer to give.

He wasn't concerned with their opinions or reactions. They would never totally understand and that was fine with him. His only thoughts were to get back to Julie. He no longer had the burden to carry a tough, hardened image, an image he had needed all his life simply to survive; now all he needed to survive was Julie.

"Julie was an amazing woman. She accepted me for who I am and above that, she totally changed who I was. She not only loved me unconditionally, but taught me how to love her in return. I say taught me because before her I literally didn't know how to love. It had never been a priority to me. My previous life had no room or tolerance for love or any chance of it ever playing a role in it. She changed all that."

Both the Chancellor and Ambassador gave Kmyviks their undivided attention as he continued.

"She treated me with respect and kindness, even after she knew my whole story she never judged me. She was everything a man could hope to find in a woman. She was very intelligent, loving and caring, and she was a great mother.

I think one of the things I miss most about her was her

ability to make me laugh. Gentlemen, I can't remember the last time I laughed here, if indeed I ever did at all

Oh, did I mention she had the most interesting hair I have ever seen on a woman; it was actually a deep reddish color. I know we can all say none of us have ever seen a woman here with that hair color. It was magnificent and very attractive!

She had a daughter who, well lets just say, I helped with some medical issues she was struggling with. We too became very close. We had all actually become like a family, a family is another thing I never had here."

Elihu and Kreia shared a hesitant smile. They were both thinking the same thing. Kmyviks story was touching but if things didn't turn out the way he hoped they were apprehensive about how he could react.

They both knew his temperament and history of violence and drug abuse. They kept their worries to themselves.

Elihu clicked on the intercom.

"Could you please get an orderly up here to escort our guest to the deportation room, we are finished here and I'm sure our guest is anxious to get going."

Kmyviks took a deep refreshing breath. This was actually happening! While trying to remain calm on the outside his heart was skipping every other beat in excitement. He still couldn't believe he was going be going back.

All doubt was removed from his mind. He was totally convinced he was making the right decision.

He suddenly remembered Julie would frequently say a prayer to a deity she believed in and had told him about. She said during times of stress and uneasiness it brought her peace and quite frequently good results.

As skeptical as he personally was about the actual existence of this deity he put his faith in Julie's belief more than his own. He took a moment to do just that figuring he could use all the help he could get.

He wasn't sure of the protocol for these invocations, he asked for only two things...a safe return trip, and a reunion with his beloved Julie.

The Chancellor interrupted his thoughts.

"Well Kmyviks, the time has finally arrived. Allow me to say before you go, it has been a pleasure meeting you and I sincerely wish you the very best. Do you have any personal belongings you want to take with you?"

Kmyviks responded with a smug smile.

"None at all sir; I don't want to take anything that will remind me of this place. I can't thank you enough for your kindness."

Ambassador Kreia added his salutations as he shook his hand.

"Kmyviks, I empathize with your troubled past and it brings me great joy that you are now in a position to put all that behind you and start off on a new life. I wish you nothing but happiness."

The secretary entered the room carrying a brief case and small brown envelope.

"Here are the things you requested sir. I have included extra provisions and here is the money you asked for. The deportation center called, they are expecting him and have everything set up for his transport."

Elihu thanked her and stood up. He walked over to Kmyviks, handed him the clothes, the suit case and envelope.

"I hope this gives you a good start Kmyviks."

Kmyviks took the suit case and money and changed in the Chancellor's private bathroom. He returned and shook the Chancellor's hand.

"I thank you again sir, this will certainly take care of me until I can get settled."

The Chancellor returned to his seat and continued his conversation with Kmyviks.

"You will be transported to the exact same coordinates as your previous trip, I hope that will be in your favor?"

Kmyviks smiled.

"That will be perfect sir, thank you!"

He remembered exactly where he had arrived the first time. It was in a large field just on the outskirts of the town, maybe a twenty minute walk.

His thoughts were again interrupted but this time by a man in a while jump suit entering the room.

"Sir, I am here to escort the prisoner to the debarkation center as you requested."

Elihu smiled and stood up.

"Excellent! Now this man is no longer a prisoner so I expect him to be treated with respect and dignity, he is an honored guest."

The man acknowledged the information as Kmyviks also stood up. He again shook hands with both the Chancellor and Ambassador and was escorted out of the room by the orderly.

The two men walked down the hall to the elevator. Inside the elevator the orderly finally spoke.

"I have to ask, if you are not a prisoner then just what is the nature of your exile?"

Kmyviks wasn't expecting any conversation. He thought about the question before answering.

"Let's just say, I've been away for many years and I'm finally going back home."

The orderly accepted the cryptic answer without any further conversation.

Kmyviks silently contemplated his choice of words. Home, he had never really had a home. He thought about how he initially dreaded going to that planet and now he is referring to it as home. Then he came to a realization which rationalized those words...home to him was now anywhere where Julie was.

They exited the elevator and walked down the hallway to two large doors. The orderly swiped his ID badge across a keypad to the left of the doors which then slowly opened.

They were greeted by a young woman also in a white jumpsuit. She smiled and took the folder from the orderly. After glancing at the file she spoke.

"Good afternoon I am Valdis; I am your deportation coordinator and will be assisting you today. Please come with me."

She turned her attention to the orderly.

"I can take him from here, thank you."

The orderly opened the doors and left as Valdis motioned for Kmyviks to follow her.

The two walked through a lobby and into a massive lab room filled with electronic equipment. There were rows of desks each with a computer terminal. Against the wall were large mainframe computers lined up neatly side by side. These massive components featured multi colored lights igniting in alternating sequences. They were connected by a web of cables and wires.

Valdis stopped for a moment at what must have been her desk. She sat and opened the folder the orderly had given her. She glanced at Kmyviks who stood silently beside the desk.

"This will just take a couple minutes sir. I need to get familiar with exactly what we are doing today."

Valdis studied the file adding notes to a clipboard she had taken from the desk. Kmyviks surveyed his surroundings. They were very familiar to him, he had been here before.

He remembered the whole ordeal. The guards with prod sticks jabbing him mercilessly as they too entered the same elevator. He remembered the surgeries prior to departure which inserted the interpretation device into his vocal chords and the data chip in his brain. He was thankful he could skip those painful processes because those items were still inside him.

He then remembered the tracking device they had told him they had attached to his spinal chord. The Chancellor said he would not have that this time yet he couldn't remember it being removed.

While this wasn't a deal breaker he wanted to know the status of it. He turned to Valdis and spoke politely.

"Excuse me for a moment, may I ask you a question?"

Valdis smiled.

"Of course you can Kmyviks, what can I help you with?"

He took a deep breath and tried to word the question appropriately.

"Well, I was implanted with a tracking device which, at the time, they had told me would not be able to be removed. Now I am being told I would be able to be tracked. I was just wondering how this was possible."

Valdis smiled and reexamined his chart. After a couple moments she replied.

"That's very easy to answer. Both things you were told are correct. You were indeed implanted with a spinal tracking apparatus which cannot be removed without causing permanent damage.

I see though that upon your return, for whatever reason, it was completely deactivated. So yes, it is still in place but it is inoperable. That being said, there is no way you can now be tracked. I hope that answers your question"

How interesting he thought. Being tracked was actually at the bottom of things to worry about. He liked the Chancellor and trusted him.

He didn't foresee any problems in this area. He knew the two of them had a mutual understanding. They would have no reason to call him back and they understood he had no interest in coming back.

Valdis turned on her computer monitor and fed some information into her computer. She studied the screen and made additional notes on her clipboard.

She stood up and addressed Kmyviks.

"Okay, I have everything in place; I think we are ready to proceed. If you will follow me to the transportation tubes we will have you on your way in a matter of minutes."

He followed her through two doors which again opened after she had swiped her ID card through the keyboard to their right. They entered a smaller room.

Dominating this room was a row of cylindrical tubes connected to a large computer by a number of cables and thick chords. The cables all eventually connected at a main terminal which was showcased by three monitors.

Valdis sat at the desk and typed in a number of commands on the keyboard. She smiled at Kmyviks as an attendant tapped him on the shoulder.

"Please grab your suitcase sir we're ready. If you will come with me sir this first portal has been set up with your coordinates. Please watch your step. Once inside all you need to do is to stand perfectly still in the blue circle on the floor. I will then close the door behind you.

We will handle everything from the terminal. All you will notice will be a bright flash of light. There will be no pain involved at all but you will initially feel..."

Kmyviks interrupted him.

"I know exactly what I will experience; I have been through this before but thank you. Now can we just get this formality over with please?"

The attendant replied.

"I understand. Please place your suitcase within the circle so it will accompany you on your trip. I wish you the best of luck"

The attendant smiled and walked out of the cylinder. Pushing a button on the exterior the clear door slowly slid shut behind him, latching tightly with a distinctive clink.

Memories of his first encounter with this scenario flashed through his head. The apprehension he felt wondering if he wouldn't simply be disintegrated in transit. Then of course of the dreadful year ahead of him in the event he wasn't.

His thoughts were entirely different this time. He knew the thing worked to perfection. He knew his new home was nothing to dread at all. His apprehensions were now centered entirely on Julie.

He remained perfectly still waiting for the flash of light he knew initiated the process. His wait was a short one. No sooner had he closed his eyes but the flash filled the room and he blacked out.

# 49

Kmyviks was slowly regaining consciousness. His first sensation was a pounding headache. He found himself laying face down in a field of tall grass. The sun was bearing down on him. He quickly remembered how much warmer this planet was than his own. He also remembered the reason.

Their planet was much closer to their sun and this revelation also reminded him of how much brighter it was than on his planet. He hoped they remembered those protective glasses they had provided him for his first visit.

He tried to sit up. He was dizzy, groggy and his stomach was nauseous. He got to his knees and attempted to stand upright. He legs gave out, he was wobbly. His whole body was tingling as if it were being reassembled. In actuality, it was.

He decided to use this down time to search through his suit case for those glasses. He had to squint just to find the satchel. The sun literally hurt his eyes.

Just as last time, he rejoiced to find them right on top. He put on the glasses and while still on his knees surveyed the area. Memories were coming to him at an incredible pace. Those tall plants which he found so unusual his first trip...trees; were ever present again.

The tiny winged creatures they call birds were everywhere. He was then hit with another discomforting remembrance...he was struggling to catch his breath.

Kmyviks quickly recalled how much thinner their atmosphere was than where he had just left. He recalled how he had to learn to breathe in short, continuous breaths as opposed to taking one deep one to get the oxygen his lungs required.

A parchment in his throat was another reminder of the air quality on this planet. The minute particles in the atmosphere, unique to this world; that had caused him so much discomfort the first time were at it again. It only added to his insane thirst. They would accumulate in his mouth and feel like sandpaper when he swallowed.

His mind was woozy. There was so much he had to remember. He had to remember names, at the moment he was struggling to remember his own. Places, what things are called, he had a lot to recall.

He attempted to stand up again, this time with more success. He finally caught his balance and his breath and, now that he was able to walk, anxious to get started.

Kmyviks looked around trying to remember which way led towards town. He was totally disoriented. He thought about it for a moment and seemed to remember traversing down a slope, a small hill to get to town.

He glanced to his right and saw nothing but a woodland area in the distance cluttered with trees and thick vines. No, he didn't remember going through anything like that. He then looked to his left and noticed the field of grass continuing. It appeared that would be a more logical direction to head in.

He picked up his suitcase and started walking. He was thankful for the clothes they provided him with this time. He was wearing a thin short sleeved cotton shirt. He was rather put off by its burnt orange color; it reminded him of one of his prison uniforms which was a very similar color, but at least it was cool.

They had also given him a nice pair of pants made from that material they call denim. He was thankful his data chip was still operational; he knew he would never remember all these details without it.

Kmyviks had comfortable walking shoes; he seemed to remember Karen calling similar ones tennis shoes, which confused him at the time because he wasn't sure what tennis was.

He had been walking for what seemed like forever. The sun was really tiring him out and he could use something cold to drink. He was disappointed after checking his suitcase to discover there was nothing to drink in it.

After another ten minute of exhausting walking, he could finally see buildings ahead of him. He was relieved that he was indeed traveling in the right direction but still had so many things on his mind. He had to have a plan. The overall objective of course was to find Julie.

It had been fifteen years since he was here. He knew there was a number of things that may have happened in the interim. Julie could have found someone else or simply moved out of town all together.

He refused to speculate on any of them. He would go directly to the bar first, that was the last known location for her. A pert of that plan would he would be able to quince his now dreadful thirst.

As he neared town his thoughts went to what course of action he would take when he finally reached his destination.

. Larry's bar would of course be his first stop. He had to remember where it was. He knew, at least fifteen years ago, Julie was not only working there but living upstairs.

He remembered Julie wasn't very happy at her apartment. It was small and it seemed every week something would require the attention of Larry to fix. While she never actually mentioned the desire to move, after fifteen years Kmyviks feared she may have had enough of that place and moved. He would deal with that if it came to it.

His first thought was to go straight upstairs and

knock on her apartment door but he decided against that course of action. In the event she had moved it would be an awkward moment and probably require an explanation he wouldn't be comfortable giving.

He resolved to simply sit at the bar, enjoy a much needed cold drink and ask for either her or Larry. If she wasn't there he was positive Larry would remember him and give him the update on her.

Kmyviks finally reached the edge of town. He now walked on cement sidewalks as opposed to the grass path that had gotten him this far.

His task now was to remember where Larry's bar was. As he walked by various stores and shops he racked his brain for the name of the bar. He was frantically searching for something that would look familiar. So much had changed. He knew if he could remember the name of the bar in the event he couldn't find it someone would be able to tell him where it was. Finally it hit him, 'Upper Deck bar and grill'.

Kmyviks thought back to his first visit. He remembered first arriving in town and how thirsty he was then. His first priority then was to find something to drink. He had vowed to stop at the first establishment that looked promising.

He couldn't remember making any turns once he got to town but rather simply walking down the street at the end of the path to town. He concluded that if indeed he had followed his original path the bar should be somewhere on this very street.

Kmyviks did remember the front of the bar had two ornate doors with unusual colored glass and three or four steps leading up to them. While he knew the facades might change over fifteen years he was hoping these landmarks would remain.

After walking another ten minutes his hopes were

answered. There before him were the steps and the ornate glass doors. He looked up at the sign above the door and was struck with confusion. Now posted above the doors was a sign proclaiming 'Leonard's Lounge'.

He was certain this was the right place; perhaps they had just changed the name. The unique doors and steps instantly brought back memories, they were unmistakable. He collected his thoughts and entered the bar. How odd he thought that Larry would change the name.

Kmyviks was struck immediately by two things. The interior was dark and cool, both blessings to him. He removed his glasses and placed them in his shirt pocket.

He looked around the room and was pleased that it did indeed look familiar. He noticed the stairway against the far wall. He knew those steps led upstairs to the two apartments as he had used them countless times. Kmyviks had so many fond memories at the top of those very stairs. He was now certain he was at the right place.

His heart was racing with anticipation. His first notion was to walk right up those steps and pound on Julie's door but he decided to hold off on that for now.

He glanced to his right at the bar and was once again comforted by its familiarity. His mouth and throat were scorched; his first priority would be to get something cold to drink.

Kmyviks decided on a seat at the end of the bar. After giving it some thought he realized that was pretty close to where he had first sat during his first visit. Within a minute or two he was greeted by the bartender who placed a coaster in front of him and smiled.

It was a young man in his twenties. His blonde hair was neatly combed and his mustache finely trimmed. His smile was very congenial.

"Good after noon sir, I'm Ben, what can I get you today?"

Kmyviks glanced at the row of taps for the draft beer and pointed in their direction.

"I'll just have a glass of that draft beer please; I really don't care what kind as long as it's cold."

Ben reached down and opened a cooler behind the bar. He pulled out a frosty mug and filled it.

"Here you go sir. I think you'll like this it's my favorite. Do you wish to start a tab?"

Kmyviks wasn't sure what he meant so he reached in his pocket and pulled out the small envelope with his money in it. He couldn't remember how much drinks were so he felt safe handing Ben a ten dollar bill.

Ben took the bill and smiled.

"I'll be back with your change in a minute sir. Let me know what you think of it."

The drink was a true Godsend for him. The cool liquid felt so good going down his arid throat and it certainly quenched his thirst. He quickly gulped down the remainder in the glass and pushed it towards the back of the bar top in a silent request for a refill.

Ben returned and placed a five dollar bill in front of him. He took the hint and refilled the glass.

"I take it you liked it?"

Kmyviks nodded.

"Yes, it was very good, I'll have another please."

With his thirst now taken care, Kmyviks now steered his thoughts to another direction, to finding out about Julie. The precious memories that were flooding his mind now that he was actually back in the bar were becoming overwhelming. His heart was aching and the anticipation mounting.

He could feel her presence. He could almost visualize her standing behind the bar. The memories which had been distant and vague while he was away were now so vivid and real.

He was trying to determine the right course of action to find out more about her. He wanted to first determine if she were still in the area. He motioned for Ben to return.

"Ben, may I ask you a question?"

The bartender renewed his contagious smile.

"Of course sir, how can I help you?"

Kmyviks sighed; he was going to ask a question and the answer would determine the course of the rest of his life. A part of him was so very anxious for the answer yet a part of him was preparing him for the worst.

He had to hope for the best but, at the same time, be prepared for the worst. He wasn't sure if he had convinced himself that he would be able to do that yet. He tried to imagine all the possible scenarios.

He threw caution to the wind. He knew he would have to know sooner or later and the uncertainty was destroying him. He blurted out the question without any further thought.

"Is Julie still working here?"

The young man thought for a moment.

"Well, I'm new here; this is only my second week. Julie, hmmm...we do have an older lady who works evenings but I'm not sure of her name, we have never worked together and I've only even seen her once."

Kmyviks was surprised by the reply.

"No, that wouldn't be her. She would be in her mid thir..."

Kmyviks stopped himself in mid sentence. An unsettling thought just hit him over the head like a hammer. While he had come to grips with the fact that fifteen years had indeed passed and what he had thought were all the possible changes that might take place in that time, one had completely and inexplicitly, escaped him.

He had thought about the possibility of her finding someone else, he had accepted the prospect she might have moved out of the area, but he had neglected to take into consideration, she would have aged those fifteen years.

Kmyviks studied his reflection in the large mirror behind the bar. He was looking at a man in his mid thirties who looked exactly like the man who had stared into that very same mirror while in his mid thirties... fifteen years ago. He hadn't aged a day!

A chill went down his spine. He wasn't sure how to handle this unforeseen omission in thought. How could he not have considered that? He had so much to think about recently that was just one item that had totally slipped his mind.

Of course she would have aged! How could he not know that? He cursed himself for such an obvious lapse of insight. In fact it wasn't even insight at all; it should have been common sense! A child would have understood it and seen it coming, yet it had escaped him completely.

Now that it had entered his mind, he had to figure out exactly how he would deal with it and just how important it was in the total scheme of things.

Would it affect his love for her and desire to be with her...not at all, but that wasn't his immediate concern.... would it affect hers?

He finally has his second beer placed in front of him . His world was now dramatically different than it had been only an hour ago. This would definitely change things but how he wasn't sure.

He finally admitted that the older woman Ben had been referring to could indeed be Julie. He had to get more information; he felt he was so close.

"Do you know if she works tonight?"

Ben shook his head.

"I'm sorry, I really don't but I could get the owner out to talk with you, he's in the back."

Kmyviks was pleased with the response.

"Oh that would be great thank you, Larry's here?"

Ben now gave him a look of confusion.

"I don't know any Larry sir, the owner is Leonard. I'll go get him for you."

Now it was his turn to be confused. Who is Leonard and why wasn't Larry the owner? Well that answered the mystery of the new sign at least. Could Larry have sold the place? He didn't find that answer likely. He knew Larry loved his bar and enjoyed not only owning the establishment but also his time working there.

That compounded with the fact that Larry had owned the entire building which included the two apartments upstairs; that just didn't add up.

After a couple minutes, an older gentleman wearing an apron appeared from the back and approached him.

"Good afternoon my friend, I am Leonard, I own the place. Ben said you would like to talk to me?"

Kmyviks managed a smile to attempt to cover up his confusion.

"Hello Leonard, thank you for coming out. I am a good friend of Larry, and I was wondering if he was still here?"

Leonard looked solemnly down at the bar top and sighed. He ran his fingers through his balding scalp to collect his thoughts.

"Larry sadly passed away about a month ago. I am his brother in law and he left the place to me. You say you were a friend of his? How did you know him? Were you a regular customer of his?"

Kmyviks was devastated at the news. He had liked Larry for a number of reasons. He had given him a place to live and he knew he treated Julie well.

"I had rented the upstairs apartment from him for a

year so yes I knew him well. He was a good man. I am very sorry to hear of his passing."

Leonard nodded.

"We were all saddened by his passing. Of course it was especially hard for me because my wife was his sister and we were all very close."

Leonard noticed Kmyviks glass was empty. He took the glass and poured another beer.

"Here, this one is on the house. So how long ago did you live here? I don't remember seeing you here before."

Kmyviks thanked him.

"Oh that would have been, let me think, about fifteen years ago. I was only here for a year."

Leonard acknowledged his reply.

"Oh, well that explains it then. I'm pretty good with remembering faces but I didn't come here very often back then. I don't recall ever seeing you here the few times I was here.

You say you rented an apartment from Larry fifteen years ago? Well, you must have been pretty young back then because I sure wouldn't call you very old now."

Kmyviks took a sip of his beer. He had again overlooked the age thing and how he hadn't aged a day. It was only natural that Leonard would have mentioned that because from his perspective he would have had to have been a young teenager fifteen years ago.

He was hoping this line of conversation would end. He was pleased that he had established contact with someone he hoped could help him on his quest to find Julie. He was positive Leonard would have known her.

He wanted to seize the opportunity but at the same time, sound nonchalant about it.

"Does Julie still work here?"

Leonard was surprised by the question.

"Julie...of course she does. This place couldn't run

without her. My goodness she has been here for, gee, about twenty years now."

Leonard thought about the question.

"You say you rented an apartment here about fifteen years ago? Well then you two would have been neighbors."

Kmyviks wasn't sure where Leonard had intended on taking the conversation so he simply nodded.

"Yes we were for the year I was here. We became very good friends. Julie was unlike any woman I had ever met before. She was truly a special lady."

Leonard smiled.

"Julie is truly a wonderful lady. We all just love her here. She and my wife are very good friends as well. It sounds like she made an impression on you as well!"

Kmyviks thought this was the perfect opportunity to find out her whereabouts.

"Yes indeed she did. In fact that is why I came back here after all these years; I was hoping to see her. Does she still live upstairs?"

Leonard shook his head.

"Heavens no, she moved, it's been many years ago. They rented a house my wife and I own just outside of town. They are really happy there. When was the last time you saw her?"

Kmyviks picked up immediately on Leonard's use of the word 'they'. That could mean a number of things. His first thought was Leonard was referring to Julie and Karen, which he liked a lot better than the second thought that went through his mind.

He tried not to put too much thought into that right now. The one encouraging thing he did get out of the statement was that Julie was still in town.

"Well, I have been out of town for over fifteen years so it's been at least that long. I would very much like to see her again."

Leonard couldn't help but like his new customer. He was polite, well mannered and very friendly. There just seemed something sincere about him.

"Oh I am sure you will run into her. If it's been that long I'm sure she would be thrilled to see you again as well."

Kmyviks couldn't help but chuckle over the last comment. He couldn't promise how thrilled she would be but he sure knew she would be surprised. He was encouraged she was still in town and the fact that Leonard at least didn't make any mention of a husband.

"You say she lives just out of town? I would love to drop in and see her. Is there any way you could give me the address?"

Leonard was confounded by the request. He liked the young man but he wasn't sure if it would be proper to give out Julie's address. He wanted to get to know him a little better before he made that decision.

"Alright, you say you have been away for awhile, did you come far to see her?"

Kmyviks scratched his head and it took every ounce of restraint not to just laugh hysterically at the question.

"Farther than you could ever imagine Leonard."

Leonard nodded. He studied the man for a moment.

"You know, I have a pretty keen sense when it comes to people. I have always been able to get a feel for good people and I can't help but think you really cared for Julie."

Kmyviks finished his beer and gave Leonard a compassionate smile.

"Again sir, more than you could ever imagine."

Leonard was pleased with the answer.

"I normally wouldn't give out her address but something just tells me you are a good man and I get a hunch Julie would like to see you so in your case I am going out on a limb and take a chance.

She lives at 825 Briarcrest Road. Briarcrest is a small two lane dirt road just to the north of town. Her house is the first on the left. She's got a long driveway that has two large oak trees on each side with a big old pine tree in the corner, you can't miss it."

Kmyviks asked Leonard for a pen and wrote the address on a bar napkin.

Sticking the napkin in his pocket he got up and leaned across the bar to shake Leonard's hand.

"I thank you Leonard for your consideration. I promise you that you will not regret telling me. You don't know what this means to me."

Leonard smiled.

"Something just tells me I won't my friend."

# 50

Kmyviks started walking to the door then stopped. He had been so concerned about finding Julie he hadn't thought far enough ahead as to figure out how he would actually get there once he knew where she lived.

He remembered Julie's car broke down once and she had to get to an appointment. She called something she referred to as a cab. A car soon arrived and took her to her appointment. How convenient he thought at the time that there were people who would actually do that!

Kmyviks knew nothing about this service but thought that might be the best solution. He knew Leonard would be familiar with it. He walked back to the bar and motioned for Leonard who was standing behind the bar watching television.

"Leonard, I was wondering, do you know what phone number you use to call a cab driver? I was thinking I could use one to get to Julie's since I am without transportation."

Leonard grinned.

"I sure do. We keep the number right here for folks who indulge a little too much to drive home. We call it every night. I would be happy to order you a cab; they certainly know where we are!"

Leonard opened a drawer below the cash register, got the phone number and took out his phone.

"Cindy, hey how are you doing over there today? This is Leonard; hey I need a cab here at the lounge as soon as you have someone free. I have a man that will be leaving here and going to Briarcrest Road, and this one is sober!"

He paused as he listened to the dispatcher respond.

"Oh, that's right, give me a minute; I don't even know his name."

Leonard turned around and addressed Kmyviks.

"They need a name, I'm afraid I don't know yours."

Kmyviks thought for a moment. He wasn't expecting the question. He knew it would be wise to give him the name he was known as here and not his real one.

"Robert, my name is Robert."

Leonard nodded and finished his phone conversation.

"Okay Robert, they will be at the front door in about ten minutes she said. You must be pretty excited about seeing her after all these years."

Leonard thought for a moment while waiting for the reply; Robert...that was Julie's son's name. He remembered she had mentioned he was named after his father. This gentleman seemed pretty anxious to see her; could he be the same Robert?

He studied the man in front of him. His initial thought was that it would be a huge coincidence if he wasn't but then he quickly discarded the notion because this man was far too young to be Robert's father.

Kmyviks smiled unawares of Leonard's thought.

"Oh yes I am indeed."

Kmyviks started walking towards the door but his progress was halted temporarily by a shout out from Leonard.

Leonard went to the end of the bar and pulled out a long stem rose from a vase that Edi had brought in the other day to brighten up the place. He handed it to Kmyviks.

"Here, take this for her. Julie loves roses; it might make a nice impression."

Kmyviks accepted the rose and smiled.

"Thank you Leonard, I really appreciate it."

Kmyviks walked out of the bar and sat on the front

steps waiting for the cab. His heart was racing. He contemplated the gravity of what he was about to do and how it would affect the rest of his life.

He knew he was stuck here one way of another and that was fine with him. He had nothing to go back to. His future, what ever it may end up being, would be here. He closed his eyes and took a deep breath.

What was he going to say to her when they first met? He knew she would initially be in a state of shock seeing him after fifteen years. She doesn't even know he's still alive! How would he react if the tables were turned?

His mind then went in a direction he hated to even have to entertain but he knew he would have to be prepared for. What if Julie had indeed moved on and found someone else?

His heart was racing as he waited for the cab. What would he say to her? He had run out of time to think, the cab pulled up.

He took a deep breath still trying to come up with the proper words to say as he sat in the cab. He gave the driver the address and sat back deep in thought. He couldn't get over how nervous he was. He tried to calm himself with the thought that it wouldn't be so much what he said to her, but rather the situation she was in, that would control his fate.

He had always mastered the ability to control his own destiny. Being in charge had been a survival tactic. He had been in many precarious positions in years past and only survived by remaining totally in charge. Now he was faced with a situation over which he had no control and that factor only added to his discomfort.

After about five minutes the cab turned off the main road and on to a small two lane dirt drive. The avenue was shaded on both sides by large trees which created a canopy overhead almost completely covering the roadway.

The cab began to slow down; they had finally reached a clearing. He could see a house on the left side set back from the road with a long dirt driveway connecting it to the street. This had to be Julie's house. Leonard had described it perfectly. At the end of the driveway were two large trees and the pine tree he had mentioned was standing alone, majestically in the corner of the yard.

The cab pulled in and stopped, so did his heart momentarily. He sat silently in the back seat in a trance as the driver turned around for his fare. This was the moment he had been waiting for; he was finally actually at Julie's!

His emotions wavered back and forth from the extremes of being totally exhilarated to the exaltation of total terror. The rest of his life would soon have a direction, one way or another.

He paid the driver and exited the car. Looking towards the house he noticed something that immediately didn't seem right. Perhaps it was simply his nerves, his over active imagination or outwardly expressing his deepest fears but it bothered him.

Much to his chagrin, he discovered there were two cars, parked side by side, in the driveway.

It wasn't so much the sight itself that unnerved him but rather what it could imply. While it would make perfect sense for Julie to have one car, he knew she would have no reason to have two.

While in his mind he knew there could rationally be more than one explanation for this anomaly, his insecurities only allowed one to come to mind. The second car could very well be her husband's.

His heart sunk, he couldn't fight his negative feelings. He became so distraught he even considered just returning to the bar without actually facing what now appeared to have the potential to be a very bad scenario.

Kmyviks turned around to see the cab driving away. With no way of calling another cab, retreat was no longer an option. He would have to face his fate.

His heart was racing as he tried to return his breathing to somewhat of a normal pattern. He stared at the front door and sighed. He had faced death in a number of forms over the years but could never remember feeling the apprehension he did at this moment.

For just a second he found himself wishing he had Julie's faith in that divine being, it was times like this that such a faith could do wonders.

Mustering up all the courage he had, he approached the door with great hesitance. He slowly walked up the porch steps finding him self getting more nervous with each step he took. After much trepidation, he finally reached the top step. He stood silently at the door for a moment. He caught his breath and surveyed the front yard.

Kmyviks was pleased she had found such a nice place. She had a very nice front porch with the swing he had remembered Julie saying she had always wanted.

They had a beautiful front yard with decorative trees and foliage and a bird feeder which he had remembered Karen saying she had always wanted. This did appear to be their dream house.

He tried to feel happy for her but was too deeply wallowed in self pity to put too much sincerity into that thought. He had to hold back a tear for this was exactly what he had hoped someday to help her get and to enjoy together. He had to refocus.

Realizing he had no other options at the moment he finally knocked lightly on the door. If indeed his life was to be destroyed he wanted to get it over with as quickly and mercifully as possible. He would deal with the aftermath when necessary.

After what seemed like an hour the door was slowly opened. A man stood at the door with a perplexed expression on his face. This only reinforced Kmyviks deepest fears.

The stranger was an attractive man about his same age. He was well built with noticeably expressive blue eyes. His dark brown hair was neatly parted to one side and his youthful face cleanly shaven.

Kmyviks studied the stranger with intrepid eyes. This would explain the second car, at this point he had no other choice than to look at the man as his advisory. His worst nightmare was appearing to come true. There was indeed another man in Julie's life.

Rick opened the door wider and examined the stranger who now stood on the other side of the screen door. He had never seen him before.

Rick's impertinent expression only caused Kmyviks more discomfort. Of course if the man were involved with Julie he would not be pleased to see a strange man standing at her door.

There was a distinct tension rapidly being created. Kmyviks was not pleased with seeing the man greet him and at the same time, the man didn't appear pleased at seeing him. His mind was now racing with thoughts, none of them good.

He wondered if Julie could really be interested in a man so many years younger than her. Then, he rethought that, remembering that would be exactly what he was hoping she would be, only with him.

Kmyviks had to be honest about what was going on. In this particular situation he was the antagonizer, it was his appearance that was disrupting the normalcy. If Julie were indeed involved with this man he would play the role of the outcast. Of course he wouldn't be welcomed with open arms.

With that thought in mind, he had to come up with a way to disarm the confrontation. He cleared his throat and spoke softly and straight forward.

"Excuse me, is Julie Wells here?"

Rick was thrown off by the man's request. He didn't know quite what to think of a strange man suddenly appearing at the door asking for Julie. He hesitated and again sized up the stranger.

Before he had a chance to reply, Karen came to his side. She put her arms around his shoulders.

Kmyviks took immediate notice of this action. He first immediately recognized Karen and took stock of what he was witnessing.

It appears the strange man at the door was not the threat he had originally perceived him to be. It now appears the man is with Karen! He was now finally breathing a sigh of relief and hope had returned to his arsenal of emotions.

It took him a moment to accept Karen as the mature adult she was and not the troubled teenage girl he had remembered her as. Again the age thing was troubling him.

Much to his delight, Karen kissed her boyfriend on the cheek and spoke.

"Who is here Rick?"

She peered through the screen door and turned as pale as a ghost. Her mouth opens but temporarily no words are able to breech her lips. She is shaking, she instantly recognized the intruder. That came easy to her because he looked exactly as he did the last time she saw him, fifteen years ago. She again attempts to speak but her words are stuttered.

"Oh...my...God...Robert...is that...really...you?"

Kmyviks smiles

"Yes, it's really me. I know this must come as quite a surprise to you but I can assure you it is me."

He looks her over admiring the beautiful young woman she has become. She was only fifteen the last time he had seen her.

"Karen...my goodness I can' get over how you have grown!"

Karen stands trembling, in a total state of shock. Her mouth dropped to the floor desperately trying to find words to say. She innocently utters the first thought that came to her mind.

"And I can't get over how you....haven't"

She turns to Rick in a total state of shock. She then turns around, her voice notably quivering.

"Mom...ahh....there is someone here to see you."

Julie replies from the kitchen.

"I'm really busy at the moment sweetheart; I've got to get this roast out. Find out what they want!"

Karen replies instantly.

"No mom...you really need to come to the door!"

Julie replies in a frustrated voice.

"I told you Karen I am busy now find out what they want."

Karen replies in a frantic voice.

"Mother, come to the damn door!"

Julie could be heard mumbling from the kitchen. She was appalled at her daughter's attitude much less language she used to express it.

"Karen Renee I don't know what has gotten into you! I tell you I am busy trying to fix dinner for everyone and you...."

As she reaches the door and looks through the screen she stops herself in mid sentence. She had instantly identified the visitor!

She grabbed her chest and stumbled into the open door. She was gasping for breath.

Karen turned and held her seeing her distress.

"Mom, are you alright?"

Julie gaped at her daughter and screamed, panting for breath.

"I am anything but alright...how could I possibly be alright!"

Kmyviks was scared for her, he panicked. He thrust though the now open door and grabbed Julie.

"Sweetheart, it's okay, I'm here."

Julie, in a complete state of hysteria, broke free from his embrace and screamed.

Karen tried to reach for her as her mother screamed again, waving her arms frantically.

"Don't touch me! Nobody touch me!"

Kmyviks looked helplessly at Karen who simply shrugged her shoulders in alarm.

"Mom, take a deep breath, relax, can't you see...."

Her mother, still gasping for air shouted.

"Oh yeah, I can see just fine dammit, but what I think I can see just...it just...it just isn't happening!"

Kmyviks put his hand on Karen's shoulder in an attempt at support and encouragement. Karen acknowledged his effort with a concerned smile.

Julie braced herself against the wall trembling. She glanced at Karen, then at Robert, and then just shook her head madly, still shuddering uncontrollably. She was in a total panic attack. Her eyes were bulging out of her head and her breath extremely labored. She was waving her arms aimlessly.

Julie slumped down slowly against the wall until she found herself curled up on the floor in a fertile position.

Karen looked helplessly at Rick and Kmyviks. The three of them didn't know what to do as Julie continued to suffer, totally engulfed in a world of panic all her own.

Julie finally put her head in her hands and took a deep breath. She turned to Kmyviks and pointed at him.

"You...you are not here. This is just a crazy dream and you are not here!"

Karen tried to console her mother.

"Mom, it is not a dream. I see him too and so does Rick. Mom, he is back."

Julie continued to shake her head in defiance.

"That's impossible! He....you, died fifteen years ago!"

Kmyviks knew he had to do something to convince her that he was indeed back. He didn't want to frighten her any more than she already was. He was momentarily confused as to what the best course of action would be.

He glanced at Karen for any support she could give him and again was acknowledged with a weak smile.

"Sweetheart, I am here, this is not a dream. I can explain everything if you can calm down and give me a chance."

Julie just shook her head.

"You died fifteen years ago!"

Karen had to speak up.

"Well mom, if that' true then he sure makes a good looking ghost, and very realistic. Mother, this is not a freaking dream!"

Karen's initial shock over seeing Robert has now taken a back seat to her concern over her mother. She turned to Robert with an expression of grave despair.

Kmyvoks felt so helpless. He then remembered the rose Leonard had given him that he had been holding in his hand.

He showed it to Karen who nodded her approval. He got down on one knee so he would be at eye level with her. Once he was assured she took notice of him, he kissed the rose and handed it to her.

Julie looked at the rose then at Kmyviks. She slowly took the rose from him with one trembling hand, and then gently took his hand with her other.

Kmyviks took hold of her hand and softly stroked it with his fingers. He smiled with all the love in his heart.

Karen grabbed Rick's hand and squeezed it for support. She then smiled at her mother. She placed her hand on Kmyviks shoulder emanating reassurance in hopes that this gesture might bring her mother around.

Kmyviks touched Karen's hand and smiled. He then smiled at Julie in an attempt first of all to prove he was real and secondly as a gesture of solidarity. If Karen could accept the fact that he was really there, then maybe her mother could as well.

Karen, Rick and Kmyviks stood silently by Julie, waiting for any kind of encouraging response.

# 51

Julie touched the rose. She ran her fingers across it gently, admiring it and then placed it under her nose and savored the sweet fragrance. She looked at the rose then at Kmyviks.

While her attention was diverted she pricked her thumb on a thorn that had been hiding on the stem. Two droplets of blood oozed from the wound. Kmyviks took immediate notice of this.

"Sweetheart, you're bleeding! Look, the blood is real… that should convince you that I am real as well. Look at the blood honey, this is not a dream!"

She smeared the blood on her thumb, deep in thought. She closed her eyes and took a deep breath. Tears started flowing from her eyes. With the aroma of the rose still engulfing her senses reality all of a sudden just kicked in.

As she pressed on the small wound she felt a tinge of pain; she stopped and thought for a moment. She could never remember actually feeling pain in a dream. She couldn't deny the blood on her thumb. …this had to real.

She looked at Kmyviks then slowly raised her hand. She touched his face, ran her fingers across his lips.

"You're really here…Robert, you're really here! I'm not dreaming you."

Encouraged by these remarks, Kmyviks placed his hand on her head and softly stroked her hair. He smiled and nodded.

"Yes sweetheart, I am really here."

He glanced up at Karen who was now all smiles. He noticed a tear coming from Karen's eye as well. He smiled at her.

"Your mom is going to be just fine; we all are going to be just fine!"

Karen hugged Rick in joy. She reached down to her mother.

"Mom, let me help you up."

Julie extended her arm and Kmyviks and Karen raised her up. Julie slowly stood up clinging to her cherished rose. She again examined the rose then turned her attention to Kmyviks.

"You gave me a rose. You have never done that before. I love roses. I had always hoped some day you would give me roses and today you did, somehow you knew."

Tears were now flowing uncontrollably from her eyes. She gently touched his face again, if for no other reason than to convince herself it was as real as the rose.

Kmyviks could see she was struggling and assisted convincing her by softly kissing her hand.

Confused and still a bit disoriented about what was real and what wasn't, she managed a weak smile.

"The rose is real, so is the blood, I can only hope and pray with all my heart that you are as well."

Her words hit his heart and told him two things. She was alright and seemingly coming back to reality, but more importantly, she still cared about him and therefore must not be involved with anyone else.

Karen was so relieved to see her mother was alright as more tears flowed from her eyes. She impulsively embraced Robert.

"It's wonderful to see you again Robert. I have missed you and I know that goes even stronger for my mom. You really made her happy, you made us both happy. I am so glad you are back."

Kmyviks hugged her tightly and held back tears of his own.

"I never knew happiness until I met your mother.

Being back here is a dream come true, one that I feared would never come true."

Karen smiled and took his hand, she squeezed it tightly.

"I wouldn't be the person I am today if it weren't for you, we both know that. I haven't gone a day since you left without thanking you in my prayers, thanking you not only for what you did for mom, but what you did for me as well. In those same prayers I asked God to somehow, someday, return you to us and he has."

They watched Julie slowly make her way to the bathroom and continued their conversation. Kmyviks took a deep breath releasing it slowly.

"I hope you both know leaving was certainly not my idea, I had…"

Karen interrupted him.

"We know that Robert, we thought you were…"

Kmyviks now interrupted her knowing exactly what she was about to say.

"I know Karen, I was so sorry about that. I had no way of letting you know I wasn't. I never even had the chance to say goodbye. Those things have haunted me over the years.

I came back the moment the opportunity first presented itself. I wasn't sure just what I would be coming back to; a lot of years have passed.

I didn't know if your mom might have…"

It was now Karen's who accurately predicted what he was going to say and stopped him before another word left his lips.

"That never entered her mind Robert, not for a second. She has been hopelessly devoted to you and has never stopped loving you, to this very day, nor have I.

I was so hoping for your return, not only for her sake

but to allow me to thank you for all you have done for both of us."

Kmyviks again squeezed Karen's hand.

"It is I who should thank the two of you for all you have done for me. I will never be able to appropriately express what knowing you both has done for me.

You two have totally changed my life in ways I couldn't have previously even imagined. Your mom has made me more of a man than I ever dreamed possible."

Julie returned after having freshened up. She noticed her daughter and Robert bonding so nicely, this also brought tears to her eyes. She was still struggling with the reality of this really happening.

This was something she dreamed of and prayed for but never in a million years expected to actually happen. She was totally convinced he was dead. She had no reason to think otherwise.

Her family was finally reunited. She stood silently in deep appreciation, almost in awe of the sight and said a silent prayer thanking God for this incredible and totally unexpected homecoming.

She walked over and wrapped her arms around both of them. The three of them embraced and cried together as one.

The trio finally released their embrace and Julie wiped the tears, now finally tears of joy, from her face. She looked at Karen and cherished the smile. She knew her daughter's merriment was mostly directed at her.

She then turned her attention to Kmyviks who stood silently next to her. She slowly wrapped her arms around his waist and pulled him close to her. She gave him a long, deep kiss gently on his lips.

After a minute or so, she withdrew her lips and just looked at him. One kiss wasn't enough; she had fifteen years of pent up passion mixed with the remorse of thinking she would never see him again, to make up for.

She pulled him close again but this time with a romantic fervor he wasn't expecting. Their lips met with a fury of heated passion.

Finally releasing him, she smiled with the adulation usually only found in a harlequin romance novel. She ran her hands up and down his body, again in an attempt to convince herself this was real. She finally got the motivation to attempt to speak, her voice quivering.

"I don't know how this came to be. I don't have any understanding about how you are standing here beside me again and I don't care at all. All I do know; is that you are here and you are real. We are together again and that's all that matters to me!"

Kmyviks gently massaged her shoulders and gave her a tender kiss.

"You couldn't imagine the hell I have been through these past years. Now I mention that not to illicit sympathy, because I am sure you have endured your own hell as well.

I mention it only to tell you, I would gladly face it a thousand times over again if I were ensured I would end up back here with you and Karen. You never left my heart and the hope of someday seeing you again, as unlikely as I was beginning to think it might be, gave me the strength to survive."

Julie shook her head in disbelief.

"That is the sweetest thing anyone has ever said to me."

She then stepped back and looked at him, studying every detail. As much as she tried to hold it back s tear forced its way out of the corner of her eye.

Kmyviks noticed it and gently wiped it away.

"What's wrong sweetheart? It seems something is

bothering you. This is a joyous time what could possibly be troubling you?"

Julie touched his face, running her fingers over his forehead, then his cheeks and chin. She closely examined every detail in his face and allowed another tear to emerge.

"You...you haven't aged a day. You look exactly like you did fifteen years ago. I don't understand how this can be true but somehow it can't be denied.

I don't know how this could be possible but I do know, sadly I have aged every day of those fifteen years. I am an old woman with gray hair, baggy eyes and wrinkled skin and..."

Kmyviks put his fingers over her lips and smiled.

"Julie, my dear Julie, you are as beautiful as the day I met you."

She couldn't help herself, she practically jumped in his arms almost knocking them both down. She held on to him to prevent him from falling backwards and kissed him.

"I retract that statement I said earlier...what you just said was the sweetest thing anyone has ever said to me."

Karen had to speak up.

"It is so wonderful to see you two together again. I don't understand how you could come back Robert, why it took fifteen years or why you haven't aged but none of those things matter; what matters is we are together again."

Both Kmyviks and Julie planted kisses on Karen's cheeks.

Karen pulled Rick over and introduced him to Robert.

"Robert, I want you to meet Rick, my boyfriend. Rick, this is Robert, he is...well, a very dear family friend. You know, the man I told you about."

Kmyviks smiled and shook Rick's hand.

"It is a pleasure to meet you Rick. You have got a wonderful lady here, now you take good care of her."

Rick smiled and held Karen's hand.

"Oh I know that sir and I promise you I will. Wonderful women seem to run in the family. Both she and her mother have spoken often of you. It's a pleasure to finally meet you Robert."

Kmyviks nodded and glanced lovingly at Julie. He liked Rick already.

"That is very true Rick; we each have a very wonderful lady!"

Julie suggested they all go and sit in the living room and she will bring out refreshments. Karen and Rick sat on the couch saving room for Julie. Robert sat against the opposite wall in the corner facing the couch.

Julie called out from the kitchen for Robert to come in and help her bring out the refreshments. He got up and joined her.

Julie took a break from pouring glasses of iced tea to walk over to him and kiss him one more time.

"Sweetheart, I am so very happy right now. I can't find the words to express it but I hope you know. This is a day I have dreamed of for fifteen years.

There is so much I want to tell you but please allow me to say this now, from my heart, I have never fallen out of love with you and I have never strayed from us. That never even entered my mind. I have never given up hope that one day this would happen."

Kmyviks smiled and picked up the tray of glasses.

"I will take this in for you sweetheart."

Julie held up one finger in a silent request for him to hold off a minute.

"Robert, there is something I had always wanted to ask you but, well I never got the chance. Well now I do. Could I ask you a silly question?"

Kmyviks grinned and nodded.

"You can ask me anything you like."

Julie rubbed her chin in thought.

"Well, this is silly I know, and really not important but it is just something I have always wondered about. Would I be correct in assuming that Robert isn't your real name?"

Kmyviks couldn't help but chuckle.

"No sweetheart, that was just a random name I chose when I arrived to, well make things easier. I feared my real name might, raise a few eyebrows and with that, a few suspicions. I wasn't in a position to take any chances."

Julie nodded but insisted on an answer.

"I kind of figured that, well sweetheart, what is your real name?"

He was hoping she wouldn't pursue it but decided she deserved an honest answer.

"Kmyviks Bhuk'aik."

Julie's eyes grew as big as saucers.

"Oh my....well, okay...what's say we just stick with Robert, it's a nice name."

They both smiled. Julie made a silent vow that if they were to ever get married she would have to finagle a way to convince him they should use her last name.

They carried the refreshments into the living room. Julie set the chips on the coffee table and sat on the couch with Karen and Rick. Kmyviks placed the tray of drinks next to them and after grabbing a glass, returned to his chair in the corner.

The four of them engaged in lovely conversation. Karen joyfully told Kmyviks how she and Rick had met and about how they got their own apartment and how much she likes her job.

Kmyviks was thrilled to hear every word of it. He thought back to when he had first met that troubled young teenage girl and how she has metamorphosed into the beautiful, happy, mature woman she is today.

Somewhere, deep in the catacombs of his mind, he was also pleased that he could have played a role in that transformation.

Confident now that this was real and not a dream, Julie reminisced about the many wonderful times she and Robert had during the year they were together. Kmyviks would add his little antidotes on each escapade. Her spirit was now reborn and she was rejoicing in having him back. They were truly a family again. The four of them were laughing and having a wonderful time.

At no point during the conversation was there any mention of Robert's true identity, where he came from or how he had spent the last fifteen years.

Karen and Julie had not mentioned any of that to Rick and it was silently, but mutually, agreed upon by the three not to make mention of it today.

They ordered pizza and everyone was having a fabulous time. Rick and Robert were getting along like old friends, conversing about a number of subjects.

Rick was fascinated by Robert's knowledge of astronomy and confessed it had always been a passion of his. Julie and Karen were both pleased the guys were really hitting it off so well.

The girls winked to each other in mutual understanding how humorous the astronomy connection really was, keeping the true irony of it their own personal secret.

The party was interrupted by a sound coming from the foyer. The door was being unlocked and opened. The screen door was slammed shut and then the front door followed with an equally loud thud.

Thinking nothing of it originally and knowing the origin of the commotion, Julie and Karen chucked and shook their heads. Robert took notice of the disturbance with more of a surprise. He glanced at Julie.

"Who would that be?"

Before she had a chance to reply, a young man's voice came bellowing from the foyer.

"Hey mom, I'm back."

Without thinking Julie finally blurted out what would normally be an innocent reply.

"Oh that's just my son."

The instant after the syllables left her lips, she realized the added weight those words would carry. A terrified thought just came to her mind. She remembered Robert still doesn't know he has a son.

She had full intentions of telling him but had gotten so wrapped up in the elation of seeing him again she hadn't gotten to it just yet. Oh my God, what must he be thinking!

Kmyviks sat in the corner dumbfounded and shocked. The words pierced his heart like a knife. They were the last thing he was expecting to hear.

She has a son? He remembered she had just confessed to never having strayed but...then how could she have a son? He was mortified! He couldn't come to grips with his actual feelings which, at the moment, were bouncing back and forth from angry to horrifically disappointed. He sat speechless and in a complete state of shock.

He conceded to the fact that she had lied to him earlier. He wondered how she would have eventually explained this after such a sentimental confession.

Were all the emotions she was displaying sincere or was he now looked at as a merely back up plan for what had obviously turned out to be a failed romance in his absence.

While he had tried to prepare himself for her being with someone else he never thought she would lie about it.

A million other thoughts raced through his mind too quickly to properly analyze each one. None of these thoughts were good.

This could change everything. As much as he had preconceived notions that this might happen, no amount of anticipation could prepare him for actually hearing it.

Before he had a chance to address the issue a young man came bouncing in the room, completely innocent of the turmoil his presence was about to create.

"Mom, Brian and his family are going camping this weekend and they invited me to come along."

The young man walked purposely into the room and stood directly in front of his mother and sister completely unaware there was a man sitting in the corner behind him.

He couldn't help but notice it appeared his mother was immune to his words, her attention seemed diverted. It was if he wasn't even there.

Kmyviks silently stared at the young man. So this was her son...a chill ran down his spine. At first he attributed that chill to the shock of first discovering Julie had a son and then the added jolt of having that child all of a sudden standing in the same room with him.

Within a matter of seconds he further analyzed this disturbing sensation. There was more to it than just that. His mind was suddenly inundated with confusing thoughts as if his brain were trying to subtly tell him something.

He was sensing something he just couldn't put his finger on but that sensation was overwhelming and undeniable. He continued to quietly study the young man who was still unaware of his presence. There was something about him that was unsettling.

Julie sat silently on the couch trembling. Her son was not three feet away from her but she was looking right through him. Her mind was on Kmyviks who she could see over her son's shoulder.

Sensing he was competing with something for his mother's attention the young man turned around. He then first saw Kmyviks. He was startled to find a strange man sitting in his living room.

Their eyes met instantly and connected with the intensity of a laser. Their gaze was unbreakable. Their mutual curiosity linked them immediately.

They both gaped at each other in silence with bilateral reverence. Independently, and completely unaware of each other's mindset, their brains were inexplicitly on the same wavelength, and what was even stranger was, they both knew it. There was something inexplicable but over powering going on.

There before them, was a man they had never seen before yet there yet there was an odd sense of familiarity, one that couldn't be explained or denied. He had felt this sensation before.

What surprised him most was the thought didn't originate from his mind, but came directly and unsolicited from his very soul. Robert recognized the man instinctively but not by way of his eyes, by way of his mind and his heart, even though they had never met before

Always taking pride in his logic and reasoning ability he once again put his faith in it to give him the answers. This time he came up short. There was a connection between them that wasn't going to be explained by reasoning.

What he was feeling had nothing to do with logic or facts, what he was feeling now went well beyond that. Again he realized he had felt this at least one time before.

Robert's mouth opened in awe as Kmyviks sat silently totally absorbed in the young man.

The boy placed his hands on his temples in an attempt to coax an intelligent thought, one that would make sense out of all of this. Again, he came up short.

He walked over to Kmyviks and, out of politeness, offered his hand to shake.

. He spoke one word, involuntarily and with complete confidence without fully realizing its significance.

"Dad."

Kmyviks took his hand and rather than shake it, embraced it. He held it and rubbed if for a moment.

There was a preternatural electricity generated the instant their hands met. Kmyviks had never experienced anything like it in his life but it was undeniable and spoke volumes.

A tear crept from the corner of his eye. He knew the instant they touched hands, his son, whom he had no previous knowledge of before, was now standing in front of him.

He released the boy's hand and calmly replied.

"Son...sit down, we have a lot of catching up to do."

**THE END**

CPSIA information can be obtained
at www.ICGtesting.com
Printed in the USA
BVHW071533300720
585046BV00001B/5